**SYLVIE THOUGHT THAT IF
ST. IVES HAD SUGGESTED SHE BECOME
HIS MISTRESS INSTEAD OF
HIS WIFE, SHE MIGHT HAVE ACCEPTED.**

"You confuse me, my lord. Am I to marry you to save my reputation or to salvage your pride?" Sylvie demanded.

"Both!" he snapped.

"You have made a great many threats, my lord, most of them foolish, but you have yet to tell me how you intend to wed me against my will, for you will do it no other way. If you require a wife, choose among your own kind and woo her like any other man. Or, does the great Earl of St. Ives always take what he wants? Well, you shall not take me, and, I warn you, I will not be bullied."

His blue eyes were soft on her face. "I would not bet on that, Miss Fairchild," he said softly. "I would not bet on that if I were you."

"Then I think you do not know me, my lord," she replied.

"No," said St. Ives. "No, but I will. And that's a promise."

DAUGHTER
OF
FORTUNE

DAWN LINDSEY

BANTAM BOOKS
TORONTO · NEW YORK · LONDON · SYDNEY

DAUGHTER OF FORTUNE
A Bantam Book / September 1979

ISBN 0–553–12314–9

Published simultaneously in the United States and Canada

Bantam Books are published by Bantam Books, Inc. Its trade-
mark, consisting of the words "Bantam Books" and the por-
trayal of a bantam, is Registered in U.S. Patent and Trademark
Office and in other countries. Marca Registrada. Bantam
Books, Inc., 666 Fifth Avenue, New York, New York 10019.

PRINTED IN THE UNITED STATES OF AMERICA

DAUGHTER
OF
FORTUNE

Prologue
Newmarket

Miss Sylvie Fairfield, only daughter of Sir John Fairfield, Bart, of Millburn Hall, Cambridgeshire, was engaged in the homely task of mucking out one of the back stalls when the groom returned to the stables from taking her father's raking chestnut up to the Hall. She was a slight girl, with a thin, wiry figure and rather too brown a complexion, and just now, in her faded habit and carelessly pinned-up hair, she more nearly resembled a serving girl from the village than a young lady of nearly twenty summers. But since she was not much in the habit of considering her appearance, having spent the better part of her life in the company of her father, her older brother, and what few servants had managed to survive the uncertainties of her father's temper and fortunes, she had scarcely given a second glance in the rather murky mirror in her bedchamber before coming downstairs that morning.

There she had been greeted with the cheerful tidings that Sir John, who had been confined to the house for nearly a fortnight with a severe attack of the gout, had complained upon rising of a renewed twinge in his left foot and was (according to the housekeeper) in a rare taking. Hinton, the housekeeper, had then proceeded to regale Miss Fairfield, over the breakfast table, with the gloomy prediction that Sir John would likely be laid up at least another week with this new attack, and she was sure she didn't know what they were to feed him. From there she progressed naturally to a recital of all the things requiring instant attention in the Hall—ranging from the stuck drawing-room window to the latest trans-

1

gressions of the new cook—if things were not to fall
about their ears one day.

It was a list that might have caused a less strong-
minded young woman to succumb to an attack of severe
depression, but since Miss Fairfield was accustomed to
the housekeeper's frequent pessimistic utterings and had
already endured a fortnight of fetching and carrying for
her Papa, she merely answered the housekeeper very
much at random as she finished her breakfast, promised
to send Blackmer up to the Hall that afternoon to
attend to the window, and made good her escape before
a fresh topic of disaster could occur to the housekeeper's
fertile brain.

Now, at sight of Blackmer, she grinned and said in
relief, "Oh, you did manage to get him off, then. I
thought you might, if I only left you to it, so I slipped
away."

Mr. Joseph Blackmer, a middle-aged individual of
stocky build and a cheerful, weather-beaten countenance,
regarded her with the familiarity of one who had put
her on her first pony. "Now, Miss Syllie," he said disapprovingly, "I've told you often, I won't have you working in the stables like a navvy, and so I mean it! What
your Mama would have to say if she was alive to see
it I don't like to think."

"Well," said Miss Fairfield reasonably, "I don't know, of
course, since I wasn't well acquainted with her, but I would
hope she would merely have said that since Papa had
turned off the stableboy, there was too much for you to do
alone. And if you mean to try to make me believe she was
as high in the instep as all that, then it's no wonder she
was so unhappy with Papa, for you know yourself what a
shockingly loose screw he is. Not, of course," she added
with a characteristic wrinkling of her straight brows, "that
from anything I've been able to discover Papa was
entirely to blame. I *do* remember that Mama used to
cry all the time, which I own makes me think she cannot
have had much common sense, for nothing is more certain
to put Papa out of temper. So very likely it was just as
well she died when she did."

She saw then she had shocked the groom, and added,
"But I am well aware that you had a veritable *tendre* for

her and will hear no word said against her. The truth is, I have something particularly unpleasant to ask of you, and since you were looking so cross this morning I thought I'd do well to get in your good books by helping you. Hinton has requested you to kindly step up to the Hall when you have a moment and take a look at the front drawing-room window, which she says is sticking."

The groom grinned at that. "Aye, only I'll be bound that wasn't the way she put it."

Miss Fairfield laughed. "No, indeed! What she did say was that she was certain any noddy in the village would know how to go about the job better than you, but you might as well make yourself useful for a change. *Naturally* I have no intention of repeating that! Anyway, there's no sense in getting upon your high ropes, for I'm nearly done now, and I'm quite content to have you finish for me. I mean to ride into the village after luncheon and see how poor Mr. Nidd is doing and then see to some other matters I've been neglecting since Papa has been home. Was he very difficult this morning?"

"Aye, well, I won't say it weren't a near-run thing," admitted the groom. "He'd have hedged off just as I'd gotten him up to the post, so to speak, if I hadn't nabbled the rust by dropping just the merest hint into his ear that Lord Twynham had his eye on that particular filly I'd told him about. Not but what he didn't damn my eyes proper just out of general cussedness!" he added cheerfully.

She laughed again and brushed down her shabby skirts to remove any loose straw clinging to them. *"What* an admirable man you are, Joe!" she said. "I would wish you groom to a duke at least if only I knew what I should do here without you. *Is* Lord Twynham interested in the filly?"

"No, nor will your Papa be, once he's discovered she's a trifle too short in the knee, let alone having very little wind. But it'll serve to get him out of your hair for the day, and I don't doubt but what he'll find something else to take his fancy easy enough."

"Oh, Joe, you wretch; of course he will! And here was I priding myself on how clever we'd been to get him out of the house! Oh well, I don't suppose one more horse eating us out of house and home will matter much. And it will be worth it if only it serves to take his mind off his gout and convince him he's well enough to leave."

This unfilial statement apparently failed to shock the groom as the first had done, since it was a sentiment he found himself in complete agreement with, but he merely grunted and said, "You ain't forgot it's the autumn meeting next week have you, Miss Syllie?"

Since they lived close enough to Newmarket to make it convenient for Sir John to take up residence at the Hall to attend the races, she looked up in dismay. "Oh, no, is it? Then Papa will be here for another week at least. It is only to be hoped his gout may have prevented him from inviting anyone, for I've not the least notion what I'm to feed them. What with the new cook burning nearly everything she sets before us and complaining that she can't get the hang of the old stove—!" She sighed, then grinned mischievously. "Well! It just goes to show that there's something good to be gotten out of almost anything, doesn't it? I must own I've been in flat despair over the cook, for even Hinton says she can't believe the woman was ever a cook before. I would already have dismissed her if it had not occurred to me in the nick of time that Papa would become so disgusted he'd leave, no matter how badly his foot was paining him. But I never dreamed I would be able to turn it to such good account! If Papa has invited anyone to stay, you can depend on it they won't remain long once they've partaken of their dinner!"

The groom was perfectly aware of how things stood up at the Hall. Sir John, like most men of usually robust health and uneven temper, had been a very bad patient, running his daughter and the housekeeper ragged dancing attendance on him. At the best of times he was not a warm man, and he had never made the slightest push to engender any affection in either of his offspring, who for years had been left to the tender ministrations of his old groom and housekeeper eleven months out of the twelve. Miss Fairfield might thus be forgiven for wishing they might soon be relieved of his demanding presence.

Kendall, his son and heir, presently away at Oxford, Sir John frankly considered a paltry fellow, with nothing to recommend him but a great many impractical notions culled from his books. Since he was bookish, besides having possessed a limp from childhood that rendered him incapable of participating in the sports that comprised his father's chief pleasure, Sir John was accustomed to hold him in mingled awe and contempt.

Miss Sylvie might have had more claim to her Papa's affections, for she shared his passion for horses and had managed his stables for years with an efficiency he himself had never achieved; but Sir John seemed to find little more to please him there either. He would only say that she was in danger of becoming a complete hoyden if she didn't watch out, and he had never seen a girl with less to say for herself.

No doubt if she had been possessed of looks she might have been able to get around him, for he was no more proof against a pretty young girl than the next man. But Miss Fairfield was not pretty, and had, moreover, an even more severe disadvantage in her Papa's eyes. In his company she tended to become reserved to the point of reticence, seldom offering anything but the merest commonplaces to whatever was said to her, leading Sir John to exclaim once that he didn't know what he had ever done to be blessed with a regular jack-pudding for a son and a daughter who was both Friday-faced and dim-witted into the bargain.

That her reticence was caused not by shyness or stupidity, as her Papa supposed, but by a strong dislike of her only parent, had naturally never occurred to him. Nor would it have troubled him. He made no secret of the fact that he considered both his children sad disappointments, and he spent as little time in their company as his always-inadequate income would allow. He frankly disliked the Hall, and it had been allowed to go to wrack and ruin for so many years that Miss Fairfield no longer noticed its many discomforts, unless it were to wish now and then that the fireplaces in most of the rooms did not smoke when the wind was in a certain quarter, or that the public rooms did not remain so chilly despite every attempt to warm them.

The house was not of great antiquity, but none of the casements fitted properly, as Hinton had justly complained, and in winter the drafts whistled through the rooms, making it necessary to wear one's heaviest woolens even on the mildest days. The furniture was outmoded, the carpets and draperies threadbare, and the grounds and pleasure gardens allowed to go to weed. It would have taken a fortune and an army of workers to set things right. And since neither were forthcoming, not to mention the wherewithal to modernize the kitchen so that a cook would stay above a fortnight, Miss Fairfield had contrived to live there for the most part in content.

Blackmer had finished spreading down the hay now, and Miss Fairfield willingly accompanied him out into the cool overcast morning. As they walked down the long lines of stalls, a black head came over one of the loose-box doors, and Miss Fairfield obediently stopped to run a hand down the soft nose stretched out to greet her. "Yes, yes," she said, laughing, "you're looking for a gallop, aren't you, old fellow? Well, so am I, but I warn you there's no carrot in my pocket, so don't look for it!"

The groom grinned. "Spoiled is what he is, Miss Syllie, and no wonder, the way you cosset him. Aye, but he's been fretting his head off lately though."

As another head emerged a little way down at the sound of her voice, she went to pull the chestnut ears as well. The groom followed her, eyeing the mare. "She's doin' well enough. I expect she'll drop her foal by the weekend."

"Yes, I had a look at her this morning. I own I'm a little concerned. She's still very young, and this is her first. I hope we don't have trouble with her."

Blackmer gave it as his comfortable opinion that nothing was to be gained by inviting trouble, and since this eminently sensible statement was inarguable, she followed him into the tack room.

The groom settled himself immediately to his task of polishing brass, and she perched herself on a convenient crossbar to watch him. "Oh this is pleasant," she said. "How glad I am to be out of the house for a while. Which reminds me. Do you have a sure thing for me for the races next week, Joe?"

"I do not, and you're far too old for such tricks and well you know it, Miss Syllie."

"Yes, and I was too old last year, you old fraud, so don't think to fool me," she retorted. "I've laid a pound by, and I mean it to mend our fortunes, so I warn you I'm depending on you."

His faded blue eyes began to twinkle. "Aye, well, *if* I was a gambling man, which I don't say I am, mind. I don't doubt but what I'd put my blunt on Little Incognita out of Fancy Belle."

She looked up quickly, her face alight with laughter. "Oh, no, Joe, who could have named her that?"

He shook his head. "As to who named her, I'm sure I've no idea. But I hadn't ought to have said anything, and don't you go repeating it."

"No, indeed, that would be *most* improper, and me so missish too!" she said, laughing at him.

"Now adone-do, Miss Syllie! She's out of the Earl of St. Ives' stables, and more than that I can't tell you. But if you're determined to sport your blunt, she'd be my choice."

"The Earl of St. Ives?" she asked. "Well, that explains the name, at least. By all accounts he has any number of little incognitas—" She glanced up at the groom and grinned. "I *meant* to say, of course, the sort of female that I, naturally, know nothing about!" she amended. "Which little incognita is this one named for?"

"I'm sure I wouldn't know, Miss Syllie," said the groom. "Unless it happened to be the one I was hearing some tale about his having stolen right out from under Lord Lambeth's nose."

She laughed. "How very glad I am you told me, Joe! Little Incognita it shall be. I believe I'd like anyone who managed to do Lord Lambeth an ill turn."

Blackmer, who had no more reason to be fond of that particular peer than she, abandoned his polishing and met her eyes. "That's as may be, Miss Syllie," he said bluntly, "but what I say, and hold by is, if your Papa has gone and invited anyone to stay with him up at the Hall, you're to go to Miss Emmy's in the village, Lord Lambeth or no."

She smiled at him with a great deal of affection. "I won't, of course, but thank you, Joe. I've often wished, you know, that you had been my Papa," she added simply. "Does that shock you?"

He was not shocked, but he was a good deal touched, and he cleared his throat of an unexpected obstruction before saying gruffly, "Aye, and a fine thing that would be. I'll thank you to remember you're a lady-born, Miss Syllie, however some people may choose to disregard it."

"Oh, Joe, I may be a lady-born, but little good it's ever done me, or is likely to," she said. "No, I think I should have been very much happier if you had been my Papa. I should have looked after you and kept your cottage clean and cooked for you. And I have no doubt you would have loved me and spoiled me very much, and in the end married me off to a promising young under-groom on the next estate."

He could not help thinking that if she had been his daughter he'd have taken precious better care of her, but he only said, "You'll not distract me with your foolishness, Miss Syllie. You're to go to Miss Emmy's and so Hinton and I are agreed."

Since Hinton and Blackmer had seldom been known to agree on anything, she looked a little touched, but only shook her head. "You know perfectly well, both of you, that you've only taken this maggot into your heads because of that stupid incident last spring. I assure you I've already forgotten it, and I can promise Lord Lambeth has. And really, you know, I can't help but think it was probably a good deal my own fault. If I had not been so foolish as to make a scene—for he only tried to kiss me, and he was odiously foxed—I have no doubt that would have been all there was to it. It is only that I cannot like him, besides thinking him a very bad influence on Papa. He treats Papa—oh, I don't know!" she said, "almost as if he held him in contempt, which makes me want to fly up into the boughs! Though why it should I don't know, for I must own I hold Papa in contempt myself."

Then, since Blackmer was still looking troubled, she gave a little shake of her head and said with a mock sigh of despair, "But the sad truth is, I fear, I was only put out of joint because no one else has ever tried to kiss me. It makes me fear there is no hope for me, for in general gentlemen do not appear to be in the least discriminating. I saw old Sir Bonamy Wingham's mistress when he brought her to the races one year, and I can tell you I was never so disillusioned in my life! She was quite plain, besides being very stout and red in the face, and though she looked to be amiable and even nodded to me in the friendliest manner, which I can't help but feel was most improper in her, I was never more taken in! I had certainly believed, from all that I've read, that Paphians must be beautiful, but it seems to be no such thing! I can only hope that the one Lord St. Ives stole from Lambeth was at least pretty."

"*What* did you say, Miss Syllie?" thundered Blackmer.

She opened her eyes wide. "What, have I it wrong? No, no, I'm sure I haven't, for I got it from Kendall, you know. It's classical, which no doubt explains why he knew it."

"And well for him if he hadn't! Or at least had refrained from passing it on to his younger sister. I'll thank you not to go repeating it in polite company!" said the groom.

"Oh, no. And particularly when you yourself have always taken such great care not to mention incognitas or game pullets in my hearing."

He had the grace to redden, but for once her non-sense failed to distract him. He was well aware that she was too much in his company, aye and her brother's, though usually Kendall could hardly be brought to notice what was going on beneath his nose, let alone go about repeating improper stories to his sister. She needed a female to guide her, and not that pesky Hinton either, with her gloomy grumblings. Things weren't right up at the Hall; no, nor had they been right for years. Miss Syllie might make light of it, but she couldn't fool him into believing she was happy. How could she be, when she had no friends her own age and a Papa who could scarcely be brought to remember her existence?

What Miss Syllie wanted was a husband. But how that was to be achieved when she seldom went beyond the nearest village, and when most of the respectable folk hereabouts had long since ceased to call upon Sir John, had Blackmer in a puzzle.

It had been exercising his mind for some time now, but never more urgently than after that incident with Lord Lambeth last spring. She might make light of that,

too, but he knew what he knew, and he didn't like to
think what might have happened if Hinton hadn't come by
and pretended urgent business with her young mistress.
Precious little reliance did he place upon Sir John's pro-
tecting his own daughter.

If Sir John had ever considered what was to become
of her he had given no hint of the fact. No mention had
ever been made of Miss Syllie making her come-out or
attending any of the assemblies held in Kentford or Newmarket, and her Papa seemed quite content to allow her
to dwindle into the life of an old maid. Didn't want to
lose her services most like, thought the groom. And the
only gentlemen Sir John was likely to bring home with him
were his hunting cronies, most either married or far too
long in the tooth for Miss Syllie, let alone that they were
a bunch of queer nabs, as loose in the haft as Sir John
was himself.

Nor, if the truth be admitted, did Miss Syllie seem to
shine in company. Blackmer might know she possessed a
keen wit and a sense of the ridiculous that was sometimes the despair of both him and Hinton; and that the
mischievous smile, breaking as it did in her usually somber
little face, could charm the heart out of one. But Blackmer
had known her all her life. Among strangers she tended to
appear shy and colorless.

So here she was, nearly twenty, and all but on the
shelf. It was a shame, was what it was.

Blackmer polished fiercely and unseeingly at the piece
of brass in his hand, and he burst out at last, "Miss Syllie,
you've got to get away from here!"

She looked a little startled, but after a moment she
said gently, "Why, and so I will, Joe. I don't mean to
stay here forever, you know that. Apart from the fact
that I am not—fond—of Papa, I can see there is no
future here for me. As soon as Kendall is down from
Oxford we mean to set up housekeeping together. I have
a little money coming to me from Mama, and Lord
Summerhill has been kind enough to promise Kendall a
post, so I don't doubt we shall do very well."

Blackmer had his own thoughts on this projected
scheme, but he only said, "And what's to happen till then
is what I'd like to know?"

"Why, I suppose I go on as I have been. You mustn't think I've been unhappy, Joe. How could I be with you and Hinton to take such good care of me?"

"And the next time your Papa brings home some of his fine friends and Hinton doesn't happen to be passing by if one of 'em gets in his cups?" he demanded.

"Why, I shall call for you, and you will no doubt come and rescue me as you have done so many times before when I have gotten into a scrape!"

Then the stable clock struck, and she looked up in astonishment, everything else forgotten. "Oh, Blackmer, no, it can't be noon already! I promised Hinton I would not upset the cook by being late to luncheon again!" She darted up and scandalized him by dropping a quick kiss on his cheek. *"Dear* Joe, what a worrier you are! And how lucky I am to have you. But oh dear, how dreadfully late I shall be!" She laughed and picked up her skirts, as she had done when she was a little girl, and ran with most undignified haste toward the Hall.

He watched her go, torn between affection and despair, and wondered, as he had done a hundred times before, what was to become of her.

BOOK ONE

I
London

The hour was considerably advanced, and all but the most hardened of gamesters had long since sought their beds, when Lord St. Ives strolled into one of the more discreet of the hells in Conduit Street. He was dressed, as usual, as if it mattered little to him to be *point-device,* his cravat indifferently arranged and his midnight blue coat cut so that he could shrug himself into it unaided. He looked tired—or drunk—his countenance set in oddly disillusioned lines for one of his years. But it was a handsome face for all that, with a pair of unexpectedly brilliant blue eyes.

He had been absent from town for some weeks, and several gentlemen called out greetings to him; but he acknowledged these only briefly and passed on through the room, his hands in his coat pockets and his tall figure very much at ease. He did not halt until he had reached an inner room, quieter and more discreetly lighted than the rest, where faro seemed to be the order of the day. Perhaps a dozen gentlemen in all, in varying degrees of inebriation, sat around a table, engrossed in the game at hand.

An older gentleman with a thin, somewhat weary face raised a pair of hard gray eyes. For a moment he looked faintly surprised, but then his habitual bored expression descended once more and he raised a languid white hand. "Well, St. Ives, where did you spring from?"

His words had an unexpected effect on his listeners. Several glanced up, and a young man seated with his back to the door twisted around and demanded, "What, is St. Ives back?"

My Lord Rockingham allowed a smile to touch his lips. "Wentworth here was beginning to think you were avoiding him, St. Ives," he drawled.

St. Ives strolled across and perched himself negligently on the arm of a chair. "Oh, have you found a rich widow in the last fortnight, Jack?" he inquired. "I warn you, I've no further need of your vouchers as shaving papers."

Wentworth grinned, and Lord Farnham, halfway down the table, delicately plied a gold toothpick and invited in his slightly mincing voice, "Will you take a hand, my lord? Though I fear Rockingham and Yates here are like to ruin us all before the night's over."

"Then I believe I will spare myself a fleecing, thank you," replied St. Ives carelessly.

"Aye, fleecing is the right word!" agreed a stout red-faced gentleman. "I protest, we've none of us stood a chance. Do you know Fleetwood, here, by the way, St. Ives? Has estates in Northamptonshire—or was it Nottinghamshire? I can never get the names of those blasted places straight in my mind."

His companion, a somewhat sober young man in a brown coat and neatly tied neckcloth, allowed this to pass, and glanced at his lordship's careless figure rather curiously. "How do you do, my lord?"

St. Ives nodded carelessly and turned away to say something in a low voice to Rockingham.

"Advise you not to play against St. Ives," Lord Chedbury cautioned Fleetwood in what he imagined to be a whisper. "Has the devil's own luck, you know."

Mr. Fleetwood glanced again at his lordship. "I appreciate your warning, but his lordship's reputation is not unknown to me," he said a little dryly. "Indeed, I doubt I am gamester enough to interest Lord St. Ives."

My Lord Farnham, amused, leaned back in his chair
and said a little maliciously, "St. Ives, I believe Mr. Fleetwood here don't approve of you."

St. Ives shot him a quick look.

Mr. Fleetwood colored slightly. "You mistake, my lord.
It is hardly my place to disapprove."

St. Ives's blue eyes turned to Fleetwood. "No," he
agreed insolently. "Perhaps you should return to Northamptonshire—or was it Nottinghamshire?"

Fleetwood turned a violent shade of red, and Lord
Farnham's unpleasant laugh sounded. After a moment
Lord Rockingham pulled out his snuffbox and regarded it
for a moment, then observed, "For my part, I have always
found the country completely incomprehensible. I believe it is reputed to be quite healthy for one, but the
only time I ever visited farther than Somerset, I was
obliged to require my host to set a lad to walk back and
forth under my window with a cart all night before I was
able to get a wink of sleep."

St. Ives's expression relaxed. "And did you stay, Jarvis?"
he asked in amusement.

Rockingham put up his thin brows. "No, how could I?
Brancton declared it was ruining his south lawn; and anyway the lad proved most unreliable. He seemed to be
always falling asleep at his post, which meant that I kept
waking all night long. For the sake of all of our health, I
was obliged to post back to London immediately."

Amid the general laughter, Mr. Fleetwood rose somewhat stiffly and bowed. "If you will excuse me, gentlemen, I will take my leave of you. You need not accompany me if you are not ready to depart, my lord," he
added as Chedbury half rose in his seat. "I believe I
know my way."

Chedbury shrugged and resumed his seat, and Lord
Rockingham dusted his sleeve with his handkerchief.
"Really, Nicky, I believe I will have to find a new place,
now that the riffraff has discovered this one," he complained.

St. Ives glanced at him. "Getting too common for you,
Jarvis?"

"Oh, it's a dull dog," interposed a bluff man at the end

of the table. "But are we to sit all night discussing him?"

A fair-haired youth seated next to Wentworth ignored that and unsteadily splashed some burgundy into his glass. "We hear you've succeeded where the rest of us have failed with the fair Fagiani, St. Ives," he complained, slurring his words. "I protest, it's that damned Byron's doings! Nowadays a female won't look at a man unless he's as black as bedamned and has the look of a cursed pirate."

Farnham inquired in his mincing voice, "Oh, had you interests there, Leyburn? Is that why you've been going about as sulky as a bear for the last two weeks?"

"I believe it was my pocketbook, not my countenance the lady found irresistible," said St. Ives cynically.

Lord Chedbury looked up incredulously. "What, never say it was you bought her that coach-and-pair she's been flaunting all over town? Good God! That must have cost you well over five hundred pounds!"

"Rather more, as I recall," yawned his lordship.

Chedbury, a man of sedate habits, studied him as if he were a rare specimen. "Aye, well, you know your own business best, no doubt," he said at last. "Myself, I wouldn't have thought any of 'em was worth it."

"They aren't!" agreed St. Ives.

Chedbury shook his head. "Egad, why do you stand the nonsense, then?"

"It is a question I have frequently asked myself."

"And have you found an answer, Nicky?" Rockingham inquired.

St. Ives looked across at him, a sudden gleam in his blue eyes. "Ah, one finds so few answers, Jarvis."

My Lord Rockingham's shoulders shook slightly, but a heavy-eyed man at the end of the table looked up then and said, "Newbury is right! Are we to play or sit chit-chatting all night? I for one have had a bellyful of St. Ives's affairs!"

St. Ives seemed to become aware of the presence of Lord Lambeth for the first time. "Hello, Lambeth," he said easily.

One or two others glanced at Lord Lambeth, wondering if there was to be trouble. Lambeth had been the chief contender for the Fagiani's favors before St. Ives entered the lists, and there was no love lost between them.

Lambeth was not drunk, but he had consumed a great deal of brandy. He nodded shortly and splashed some more into his glass. "Well, St. Ives! Is there any end to your accomplishments?" he sneered. "If we are to listen to these fools tonight, your prowess with the ladies even exceeds your offensiveness. Accept my congratulations."

St. Ives's eyes had not left Lambeth's face. "Oh, no. I have no doubt my offensiveness more than exceeds my prowess with the ladies," he said, "but it is you who is to be congratulated, I understand. Your nuptials seem to be as unexpected as they were timely."

One or two gentlemen snickered, and Lambeth turned an ugly color. Everyone present knew that to escape his gambling debts, Lambeth had recently wed the vulgar daughter of a wealthy merchant.

"Come, come, Lambeth!" interposed Chedbury. "No offense was meant, I'm sure."

Lambeth had half risen in his seat. "My Lord St. Ives overreaches himself!" he said angrily.

St. Ives smiled. "Oh, I don't think so!" he said sweetly. "But then you know what to do about it."

Lambeth hesitated, then laughed harshly and resumed his seat, tossing down the remains in his glass. "Yes, I know what to do about it!" he said. "You tempt me, my lord, to rid us all of your presence once and for all. But I believe my question still stands. Are we to play or sit chitchatting all night?"

After a moment the gaming continued. A slender gentleman in a buff coat and an intricately tied neck-cloth had observed the whole somewhat sleepily, but he said now as St. Ives came up, "Well, dear boy, you are, I see, as popular as ever."

St. Ives put up his brows. "Slumming, Frederick?"

The Honorable Frederick Strickland yawned, pulled out his snuffbox, and flicked it open with one finger. "Thought I'd see the newest hell," he said. "But I trust I have lost the requisite number of guineas and may soon retire to my bed. By the by, Nicky, was that really necessary?"

St. Ives shrugged. "Lambeth begins to bore me. If he

wishes the lady, he has only to outbid me. She means nothing to either of us."

"It would be useless, I collect, to point out that Lambeth ain't the fool you think him?"

But St. Ives was no longer attending. He was observing through his quizzing glass the late arrival of a stout gentleman in a waistcoat of startling design. "Good God. I'd no idea I'd stumbled on a family party."

Mr. Strickland merely yawned again and watched without surprise the advent of his lordship's uncle.

Lord Timothy Desborough, a gentleman of indeterminate years, with an amiable, slightly hedonistic countenance, halted to say a word to the waiter at his elbow, then came strolling in, waving two fingers at his nephew. "Hallo Nicky," he said cheerfully. "Thought you was still in the country. As it happens, I'm glad you're back. I'd something to say to you."

"How much?" inquired his undutiful nephew.

Lord Timothy blinked. "No, no, nothing like that. Though if you *could* see your way clear to lending me a monkey, I'd be obliged to you! Oh, hallo, Strickland, is that you?" he added as that worthy made some slight sound in his throat. "Not your usual haunt, is it? Well come to that, it ain't mine either, but I thought I'd best come around and see the newest hell. White's is grown damned respectable and even Watier's is devilish dull these days. Which reminds me, St. Ives," he added, turning back to his nephew, "have a sip of this and tell me what you think of it. Fellow—what's his name?—landlord here, tells me he's got three dozen bottles of it laid down."

St. Ives accepted the glass and lounged into a chair. The light from a branch of candles nearby fell partly on his face, making his blue eyes appear to glitter strangely in his dark face and casting deep shadows that accented the cynicism in his eyes and the arrogant twist to his mouth.

Then he moved his head slightly and the illusion was lost. He studied the contents of his glass and tossed it down in one swallow.

"Here!" protested Lord Timothy. "That ain't the way to treat a good wine. You're drunk, St. Ives!"

"Devil a bit! I drove down from Cheltenham tonight,"

said St. Ives. "I'll take half of whatever he'll let you have of this, Timothy. This is quite decent."

"Decent!" snorted his uncle. "It's damned good, and you know it. Where the devil did that rascally fellow get to—oh, you're there are you?" he added as the landlord appeared silently at his elbow. "I'll take whatever you've got of this brandy; and see that it's up to the quality of this bottle. You can send the bill to the Earl of St. Ives, here."

As Mr. Strickland looked faintly bemused, Lord Timothy grasped a button of his nephew's coat and added in confidential tones, "Tell you what, Nicky, it wouldn't do a mite of harm to have a look-see through the fellow's cellars as long as we're here. I'd go bail this stuff never paid duty at any port."

As his lordship looked sleepily interested, Lord Chedbury groaned, "Don't encourage him, St. Ives!"

Lord Timothy looked around. "What, is that you, Chedbury?" he asked. "Didn't see you there. Here, have a swallow of this brandy and tell me if you've ever tasted finer."

Lord Chedbury shook his head in resignation. "Come and take a hand or two. Rockingham has had all the luck for the last three nights running."

"What, is Rockingham here? Damme if it's not a good thing I looked in. He owes me three hundred pounds." Lord Timothy wandered over to observe the game in progress and in a moment had pulled out a chair and could be heard inquiring, "Is that your bank, Rockingham? What's the stakes?"

He glanced up when St. Ives reached across and firmly relieved him of the brandy bottle, but he made no objection, and soon a pile of papers and coins lay before him and he appeared oblivious to all else.

When St. Ives yawned and pulled himself up out of his chair at last, it was nearly dawn. Lord Timothy looked around absently. "What, you off so soon, Nicky?" he called. "Well, come and see me tomorrow. Not too early, though. Here!" he broke off to protest, "is that your queen, Ashbourne? Devil take you, I thought you'd played it an hour ago."

He then waved a careless hand, drained the wine in his glass, and called loudly for another bottle.

As they descended the stairs, Mr. Strickland, who had undertaken to walk part way with St. Ives, observed, "You've wasted your blunt, Nicky. He'll have the lot drunk before he goes home tonight."

St. Ives merely shrugged and turned up his coat collar as they emerged into the clear, cold dawn.

II

. The next morning the Earl of St. Ives found himself with an hour on his hands and obediently strolled around to the lodgings of the most congenial of his relatives. Though it was nearly noon, he found that aging dandy, still in his brocade dressing gown, sitting before the remains of a substantial breakfast and going through his morning's post.

Lord Timothy was a trifle heavy-eyed, but at the sight of his nephew he waved an indolent hand. "Oh, it's you, is it? Had a notion I remembered seeing you last night. You wasn't at White's, was you?"

St. Ives came in and propped his shoulders against the mantel, running a sardonic eye over his uncle's large figure. "No, the Nonesuch."

"Is that where it was?" grunted Lord Timothy. "Knew I'd discovered a remarkable brandy, but couldn't for the life of me remember where I'd been. By the by, did you have some, Nicky? I bought thirty bottles of it."

"Given you a head, Timothy?" inquired St. Ives with a grin.

Lord Timothy sighed. "Worst head I've had in years. I'm getting old, is what it is. Here, pour me a glass of that burgundy over there, will you, m'boy? Have one yourself. It won't do you a mite of harm."

St. Ives did as he was bid, pouring out two glasses and

handing one to his uncle before hooking forward a chair. He slouched into it, one booted foot flung over the arm, and raised his glass in mocking salute.

"Aye, that's cleared my head a trifle!" said Lord Timothy. He poured himself a second glass and disposed of the correspondence in front of him. "I'd something to say to you, but it's gone clean out of my head for the moment. Never mind! I've a piece of advice for you, m'boy. New hell: forgotten its name, but you know the one I mean—run by that Irish woman calling herself Lady Something-or-other. Advise you to steer clear of it. Fuzzes the cards," he added simply.

St. Ives regarded him with lazy interest. "You lose a bundle, Timothy?"

"Come to that, whenever did I not?" replied his uncle. "I tell you, Nicky, if my luck don't change soon, I may have to give up faro and take to whist. I lost a millaleva last night." He sighed gloomily, then roused himself to ask, "I don't owe you anything, do I?"

St. Ives had leaned back after a moment and closed his eyes, but now he opened one. "A trifle; a few thousand only," he admitted. "Why? You wasn't thinking of paying it back, was you?"

"Not unless my luck changes soon," said Lord Timothy truthfully. "But if I'm in to you already, leave it. I'll find the money elsewhere."

St. Ives closed his eyes again. "Wicken will give you a draft on my bank."

"Aye, well, it won't come amiss, I can tell you. Never saw such a cursed run of bad luck in my life. But if you're short, I can always ask Wraxham for it. Though it's something I'd as lief not be obliged to do, if I can help it," he admitted. "He's become damned prosy since he married that cheeseparing wife of his."

"I have enough for my needs," replied St. Ives.

His uncle regarded him with something akin to awe. "Well, if that's true, you must be the first of the family ever to say so! *I've* never been able to keep my head above water, God knows, and Ariel was forever in the clutches of some moneylender or another, until your father found out and put a stop to it. I doubt she ever knew how much she owed, from first to last, bless her!

Never knew such a female for running through the ready. Must be more of your father in you than I thought, Nicky."

St. Ives appeared unmoved by this tribute. "Then it must enjoy the distinction of being the only thing my sainted parent left me with his blessing," he said cynically.

"Aye, well, James was a dull dog," admitted Lord Timothy. He drained his second glass and leaned back in his chair. "Aye, that's got it! Knew I'd something to say to you! Thought I'd best warn you, Nicky: Laura's in town."

"Oh, God, is she?" said St. Ives wearily.

"Aye, caught me outside old Conyngham's house and kept me standing for the better part of an hour!" said his lordship. "How you stomach that she-dragon, Nicky, is more than I can understand!"

"I don't," St. Ives said briefly.

"Aye, devilish ill-bred woman! As much as accused me to my face of encouraging you. As if you ever needed any encouragement of mine, and so I told her. James may have been a dull dog, but how even he could have inflicted us with that—" He broke off and cocked a weather eye at his nephew. "Oh, well, never mind," he said. "No wish to say anything against your father, after all, dear boy."

"You've no need to hold your tongue on my account. I believe there was never any love lost between us."

Lord Timothy regarded him curiously. "Is there anything you're fond of, m'boy?"

St. Ives shrugged and reached for the decanter at his elbow.

"No, dear boy!" protested his uncle. "Must care about something."

St. Ives glanced up, his blue eyes hardening. "Sermon, uncle?"

"No, damn it, advice," said Lord Timothy. "And that's put me in mind of another matter, blister it! Prinny's got wind of that affair with Lambeth."

St. Ives, in the act of removing a pinch of snuff from a plain gold box, lifted suddenly narrowed eyes to his uncle's face. "So?"

"He ain't pleased, m'boy!" said Lord Timothy. "Asked

me to my face when you meant to settle down and quit kicking up scandals."

"Am I to quake in my boots because the Prince of Wales expresses disapproval of my actions?"

"Lord, it's nothing to do with me if you want to set up a damned harem! But Prinny's another matter. Mark my words, he'll be Regent before the year's out, and he can't afford another scandal just now. That affair with Colchester was bad, Nicky, and it ain't as if you cared anything for the chits! Never see you myself but what you're involved with some female or another. *I* never found the creatures worth it, bless 'em!" he added, momentarily losing sight of his object. "If they ain't got their little hands in your pocket for some gewgaw or another, they're enacting you Cheltenham tragedies over the breakfast table."

St. Ives's expression had become a little dangerous, but at that he laughed. "I always suspected that prime bit of virtue you had in keeping two years ago was a virago, Timothy."

"What—you don't mean Fanny?" asked Lord Timothy.

"No, the one before Fanny. Redhead. Can't remember her name."

Lord Timothy's brow cleared. "Oh, you're thinking of Sophia. Aye, what a temper! Once threw a teapot at me. But she was nothing to a little bird of paradise I once knew," he added. "Before your time, that one was, but she once took a knife out after me, little spitfire. Nearly skewered me, too!"

"What happened to her?"

"Lord, I don't know. Heard she turned respectable. Now what was her name? Sarah? Sally. Aye that was it! I don't like to think what she cost me, first to last, but what a little beauty she was."

He shook his head, dwelling on the memory for a moment; then it seemed to occur to him that these reflections were scarcely felicitous, for he frowned abruptly and said, "Plague take it, don't I keep telling you it's serious this time, Nicky? Don't keep changing the subject! You kick up a scandal over this, and Prinny won't wink at it like he did the last time. You be warned!"

St. Ives closed his eyes again. "You will forgive me if

I find such strictures a little hard to stomach, under the circumstances."

Lord Timothy glanced up at his nephew, his countenance for once unnaturally solemn. "Aye, you're a cool one, ain't you!" he said. "I never listened to Laura when you was younger, Nicky, for one thing because I can't stand the female, and for another because I thought you'd grow out of it. But damned if I'm not beginning to think she's right. There's bad blood in you, St. Ives! It ain't natural to be so cynical at your age."

St. Ives had risen. "If I didn't know better, I'd think the wine had gotten into your head, Timothy. If you're finished, I'll take my leave of you. I have known you more entertaining."

Lord Timothy met his hard stare for a moment, then sighed and relented. "Oh, very well, I've done!" he said. "But I warn you, you'll go too far one of these days, Nicky, and even I will wash my hands of you. And if you don't know it, I'm just about the last friend you have left."

"My God, would I survive?" mocked his lordship. Then, as Lord Timothy started up, an unnatural flush on his cheeks, St. Ives frowned and thrust out a hand to push him back. "Very well, Timothy, your warning is taken! But you're growing damned moral in your old age. I would never have thought it of you."

"Well, if that don't beat all! After I spent the better part of the last two weeks doing nothing but defending you!"

St. Ives's expression hardened again. "You're outside your role, Timothy," he said. "My business is my own, whatever I choose to do."

"If you want to keep your affairs your own, don't conduct 'em in gambling hells!" snorted his uncle. "And if you think you do well to make an enemy of Lambeth, you're an even bigger fool than I thought you."

"Good God, I don't fear Lambeth," St. Ives said contemptuously. "Now for God's sake, leave it, Timothy! You're the only one of my relatives I can stomach, and that's only because you're a licentious old reprobate."

After a moment Lord Timothy abandoned his effort. "Trouble is, you ain't got enough to interest you, Nicky," he said. "Damme, if Laura and Prinny ain't both right, plague take 'em! It's time and more you was thinking of setting up your nursery and quit kicking up scandals wherever you go."

"Following in your footsteps, uncle?"

Lord Timothy, a confirmed bachelor, had the grace to blush. "Aye, but that's not to say I wouldn't have done things differently if the succession had ever been in doubt," he said stubbornly. "And that's another thing. You can't tell *me* you want that cousin of yours stepping into your shoes, because I won't believe you."

St. Ives swore softly. "No, I don't want to see Michael in my shoes," he admitted. "My very respectable cousin and I don't see eye to eye."

"Aye, and you needn't try and humbug me, as Laura did, that no decent girl would have you. You may have a bad reputation, m'boy, but you're handsome enough, besides having a great deal more money than's good for you, and I've seen the way the silly chits look at you. You could have any one of the gals on the marriage mart for the crooking of a little finger."

"That is the one mistake, for my sins, I have no intention of making. I've seen enough of wedded bliss to last me a lifetime," said St. Ives cynically.

He tossed down the remains of his burgundy and rose, looking lazily down at his uncle. "If you've nothing of more interest to impart, I'll leave you, beloved. I'm off to Newmarket tomorrow. Will I see you there?"

Lord Timothy shrugged and said vaguely, "Yes—no—that is, I haven't decided yet. Prinny and I may have a look-in later in the week. Do you have anything running?"

They discussed the relative merits of various horses for a few minutes before St. Ives, with a glance at the clock, moved toward the door. He was halfway through when he glanced back and added, "Oh, and you may tell His Royal Highness for me, Timothy, that if and when I decide to wed, I will at least confine myself to one bride at a time."

"Now, Nicky," protested his uncle, "you know that story was never proved."

"Never mind. I'll tell him myself. I never thought I'd see the day you two court cards would set up as moral arbiters. It's damned disagreeable, I can tell you."

He closed the door behind him before Lord Timothy could think of a suitable retort.

III

News of St. Ives's return to London and his brief exchange with Lambeth reached a number of interested parties by the next morning. One of them, a rather bluff man of considerable bulk, glanced at his companion and said, "There's likely to be trouble there! Not that it would distress you much, eh? You'd be well rid of him, from all I hear."

His companion, Mr. Michael Staunton, was a rather grave-looking young man with nothing of his flamboyant cousin's habits. He merely smiled now and said calmly, "*If* St. Ives lost, which is by no means certain, you know. You've not seen him with a pistol. But I assure you I have no desire to see any harm come to him. I only hope he may not allow his temper to overcome him once too often."

Winterbotham eyed him curiously. "Aye. You ain't much like him, you know."

Michael grinned. "If you mean I lack his ability to get myself talked about from one end of London to another, I must count that as a compliment."

"Aye, he's a devil from all I hear," admitted Winterbotham. "Aldersley was telling me some rubbishing tale of his having shot out the wicks of the candles in Watier's t'other night. Dead drunk, too, if you can believe Aldersley."

"Yes, I was there. A stupid trick, no more. But St. Ives has always been an excellent shot."

"Well, he must be if he was drunk! What'd he do it for?"

Staunton shrugged. "Oh, it was a wager, I believe. But

you wrong St. Ives, you know. He has never required a
reason. To say he was drunk is enough."

He spoke lightly; but, there was a faint bitterness in his
tone. Winterbotham glanced at him again, but then several
others came up and the conversation became general.

The Countess of St. Ives received the news of her
stepson's return to London with scarcely more joy. She
had come up from Bath expressly to see him, but, since
she had grown accustomed over the years to his unpre-
dictability, she had not been surprised to discover that
he was away and that his servants had no idea where he
had gone or when he would return.

She was a cold woman, of a somewhat intolerant nature,
and St. Ives had been a thorn in her flesh for many
years. As a boy he had passionately resented his new
and forbidding stepmama; as a young man he had in-
dulged in every excess, purely, she was convinced, for
the purpose of humiliating her; and even now she seldom
went anywhere but what she was confronted with some
fresh scandal of his.

She had often been heard to remark, in her measured
way, that if dear Nicky were not so very much a Staunton,
one would almost believe that Ariel had played her
lord false, for one could never quite imagine that dear
James had fathered such a wild, unmanageable boy. Nicky
had been that way since she had known him, and no
one had ever had the slightest influence over him, unless
it had been Lord Timothy Desborough, and on *that* subject she would say no more. But then she did not mean
to complain. One could only suppose, from the things one
heard, that St. Ives had taken after his Mama in temperament, if not in looks.

Since she made her home for much of the year in
Bath with her only daughter, a rather lively damsel of
seventeen, and seldom came up to London anymore, it
might have been supposed that the ruinous activities of
her stepson had ceased to disturb her. But anyone who
thought that was ignorant of the rapidity with which gossip
traveled in her large circle of friends, and of her ladyship's own indomitable will. Her husband, the late earl,
had been a man of strong principles, and she prided her-

self that she had never once failed to do her duty toward his only son and heir, however much that duty may have weighed upon her.

The complaints she had recently lodged with Lord Timothy had been more in the nature of spite than from any conviction on her part that her words would have an effect. She had never been able to rouse that amiable dandy to a sense of his responsibilities. Indeed, she did not hesitate to place a great deal of the blame directly at his door. One might talk all they pleased of the wild blood of the Desboroughs, but she was of the opinion that Lord Timothy had always encouraged his nephew just to thwart her.

Since Timothy had also taken it upon himself to introduce a younger St. Ives to the notice of such persons as he thought would be useful to himself, Lady St. Ives might be considered somewhat justified in her dislike of her late husband's brother-in-law. Lord Timothy was a member of the Carlton House set, those intimates of the Prince of Wales who were considered as amoral as the Prince himself and were famed for gambling for disastrous stakes, drinking quantities of liquor, and being lax in almost everything but matters of play and pay.

Society might have managed to over look these things, for young men were expected to sow their wild oats, after all, and there were few eligible bachelors who combined St. Ives's rank and fortune with his romantic face and figure. But when St. Ives culminated a series of open liaisons with a disastrous affair with the wife of a prominent politician—who subsequently divorced her and then shot himself—the more respectable doors began to be closed to him, and matrons of eligible daughters regretfully turned their attentions elsewhere.

Spiteful persons might say that it was only to be expected, after all: his Mama's indiscretions had been an open secret for years before her death; and Lord Timothy, however amiable, was frankly hedonistic and had lived on the edge of ruin for more years than anyone cared to remember. But they had always been good *ton*. St. Ives, on the other hand, capped his disgraceful conduct by seeming totally indifferent to what was said about him, and, instead of showing proper regret for his ouster, he had never betrayed the slightest desire to figure in that society his name and rank entitled him to adorn.

Never one to put off an unpleasant duty, Lady St. Ives sailed forth the very next morning to call on her stepson. She succeeded in bullying a footman into admitting her and descended upon St. Ives while he was still sitting over his breakfast.

St. Ives had had very little sleep the night before, and he was looking a trifle pale, but he glanced up without surprise at his stepmother's entrance and said smoothly, "Ah, Laura, I might have known I could expect a visit from you this morning. You have eaten, I suppose?"

His stepmother raised her eyebrows. "Good morning, St. Ives. I breakfasted hours ago, thank you. I hope you can spare me a few minutes of your time. I have something to discuss with you."

"Yes, I rather thought you might have," he observed. "Where's Kitty, by the by? Is she with you?"

"Kitty has gone shopping with the misses Mildmans." She could not resist adding, a little spitefully, "I doubt you would know them. They do not, I believe, frequent the same circles as you do."

A glint of amusement stole into his lordship's eyes. "Ah, Laura, no matter how long we've known one another, you never disappoint me."

Lady St. Ives's sallow cheeks took on an unaccustomed redness, but she said shortly, "As a matter of fact, it's about Kitty that I wished to speak to you. You must know—or rather you would if you had ever paid the slightest interest in your sister—that Kitty will soon be eighteen."

"On the contrary," corrected St. Ives, leaning back and calmly slicing a peach with his long fingers, "I am perfectly aware of Kitty's birthday, since I sent her a present only last month. And a very handsome one it was, too, if I recall."

Lady St. Ives allowed herself to be goaded into an unwise retort. "I hope you don't expect me to believe you remembered the date yourself!"

He shot her a quick glance. "Of course not," he admitted maliciously. "Wicken reminded me."

Her bosom swelled visibly, but she managed to choke

back the words trembling on her lips. "Never mind! You must know that Kitty has her heart set on making her come-out this spring."

His black brows rose, but he only said, "She'll elope with the first rattle in a scarlet coat."

Since the Lady Catherine's propensity for flirting with the members of the military formed a major part of the reason her Mama had consented to put forward her presentation, Lady St. Ives said, "I do not find that amusing, St. Ives! Kitty has a—a lively disposition, but I have every hope that a little town bronze will do a great deal to settle her down."

He took her up in an unfortunately literal manner. "Ah, has the Twelfth Foot been gazetted back to Bath?" he asked in amusement. "Really, Laura, if you can't control the chit in Bath, how the devil do you expect to do so in London? Well, you will do as you wish, no doubt. I presume you didn't interrupt me at my breakfast to ask my permission?"

Lady St. Ives regarded him with undisguised dislike. "It is clear you cannot have fully considered the matter, St. Ives. However little you may like to acknowledge the fact, Kitty is your sister, and, I may remind you, every bit as much a Staunton as you are. What do you suppose the world will have to say if she makes her bow, not from her brother's house, but from the house of her maternal grandparents?"

"Ah, so that's what you're up to, is it? I will remind you that it was your decision to immure yourself in the fastnesses of Bath. I have always tried, at least, to remember that my father chose to marry you."

Lady St. Ives's mouth thinned in anger, and she lost sight of her object in an old grudge. "And the moment we arrive in town, you'll be off to one or another of your country houses, I make no doubt!" she snapped.

"What else?" he inquired sweetly.

"I will remind you, St. Ives, that you are Kitty's guardian—an arrangement I was neither informed of nor approve! Up to now you have stirred yourself not one whit in her behalf, which," she added tartly, "I should no doubt be grateful for, since you seem to delight in making yourself notorious from one end of England to another! But you will not—I repeat, you will *not*—demonstrate to the world what you think of us by posting off as soon as we cross the threshold!"

"Oh," he protested mildly, "I don't object to Kitty coming, if she behaves herself."

Lady St. Ives rose to her not inconsiderable height and stood glaring down at her stepson. "I have done my best over the years to overlook your disgraceful conduct," she said, "but when I remember the scandals you have engaged in and the pleasure you seem to take in making yourself the object of gossip in the face of all my friends and acquaintances, I can only be thankful that poor James is not alive to see it. I cannot tell you the number of times *I* have had to blush with shame at the connection between us!"

He sat up and said in a deceptively soft tone, "Have you, ma'am? It is remarkable that your shame does not seem to stand in your way when you want something. And I will remind you that this is *my* house. Kitty may come or not, as she chooses; it makes little difference to me. But if you had contrived to keep a vestige of control over her, she might not now be the worst little baggage it's been my misfortune to meet."

Enraged, Lady St. Ives picked up her gloves and scarf. "I can see there is no talking to you in this mood, St. Ives. I might have known I could expect nothing but rudeness from you. And one more thing—if you could contrive to keep your name from being bandied about, at least until I have returned to Bath, I would consider it a favor."

He smiled silkily at her. "Ah, you almost tempt me, Laura! If I could only be certain that would be soon, I might even try to accommodate myself to your wishes this once."

She swung on her heels and swept out, her demi-train swaying angrily behind her.

He watched her go, then abruptly rose and crossed to the fireplace. He had not meant to let her anger him, but in talking about his stepsister she had trod on a corn, however little he might like to acknowledge it. He had been aware for too many years that in neglecting his responsibilities he had condemned the lively young Kitty to just the sort of childhood he himself had endured. And no one knew better than he what that meant.

He frowned into the grate. It was useless to tell himself that he could scarcely have done anything else. He had hardly attained his majority when his father died, and he certainly knew nothing of the requirements of infants scarcely out of leading strings. Nor would Laura have viewed with anything but extreme disfavor any attempt to take away her only child.

But he knew that he had made no attempt simply because he had not wanted to trouble himself. Aye, he was a Staunton, all right, for all Laura's sly innuendos, and when had a Staunton ever cared for anyone but himself?

He shrugged impatiently and crossed the room, preparatory to going out, when he suffered his second uninvited visitor of the morning. The door flew inward beneath his hand, and the laughing face of a young girl was peeped round the panels.

"Oh, good, she's gone!" the girl said naughtily. "I made Chelmsford let me hide in your study until I heard her leave."

She danced into the room. "You must have made her dreadfully angry, Nicky! Her face only looks purple like that when she's particularly enraged!"

He regarded his young sister without surprise. "Hallo, Kitty. I'm surprised you weren't listening at the keyhole."

She appeared to accept his remark as a compliment, for she admitted, with a gurgle of laughter, "I meant to, only Chelmsford caught me and made me come away."

The long-suffering butler appeared at the door at that moment. "I beg your pardon, my lord. Lady Catherine was particularly desirous of speaking with you, and I thought, seeing as how you had her ladyship with you, I'd best let Lady Catherine have her way. As for Lady St. Ives, sir," he added stiffly, "I've already had a word with young Jonathon. It won't happen again, my lord."

"Very well, Chelmsford," St. Ives said, "you can go and leave this brat to me."

When the butler had withdrawn, Kitty asked, "Have you warned your servants not to admit Mama, Nicky? Won't she be livid when she finds out!"

"No, I haven't warned my servants not to admit her, brat! But if you don't take care, I may issue such an order about you. Now what is it you want? I'm already late."

It was apparent that she stood in no awe of her formidable brother, for she merely laughed and danced across the floor, saying, "Very well, ten minutes. But you must look at me, Nicky, because I have something I particularly wanted to ask you."

His lips quirked slightly, despite himself. She saw it and said sunnily, "There, I knew you could not be so cross as you looked!"

"Don't try your wiles on me, my girl. How much do you want this time?"

She opened her eyes very wide and attempted to look demure. "I promised you last time I would stay within my allowance, Nicky, and so I have." After a moment she amended, "Well, almost! Anyway, that isn't in the least what I came to see you about, but now that you mention it, I am a little short until next quarter's allowance. Lydia and Susan and I were playing whist in the back parlor the other morning when Mama thought we were practicing our French, and I lost twenty-five pounds." She peeped at him from between her lashes. "I hadn't meant to ask you. As a matter of fact, I think Lydia must have been cheating, for as a rule I nearly always win. But you know yourself that debts of honor must be paid immediately."

He pulled several notes out of his pocketbook. "Does Laura know you're gambling?"

She took the notes, counted them, and then threw her arms about his neck. "Oh, thank you, *best* of my brothers!"

He removed her hands from their clutch on his neck-cloth.

"You must know Mama doesn't approve of gambling, Nicky. I think she's afraid I'll grow up to be like you."

"No doubt. But if you're going to play, at least make certain you know how. You'd better come to me and I'll teach you." He went to pour himself another glass of wine. "But what was of such importance that you must disturb me at the breakfast table?"

Some of the animation disappeared from her face.

"Yes, well—d-did Mama tell you she's thinking of putting forward my come-out?"

"Yes, and I must confess it made me wonder what you'd been up to, to make her consider a step she was violently against the last time I spoke to her."

She blushed a little. "Well, I did get into a scrape. But we *weren't* eloping, whatever that silly Mrs. Williams said! And for Mama to say that if I didn't watch out, people would begin to think I was every bit as b-bad as you, and I would never obtain vouchers to Almack's or anywhere else is not true!" she cried. "And anyway, I wouldn't care if it *was* true, for I don't know anyone I like as well as you, and Uncle Timothy, and Grandmama Wraxham, for you never scold me or make me think I'm bad just because I want to have a little fun and not be so deadly serious all the time. Oh, Nicky, I think I shall die if I have to go back to another year with Mama in Bath!"

He stood looking down at her. She was an extraordinarily pretty young girl, dressed expensively and becomingly in a sky-blue pelisse buttoned up to her chin and trimmed with fur. A muff of the same fur was thrown carelessly on the chair, and a dashing bonnet was perched on her dark curls. She did not much resemble her brother, but the tearful eyes fixed so meltingly on his face were very like his own.

When he made no answer, she said, "Mama says you don't care a fig about me, but you do, don't you, Nicky? And you are my guardian. If you were to decide to bring me to stay with you for a little while, just until I made my come-out, Mama could have nothing to say. Oh please say you will, Nicky!"

"I imagine your Mama would have a great deal to say," he corrected. "No, Kitty, even if I wanted to, the whole thing's impossible."

She would have tumbled eagerly into speech, but he held up a hand.

"No, listen to me, for I won't repeat it! Even if I wanted to have you with me, Laura would have a good deal to say, and most of it true. You've listened to her long enough to know that I am the last one to be charged with bringing a young girl out. And even if I were, you would need a chaperone, someone to tell you the ins and outs and what to wear and all that nonsense that I know less than nothing about. I'm sorry, Kitty. I understand—perhaps better than you think—but it wouldn't work."

"If you d-did understand," she cried, "you w-wouldn't be so cruel! I warn you, if you w-won't help me, I'll d-do something desperate! And I can, too, for I'm considered quite an heiress, and I've already met a number of m-men who would like to marry me. And if I do, it will be all your fault!"

He controlled his temper with an effort. Damn Laura. Things were even worse than he had thought. What the devil was he going to do with the chit?

"If I did take you, you'd not get by with these tantrums! You've been badly spoiled, and someone should have taken a hairbrush to you years ago."

Her face cleared like magic. "Yes, but I daresay I wouldn't be if I were happy. Oh please, Nicky, say you will?"

His mouth twisted. "What the devil am I to do with you?"

"Well, I've thought about that, too, and I think I know the exact thing! If you were to marry right away, your wife could chaperone me, and Mama would be left with nothing to say. You know yourself she's always saying that if you would only marry and quit making scandals everything would be perfectly all right, and people would no longer gossip about you."

"And do you have a candidate in mind? Someone I can woo, wed, and induce to take my naughty young sister under her wing, all in a few short months?"

"Well, I did think either Lydia or Susan might do—they're the Mildmans you know—because they think you're enormously romantic. Lydia says you're a rake, and women are always partial to rakes," she added with a grin.

"Oh, my God!"

"Well, I do see now that they may be a little too young for you. Grandmama Wraxham says you usually prefer riper women. I don't know *precisely* what that means, but I think it must mean older and more sophisticated, like your opera dancer. Only of course you can't

marry her! But I'm afraid that leaves Susan and Lydia
out because they're not much older than I am."

"Go on, whom have you selected? Let me know the
worst."

She regarded him with a hint of apprehension. "No
one, honestly! Mama's always saying it's disgusting the
way everyone throws their caps at you, so you should
have no trouble finding someone who's willing to marry
you. But I quite see that it's very important to have
someone we both can like. And I've even made up my
mind not to complain if it has to be Julia Horneby, even
though she does treat me as if I were the same age
as that dreadful little sister of hers!"

"I am beginning to think your Grandmama Wraxham
and your Mama talk a good deal of nonsense!" he said.
"Perhaps it is time that I did something about you, but
you'll be lucky if I don't find some female dragon for you
and retreat permanently to the Priory."

She smiled sunnily up at him. "Oh, best of my brothers!
You won't really leave me alone, will you? It would be
so much more fun with you here. But I won't say anything more, and I must run, or Mama will begin to wonder
where I am. I bribed the butler to say I'd gone to the
library with Susan Mildman." She waltzed toward the door,
and as she was leaving, stuck her head back around the
panels and said, "But you will at least *look* for a bride
before February, won't you, Nicky? It would make everything so much nicer!"

He swore and watched her go. Damn Laura. It was
clear he was to have no peace until he'd settled the
problem of Kitty. No doubt the easiest way would be to
find some respectable woman of good birth to come and
look after her. He searched his memory for a suitably
respectable woman and was in the end forced to admit
that his acquaintance boasted few who could fit the
description.

He tossed down his wine and thought about marrying
Julia Horneby, as Kitty had suggested. She would make a
good countess, she would not be shocked by anything he
might choose to do, and she would probably bear him the
son he needed to succeed him. And it would be no great
sacrifice, for she was both beautiful and willing. But the

thought of being married to her for the rest of his life moved him to profound boredom.

He pulled violently on the bell to order his curricle. Then, consigning his various relatives to hell, he went off in search of distraction. That, at least, he knew how to find, and with a vengeance.

IV

His lordship was evidently still seeking distraction when he left for Newmarket that afternoon. He had set his whole staff about their ears with his temper, and he drove at such a reckless pace that Wicken, his groom, wondered what mischief was brewing now.

Mr. Strickland, the only other occupant of the curricle, was moved to inquire politely after the first few miles if St. Ives was meaning to kill them all, in which case he preferred to be set down at the next posting house.

St. Ives glanced at him, then passed the vehicle ahead of them with only inches to spare, nearly sending its hapless driver into the ditch. Wicken remained impassive, but Strickland clutched the side of the curricle and turned pale, eyeing his friend with a distinct lack of favor.

Despite Mr. Strickland's obvious doubts, they managed to reach Newmarket without mishap, and early enough for dinner, a circumstance that did much to restore Mr. Strickland to charity with his friend. But St. Ives, despite Mr. Strickland's example, partook only sparingly of the excellent meal that was set before him and stayed drinking alone before the fire until a late hour.

The following day dawned cloudy and cold, leading Mr. Strickland to predict they were in for rain, an opinion shared by a great many others. But though the sky remained overcast, the expected rain did not fall, and the course was excellent. St. Ives's colors did very well, and a particularly promising four year old he had just bought took the field against all odds.

But St. Ives remained unmoved by his victories. He drank heavily each evening, seldom going to bed much before dawn, and he was gambling deeply as well.

The Prince of Wales, with his friends, came up briefly on Wednesday, when one of the prince's favorites was running. But since the Regency crisis was still unsettled and the old king's health reportedly deteriorating every day, no one was much surprised when he did not linger.

Lord Timothy, accompanying His Royal Highness, had time to speak only briefly with his nephew, and then he seemed uninclined to do much more than bemoan his losses. He had received a sure tip on Jack-Come-Tickle-Me in the third race and had staked a large sum upon him only to have the horse unplaced. He was much inclined to believe that he had been robbed. But he did remember at the last moment to tell St. Ives that Laura had unexpectedly returned to Bath. He grinned wickedly, clapped his nephew on the shoulder, and started off, only to turn back again with the intelligence that Kitty had been to see him full of plans for her come-out, with some fal-lal tale of St. Ives having agreed to take her off Laura's hands. Timothy listened cynically to St. Ives's explanation, but at an urgent summons from his prince he hastened away.

Late on Thursday the expected storm broke, drenching the field and driving the hapless spectators to seek shelter. St. Ives, apparently indifferent to the steady downpour, would have headed back to the inn had not Mr. Strickland vetoed the suggestion in uncustomarily strong terms.

His reason soon became obvious. When St. Ives had frowned and impatiently pulled up under the shelter of a low-spreading tree, his companion anxiously examined his elegant pearl gray beaver. Reassured it had suffered no lasting hurt, he sighed and said, "Damn it, Nicky, you would bring your curricle! I just had this hat from Welting last week."

"I wonder why I put up with you, Frederick," St. Ives

said snubbingly. "You won't melt for a little wetting, you know."

Mr. Strickland flicked an imaginary speck of dust from the spotless white top of his boots. "Really, Nicky," he observed, "you must know that practically your only claim to fashion is that I notice you. *Where* had you that coat, by the by? I warn you, if I had glimpsed it before I consented to accompany you, nothing in the world would have prevailed on me to be seen in your company."

"A little more of that, Frederick, and I'll set you down and let you walk back." He ignored his friend's indignant protest. "What I won't do is keep my horses standing in this weather. Believe me, I care a great deal more for them than for your damned hat."

"Then you can set me down here," Mr. Strickland said. "I'll be damned if I'll have my teeth rattled and my boots splashed for the sake of your blasted grays, St. Ives. I know your neck-or-nothing style!"

St. Ives's groom had been listening with great appreciation to this exchange, but since he was well acquainted with Mr. Strickland, he said kindly, "Now, sir, you don't need to go worriting about anything. I've never known his lordship to splash anyone." He glanced at his master's sardonic expression and added, "Leastways, not *accidental,* that is."

Mr. Strickland allowed his pose to drop. "That's precisely what I'm afraid of, Wicken," he said with a grin. "Advise me. Dare I trust him after his ill temper of the past week?"

Wicken shrugged, grinning, but St. Ives said promptly, "And be damned to you, Frederick! The sight of your dandified face is enough to put anyone into a temper. And I give you fair warning, I can't guarantee I won't overturn you if you make my horses stand much longer in this rain."

Mr. Strickland began to look alarmed, but Wicken, his precious grays maligned, said roundly, "Now, that's enough, my lord! You know perfectly well these grays is perfect lambs, rain or shine."

Since those same lamblike grays were known to be an extremely difficult pair and were showing unmistakable signs of growing restive, Strickland did not seem convinced. But at that moment a gentleman from a little party that had gathered under a group of trees nearby rode up and hailed them.

He touched his hat and said, "Ah, St. Ives. Thought I recognized those grays of yours. There's a house not more than a mile from here where we can take shelter. Belongs to a chap by the name of Fairfield. He's invited any that cares to, to take their potluck with him and sit out the storm."

Mr. Strickland, still thinking of his hat no doubt, said, "Fairfield, eh? Do I know him?"

"Oh, I'm sure you know who I mean," said Captain Roth. "Big chap, rides about fourteen stone. Bit of a fool, really, but a good man to hounds. No need to fear. There'll be enough of us there to pass a tolerable enough evening."

"How do we find the place?" inquired Mr. Strickland.

"Oh, just follow the road till you come to the tollgate, then take the left turning. Fairfield says you can't miss it. Big stone house." He pulled his hat down over his eyes, saluted with his riding crop, and splashed back to his companions.

"I know Fairfield," said St. Ives. "He's a hanger-on, half flash and half foolish."

"Yes, dear boy," said Mr. Strickland, "but you're forgetting my hat."

St. Ives laughed and whipped up his team.

Several hours later the rain still showed no signs of stopping. It pounded against the heavily curtained windows of the untidy room in which the party sat, and an occasional low growl of thunder could be heard.

The room was poorly lighted, and since no one had come in to make up the fire in the last hour, it was growing steadily colder. But few of the gentlemen seated around the large table gave much sign of being aware of either fact.

It was not a large room, but it had been handsome once, with dark-paneled walls and small-paned windows. Now it showed unmistakable signs of neglect: the hangings at either side of the window were threadbare and the Turkey carpet on the floor was worn. Bits of bridle, riding crops, and bills, along with back copies of the *Turf Remembrancer* and the *Morning Gazette*, were tossed on every available surface.

The cloth had been removed from the table and the remains of the meal taken away, but the faint odor of overroasted meat remained among the brandy fumes.

For the most part, there was little sound in the room aside from the low-voiced placing of bets and the occasional shifting of a log in the fireplace. The play was deep, and most present were too much the hardened gamesters to waste time with idle chatter.

Sir John Fairfield allowed his eyes to wander around the room. He was a large man, still trim and fit for his forty-six years, though his face was no longer handsome. Too many days spent in the saddle and too many nights like this had taken their toll, and the lines of dissipation stood round his eyes and mouth. He was a bluff, hearty man, a widower of many years standing, but since his relationship with his wife had never been close, he had been much more comfortable since her death. If he sometimes regretted the fact that neither of his children lived up to his expectations, he did not often let his feelings disturb the even tenor of his days.

If anyone had asked him, he would have said that he was quite content with his life. There was never enough money, of course, but he always managed to find what was required for his own entertainment, and his responsibilities had always sat lightly upon him.

He had been drinking more heavily than usual tonight, a little flattered at having at his board gentlemen who had seldom troubled to acknowledge his existence; and he had momentarily allowed his vanity to overcome a certain native shrewdness. Now he thought that perhaps he had had too much to drink, for the brandy had failed to dull his senses. It seemed, instead, to have sharpened his intellect, so that he saw himself as he must appear to others. It was not a pleasant experience.

The men at his table were well known in society for the most part, fashionably dressed and carelessly at their ease. Most of them wore stained buckskins and mud-splattered top boots, their cravats loosened and their faces flushed with drink, but they still somehow contrived to make the room look shabby and not overclean. To Fairfield's brandy-soaked brain there seemed a faint atmosphere of aristocrats slumming—eating his food and drinking his brandy and sneering at him behind his back.

He was not ordinarily fanciful, and now he shook his head to clear it. Hell, he was getting maudlin. He knew these arrogant young bucks for what they were. He had known most of their fathers before them.

His eyes felt scratched and bleary. He glanced around the table. My Lord Farnham said something in his mincing voice to Mr. Strickland, then laughed unpleasantly as Mr. Strickland put up his brows in distaste, and Fairfield was suddenly convinced that they had been laughing at him. Goddamn them all! Let them come and sneer at him, with their fine airs and mincing ways. He would show them.

A branch of candles on a side table flickered, and he rubbed his eyes again. He couldn't remember when he had last been this drunk. The cards in his hand blurred before his eyes and he had trouble making out their numbers.

Lord Lambeth, to his right, raised heavy-lidded eyes for a moment, as if aware of his host's condition, then looked back at his hand. "Very well, then. I'm in," he said indifferently and pushed forward a little pile of coins. "Five hundred to you, Fairfield."

Fairfield concentrated on his own cards. They meant little to him. He had won fairly frequently at first, but he seemed to have been losing steadily for the past hour.

Then the sum Lambeth had named pierced his foggy consciousness. Even in the deeper clubs in London the stakes were seldom so high. He moistened his lips, sober enough to know that if he lost his nerve he was finished, and longed for that earlier blind euphoria. He recklessly downed the brandy in his glass and thrust forward nearly all the coins in front of him before he had time to change his mind.

The play moved around the table. Captain Roth protested the stakes, but was overruled, and Wentworth hiccuped slightly and unsteadily pushed forward the last of his coins. "Burn you, St. Ives," he said without heat. "I'll have a nine or better."

The Earl of St. Ives, who held the bank, turned up a three. Wentworth swore loudly and refilled his glass.

Fairfield, discovering that he had miraculously emerged the winner, was scarcely aware of any of them. He swallowed and gathered his winnings with trembling hands.

Lambeth again glanced at him with a faint sneer, then pulled out his snuffbox and took a pinch, his hooded eyes veiled.

St. Ives, seated at the foot of the table, was sprawled in his chair, his dark locks romantically disarranged and one arm hooked over the back of his chair, his booted legs thrust out before him. He looked three parts asleep, his eyes half closed, but for a brief moment they lifted, too, to rest expressionlessly on Fairfield's face. Fairfield had the uncomfortable impression that they looked right through him.

St. Ives looked away again, his eyes coming to rest on Lambeth, then he leaned forward to splash some more brandy into his glass, his hand perfectly steady. He said lazily, "I think the stakes are too tame for Wentworth, here. Raise you to a thousand, gentlemen."

Lambeth shot him a quick glance, and Mr. Strickland, still immaculate though he had broached his third bottle, said, "Damn it, Nicky, it's too steep. Five hundred's enough. This ain't the Daffy Club."

"Raise you to a thousand, gentlemen," repeated St. Ives.

"Oh, very well," relented Mr. Strickland. "A thousand to you, Lambeth."

Lambeth, his habitual sneer rather more pronounced than usual, said, "If it's too steep for you, Strickland, stand out!"

St. Ives's eyes lifted. "It would seem you've grown more daring since last we played, Lambeth," he drawled. "Or is it that your bride's money makes you suddenly bold?"

Lambeth's face stilled, and there was a sudden silence.

Then his heavy lids came down once more, concealing his expression. "We'll see who rises a winner by morning, my lord!"

"Perhaps you'd care to make a small side wager on that possibity. Say a thousand pounds?" St. Ives said.

Lord Skeffington, standing with his back to the fire, said angrily, "St. Ives has the devil in him tonight! We'll see trouble before the night's out."

His companion's thin brows rose. "Oh, St. Ives is drunk," Cranborne said, "but that don't signify. He and Lambeth have been at each other's throats since the Fagiani affair, although Lambeth isn't fool enough to challenge him."

Wentworth, in the meantime, had drunkenly latched onto the proposed wager. "A bet! A bet! Aye, that's it, Lambeth! Five hundred says you'll not break St. Ives's bank by morning."

St. Ives's eyes were still on Lambeth's face. "I'm afraid you'll have to stand in line, Wentworth. Lambeth is engaged to me. Well, Lambeth?"

If Lambeth hesitated, it was only infinitesimally. "Certainly, my lord," he said with his faint sneer. "Let us hope your legendary luck will have deserted you this time. You are, I believe, reputed to possess—er, shall we say— uncanny fortune?"

"Thus disproving the old adage, 'Unlucky in cards, lucky in love,' eh, Lambeth?" inquired St. Ives.

Wentworth laughed loudly, and Lambeth's face darkened. Fairfield, by now too muddled with drink to be aware of the undercurrents, shook his head a little and thrust forward nearly all of his winnings, convinced that the luck had veered in his favor.

The betting went on round the table, and Captain Roth complained, "Damn it, St. Ives, Strickland is right. It's too steep. Make it five hundred."

"It's a thousand to you, Roth. Put up or stand out," said St. Ives indifferently.

Roth glanced around, his good-looking face flushed with drink, then he shoved back his chair. "I'm out, then!"

"Oh, come man, you can stand a thousand," said Strickland, blithely switching sides. "St. Ives can't win all night. The luck's bound to change."

Lambeth laughed heavily. "So we would presume. Even St. Ives can't continue to win forever."

Everybody ignored him, and Roth went to stare out the window at the rain, his back to the group at the table.

Wentworth looked down at the few coins left before him, then searched through his pockets, pulling each one out as he emptied it. "I make it fifteen guineas," he pronounced carefully. "Can't bet with fifteen guineas. Tell you what: give you my voucher." He pulled out a slip of paper and scribbled his name on it, then pushed it into the pile of coins already in the center of the table.

St. Ives watched him through half-closed eyes and drew out his cards. The play continued. Money changed hands across the table, but at the end of another hour's play St. Ives was still easily the winner.

Strickland, who had started punting on tick now as well, threw down his cards and yawned. "Plague take you, St. Ives! I'm done for." He drained his glass and pulled out his enameled snuffbox, studying it carefully, as if he had not gone down to the tune of several thousand pounds.

St. Ives raised his eyes to Lambeth's face. "Well, gentlemen, do we continue?"

Lambeth, who had been losing heavily as well, said unpleasantly, "I believe we have a wager, my lord! Unless, of course, you don't intend giving us a chance to recoup our losses." When St. Ives merely shrugged, he added deliberately, "I believe it stands at eight hundred pounds. To you, Fairfield."

Fairfield gazed blankly at the pile of coins and papers that lay before St. Ives. His brief moment of insight had long ago been drowned, and he was scarcely aware of what was going on.

He had won again for a while, reinforcing his belief that the luck had indeed changed, but then it had seemed to veer again, and he had been losing steadily. He no longer had any clear idea how much. Like Strickland and Wentworth, he had been scribbling his name on voucher after voucher. Now some part of his native shrewdness reasserted itself, and he protested weakly, "My lords, I fear you'll ruin me. I protest, the play's too steep."

Lambeth glanced at him with contempt, and Wentworth said drunkenly, "Stick to it, that's my advice. Luck's bound

to change, you know." He stood up suddenly, almost over-
setting himself, and added, "Tell you what!" He solemnly
removed his coat and turned it inside out before re-
donning it. "S'what m'father always said to do when the
luck's going against you. You try it! Bound to help."

Since Wentworth's father was known to be an extremely wealthy and tolerant man, never failing to rescue his son from his frequent pecuniary embarrassments,
Fairfield blinked and declined to follow this example. He
was vaguely aware that he could no longer afford to pay
his losses, but the gambling fever still gripped him and he
seemed unable to draw back. He nodded and said in a
hoarse voice, "Eight hundred pounds, then."

After that, he went down heavily, then heavily again,
feverishly thinking the bank could not continue to win.

If it was any comfort, Lambeth was losing badly too. He
was drinking steadily as well, and his temper was nasty.

Lord Skeffington and Cranborne had long since wandered away. Mr. Strickland was dozing in his chair, and
Wentworth had reached the rollicking stage, cheerfully
scribbling voucher after voucher, his cravat loosened and
his inside-out coat lending a hilarious note to the pro-
ceedings. Fairfield felt as if he had inadvertently wandered into a madhouse and could think only of his bed.

Of those present, only St. Ives, and perhaps Farnham,
showed little effects from the long night. Farnham was
observing everything with detached, slightly malicious interest, and St. Ives continued to slouch in his chair, only his
eyes, glittering strangely under his sleepy lids, betraying the
quantity of brandy he had consumed.

At last Wentworth threw down his cards. "That's done
it for me!" he cried. "The luck's with you, St. Ives."

Lord Lambeth looked up. "If you ask me, the luck's a
little too uneven for my taste."

There was a second of stunned silence, and then
Strickland, who had roused a little, said irritably, "Well,
no one asked you! Don't be a fool, man. The luck's always
uneven."

But St. Ives had fixed his eyes on Lambeth's face,
suddenly alert. "Hush, Frederick," he said softly. "I believe Lambeth has a complaint about the game."

Lambeth, as if glad to give full rein to his temper,

repeated, "I know when the luck's too uneven for chance, my lord!"

Farnham's eyes flickered, but he said nothing. Strickland, wide awake now, said, "Leave it, Nicky! He's drunk."

St. Ives still slouched in his chair, but his eyes did not leave Lambeth's face. "So am I drunk, Frederick. But I know when a man calls me cheat."

Strickland's hand came down heavily on his shoulder. "Lord, you'll never care what's said after the third bottle! Take it back, Lambeth!" he said angrily. "No one else has any complaint."

St. Ives, an odd little smile on his lips, shook off Strickland's hand and leaned forward. "For shame, Frederick!" he chided gently. "I believe Lord Lambeth has been awaiting this moment for a long time. Never let it be said I refused to oblige any man. I am completely at your service, my lord!"

Skeffington and Cranborne had returned at the sound of raised voices, and Cranborne now said in his authoritarian way, "It's late and we're all tired! I'm certain no insult was intended, St. Ives. Let us have no trouble."

Skeffington had meanwhile drawn close to Lambeth and whispered urgently, "Apologize, man! You know you're in the wrong."

Lambeth's unpleasant smile did not falter, but his brain was working quickly. He was aware he had allowed the amount of liquor he had consumed and his hatred for St. Ives to momentarily cloud his judgment. He had a score to settle with St. Ives, but to be pushed into doing it over pistols at dawn in a frozen field scarcely suited his purpose. Not only was St. Ives the superior shot, but if by some unlikely chance Lambeth should succeed in killing him, he would undoubtedly be forced to flee the country. St. Ives had enough relatives in high places to insure that.

"I fear Lord St. Ives's well-known temper will have him at pistol point continually," said Lambeth at last, "but I assure you I have no aspiration to be one of his victims. If I spoke hastily, I beg your pardon. I intended no insult, my lord."

It galled him to say it, and he was forced to see the steely look in St. Ives's eyes give way to one of contempt. St. Ives leaned back, making no answer, and tossed down the contents of his glass.

The others relaxed, and Skeffington said, too jovially, "I for one am for my bed. It's nearly three."

Strickland seconded it. "Aye, we've all had enough to-night. I'm for my bed as well."

St. Ives looked up at him with lazy mockery in his eyes. "What, Frederick, not done up yet? The night's still young."

"Devil take you, Nicky!" said Strickland, relieving some of his feelings. "We're all three parts asleep. There's no harm in getting to bed for once before the cock crows."

"You forget that a wager still stands between Lord Lambeth and myself." St. Ives turned to Lambeth once more and made no attempt to lessen the insult of his tone. "Or perhaps you've had enough, Lambeth?"

Lambeth's knuckles showed white on the glass he was holding, but he had himself well in hand now. "Oh, I do not dispute your victory tonight, my lord," he said. "Let us hope my luck will not have deserted me another time."

St. Ives laughed and carelessly pocketed his winnings. "Very well, Frederick, you may seek your bed, then. But I'm not returning to Newmarket. Wicken is bringing my baggage around. I'm for London tonight."

"London! Good God, Nicky, you'll never set out at this hour for London. You're drunk, man!" said Strickland in astonishment.

St. Ives laughed again, his blue eyes glinting. "So you've accused me. But not so drunk I can't drive. I have an engagement at noon. It would never do to disappoint a lady," he added, his eyes on Lambeth. "So let us settle up, gentlemen, and I will bid you good night, so that Frederick here may retire to his bed."

Wentworth had been laboriously counting his vouchers, and now he groaned, "Lurched, begad! I make it ten thousand pounds, St. Ives. My man will be around to you as soon as I return to London."

"At your convenience," St. Ives said.

Lambeth had likewise totaled his losses, and the sum had not sweetened his temper. He had lost well over ten thousand pounds and been made to look a fool, but he was a hardened enough gamester to hide his feelings. He had no intention of blundering a second time in one evening.

Fairfield, however, was scarcely aware of what was going on around him. He, too, had retrieved those carelessly scribbled vouchers, and he stared in disbelief at the figure before his eyes. He had lost nearly eight thousand pounds tonight. If he sold everything he possessed he could scarcely raise such a sum. While they joked about their losses, utter ruin was staring him in the face. For a moment he felt physically ill, and there was a great roaring noise in his ears.

But everyone seemed to be looking at him now, waiting for him to make some arrangements to settle his debts so they could be off.

He made an effort to pull himself together. He licked his dry lips and said hoarsely, "My lord, I cannot— I fear I must have some time—"

St. Ives only looked bored, but Strickland, possessing a kind heart, said awkwardly, "No hurry, I'm sure, if you're short."

Fairfield suddenly threw back his head and laughed wildly. "Short! By God that's rich! If I sold the building around my ears I couldn't pay such a sum! Short!" The wild laugh broke from him again. "I tell you, the only thing in this house St. Ives doesn't own now is my daughter and myself!"

Strickland was looking ill at ease, and the others had turned their eyes away, as if observing something faintly indecent. Only Lambeth, deriving a perverse satisfaction out of the discomfiture of another man, appeared to have heard Fairfield's wild words.

His eyes narrowed and he leaned forward, a smile beginning to play about his mouth. After a moment he said, "Now there's a wager for you, St. Ives. You profess to be a gambling man. All you've won from Fairfield tonight, staked against his daughter."

Farnham was watching, a sudden speculative gleam in his eyes, and someone else gasped. Then St. Ives, who had been absently swirling the dregs of wine in his glass, looked up, tossed off the remains of his wine, and laughed. "Why not?" he said. "But why stop there? Everything I've won tonight against Fairfield's daughter—one draw of the cards, winner to take all."

"Good God, you must have won fifty thousand pounds tonight!" said Skeffington in disbelief.

St. Ives merely shrugged, but Mr. Strickland, always practical, said, "Good Lord, Nicky, don't be a fool! You ain't even seen the chit yet!"

St. Ives showed his teeth in a brief grin. "If I don't want her, you can take her off my hands for me, Frederick. Well, Fairfield? Are you game? Your daughter against all I've won tonight?"

Fairfield stared feverishly at him, running his tongue over his lips. He hesitated for only a moment, then nodded mutely.

Without another word St. Ives drew forth a fresh pack of cards and offered it to Fairfield. Fairfield's hand shook so badly he could scarcely control it. A fortune balanced against utter ruin. He broke the seal and cut the pack, then abruptly turned over a card. A knave of diamonds stared up at him.

He closed his eyes, suddenly faint, and scarcely heard Lambeth's gloating laugh. "Well, the bank may be lost after all St. Ives."

St. Ives carelessly reached out a hand and turned over his own card.

Lambeth swore suddenly, the smile gone from his lips, for St. Ives had turned up the king of spades.

"Well, St. Ives, it would seem you now possess *everything* in this house," drawled Farnham.

Suddenly the reality of what he had done seemed to penetrate Fairfield's befogged brain. He looked up and whispered hoarsely, "You will—you will marry the girl, St. Ives?"

St. Ives shrugged. "So it would seem." He scribbled something on a piece of paper and carelessly tossed it across the table.

Fairfield stood up, sending his chair over backwards behind him, and strode to the fireplace. He yanked furiously on the bellpull, then crossed to the door and flung it open, setting up a harsh bellow up the stairs. "Hinton! Hinton! Goddamn it, get down here!"

He stood at the door until an old woman, sketchily

dressed, came stumbling down the stairs. "Wake Miss Fairfield and have her come down!" he barked. "I want to speak to her."

The old woman glanced around the room, taking in the oddly still figures, then without a word did as she was bid. Strickland exchanged a frowning glance with Cranborne, but no one spoke.

Fairfield had returned to the table, and sat there with his head bowed in his hands. St. Ives had not moved and seemed to be supremely uninterested in what was going forward.

It could not have been more than ten minutes later that the old woman returned, followed by a plainly dressed girl. Her hair was hastily pinned up, and she appeared both very young and very frightened. There was a question in her wide dark eyes, and she, too, glanced around the room, then came to stand before her father.

Fairfield looked up and said harshly, "Pack your things! You'll be leaving with Lord St. Ives."

She paled. "Papa—?" she said in disbelief. At his expression, she faltered.

He evaded her eyes and said furiously, "Don't stand there staring at me, you stupid fool! Do as I say! Hinton, pack her things. Hinton, do you hear me?"

Still the girl did not move. Strickland, completely sober now, rose abruptly and said in disgust, "No, this is madness! She's little more than a child. You can't do it, Fairfield!"

For answer, Fairfield shouted again at his daughter to hurry. "And don't look at me with those accusing eyes of yours, damn you!" he raged. "You'll live to thank me for it. Marriage to an earl, by God!" He gave a short laugh. "Aye, you may stare, but he'll marry you right enough. I have his signature on it. God knows you'd get a man no other way." Like many weak men, he had managed to work himself up into a rage to hide from himself the knowledge of what he was doing.

Even now she did not move. Suddenly beside himself, Fairfield raised his hand as if to strike her.

To the fascinated onlookers it seemed that St. Ives had not once raised his eyes, but now he spoke, his voice menacing in its softness. "I would not do that if I were you."

Fairfield's face turned purple, but after a moment he allowed his hand to drop.

For the first time St. Ives turned his eyes on the girl. "Well, you have heard what your father has to say. Will you come with me or not?"

"Damn it, St. Ives, you're drunk! You can't do this," cried Strickland.

St. Ives's gaze never left the girl's face. "Why not? It has been made more than clear to me lately that I stand in need of a bride. I suppose one girl's as good as the next for my purposes."

Strickland gaped at him, and Miss Fairfield colored furiously, as if touched for the first time, and clutched her shawl more tightly across her bosom. She looked again at her father and said, almost as if against her will, "Papa, you cannot mean to do this?"

Fairfield swore and looked away, refusing to meet her eyes.

She swayed for a brief moment then, as if he had indeed struck her. Then she lifted her chin. "I will come with you, my lord," she said. She did not look at her father again.

St. Ives showed no emotion. "Very well. You have ten minutes to pack what few essentials you need. If that gown is any indication of your wardrobe, leave it behind. We return to London tonight."

Without another word she turned on her heel and left the room.

Strickland spent the time exhorting his old friend, but St. Ives hardly seemed to be listening, and the others kept oddly silent.

In exactly ten minutes she returned, wearing a bonnet and a light cloak and carrying a single bandbox, as if she had taken St. Ives at his word. He rose and took it from her, then cast a cursory glance at her coat before ordering the servant to bring a warmer one. "We're going in my curricle," he said briefly.

She accepted his statement without a word, but Strickland, forgetting larger issues for the moment, said, "Damn it, Nicky, you can't take her in an open curricle in this weather!"

He might have spared his breath for all the notice

either of them paid him. The old servant, her eyes shadowed, returned with a heavy cloak, and St. Ives placed it around the girl's shoulders.

Only as they reached the door did St. Ives seem to become at all aware of the consequences of what he was doing, for he looked up and said, "Not a word of this is to leave this room. Is that understood?"

"Certainly, St. Ives," answered Lord Farnham calmly, polishing his glass. He lifted his eyes. "Oh, and Nicky?" he added softly.

St. Ives glanced at him.

"Pray accept my congratulations on your forthcoming nuptials."

V

Wicken, waiting patiently for his lordship, his shoulders hunched against the driving rain and his collar turned up to meet his hat, sneezed violently and expressed himself bitterly on the whims of the nobility. He had a head cold coming on and should be in his bed, not capering about on a fool's errand on a night not fit for man nor beast.

He sneezed again, causing the two blanketed grays between the shafts to start nervously, and muttered darkly under his breath, "Aye, my beauties, you'd like to be safe home abed, too, wouldn't you? Well, it ain't any use showing me your tempers! *I* ain't the one had you roused out of your nice warm stalls."

Since the grays merely shook their heads impatiently and vouchsafed no answer, he sighed and returned to his dour contemplation of their ears.

Head cold or no, Wicken had learned long ago the folly of trying to cross St. Ives in one of his moods. Wicken had been with his lordship for more years than he cared to remember, and he had little doubt what was behind this latest bout of ill temper. But he disremembered the last time his lordship had allowed his stepmama to seriously disturb him—it hadn't been for many years—and he wondered what that hell-born female was up to now.

Whatever it was, St. Ives was clearly in one of his reckless, go-to-the-devil moods, and Wicken had not been particularly surprised at the sudden change in plans. He had rather been expecting something of the kind; and past his first involuntary protest, caused by a fuzzy head and sore throat, he had listened impassively to his lordship's command to pack up the gear and bring the curricle around at three. At best, St. Ives was always unpredictable, and his temper was seldom amiable. When his orders were questioned, it could descend rapidly to the dangerous.

Wicken sighed, adjusting his hat to a better angle against the rain, and hoped that if St. Ives meant to drive himself, he had not broached his third bottle. But since prudence had never been one of his lordship's particular virtues, the groom placed little reliance on that probability. Only the devil and St. Ives himself knew what maggot had got into his head that they must hare back to London on such a night. And, Wicken thought, he was as like to get the answer out of the one as the other.

There was a sound at the big front door, and the groom grunted in satisfaction. St. Ives might be capricious, but he would never keep his horses standing in such weather.

The heavy door opened, emitting a feeble light that flickered in the gusty wind, and St. Ives's greatcoated figure appeared. Scarcely noticing the rain he descended the steps and swung himself up into the curricle. It was only then that Wicken saw the heavily cloaked figure behind his lordship.

"I'm afraid you'll have to ride behind, Jeremy! We have an unexpected passenger," St. Ives said and left his groom to place what construction he might on the presence of a female at such an hour.

The hooded figure turned and gave a last look at the tightly closed door, then accepted his lordship's hand into the curricle and took her place beside him in the far corner of the seat.

Wicken, shaking his head in resignation, hurried to pull the blankets from the waiting grays. It wasn't the first time his lordship had had a female up beside him, nor would it be the last, if he was any judge, and his lordship wouldn't thank him for meddling.

Any hope Wicken might still cherish that his lordship had not been drinking heavily died in those first few minutes. Aye, he was in a proper taking, all right, and Lord knew where it would end. They'd be lucky if he didn't break their necks for them before the night was over.

Drunk his lordship might be, but it had little visible affect on his driving. His reflexes gave no sign of being impaired, and though he drove his grays with little regard for the night or the weather, he had them well in hand. But if Wicken had counted on the cold air to sober his lordship, it was soon apparent that the groom was in for disillusionment. St. Ives had frequent recourse to the brandy flask in his greatcoat pocket.

His companion remained huddled in her corner of the carriage, to all appearances asleep. If the pace, or his lordship's drinking, alarmed her, she gave no sign of it. She did not once glance in his direction.

Wicken thought that they all deserved to be clapped up in Bedlam for this night's piece of work. He muffled another sneeze and subsided miserably into his coat collar.

At the end of another half hour he had had enough. He straightened with a jerk, a martial light in his pale eyes, and prepared to do battle. St. Ives might kill them all and be damned to him, but he'd not kill those grays if Jeremy Wicken had anything to say in the matter. They were still running gamely, their heads well up, but they were flecked with foam, and it was obvious they were flagging.

"My lord!" he warned, "you'll kill them if you run them like this much longer!"

St. Ives's head jerked up, as if his thoughts had been far away. "You needn't fear for your neck, Wicken," he said insolently.

"No, but I won't say as much for those grays if you continue to push them like this!"

St. Ives's eyes narrowed. Wicken, his face set, met his gaze.

After a moment St. Ives shook his head as if to clear it and allowed his hands to drop slightly. "Damn your impudence, Jeremy," he said, sounding more himself. "You needn't look so disapproving. I'm only half sprung, you know!"

Satisfied, Wicken merely grunted.

The female turned her head then and gave Wicken a grateful look, and he studied her a little curiously in the uncertain light of the carriage lamps. His mouth fell open and all thought of the grays was driven from his mind. He had drawn his own not unnatural conclusions, but he was suddenly shaken to the core of his being. This girl—for she was little more—was not at all what he had been expecting.

A sense of extreme uneasiness pervaded him. As far as he knew St. Ives had never yet extended his liaisons to the young and inexperienced, but, unless Wicken had lost his senses, this girl was both. More than ever he wished for an end to this nightmare journey.

When they at last stopped to change horses, Wicken was given no opportunity to speak privately with his lordship, as he had planned. St. Ives jumped down to stretch his legs, while Wicken was forced to go and rouse the ostlers, and by the time the pair that St. Ives kept on the Newmarket road were harnessed to his curricle, he was ready to be off. Wicken just had time to procure a cup of tea for the young lady, which she accepted gratefully. He had half feared St. Ives would leave him to bring the grays on to London the next day, but either his lordship was more aware of the proprieties than his groom suspected, or he desired the groom's presence for some other reason, for he only said, "You may come back and get them in a day or two, Wicken," before whipping up the new team.

It was nearly morning, the sky just beginning to show the first pale color, when St. Ives pulled the weary team up before his dark house in Mount Street. The rain had ended some time before, but it was foggy and very cold, and Wicken, who had fallen into an exhausted half sleep, roused himself with difficulty and jumped stiffly down, rubbing his hands against the chill.

He was obliged to bang the knocker several times before he managed to wake anyone in the house, but then a sleepy porter put his eye to the small portal in the door. At Wicken's command to open up he looked startled, but after a considerable pause the door was cautiously opened.

Wicken thrust it wide without ceremony and ruthlessly dispatched the half-dressed porter to the horses' heads while he himself went to attempt to reason with his lordship. "What of the young lady, my lord?" he said. "You can't mean to bring her here?"

St. Ives's eyes were shadowed. "She comes in!" he said curtly, adding, "See to the baggage and keep your nose out of what doesn't concern you."

Wicken clamped his lips tightly together and went to do as he was bid.

The girl, looking bedraggled and more than a little forlorn, had descended from the curricle and now stood staring up at the door, shivering slightly. Wicken, more out of charity with St. Ives than he would have believed possible, was not proof against that air of appeal in her slight figure. He cursed violently under his breath and went to escort her, saying, "If you'll allow me, miss?"

She turned, startled, as if she had forgotten his presence, and looked around a little desperately. But then she sighed and said in a colorless little voice, "Yes, please," and allowed the groom to escort her into the wide hall.

St. Ives had thrown off his greatcoat and had gone to stand staring at the remains of the hall fire. He did not look up as they entered.

The girl glanced at him, then at Wicken, as if for guidance. The groom, having no clear notion himself of what his lordship intended to do, could only sigh in profound relief at the sight of the respectable figure of his lordship's housekeeper, in her dressing gown, standing in bewilderment near the foot of the stairs.

He hurried his charge across to her and said in a low voice, "I'm glad you're up, Mrs. Blodgett. Take Miss—" he broke off and could have willingly bitten out his tongue.

He had no idea what the young lady's name might be and was not quick enough to cover his slip.

After a moment the girl looked up without expression and supplied it. "Miss Fairfield," she said.

But the damage had been done. Mrs. Blodgett might have a kind heart under her gruff exterior, but she was no fool; her eyes, already suspicious, took in the bedraggled figure and the unattended state of his lordship's young companion, and they began to snap alarmingly.

Miss Fairfield was looking pale and exhausted, as well she might, but under the housekeeper's outraged inspection she straightened, a natural dignity coming to her aid. "Mrs. —Blodgett, is it—is perfectly right," she said calmly. "She naturally desires some explanation for this—this rather odd intrusion. I apologize for disturbing you at this hour, ma'am but you see I—"

At any other time, Wicken would have given a great deal to hear an explanation for the events of this night, but he couldn't help but feel, under the circumstances, that candor was not wanted. He had no idea what she might say, but he was well acquainted with Mrs. Blodgett's narrow moral viewpoint, so he coughed and interrupted. "Miss Fairfield has been involved in an accident, Mrs. Blodgett, as anyone but a fool could see, and doesn't need to be kept in this drafty hall talking on forever! You just see that she's put into a nice warm bed, and explanation can be made in the morning."

Mrs. Blodgett's large figure bridled. "We shall see about that!" she said sharply, looking toward his lordship for guidance.

She received none. Wicken, aware that he had made a false step, attempted to recover his ground. "Miss Fairfield is a friend of young Lady Catherine's, and his lordship thought it best to bring her to you, ma'am. Naturally we was forced to leave her maid behind—quite hysterical she was, as you can imagine—but I know his lordship can depend upon you to see that the young lady has everything she requires. Now she's exhausted and very wet, as you can see, and is longing for her bed."

Mrs. Blodgett was decidedly skeptical at this talk of maids and Lady Catherine, but it was clear the young lady had made a favorable impression. She glanced at his lordship uncertainly again, and still receiving no direction from that quarter, she bit her lip and said, "Well—"

Wicken was quick to pursue his advantage. "Now you just go along with Mrs. Blodgett, miss, and she'll take good care of you until your maid is restored to you."

This further mention of a missing maid, coupled with Mrs. Blodgett's inherently soft heart, finally succeeded in overcoming the housekeeper's scruples. Immoral goings-on in her house she would not tolerate, as anyone who knew her could vouch for; but then the poor young lady seemed soft-spoken enough, poor wet creature that she was, and hardly likely to draw even a second glance from such as his lordship. And, whatever else might be said about his lordship, he had never yet tried to foist one of his hussies on her, a thing she had no intention of standing still for, and so she'd tell him to his face.

She sniffed and said grudgingly, "Well, and what do you mean by keeping the poor child out to this hour, and in such weather too, when it's plain as a pikestaff she's fit to drop (if you don't mind my saying so, miss)? Now you just come along with me, miss," she added with gruff kindness. "Never mind your boxes. I'll find a nice warm nightgown for you and see that there's a hot brick placed between the sheets. Where is that—Oh, never mind! We'll get you out of those wet clothes, and I'll fetch a nice cup of hot milk for you myself. You'll like that, miss, and then we'll tuck you up for a nice long sleep." Half scolding, half cajoling, she had already begun to shepherd her charge up the stairs.

Miss Fairfield, as if everything were suddenly too much for her, allowed her shoulders to droop and turned almost blindly to follow her latest self-appointed protector. But on the bottom step she turned and looked at the groom. "I—thank you!" she said, then turned and followed the housekeeper's stout figure up the stairs.

Wicken, oddly touched, cleared his throat loudly and turned away to fetch in the baggage. Then he started, an unaccustomed dull color seeping into his cheeks as he discovered the blue eyes of his lordship fixed upon him.

"Very touching!" drawled St. Ives. "Your estimation of my character is most flattering."

He moved toward the stairs. "Only next time your

chivalrous instincts are aroused, make certain I have designs on the lady."

VI

Anyone who had been in the Earl of St. Ives's employ for more than a few days had come to expect the unexpected from his lordship; still, his arrival created a degree of speculation in the household. Not, of course, that anyone had seen him, since he had arrived before the household was stirring and had not yet emerged from his bedchamber, though it was nearly noon.

Young Jonathon, the underfootman, predicted cheerfully that his lordship had killed his man and would shortly be required to fly the country, as that Lord Ffolliett had done only last year.

He was preparing to enlarge on this agreeable theme, the silver tray he had been set to polish forgotten in his hands, when Chelmsford arrived on the scene and speedily put a stop to the discussion, sending them all about their business with a bee in their ears on the sin of gossiping.

Only Manley, my lord's valet, when the news was relayed to him at the breakfast table, betrayed no curiosity about his lordship's return from Newmarket three days before he was expected. Since his lordship had not required his valet's services for the better part of a week, choosing to take his groom in his stead, this surprised almost no one. It was generally agreed, belowstairs, that Manley was far from being what one would consider a proper valet for his lordship. He was quiet and unassuming, making no effort to demand his rightful place in the strict servant's hierarchy, and was, besides, a regular gloomy gus, with never a cheerful word for anyone.

Manley was perfectly aware of what was said about

him in the servant's hall, but he was inclined to consider it as yet another penance he must pay for having succumbed to the supreme sin of vanity. When the position as valet to the Earl of St. Ives had been offered him, he had allowed himself to be blinded by his lordship's rank and obvious physical attributes. Manley's previous employer had frankly lost the battle with age and stoutness and had furthermore had no interest in the *ton,* coming into London as little as possible.

But it had taken Manley very little time to discover his mistake. Not only did he disapprove of his new master's free and easy ways—not to say anything of his morals—but Manley, a high stickler, was disgusted by the shocked fascination with which most of his lordship's staff were wont to greet each new report of his lordship's scandalous doings.

Nor was St. Ives by any means an ideal employer. His temper was apt to be violent, his dress was careless to the point of indifference, he would never allow his valet to shave him or arrange his neckcloth, and he had his coats made so that he could shrug himself into them unaided. Only the fact that he paid Manley a princely sum for a very little amount of work prevented the valet from seeking a less dishonorable situation elsewhere.

The valet had another reason for being in no hurry to present himself to his lordship this morning. He had a pretty fair notion of the state his lordship's baggage would be in after a week of Wicken's ministrations, and he did not doubt it would take him hours to undo the damage—if indeed it was not already too late.

His first look at his lordship's bedchamber did nothing to allay his fears. There was no sign of any baggage—presenting Manley with horrible visions of stolen portmanteaus—but the boots the earl had been wearing, stained and muddy, had been left in the middle of the floor, and his discarded clothing had been thrown across a chair in what Manley could only describe as a Sodden Heap. He was not a man frequently aroused to anger, but such wanton destruction outraged his sensibilities, and he snatched up the offending garments and clucked over them, anxiously seeking signs of permanent damage.

He found none, a fact he attributed more to a generous providence than to Wicken's ministrations, but the clothing required his instant attention if further damage were to be avoided. All thoughts of waking his lordship fled, and he turned to the most pressing of the tasks before him.

He was in the act of attempting to brush a persistent spot of dried mud from the skirts of the earl's favorite riding coat when an irritable voice said, "Wipe that long-suffering expression off your face, Manley, and tell me what o'clock it is."

Manley, startled out of his natural calm, nearly dropped the riding coat before he recovered himself. He turned then and said, "Yes, my lord. It is near noon, my lord."

St. Ives sat up and winced as the movement set off a hammering in his head. "The devil it is," he said. "God, I feel like death."

"Yes, my lord," repeated the valet.

St. Ives looked up, a gleam of something like self-mockery in his eyes. "And be damned to me, eh?" He ran a hand over his unshaven jaw. "I have no doubt you're right, Manley. What day is it?"

"Friday, my lord." The valet spoke absently, his attention already straying to the coat he held.

The earl's lips curled. "Aye, I thought it was. I have a luncheon engagement at one o'clock, Manley."

"Yes, my lord."

"See that I get there on time."

"Yes, my lord."

St. Ives observed his valet through half-closed eyes. "One wonders if she's worth it," he said. When the valet made no answer, he leaned back against the pillows and stretched his long legs. "How old am I, Manley?"

"I believe you are one and thirty, my lord."

The cynical expression in his lordship's eyes grew more pronounced. "One and thirty. Old enough to know better, wouldn't you say, Manley?"

The valet carefully placed the coat on a chair. "I couldn't say, my lord. Will you be getting up now, my lord?"

St. Ives laughed harshly. "Wouldn't say, more like! You know, Manley, I'd give a monkey to know what goes on behind that pallbearer's face of yours."

Manley's expression did not alter, and St. Ives swung his legs out of bed and rubbed his eyes. "Yes, I'll be getting up. I doubt I'll be returning to dinner. See that the message is delivered to the cook."

Twenty minutes later he lay slumped in his chair at the breakfast table, his breakfast ruthlessly dispatched back to the kitchen with orders that he was not to be disturbed. A decanter of brandy stood open before him, a half-filled glass at his elbow, and he supported his aching head in his hands, a terrible taste in his mouth and his thoughts nearly as bitter.

He could remember little of the night before, apart from a singularly bad dinner and an even worse brandy. No doubt he deserved it for allowing Strickland to talk him into going to that fool Fairfield's.

Too many of his nights for too many years had ended like this. It sometimes seemed to him he could exchange one year for the next without being able to tell the difference. God, he must be getting old. He couldn't remember the last time anything had mattered to him.

The Fagiani, for instance. It was she he was to meet for luncheon, but at the moment he hardly cared whether he ever saw her again. She was beginning to bore him already, and that was the one fault he would not forgive. She was as beautiful as an angel, with the true soul of a courtesan, and he had snatched her in the teeth of half the men in London. He supposed he had been quite hot for her once, but now the thought of spending an hour in her company left him supremely indifferent. He would have to end it soon; although even that seemed too much of an effort. He *was* getting old.

He doubted whether Lambeth cared much more for the piece than he had, but Lambeth's pride had been wounded, and that was a thing he would not soon forgive. St. Ives toyed briefly with the idea of telling Lambeth he could have the Fagiani with his compliments, and he grinned mirthlessly at the image thus conjured up. Aye, he had made an enemy there—if it mattered. Lambeth would put a bullet through him without compunction. The situation was not without its humor.

Not that Lambeth would ever call him out. Men like Lambeth preferred a dark night in some back alley. St.

Ives discovered without surprise that the idea left him unmoved.

He wondered how much he'd won the night before. He seemed unable to lose lately, so that even gambling had lost its tang. He remembered holding Strickland's vouchers, and he thought he held Lambeth's and Fairfield's as well. He wondered if Fairfield's were worth the paper they were written on.

Something else tickled his memory, then eluded him, and after a moment he dismissed it. Perhaps he'd go away for a while. If it weren't for the damned war he could go to Paris or Vienna, or even Naples.

He swore suddenly, wondering what in the name of hell had possessed him to make that rash promise to Kitty. He'd be damned if he'd stay around and play duenna for the brat. Maybe he'd go into Somerset for a while and leave the place to Laura.

The idea appealed to him briefly, but he doubted whether it would last. He smiled, not particularly enjoying the bleak jest of his life; and it was then that an unknown voice said from the doorway, "Good morning, my lord."

His head jerked up. For a moment he thought he must still be drunk, and he passed a hand across his eyes to clear them. A pale, badly dressed young woman stood in the doorway regarding him gravely.

The flush in her cheeks grew more pronounced under his astonished stare, but she held her ground and said stiffly, "I beg your pardon, my lord. I did not mean to startle you, but your housekeeper directed me here, and I thought—that is—" She broke off and then said, "At any rate, I fear I am dreadfully hungry. I missed my supper last night, you see."

St. Ives did not often find himself at a loss, but it took him a moment to gather his wits. The girl was no lightskirt. But who the devil was she?

She was no beauty either. Her figure was thin and she was of no particular height. Her complexion was brown, her nose insignificant, and she was execrably dressed. Soft brown hair had been pulled back into an unfashionable knot, her cheekbones were too high, and her brows oddly straight, without any hint of a curve. Only her eyes

had the slightest claim to beauty. They were of a shade
somewhere between gray and black, with no discernible
pupil, so that they appeared abnormally large and clear.
It was that, perhaps, that had made him think when he
first set eyes on her that she looked like nothing so
much as a shy little brown sparrow.

She withstood his inspection and came into the room.
"I—" She broke off again. "It was not my intention to see
you again, my lord. Only I did not like for your housekeeper to think—and anyway, it has occurred to me that
perhaps it would be better if we had a—a frank discussion after all."

Something in his face must have alerted her at last. She
halted, her eyes going swiftly to his face. "Oh, good God!"
she said. "Whenever did *Papa* remember anything he didn't
wish to the next day?"

St. Ives sat observing her, his expression suddenly dangerous. "I think you had better explain that remark,
ma'am."

She lifted her chin. "So I am beginning to see!" she
said scornfully. "My name is Fairfield, my lord."

As his memory returned, his hand tightened spasmodical-
ly on his glass. Good God. He must have been drunker
than he thought last night. Fairfield's daughter. He looked
at the bedraggled girl before him and discovered that he
cared more for his name than he had ever had any
reason to suppose. The knowledge should have amused
him.

When he had agreed to the wager it had seemed to
matter little whether he won or lost. If he lost, the
money meant nothing, and if he won, at least it would
serve to solve the problem of Kitty. If he must wed,
no doubt one girl would do as well as the next. Now the
thought of taking to wife this ill-bred little baggage filled
him with unexpected disgust.

He lounged in his chair, making no attempt to hide
the contempt in his eyes, and said unpleasantly, "Well,
Miss Fairfield. Pray accept my congratulations. I think you
must be a very clever young lady."

"A clever—?" she repeated in astonishment, her face
suddenly diffused with violent color. "I see, my lord!" she

said at last. "I should have expected this after all. But I will remind you that it was you and my father, between you, who made me the prize in a game of chance. How am *I* clever?"

"You made no objection, as I recall."

The wild color grew in her cheeks, and there came such fury in her dark eyes that he was momentarily shaken.

Then she had recovered herself. "No, my lord, I did not," she said cordially. "Why should I have? I find it will suit me very well to be the Countess of St. Ives."

His doubts vanished, and along with them any intention he might still have had of honoring his part of the agreement. He might be a fool, but he was damned if he would be blackmailed into marriage by an ill-bred little chit without even beauty to recommend her.

"Over my dead body, Miss Fairfield," he said through his teeth. "I have a constitutional dislike of being taken for a fool, nor am I a gull to be caught in such an old net as that."

The fury shone from her eyes again briefly. "We shall see, my lord! You cannot deny the facts."

"I should be made to look a fool, certainly," he agreed. "But that is nothing to what would be said about you, my dear! I believe society has a name for women like you."

She regarded him in ill-concealed dislike. "Your insults serve no purpose, my lord!"

He laughed harshly. "Egad, I hope you will tell me how I may insult such a brazen piece as you! Innocent young ladies, in case you don't know it, don't consent to take part in such unsavory schemes as this, Miss Fairfield. Nor do they possess fathers such as yours. If I used you in the way you deserve, you would have no one but yourself to blame, but my tastes don't run to ill-bred little schoolgirls with ideas above their stations. Very well, how much do you think it will take to repay you for whatever 'damage' may have resulted to your reputation?"

Her whole figure seemed to stiffen. Then she glanced up and even managed a laugh. "Well, I do think you must be prepared to be generous, my lord."

"My dear girl," he drawled, "you will take exactly

what I choose to give you. If you were to shout your story from the rooftops, you would scarcely raise an eyebrow."

"Perhaps you are right, my lord," she said evenly, "but you will not deny, I hope, that you have a certain position to maintain, despite your reputation. Nor do I doubt that the world, however cynical, would be extremely interested in a certain piece of paper my father has in his possession."

He thought pleasantly of murdering her with his bare hands. "You may tell your story to whomever you please, Miss Fairfield! I have been gossiped about for years. One more story will hardly make much difference."

She put up those preposterous brows of hers. "Come, my lord! I believe this is a touch different, is it not? Surely you do not wish the world to say that the Earl of St. Ives refused to honor a gambling debt."

"How much do you want?" he repeated violently.

She appeared to consider the question. "Do you think twenty-five thousand pounds might reconcile me for the loss of my reputation at your hands?"

He did not even dignify her remark with a response. She laughed and said provocatively, "Yes, perhaps you are right. Shall we say, then, fifty thousand?"

When he still made no answer, she sighed. "Ah, well, I'd an ambition to be a countess after all. I think I shall make an admirable one, don't you, my lord?"

"Do you, Miss Fairfield?"

She flushed a little, but put up her chin. "I have never heard it said you do much credit to your name, my lord. I have no doubt we shall deal very well together."

"Allow me to return the compliment, Miss Fairfield. I, on the other hand, have no doubt that your Papa must be extremely proud of you at this moment."

The anger shone from her eyes once more. Then she shrugged and said indifferently, "That hardly matters, does it, my lord? What does signify is that my father has in his possession your signed agreement to marry me. I intend to hold you to that agreement."

"I can assure you, you would rue the day you wed me, Miss Fairfield!"

"Would I, my lord? I doubt it." At his mocking laugh she raised her eyes and said, "Whatever else you may think me, my lord, I am not a fool. But only consider: I am past twenty and unlikely to wed. As Lady St. Ives you would be bound to at least publicly accord me the respect your wife deserves, and that is all that matters to me. I would have a position of some importance, money and fine clothes, and the independence I lack now. No, my lord, I do not think I would regret it."

"What is your name?" he snapped.

She was startled. "I can assure you I am who I say I am."

"I mean your given name!"

"It is Sylvie, my lord."

"Why were you not at the dinner table last night? Fairfield said nothing of a daughter."

"I have found it advisable not to be present when my father entertains," she said. "His guests, I have found, are seldom gentlemen. At any rate, one of the mares had a difficult breech birth last night. I was in the stables until past midnight."

"And do you always discuss breech births in polite company, Miss Fairfield? What a redoubtable young woman you must be. It is no wonder you do not flinch at the thought of mere blackmail."

She did flinch at that, but said in icy tones, "I do not claim to be other than what I am, my lord! It is something you should have considered before agreeing to such a— such a—" her mouth curled over the word, "bargain!"

"Ah, do you think I was cheated, Miss Fairfield?"

When she only glared at him, he added maliciously "I am very much afraid it is you who will discover you have been cheated, my dear! There was not a single man present last night who cannot swear that you came with me willingly. I think you will find my name carries a great deal more weight than yours."

"And I think you are forgetting the paper my father has."

"Ah, yes, but you see, Miss Fairfield, I have suddenly remembered even more of last night. And unless I am much mistaken, I have in *my* possession a number of

vouchers in your father's hand. I imagine we will be able
to reach an arrangement agreeable to us both, don't
you?"

She paled a little, but did not admit defeat. "We shall
see, my lord!" she said. "There is still my word against
yours. And I can assure you I will not hesitate to carry
my story to the proper persons."

He straightened, sick of the whole. "I presume you
brought some sort of bandbox with you, Miss Fairfield," he
said. "Get it!"

"Where do you intend taking me, my lord?"

"You were less curious last night, as I recall, Miss Fairfield. Perhaps it would have been better for you if you
had been. You should have taken me up on my earlier
offer. It is unfortunately no longer open to you. I have a
constitutional dislike of being bled by such a doxy as you!
You'll get not a farthing out of me, but I'll save your
reputation for you—if you care. I intend to take you
to my grandmother until I can decide what is to be done
with you. And I would advise you to choose a greener
man for your next victim."

"And if I refuse to come with you?"

In a moment he was beside her and had grasped her
wrist, letting her feel the strength in his hard fingers.
"I am not a patient man, Miss Fairfield," he said in a
mild tone, "and I give you my word I would as soon
throttle you as look at you. Don't tempt me too far."

After a moment she nodded, her head held proudly.
"Very well, my lord. I will accompany you. But do not
dare to touch me again!"

He laughed and carelessly released her wrist. "Surely
one in your position cannot afford to be so squeamish,
Miss Fairfield?"

"I have said I will accompany you, my lord, but do not
imagine you have heard the last of me. I mean to be
the Countess of St. Ives."

He threw open the door and shouted for the butler.
As Chelmsford hurried forward and a footman started up
out of his chair in alarm, St. Ives said softly under his
breath, "I'll see you damned first, Miss Fairfield!"

VII

The Dowager Duchess of Wraxham lived somewhat retired from the world, but that circumstance did not prevent her from being abreast of every *on dit* and scandal
in town. More than one of her numerous offspring, all of
whom she frankly bullied, had had reason to animadvert
bitterly on her "blasted network of spies."

The accusation, though seldom made to her face, was
true. She had been a reigning toast in her day and had
led society for nearly sixty years, and she saw no reason
to allow her advancing age to alter anything. She might
seldom leave her quiet house in Arlington Street these
days, but, as one of her more cynical acquaintances murmured, why should she? One was sure to meet anyone of
importance in her drawing room if only one waited long
enough. The dowager's days were spent in visits and
correspondence with her old friends, whose number included almost anyone of any consequence in London,
and they saw to it that she was kept informed of every
occurrence, from the latest gossip to the inner workings
of the Home Office.

She was a small woman, no longer handsome, but still
upright and imposing for all her years. Indeed, the only
concession she had ever been known to make to her age,
besides the particular vanity of admitting it freely to
everyone, was the ebony stick she carried. But since
it was used primarily to emphasize a point or gain someone's attention, it fooled almost no one.

The dowager had been widowed for many years, a
state she frankly enjoyed, and, although she invariably
wore black, it was—she said—to remind herself of her
freedom, and any resultant somberness was more than

offset by the large collection of jewels she wore about her person.

It was the possession of those jewels, as a matter of fact, that was one of the major causes of the longtime breach between herself and her eldest son, the present Duke of Wraxham. A large proportion of them were technically a part of the Wraxham family jewels, though it was a technicality the dowager steadfastly refused to acknowledge. On the occasion of her son's marriage, she had declined to hand them over, on the perfectly reasonable grounds that his bride was an encroaching Cit and she couldn't imagine what Wraxham saw in her.

Her son, torn between fear of his strong-willed Mama and awe of his sharp-tongued wife, had not known which way to turn, with the result that the dowager remained in possession of her jewels, along with other odd pieces of furniture and bric-a-brac she considered her own property, and retired to her house in Arlington Street in triumph. The new duchess, equal to the battle, refused to call on her mama-in-law—until it was borne in upon her that such a stand disturbed the dowager not at all and was the source of much amusement to the polite world. Since that time an armed truce had been maintained, while the hapless duke, caught between two superior forces, had quietly retired to his clubs.

The dowager, who ruled her children and grandchildren with a will of iron, never failed to speak of the present duke as that Great Booby. The duchess she seldom spoke of at all.

In fact, among her closest friends it was generally agreed that the only one of her children the dowager had ever cared two pins about was her youngest, the willful and beautiful Ariel. She never spoke of her, of course, but a few still remembered the stricken look she had carried for months after Ariel's death, and it was said that if her heart still retained a soft spot, it was for Ariel's only child, the wild young Earl of St. Ives. She frankly characterized Lord Timothy as a worthless fribble; and she unashamedly bullied her only remaining daughter, Venetia, who lived with her most of the year.

The dowager was engaged at her escritoire when the Earl of St. Ives was announced. She continued to move her hand across the page until she had completed her letter. She carefully sanded it, folded and directed it, and put it aside, and only then did she raise her eyes to her grandson's face.

"Well, St. Ives?" she said.

The earl came forward and gracefully kissed her hand. "Good morning, Grandmama," he said with deceptive sweetness. "I hope I find you enjoying your customary health?"

"Hmph!" said the dowager. "Don't think to play off your tricks on me, for I'm more than a match for you. I thought you were still at Newmarket. Is that opera dancer I last heard about still leading you around by the nose? I can assure you, in *my* day we had a name for women like that."

"I'm certain you did, ma'am," said the earl. "Does anything happen that you don't know about?"

"Not much," she admitted. "But then, no one told me you were back in town. But I don't suppose you've come to see me just to inquire after my health. What have you done now?"

The earl had gone to pour himself a glass of brandy, but he looked up at that. "As usual, ma'am, you are exactly right. God, we're a family, are we not? Is there a scandal we haven't engaged in at one time or another?"

"Aye, you've more Desborough in you than Staunton," admitted the dowager grudgingly.

He raised his glass. "To the Desboroughs, then!" he said flippantly. "I want you to keep a certain young lady for me until I can decide what to do with her. Will you do it?"

The dowager had been idly toying with the ornate gold head of her stick, but now she glanced up, her bright dark eyes scanning his face. Then she nodded, apparently satisfied. "You'd better sit down and tell me the whole. I don't say I'll help you, but at least you ain't afraid to come and tell me about it. Not like that Great Booby Wraxham. But I won't have one of your light-skirts, mind. Who is she?"

St. Ives poured himself a second glass of brandy and sank into a gilded chair. Then without varnish he told her the events of the night before.

She listened, her eyes half closed in a trick that St. Ives himself often made use of. When he finished she sat for a moment longer; then she stood up and crossed to pull the bell.

"Well, you're a fool, St. Ives, but you don't need me to tell you that," she said. When his mouth tightened, she added, "But then you're Ariel's son for all that. My grandson too, if it comes to it."

He smiled at her disrespectfully. "I was wondering if you meant to admit it, ma'am. From all I've ever heard, you led my grandfather a merry dance."

"Aye, I don't deny it. But the difference is you must stay within your own class—or keep to the little bits of fluff you young men are so fond of sporting. That opera dancer of yours—what's her name?—Fabriani or some such nonsense—is all right because she expects nothing but a few expensive baubles. Even your liaison with Julia Horneby can be sanctioned." She saw his eyes narrow and smiled sourly. "Oh, yes, I know about that too. But she can be depended on to play by the same rules as you do. However, this Fairfield chit is another matter. Did you really mean to marry her?"

"Since I played at all, I suppose so! But I discover I have a dislike of being blackmailed; nor will I marry such a grasping little bitch as that. She thinks to threaten me, but she will soon discover her mistake. I want you to keep her and swear, if necessary, that she's been with you from the beginning. She may try to spread her story, but she'll find that hers is the only reputation to suffer. In the meantime, I'll deal with Fairfield. Is my Aunt Venetia with you, by the way?"

"No, she's gone to stay with Wraxham. One of his brats is sick. Do you think you can keep the rest of those fools quiet?"

"I mean to try. They were all drunk, and may not remember more than I did. There's one that would do me an injury if he could, but I know how to deal with him," he said deliberately.

"Well, I don't mind admitting it's this paper she mentioned that has me worried. Did you sign anything?"

"It's possible, for I was as drunk as the rest."

The dowager mulled it over for several minutes. "At any rate, you did the right thing by bringing her to me. I'll keep her for you." She looked up. "But if she's telling the truth about that paper, you haven't a hope in hell of even buying her off. You'll have to marry her. You ain't a Wraxham, but I won't have it said you played fast and loose with a gently bred girl. Fairfield's daughter, is she? He's a drunk and a fool, but it could be worse, I suppose."

"I assure you, I don't need you to tell me my duty, ma'am, but I won't be made a fool of. Not by her, or by you."

"All right, all right! You needn't jump on your high ropes. Pour me a glass of that claret over there and I'll see this girl of yours. You should try it instead of brandy. You drink too much anyway. By the way, what *do* you intend to do with the chit? Is she pretty?"

He laughed. "No, damnably plain! It is perhaps the cream of the jest. I feel sure you will be able to appreciate the humor of it, ma'am. As for what to do with her, I am open to suggestion. My own inclination at the moment is to wash my hands of her, but doubtless I will be able to restrain myself."

Her grace merely looked up calmly. "Ah, there you are, Horsham. I believe there is a young lady waiting downstairs to see me. Show her up. Oh, and Horsham, see that the yellow room is prepared. We will be having a guest for a few days."

When the butler had withdrawn, she said, "What's this I hear about young Kitty? You aren't seriously thinking of taking her?"

He swore. "I don't know. Laura's ruining her, but that's nothing new! She'll run off with the first half-pay officer who makes up to her, not that I'm certain I care. While you're being so obliging, you might keep a lookout for some genteel widow to keep an eye on her for me."

The dowager put up her brows. "And how long do you think you'd stand for that?"

"Devil take the chit!" he said impatiently. "But it's clear Laura can't handle her, and I don't know if even I can condemn her to another year among the Bath quizzes."

"Well, there is a solution."

"It may surprise you to know I've considered it," he retorted. "Why do you think I'm in this present mess? Do you fancy Julia Horneby for a granddaughter-in-law?"

She glanced up sharply, but it was impossible to tell if he were serious or not.

Miss Fairfield, when she was shown in, was not looking her best. She glanced defiantly at St. Ives before acknowledging his mocking introduction.

The dowager unhastily examined her from head to toe, her quizzing glass held up to enable her to get a better look at the girl's pale face. Then she said coolly, "Very well, child! Come and sit here."

Miss Fairfield remained where she was. "I prefer to stand, thank you ma'am."

The dowager's thin brows rose. "Ah, do you? You must forgive me, my dear, and humor an old woman for a moment. I cannot get around as easily as I once did."

Defeated, Miss Fairfield stiffly took the indicated seat. St. Ives moved to lean against the mantel, his arms crossed over his chest, enjoying himself.

"So," said the dowager calmly, "you mean to marry my grandson, do you?"

"Yes, ma'am, I do!"

"He is no prize, my dear," she said dryly. "Do you think you can handle him?"

Miss Fairfield looked surprised. "I don't know, ma'am," she said honestly. "Once we're married, he may do exactly as he pleases. I intend to do the same. I can assure you I have no illusions about this marriage, if that is what you mean."

The dowager smiled. "Ah, my dear, then you are very brave, or very foolish, and I intend to find out which." She glanced up at her grandson and added, "You may leave us now, St. Ives! I will talk to Miss Fairfield. If you wish you may return in the morning."

St. Ives straightened lazily. "Very well, ma'am. Miss Fairfield, your most obedient." He bowed, and at her look laughed and strode from the room.

Miss Fairfield, brilliant color high in her cheeks, watched the earl's departure. Then she seemed to become engrossed in the strings of her reticule. "I d-do not think there can be anything more for us to discuss, ma'am," she said, stammering badly. "You cannot dissuade me, but I want you to know it was never my intention to foist myself upon you."

"Only upon my grandson," murmured the dowager.

Miss Fairfield flushed even more deeply, but she lifted her eyes and said, "Yes, ma'am! But there is no need for me to impose myself on you as well. I am perfectly aware of what you must think of me. I will go now." She stood and went to the door, not looking back.

The dowager watched her go, and only when she had reached the door did the older woman say quietly, "Just a moment, my dear."

Miss Fairfield hesitated. "I mean to hold your grandson to his agreement! Nothing you can say will change my mind, ma'am."

Something very like a smile touched the old woman's lips. "Do you, my dear?"

"Y-yes!" said Miss Fairfield.

"Then why are you crying?"

Miss Fairfield sniffed audibly and said in a small voice, "I'm n-not!"

"Ah!" said the dowager. "Come here, my child."

Miss Fairfield stiffened and took a step toward the door. Then she halted and turned back, her head high.

The dowager studied her for a long moment, then nodded. "You don't mean to marry him at all, do you, my child?"

Somehow Miss Fairfield, who had endured a trying twenty-four hours, found herself on her knees, sobbing into the skirts of the forbidding Dowager Duchess of Wraxham. The dowager, as if such a thing were a common occurrence, removed her guest's bonnet and smoothed her hair, saying, "Yes, my dear, you have a good cry, and then we'll talk."

Sylvie gulped and searched vainly for her handkerchief. When the dowager handed her one she accepted it and self-consciously dried her cheeks and blew her nose. "I'm sorry, ma'am—!" she said. "I know what you must think of me."

"I will tell you that when I know," replied her grace briskly. "For the moment, pour us both a glass of that claret over there, my dear. No, not the stuff in the decanter. I keep that for guests I want to get rid of. Horsham keeps a bottle in the cabinet for me."

That made Sylvie laugh a little through her tears, and she jumped up and went to do as she was bid.

"Good," said the dowager when she had returned with the glasses. "Now then, don't you think you'd better tell me the whole story?"

Sylvie turned her glass nervously in her fingers and did not meet the dowager's eyes. "Yes, ma'am," she said at last, "but I think I have done enough harm already. Couldn't we please just leave it that I—that I have changed my mind, and that your grandson has nothing to fear from me?"

"If you are worried about shocking me, my dear, I should tell you that St. Ives has already told me the whole," said the dowager. "He may have many faults, but at least he don't hesitate to own up to 'em. Now I'd like to hear your version."

Sylvie sighed and did as she was bid. She made no attempt to excuse her own part in the incident, but since she had been absent for the greater part of the previous evening, that portion of her story was naturally sketchy. Only when she got to the events after they had reached London did her grace sit up and say with sudden energy, "Yes, now you are getting to the part that interests me!"

When Sylvie blushed, she snapped, "Oh, don't be missish, girl! I didn't mean that. If St. Ives had touched you, he'd scarcely have brought you here."

Sylvie had to smile at this novel moral viewpoint. "No, ma'am. In fact, I think he'd forgotten all about me by then," she said. "And I don't think it was ever his intention—his intention—" She blushed again. "It is rather my fault, for I had meant to go to my old nurse's home, only I was so very tired, and it was so late that when his lordship's groom—such a kind man!—offered to help me—well, I have been very stupid, but I didn't think—" She shook her head. "The rest I think you know, ma'am. When I saw St. Ives the next morning he—"

"Assumed the worst, no doubt," supplied her grace.

"Well, not at first, I don't think," conceded Sylvie, "but it was clear that he didn't remember a thing. Papa never does either when he'd rather not. Only when I told him who I was, he said—" Her eyes sparkled in memory. "He said that I was very clever, and that Papa should be proud of me! That was when I lost my temper, ma'am, and said that he *should* marry me, and that I thought I should make an excellent countess. But I never meant it to go so far, ma'am," she said wretchedly. "I know I said the same to you, but I was still angry, and I never dreamed I would have to confess everything to you. I beg your pardon, but I'm *not* sorry I said what I did to your grandson, for he deserved it!"

"Of course he did," said the dowager. "Any woman of spirit would have done the same. But that's neither here nor there. The question is, what are we going to do with you?"

"Am I ruined, ma'am?" asked Sylvie.

The dowager gave a short laugh. "You take it calmly, I'll give you that."

"Well, there would be little point in shedding tears now. It is my own fault, after all. I know little of the world, but even I am aware that young ladies do not—do not spend the night in a single gentleman's residence."

"Especially not my grandson's!" conceded the dowager.

Sylvie smiled. "Yes, ma'am. The thing is, I had intended to find employment as a governess, just until my brother is down from Oxford in a year. Do you think that is impossible now?"

The dowager had been frowning, as if pursuing her own thoughts, but she looked up sharply. "Oh you had, had you?" She eyed Sylvie for a moment, then seemed to come to some conclusion. "You've got spirit, I'll grant you that. Well, I told you the truth. St. Ives is no prize, but I won't stand by and see him ruin a gently bred girl. He'll marry you if I've any say in the matter."

"Thank you, ma'am," said Sylvie. "I know what that must have—must have cost you. But I told you the truth. I hope you will believe me, but whether you do or not, it was never my intention to force St. Ives into a marriage he must despise. He is no more to blame than I am, or my father." She smiled a little crookedly. "Besides, what sort of marriage would it be?"

"At least you'd have the protection of his name. And

it might do St. Ives well to have to suffer the consequences of his actions for once in his life."

"I do not think I would enjoy being the bitter medicine, ma'am."

Her grace nodded reluctantly. "Very well. Perhaps you are right after all." She sat up with sudden decision. "I can see I will have to take a hand in this, or between the pair of you you'll ruin everything. If you won't have St. Ives, we'll have to find something else to do with you, but let's hear no more about being ruined, or hiring yourself out as a governess! I'm still somebody, I hope, and if I say you've been with me from the beginning, and that my grandson was commissioned to bring you to me, I would like to know who will question it! But that don't solve the problem of what to do with you. I'm too old to take you myself and see that you are introduced to the *ton* as you should be. Surely you must have some relatives?"

If Sylvie thought there might be a great many people who would challenge her grace's blithe statement, she wisely kept it to herself. "I—well, I do have an uncle, ma'am. But he and my father quarreled years ago, and I wouldn't ask him to help me."

The dowager frowned and tapped the head of her stick. "I might make that Great Booby Wraxham take you," she said with sudden malice. "It would be almost worth it to see my daughter-in-law's face."

Sylvie said nothing. Then she frowned. "There is my godmother," she said hesitantly. "I've never met her, but she was my Mama's closest friend in school and she sent me a very handsome christening gift. And I do know she has a house in town. Do you know Lady Bridlington, ma'am?"

The dowager sat up. "Sophia Bridlington? Of course I know her! So she's your godmamma, is she?"

"Do you think she would consent to have me, just for a few weeks?" Sylvie inquired anxiously.

"Sophia Bridlington is a foolish creature, but she has a good heart. You just leave her to me." The dowager leaned back, her mind full of schemes, and she was only brought back from her reverie by Horsham returning to collect the glasses. "Oh, it's you, is it, Horsham? Good!

Leave these things till later. Show Miss Fairfield to her room, now, and then send up a footman. I have a note I want delivered immediately."

She reached out to pat Miss Fairfield's hand. "You go with Horsham, my dear. You can safely leave the rest to me. I may be an old woman, but I'm not in my dotage yet."

Sylvie colored and tried to express her gratitude.

"Poppycock!" said her grace, "I haven't enjoyed myself so much in years. Go along with you now. I've things to do."

She had reached the door when her grace added briskly, "And my dear?"

Sylvie looked around quickly.

"I knew your mother well. You're very much like her," said the dowager matter-of-factly.

Sylvie smiled, blinking suddenly damp lashes, and turned to hurry through the door.

When she had gone, the dowager leaned back in her chair for some moments, a smile playing about her mouth. Julia Horneby indeed! That had seriously alarmed her, for she knew exactly how long St. Ives would be faithful to such a one. No, she had made a fatal mistake with Ariel all those years ago, and she did not mean to stand aside and watch Ariel's son commit the same folly. Perhaps she could atone, in some small part, for all his unhappiness since.

For a moment, as she looked back over the years in some bitterness, she seemed every bit her age. For that one moment only did she permit herself such weakness. Then she pulled herself together again, sat up briskly, and reached for a piece of paper.

VIII

Lady Bridlington, upon receiving an urgent summons from the Dowager Duchess of Wraxham, hardly knew whether

to be flattered or dismayed. She had known her grace
for nearly twenty years, but their acquaintance had never
extended beyond a polite bow in the park or a nod at
Almack's. She had certainly never been invited to pay
her grace an afternoon visit at her house in Arlington
Street.

Lady Bridlington was generally well liked, and she had
entrée everywhere, but she had never figured in the exalted circles of the *haut ton*. She had been a handsome
girl in her youth and had married well, in the midst of
her first season, but neither her modest wealth nor her
beauty had been sufficient enough to permit her to take
her place on more than the outskirts of fashionable
society. And though the Bridlingtons were an old family,
they had never boasted more than a simple knighthood
and good sound management of their land.

All that had been thirty years and more ago, of course.
Lady Bridlington had dwindled into a slightly plump, slightly silly woman of no more than common sense, but with an
easygoing nature that allowed her to dote on her only
son, a rather stuffy young man of some nine and twenty.
She was seldom unkind to her servants; she subscribed to
whatever charity was fashionable at the moment; and if
her intellect was not strong and her conversation com-
posed primarily of platitudes, few were unkind enough
to characterize her as a shatterbrained woman with more
hair than wit.

Her son was not so fortunate. The fact that his father,
Sir Wilfrid Bridlington, had died at an early age, leaving
both his title and his wife to the tender care of his only
son and heir, had served to exaggerate an already somber
disposition and an inclination to be uncompromising in
what young James considered to be his duty. The result was
that James was almost completely devoid of a sense of
humor, and he had fallen into the unfortunate habit, from
having his word treated as law in his own home from far
too early an age, of weighing up his opinions and then
carefully delivering them in a manner designed to put
an end to any discussion. Since his intellect was not a
great deal higher than his Mama's, and he lacked her
easy amiability, he was not a general favorite. Though to
do him justice, he had no desire to be one. He was con-

temptuous of the dandy set and indifferent to either the
lure of the cards or the dice tables.

Lady Bridlington, who enjoyed a friendly game of silver
loo or whist as well as the next, had begun to find James's
rigid attitude extremely depressing. In fact, it had recently been borne upon her ladyship that perhaps she had
been guilty of spoiling James, just a little, and had allowed
him to become far too autocratic and set in his ways. At
the time, of course, it had been so comforting to let
James make all the decisions and deal with the hundred
and one details consequent upon her husband's untimely
demise.

But within the last few months she had begun to realize
exactly how stolid James had become. He had never
been frivolous, of course, disdaining routs and balls, as
well as the less innocent diversions favored by young
gentlemen of birth, but she was sure he had never been
hard and unfeeling before. Lately, he seemed to go on
and on about funds, and the need to retrench, and re-
investing on 'Change. It was impossible for her to understand how the war, however tired one might be of it,
could have anything to do with her capital; and as for a
Bubble someplace she had never even heard of—! Why,
Wilfrid may have been an unsatisfactory husband in many
ways, but on *financial* matters at least he had always behaved with perfect propriety.

Not that James ever actually tried to interfere with
his Mama's pleasures. Only he would pull down his mouth
in that disagreeable way of his and say that naturally she
must do as she liked—a generous permission guaranteed
to result in her abandoning whatever scheme she had
put forth. Ordering a new gown, or choosing new curtains
for the drawing room when the old ones were positively
threadbare—as well as being a color she had never liked
—lost all enjoyment when James, without ever saying so,
could contrive to make one feel as if one were being
monstrously selfish and extravagant.

In fact, so little in charity was she with her only son
these days that she had almost begun to wish that James
would find himself a wife. It was something she had not
looked forward to, but at least then she might have the
excitement of a wedding to look forward to, with all its

attendant balls and parties. But James, when she had ventured to broach the matter to him, had only given her
an impatient look and said that he could not think of
marrying until he had straightened out his affairs. Which
of course only served to remind her of just how unhappy
she was.

She allowed her shawl to droop listlessly from her fin-
gertips, ignoring the complaint of the fat pug who had
been asleep in its folds, and regarded again the note
that had been delivered by hand that morning. Ten to
one it meant she had contrived to offend the dowager
and could shortly expect to be ostracized from society—
cut by all but her dearest friends and forced to live out
her remaining days in poverty and unhappiness, alienated
even from her only son. For she had so far forgotten herself that morning that she had snapped at James when he
had pointed out patiently that he failed to see how his
Mama could have offended the dowager, since it was well
known she seldom went into society anymore; nor did he
understand what difference it made, since he doubted
he had set eyes on the woman above a dozen times in
his life.

She had not meant to lose her temper, of course;
but really, it only showed how ignorant of the world James
was. Lady Bridlington was perfectly aware that the
dowager had not relaxed her influence one whit. She
was related to half the noble houses in England, and was,
furthermore, the intimate of such powerful women as
Lady Jersey, Lady Cowper, and Mrs. Drummond-Burrell,
three of the most important patronesses of Almack's. One
word from any of those ladies, and Lady Bridlington might
as well leave England forever. Not, of course, that one
could leave England, with the war going on in Europe.

The fact that she seldom mixed in such exalted circles,
and that she was uncertain whether at least two of the
patronesses even knew her name, was unimportant. She
had been content among her own circle of friends, and
her parties were always well attended, if not so crowded
as to make them fashionable squeezes. But she had
never been quite able to abandon her first ambition to
cut a figure in the polite world.

She dabbed tearfully now at her eyes with a wisp of

handkerchief. She had apologized to James, of course, but he had retreated sulkily to his club and left a message with Saltish that he would not be home to dinner, leaving her to support this latest ordeal on her own. It did not occur to her to ignore the summons, or to plead illness. One simply did not ignore the Dowager Duchess of Wraxham.

By the time she had been dressed by Crimping, her dour maid, and at last presented herself in Arlington Street a few minutes before the appointed hour, she had managed to work herself up into such a state that she was required to fortify herself with a few sniffs at her vinaigrette before she dared descend from the coach. Not even the fact that she was looking quite modish, in a gown of the new straw-colored satin that was all the rage, had the power to raise her spirits. The Dowager Duchess of Wraxham had always terrified her.

Nor were her nerves improved by the intimidating old butler who left her for a good quarter of an hour in a small saloon before the dowager condescended to receive her. The dowager was not a tall woman, but she had always managed to overpower all but the strongest of wills. She easily did that now, leaning heavily on her stick as she came into the room dressed in her usual black silk and bedecked with diamonds.

She looked her guest slowly up and down, her eyebrows slightly raised, and remarked dryly, "Well, Sophia. You look the same, I see. You've grown stouter, but the years sit well on you. You always did favor colors that didn't suit you. That straw makes you look pasty." Having neatly bestowed a paean and taken it back again, the dowager lowered herself into her chair with the aid of her cane, and then rang for her butler.

Lady Bridlington managed a feeble smile and asked after her grace's health. The dowager informed her with perfect accuracy that she was never ill and had no patience with females who were always dosing themselves. Lady Bridlington clutched her reticule nervously and murmured that she was delighted to see her grace looking so well.

Her grace gave a bark of laughter. "You mean at my age, no doubt! Well, I don't mean to stick my spoon in the wall just yet, and so you can tell them. They'll discover I'm still a force to be reckoned with when I choose."

Lady Bridlington turned pale and groped blindly for her vinaigrette.

Her grace, seemingly unaware of her guest's odd behavior, looked up and said, "Ah, there you are, Horsham. You needn't stay. Lady Bridlington will pour."

The aging butler arranged the silver tea service to his satisfaction, inspected the room for anything out of order, adjusted the angle of a vase on the mantelpiece, and then bowed and carefully closed the doors behind him. Lady Bridlington, calling on reserves of strength she did not know she possessed, managed to pour the tea and hand her grace a cup.

The dowager sipped distastefully for a moment, then thrust her cup aside. "Ah, bah, it don't do to go muddling your insides with tea at this time of day. In *my* day we didn't sit about drinking the stuff from morning till night. But that's neither here nor there. What do you know of Marianne Fairfield's girl?"

Lady Bridlington, thrown completely off her stride, spilled tea on her new straw satin. "Marianne Fairfield?" she repeated. "Why, I don't—"

The dowager's mobile brows rose. "Hmmm. Said she knew you."

Lady Bridlington gasped. "Why, I've never laid eyes on the girl! Is *that* why you wanted to see—Well, really, ma'am! I assure you that whatever the girl has done, I know nothing of it. And furthermore, anyone who told you I knew her is either a mischief-maker or a liar!" She dabbed at her ruined skirts and almost flounced in her chair.

The dowager, her shrewd eyes hooded, said, "Who said she's done anything? I merely asked if you knew the girl. I was told you were her godmamma."

Lady Bridlington's mouth jerked open foolishly, brilliant color staining her cheeks and rectifying any tendency she had of being pasty-faced. "M-marianne Fairfield—? Good God! You can't mean Marianne *Spencer*? Why of course I know her—or did," she said. "She's dead, of course. Now that I come to think of it, I did stand godmam-

ma to her eldest daughter, but I've never seen the girl.
What was her name? Sadie? Sophie? No, no, Sylvie! Yes,
of course, I remember now. It was Marianne's Mama's
name."

The dowager, looking satisfied, sat back in her seat and
fingered the head of her stick. "So you are the girl's
godmother?"

Lady Bridlington, her gentle temper roused at last,
said, "Marianne Spencer was my dearest friend in all the
world, and I won't hear a word said against her! If that's
what you brought me here to tell me, I can only say
you've wasted your time. I can't believe she's done anything to offend you. As a matter of fact, she couldn't
have. She's been dead these fifteen years and more. And
if you mean to tell me you've been harboring a grudge
for all these years, why I've never heard of anything so
ridiculous!"

The dowager listened to this speech with uncharac-
teristic patience and only said calmly, "Aye, you always
were a flighty woman, Sophia, but I'll say this for you.
You've a good heart under that silly exterior. I want
your help."

Lady Bridlington was by now wholly bewildered. "My
help? Well, I'm sure I'll do anything I can, but I really
don't see—?"

When informed that her grace wished her to take
Marianne Spencer's daughter to live with her for an in-
definite period and present her to the *ton*, Lady
Bridlington's spirits underwent a remarkable transforma-
tion. Indeed, she hardly knew why the idea had never
occurred to her before. To have a young girl about the
house would be almost as good as having the daughter
she had never had, and there was nothing better to take
one's mind off one's troubles than being obliged to introduce someone to all one's friends and to undertake the
rigors of outfitting them in the first style of elegance,
generally showing them how to go on in a society where
one might not be of first consequence, but one certainly
knew almost everyone of note.

Lady Bridlington had not, for some reason or another,
kept up with her goddaughter, and had nearly forgotten
her existence, but she had told the dowager the simple

truth. Marianne Spencer had been her dearest friend in all the world before she had married Sir John Fairfield and gone to live somewhere outside of Newmarket. It had not been a successful marriage, by all accounts. Sir John had been an abrupt, rude man, with little charm, though handsome enough in his day. Now her heart positively ached at the thought of poor Marianne's motherless child.

Her flight of fancy descended. "But how is this, ma'am? Surely Fairfield has not died? I'm certain I would have heard if he had. And I'm sure I never heard that the Fairfields were in anyway connected to the Desboroughs. How do you come to be involved?"

The dowager's expression did not change. "You're not as stupid as you look," she conceded. "I can see I'd better tell you the whole."

When she had finished, Lady Bridlington was up in arms. "Well, I never!" she gasped. "It's positively wicked! They were all drunk, I make no doubt! But to be staking the poor child at a game of cards as if she had been no better than a common—! Well, it's hardly more than I could expect from that father of hers—and as for St. Ives—! And to think I was just the other day wishing that James might be a little more—Well, never mind! I beg your pardon, ma'am, but I've never heard the like. Of course I'll take her. Where is she?"

"Upstairs," said the dowager dryly. "You may see her in a few minutes. We've important things to discuss first."

Lady Bridlington, preparing to embark upon exactly the sort of intrigue she enjoyed best, said, "Indeed we do, ma'am! But do you really think it can be kept quiet? I won't have the child's reputation ruined because of the disgraceful conduct of a few drunken men!"

The dowager raised her brows, but only said, "We have to rely on St. Ives to try to keep those fools from talking. I'll do what I can, of course. As far as anyone is concerned, the girl has been in your care since yesterday morning. Can you trust your servants to keep their mouths shut? Good. What will you say when people ask why she's with you instead of her father?"

"And what is more natural than having her come to her godmamma for her come-out?" said Lady Bridlington, warming to her role. "I can't think why it never occurred to me before. Poor Marianne's daughter!"

"Aye, you just keep that up. You know the style. I'll see that she's accepted, vouchers to Almack's and that sort of thing. Just quietly, mind you, as a favor to the daughter of an old friend of Ariel's."

Lady Bridlington suddenly began to perceive that there might be unexpected dividends to the affair. If she had feared being in the dowager's black books, she now saw that there was very little the dowager might not do if she were indebted to her. After all, she was saving not only the young girl's reputation, but the dowager's graceless grandson's as well. Not that he didn't deserve to have the whole thing descend about his ears. If it hadn't been for Marianne's daughter, she'd be tempted to step aside and let it do just that. And as for Fairfield—! She intended to write him a long and extremely frank letter telling him exactly what she thought of him.

A new thought struck her then, so dazzling it nearly took her breath away. She toyed with it briefly, allowing it to develop in her mind. She might despise St. Ives's part in the affair, as well as disapprove of his general conduct, but it would be foolish to allow mere scruples to interfere with more practical considerations. Besides, the boy was so very handsome.

Feeling this was not the moment for deviousness, she looked up and said, "And if it does leak out, ma'am? What then? Is St. Ives prepared to do the right thing by her?"

The dowager regarded her with disconcertingly knowing old eyes. "I've already said he'd marry her—if she wants him." She gave a harsh laugh. "The girl says she won't have him."

Lady Bridlington's image of a sweet innocent child suffered a severe check. Her eyes rounded in astonishment and she gasped, "Won't have him—! *W-won't* have him? One of the richest men in England? You just leave her to me, ma'am."

The dowager sat up and said in a voice that brooked no argument, "No, you leave her alone! She's got a head on her shoulders, that one. She's not one of those flighty modern die-away misses. I won't scruple to tell you that I'm concerned about my grandson," she added. "It's no secret that he's wild—I don't hold that against him, mind. What young man worth his salt doesn't sow a few wild oats? But it's time he was settling down and seeing to the succession."

She looked up. "I don't say that in the normal run of things I'd consider a match between a Fairfield and a Staunton an equal one. He's not a Desborough; still, he might look as high as he pleases for a bride. But since this unfortunate affair has happened, I don't say it mightn't do very well. And I won't even deny that I've taken a liking to the girl."

Lady Bridlington was trying to contain her elation. St. Ives—! Who would have thought? "Oh, ma'am, it is plain it is the only solution!" she cried. "I saw that at once! And successful marriages have been based on far worse circumstances, as we both know. You'll not regret doing the right thing, I assure you."

"Hmph," said the dowager. "That remains to be seen! But you don't know either of them if you think they'll be driven. I've said I'll see this through, and I won't go back on my word, but it will take careful handling. You leave it to me and concentrate on making the girl presentable." She laughed. "There, I've been more frank than I like, but I know I can rely on you."

Lady Bridlington eagerly assured the dowager that she might indeed rely on her, her mind already busy weaving plans and stratagems. To snare the most eligible matrimonial prize on the market! And to think that only an hour ago she had been in flat despair.

Then she remembered James and his wretched balloon, or whatever it was. Well, she would absolutely refuse to allow James to ruin what bid fair to be the best piece of work she had ever done. Retrench indeed, when she had the opportunity of pulling off the coup of the season. St. Ives—? Well, well, well. He was a devil, all right, but what woman hadn't a soft spot for a rake, especially one as handsome as St. Ives? And the fortune—! If he hadn't been able to run through it by now there was no telling what he might be worth. And it was no secret that he was the dowager's favorite. The old woman had a tidy bundle set aside, if rumor were to be believed, and no doubt intended to leave it all to St. Ives.

Lady Bridlington frowned, attempting to do mental sums in her head, and was gratified by her conclusions. But James was likely to prove difficult. He could be guaranteed to object to having a strange girl thrust upon him, and he wasn't likely to be in the least swayed by the circumstances surrounding the affair. He was far more apt to consider it exactly the sort of thing he wished his Mama to have nothing to do with. And the expense of presenting a young girl to the *ton* was not negligible, however one might scrape. Not, of course, that she had the least intention of scraping when the stakes were so high. Well, well. Who would have thought it of Marianne Spencer's daughter?

Still, it wouldn't hurt to at least broach the matter, in case James proved completely intractable. So she said carefully, her color a little high, "I dislike being obliged to bring it up, ma'am—not that I would begrudge the poor child anything, as I hope you know! But I fear things are a little—unsettled—at present, and I—"

Unfortunately, the dowager took her up literally. "Ah, I heard you'd lost a packet in the last South Seas scheme? That's what comes of putting money in anything but good sound English stock. But fools will never learn when they think there's money to be had for nothing. Ah, well, from all I've ever heard that son of yours is a dull dog, although sounder than his father. I don't doubt he'll set it all to rights. Pinching pennies, is he?"

Lady Bridlington, two bright spots of color in her cheeks, made haste to disclaim, but she forgot all inclination to be indignant at the dowager's next magical words. "Never mind. I meant, naturally, that I would frank the girl. Send all the bills to me."

But Lady Bridlington's spirits were a little daunted by her first sight of the girl. It was obvious that Miss Fairfield had brought little more than nightgear in her bandbox, for not even the dowager's own dresser had been able to remove from her gown all traces of last night's storm. She looked pale and decidedly ill at ease, and she came slowly into the room, a question in her wide dark eyes, and stood regarding them gravely.

Lady Bridlington, her mind already busy, looked her

over critically. The child was certainly no beauty. Her hair was unbecomingly arranged, her dress was a disgrace, and she was as brown as an Indian. Leave it to a man to allow a girl to run wild with no protection for the complexion. Thank goodness, at least she had no freckles.

The dowager, watching Lady Bridlington in some amusement, said, "Well, what do you think?"

"We'll have to see what we can do with that complexion," said her ladyship gloomily. "Cucumber slices, I think, though whether even that can do any good in such a short time I've no idea."

The dowager snorted. "Cucumbers! Nonsense. Crushed strawberries."

Lady Bridlington was momentarily diverted. "Crushed strawberries? I've heard of laying lemon slices on the complexion, but never strawberries. Tell me, what do you recommend for spots?"

The dowager recalled her to the subject at hand with a rude recommendation not to be such a nodcock if she could help it. Her ladyship took it in good part, only saying, "Well, I daresay it would be almost impossible to obtain any strawberries at this time of year, so it will have to be the cucumbers. In the meantime, I think, champagne and straw. And perhaps the palest yellow?"

"Just see that you don't deck her out in whites and blues."

"I should hope not, with that complexion!" said her ladyship, bridling slightly.

"Aye, aye, you'll know how to do the thing," the dowager said. "Just don't turn her into a milk-and-water miss is all I ask."

"I don't think I could if I wanted to. But what do you think, ma'am? Dare we try green—or even crimson?"

The dowager's dry laugh cackled. "Just what we want! We'll make them sit up and take notice. If she don't suit the fashion, we'll make her the fashion! We've had enough of these simpering, fubsy-faced chits. I told you I'm still a force to be reckoned with when I set my mind to it."

"Yes, but ma'am—we'll never make a beauty out of her, and no one will believe her fortune is more than respectable. Everyone knows Fairfield has been run to pieces for years."

"Don't be such a fool if you can help it!" retorted the dowager. "I have no intention of passing her off as other than what she is. As for being a beauty, fiddlesticks! I was no beauty, and I caught Wraxham. Sally Jersey's no beauty, nor is Lady Hertford, but that don't keep 'em from being two of the most fascinating woman of their day. In fact, I've seldom known a beauty that wasn't a dead bore into the bargain."

"But I don't want to be a fascinating woman," pointed out Miss Fairfield.

Both women looked around in astonishment. "Good God, girl! I'd forgotten you," said the dowager with a grin. "What's this? Of course you do. Every woman wants to be fascinating. Precious few of 'em make it, though."

There was a look in Miss Fairfield's grave gray eyes that the dowager had encountered once before. "Forgive me, ma'am, but you are both of you being nonsensical, you know," she said. "It is very kind, but you must not think that I am so frivolous that I left home merely because I had a yearning to—to dance and go to parties."

"Nonsense!" said the dowager. "And why should you not? If your father hadn't left you to molder away in the country, none of this might have happened."

Lady Bridlington added kindly, "No, my love, this is all the merest agitation of nerves! In a few months, when you see how soon you feel exactly at home here, I don't doubt but that you will laugh at how silly and nervous you were."

Sylvie hesitated, then came shyly forward, holding out her hand. "You are Lady Bridlington, of course, ma'am. If you have really consented to let me stay with you, I am very grateful, but you must not think I wish you to drop everything and play chaperone to me. I can only promise I will try not to be any trouble to you."

Lady Bridlington, her soft heart touched, warmly clasped the hand held out to her and said a little mistily, "You are talking nonsense, my love! As if you could ever be the least trouble to me. Indeed, I can't imagine why I

never thought of having you with me, for if you must
know I've been quite blue-deviled of late. There's nothing
I'd enjoy more than having you to stay with me for as long
as you'd like. Your Mama and I were almost like sisters,
you know."

"I do know it, ma'am," said Sylvie. "It is why I dared
to hope you would help me now." She glanced at the
dowager and added, "But I cannot impose on you unless
you know the whole of the—the scrape I'm in. And I
will quite understand if you feel you cannot help me
after all."

The ready tears sprang to her ladyship's blue eyes and
she held out her arms and gathered her goddaughter to
her bosom. "Oh, my poor, poor child! Of course I'll help
you."

The dowager observed this scene unmoved, merely
commenting after a moment, "Very well, Sophia. There's
nothing to cry about."

Lady Bridlington released her burden and mopped at
her eyes. "N-no, no of course not," she said. "Here,
child, let me have a look at you. Now that I notice, you
have much the look of your Mama. Sylvie, isn't it? Not
usual, but then it's French, isn't it, and I have always
thought they have the oddest names. I remember your
grandmama very well; though, come to think of it, she
died before you were born."

She prattled on, but secretly she was busy revising
her first impression. The girl was not so shy as she had
feared. In fact, her manners seemed quite pretty. That
grave look of hers was deceiving.

Lady Bridlington's heart had sunk at her first sight of
the girl, for, whatever the dowager might intend, it was
daydreaming to suppose that St. Ives would ever look
twice at this chit when he had been used to diamonds
of the first water. Lady Bridlington had not personally seen
the opera dancer reputed to be his latest mistress, but,
according to Sally Debenham, the woman in question was
disgustingly lovely. She *had* seen Julia Horneby, of course,
and if she was not already his mistress, everyone knew
it was just a matter of time, for the way she looked at
him in public was a disgrace. It was useless to think that

this child was a match for such a poised and willowy beauty.

Miss Fairfield could, by no stretch of the imagination, be called willowy. She possessed a neat little figure, but she was not tall, and not even the kindest of critics would call her more than passable. But, although those eyebrows of hers were certainly impossible, it was unjust to call the girl plain. As a matter of fact, her eyes were unexpectedly lovely and had a trick of looking at one in an odd, grave way that gave a quaint old-fashioned look to her small face. Not that gentlemen were fond of girls who were too serious, of course; nevertheless, there was something arresting in those eyes. No, thought Lady Bridlington, with eyes like that the child could be a great deal plainer than she was, and no one would remember it.

She patted Sylvie's hand and smiled at her fondly. "Now, not another word about being a trouble to me. I swear, I can't think why it never occurred to me to have you with me. I have always wished I had a daughter. First thing tomorrow we must begin dressing you. Mirabelle's, I think, and perhaps another charming little modiste I know of in the Strand. She has not yet been discovered, but she is unbelievably clever with a needle and will know just what to do with you. Of course, it will never do to let anyone know where the gowns came from. And for bonnets—" She glanced at the dowager for approval. "Yes, I think Mme. Laurent, don't you, ma'am?"

"Oh, by all means go to Mme. Laurent. At her prices she should be able to find something to suit you," said the dowager. "And if you require any advice, you could do worse than to go to St. Ives. He's had more practice in buying women's fal-lals than almost anyone I know." She cackled rudely at Lady Bridlington's shocked expression, then leaned back into her chair a little more. "And now, I think I must ask you to excuse me. I'm not as young as I used to be, and it has been an exciting day. My dear, ring for Horsham, there's a good girl."

She closed her eyes, causing Miss Fairfield and Lady Bridlington to exchange startled glances, but when Horsham entered the room a few minutes later the dowager opened her eyes and said in her usual robust tones, "Ah, Horsham, send round for Lady Bridlington's carriage."

She held out a thin hand to Sylvie and clasped the girl's hand strongly. "My dear, you go along with Sophia and leave everything to us. I hope you will come and see me whenever you have a moment. I don't know when I was last so well entertained. And don't let Sophia turn you into a simpering ninny. Just remember that most people will accept you for what you are as long as you don't let 'em scare you." She gave a short laugh. "And that's probably the best piece of advice you're likely to get!"

She then cut short Sylvie's efforts to thank her, gave her hand briefly to Lady Bridlington, and closed her eyes once more.

As Horsham saw them out, Lady Bridlington whispered, "That's easy enough for her to say. I tell you, my dear, I may have been sometimes *tempted*, but I have never before taken a nap in front of my guests! I swear, she has always made me feel exactly as if I were back in the schoolroom, where I can assure you I haven't been in more than thirty years."

She nodded graciously to the aging butler and with great dignity led the way out the front door to her waiting carriage.

IX

Lady Bridlington's spirits remained high during the next few days, but it did not take her long to understand what the dowager had meant about her goddaughter. For Marianne's sake, she had been prepared to love Sylvie, even without the child's brilliant prospects, and after an hour in her company she was sure that there had never been a sweeter, more unaffected girl; but she could not deny that Sylvie was not just in the common way.

In the carriage on the short ride to Green Street, Lady Bridlington chatted animatedly in an attempt to put her young guest at ease. Sylvie had looked wide-eyed at the things her ladyship pointed out and had said with her quick smile, "I am afraid you will think me a regular country bumpkin, ma'am. I have always dreamed of coming to London, and it is all so much more than I ever expected."

Her ladyship had been touched and had patted Sylvie's hand kindly. "Well, it would never do, of course, to act too amazed, for I'm sure young ladies who do are considered quite provincial," she said, "but I have never thought a certain amount of enthusiasm out of place in a young girl. And I am sure no one would ever be able to think you a country bumpkin, my love! To be sure, those clothes—and we must see to your hair as soon as possible—but you remind me of what your Mama was at that age. Ah, how it takes me back."

"You are being kind, ma'am, but you know yourself what a shocking untruth that is!" said Sylvie. "Mama was reputed to be a great beauty, and though there is only one small miniature of her at home, I think it must be true, for Papa, you know, only likes diamonds of the first water."

Her ladyship had been startled. "Why, my dear, if it is so—and I do not think—but surely you can know nothing about it?"

Sylvie colored a little. "I think you mean that I should *say* nothing about it, ma'am. And generally I do not, of course. But I have been used to paying their bills for years, for Papa can never remember to do so, and I am assured that they were all diamonds of the first water. Who else could carry off a hat with seven ostrich feathers and a veil? Kendall and I laughed a good deal about that one, you can imagine, and made up fantastic tales about what she must have looked like."

"You cannot mean your Papa dared to bring such creatures home with him?" gasped her ladyship, scandalized.

"No, for Hinton would not stand for it. Hinton is our housekeeper, ma'am, and very straitlaced. I must own I was grateful, for to be obliged to entertain a great many strange women would not have been to my taste at all. I beg your pardon, ma'am; I can see you are shocked.

Only Hinton was most reliable, and generally, you know, Papa did not care to cross her. She had used to be the cook, but from one cause or another became the house-keeper, and Papa was always terrified that she would decide to leave, too, and he might have to tend to some of his own responsibilities."

She grinned then. "Kendall has always said that Hinton made a great sacrifice to stay with us, but he was her favorite and could do no wrong in her eyes, even when he fell asleep over his books one night and nearly burned the house down. For my part I've always thought she remained because she enjoyed lording it over all of us."

"But there must have been some—some respectable woman to take charge?" said her ladyship. "He could not, surely, have left you with such a woman?"

"You do not know Papa if you think that, ma'am," said Sylvie a little mischievously. "Papa can convince himself that anything he wishes to do is just what he ought to do. But Blackmer saw to things, at least until I was old enough to take over some of the responsibilities myself. Blackmer is our groom—I should say our head groom—and I don't know what we would have done without him."

Her ladyship was beginning to feel stunned. "Until you should take over some of the respons—oh, my dear!" she cried. "You must believe I had no idea things were so bad! But surely your brother—?"

At that Sylvie went off into a peal of laughter. "Oh, I beg your pardon, ma'am! Of course you can't know, but Kendall is brilliant, you see. He has a distinguished political career before him, and I would not be surprised to see him become prime minister someday. But particularly brilliant men, it seems, frequently possess less than common sense. He can unravel the most complicated Latin passage, but he is unable to make a column of figures total the same twice in succession. I have seen him forget—for an entire morning—to put on his other boot because he was reading a new treatise on government. Blackmer says he'll end by contracting an inflammation of the lungs because he'll forget to notice it is raining when he goes out one day."

Her ladyship could not help reflecting a little bitterly

that this seemed to be the least harmful idiosyncrasy in that bizarre household. "But my dear, even your *Papa* could not have left two young children with no one more to care for then than a—a former cook and a groom! I'm sure they were most capable, but to leave you quite alone with such people is unthinkable!"

Unexpectedly, Sylvie had bridled a little. "I can assure you, ma'am, we did very much better with 'such people' than we ever did when Papa was home. They at least had our interests at heart. And since Papa was never home, and both Kendall and I disliked him excessively, I don't know where we would have been without Blackmer and Hinton."

She smiled then at her godmother and added in her frank way, "You do not like me to say such things I can see, ma'am. But Papa never made the least push to attach our affections, Kendall's and mine, and he quarreled bitterly with Mama when she was alive, so I do not think you would want me to pretend an affection I cannot feel. But there is no point in talking of that. I wish instead that you would tell me about my mother, for I can scarcely remember her, you know."

Her ladyship was glad of a change of topic, and embarked upon several anecdotes she had all but forgotten. But Sylvie's story had shaken her more than she liked to admit, and after a few minutes she sighed and dabbed at her eyes. "Ah, how it takes me back! Poor Marianne dead, and so many years gone. You must believe I had no idea things were so bad, my love. But there, you are with me now, and everything has turned out for the best, I'm sure. Except for poor Marianne, of course. Can it have been fifteen years ago?" she said. "Why you must have been no more than—"

"I was four when she died," Sylvie said. "Kendall was eight, so he remembers her better. But I did not mean to upset you, ma'am, and I can see I have done so." She hesitated, then said, "Indeed, I have only told you as much as I have because I wanted you to understand a little why I—why I did what I did. I did not think I could remain at home another night after—after that."

"Oh, my poor dear!" cried her ladyship. "Oh, I do understand, and I feel for you with all my heart. Merely to

think of you at the mercy of such men—! Oh, it does
not bear thinking of! How terrified you must have been."

"To be honest, ma'am," said Sylvie with a grin, "I was
far too angry. And I did not fear his lordship, you must not
think that. I don't think he ever even looked at me.
But I mean only to forget it now. I have been luckier
than I deserve, and I will always be grateful to you and
her grace."

Her ladyship was quite overcome, and she murmured
tearfully that they need never speak of it again if Sylvie
desired. Indeed, she added, it would be best if they did
not; for one never knew who might be listening, it was
amazing how the very thing one most wished to remain
secret was what became talked of the most.

Sylvie laughed. "Yes, that is true, ma'am, but I think
we shall have to speak of it just this once. I—her grace
has been frank with me to a certain extent, and I would
desire you to be as frank, if you please. She thinks
that—she seems to believe she will be able to stop any
talk, and that I need not fear being ruined. And you have
both of you talked of my going about in society a little.
Do you think to find me a husband?" she asked. "Is that
in your minds?"

This was plain speaking indeed, and on a topic her ladyship could not help but feel somewhat dangerous. "I—
why I'm sure it would be vulgar to set your cap, my love,
but we naturally hope you may meet someone you can
—" She broke off, having had a horrible thought. "You
cannot mean you are—are *opposed* to marriage, like that
dreadful Mary Wollstonecraft?" At that point, nothing
would have surprised her.

"No, no, ma'am! I only meant that if you thought you
could find me a husband, I would be very glad," Sylvie
said. "For various reasons I had grown accustomed to
thinking I would never wed, so Kendall and I had intended
to set up housekeeping together as soon as he finishes
school. But if I could marry, I don't know but what this
whole thing won't have been a blessing in disguise. Kendall
would be far happier in lodgings somewhere, so that if
he wishes to stay up all night and forget to eat his meals
he need not worry about disturbing me."

"Does he do that?" asked her ladyship faintly.

Sylvie's eyes began to twinkle. "Oh, yes, frequently! When I thought I had no alternative, I had made up my mind I could at least prevent him from ignoring too many meals, but it would be better if I could find some way to be independent, so that he need not feel responsible for me, which I know he does now." She looked up a little anxiously. "Only, I feel I should perhaps warn you that I am not likely to *take*, ma'am," she said. "Papa says I have no more notion of conduct or conversation than a village slattern, and I fear he may be right. And I have no portion. I have a little coming to me on my next birthday from Mama, but I do not think it would be considered a portion exactly."

She sighed, a hint of mischief in her eyes. "I have made it sound hopeless. *Is* it hopeless, ma'am, and had I better resign myself to making Kendall's life miserable?"

"Don't be absurd, my love!" said her ladyship. "I feel certain any young man could learn to love you, as I have done already, and then your lack of portion would not matter one jot. But what did you think of St. Ives, my dear?" she asked coyly. "He is very wild, I know, but so handsome!"

"Now you are being absurd, ma'am!" replied Sylvie promptly. "I do not set my sights so high, I can assure you. I will be more than content with a man of good sense and an easy competence. Or even one without perfectly good sense, if he is amiable," she added teasingly. "Though I do feel for the children, poor dears. But then, beggers can't be choosers, and someone must mother all those poor silly children."

She saw then that her godmother was looking wholly bewildered, and she laughed. "No, no dear ma'am, I do not wish you to find me a man with silly children! As for my Lord St. Ives, I very much doubt if I shall ever be obliged to see him again. And now that we have safely settled the problem of my future and need not ever speak of that dreadful night again, I wish you will tell me if there is anything I can do to be useful to you. I meant it when I said that I did not mean to be a burden."

Her ladyship was naturally touched, and she made haste

to disclaim any desire but that her dearest Sylvie should enjoy her stay as much as possible. Nonetheless, she could not help wondering what James would make of this odd child.

Strangely enough, James, after his first angry reaction, seemed to be unexpectedly tolerant of his Mama's young guest. He had burst in upon his Mama on that first day as she had dozed by the fire, a cap tied over her curls and several shawls draped across her feet, and said without ceremony, "Good God, ma'am, what's this I hear about a strange girl coming to live with us?"

Lady Bridlington had started, one hand going to her cap, the other clutching at her shawls. "Oh, James!" she said. "How you startled me! What do you mean bursting in here without so much as a by-your-leave and scaring the wits out of me?"

"I beg your pardon, ma'am," he said, "But I can scarcely credit what Saltish has been telling me. Can you seriously have invited a young girl to come and stay with us, particularly at a time when you know we must exercise the strictest economy?"

Lady Bridlington, flustered, straightened her cap. She had intended to inform James in her own time, when she had decided what and how much to tell him. James was sometimes appallingly straitlaced, and she placed no reliance on his accepting the story in the proper frame of mind.

Now, thrown off her stride, she gained time by evasive tactics. "Really, James, I thought you were to dine out this evening!" she said indignantly. "I must tell Saltish to set another cover for dinner. I wish you would not change your mind like this. You know how cook resents any change in plans."

"I had intended to dine at my club," said James heavily. "But that was before I was informed of this extraordinary occurrence. Will you have the goodness, ma'am, to explain exactly whom you have invited into my house behind my back?"

"Well, if you *will* gossip with the servants, James! And I did not invite anyone behind your back. Or at least not precisely. It is Sylvie Fairfield, poor Marianne's daughter, and if you tell me I should have turned my back on her at such a time, when I am her godmama, well I would never have thought it of you. What is more, this is *my* house," she added, "for your Papa bought it for me!"

James blinked, caught off guard by this unexpected counterattack, and said a little more mildly, "Yes, well, never mind. Sylvie Fairfield? You don't mean Sir John Fairfield's daughter, surely? Is she your goddaughter? I had never heard it, but I am sorry, ma'am, that is an acquaintance I cannot advise you to continue. Everyone knows Sir John is a shockingly loose screw."

"Well, I intend to continue it!" said her ladyship. "Unless I much miss my guess, St. Ives will have her. Aye, you may stare," she added in satisfaction, "but I'd be willing to wager my diamond necklace he'll marry her. When I think of Sally Debenham's face when she finds out! And as for you," she added bitterly, rounding on her only son, "is it any wonder if I have invited my goddaughter to stay with me, when all you can do is sulk and look grave and scold me for being extravagant? I tell you, James, if you don't watch out, you'll become a dead bore before you're thirty."

James blinked again. "Yes, well, I do not mean to forbid you to do anything you think is best, ma'am. But as for St. Ives marrying Fairfield's daughter—!" He frowned. "Aside from the fact that I have heard no indication that St. Ives is thinking of wedding, I fear you are indulging in pipe dreams, ma'am. I doubt even St. Ives could be so blind to what he owes to his name."

Lady Bridlington was naturally a little annoyed at this, but she thought she would do best after all to tell him the truth. He listened gravely, and, although he certainly looked shocked, after much consideration he reluctantly conceded that his Mama had done the only thing possible by bringing the girl there. "I will not try to hide from you the fact that I cannot like it, ma'am. But knowing that the girl was at the mercy of such—well, I need say no more, I know! I only wish it were not necessary for me to remain silent about the affair. I have long thought Lord St. Ives the epitome of the type of man I can only hold in utter contempt. He has birth, wealth, and breeding, and he does nothing but throw it away.

"If he did not offer for Lady Colchester after that disgraceful affair, I think it only fair to conclude he is lost to all decent feeling, ma'am. And *she*, I need not remind you, was the daughter of an earl. No, no, we must make sure that this whole shameful incident remains hushed up, for if even one word of it should get out, I do not like to think what will be the result. I hope you may not live to regret this day, ma'am, and that is all I mean to say on the subject."

He went away to change for dinner, unaware of having said anything to anger his Mama. But after dinner, when he stopped by her dressing room again before going to bed, he seemed inclined to look with more favor on her young guest. Both the manner of her coming and of her parentage had naturally served to prejudice him against her, but he was bound to own her manners had agreeably surprised him. He was not pleased with the way in which modern young ladies were wont to put themselves unbecomingly forward, and he thought Miss Fairfield seemed to possess more modesty and rather more intelligence than was commonly met with in her sex.

He then kissed his Mama on the cheek and went away to bed, saying that perhaps it would amuse her after all to have Miss Fairfield with her, and as long as she was not too extravagant, he did not mean to forbid it. He stuck his head back in, though, to add that he hoped she meant to write Sir John Fairfield an extremely frank letter, for if she did not he would certainly do so, and with a great deal of pleasure.

Lady Bridlington found little to please her in her son's unexpected praise, for it was useless to suppose that the manners James might approve of would be to the taste of the wild young Earl of St. Ives; but it was at least a relief to know that James did not mean to be difficult. Indeed, it had occurred to her ladyship to wonder if she had overloooked a possible danger. It would be just like James to develop a stupid *tendre* for the girl, or to believe himself duty bound to offer for her; and although Lady Bridlington was already quite fond of the child, Sylvie hadn't a penny to her name and would never do for James. Besides, her ladyship had something very different in mind for her goddaughter.

She went to bed, only to dream of bridals and of a

handsome young rake tossing her goddaughter over his saddlebow and riding off into the black night—a dream that would have very much surprised its two principles, neither of whose thoughts at the moment were anywhere near so romantic.

Sylvie, wrapped in the unaccustomed luxury of a soft bed with a hot brick at her feet, was thinking that she had stumbled into a dream, and must waken soon. She snuggled deeper into the silk coverlet, trying to drown out the cries of the linkmen and the carriage wheels outside, and sleepily wished that Blackmer might see her now.

Oddly enough, however, her last thought before she drifted to sleep was not of the solid Blackmer or of her new life, but of a pair of brilliant blue eyes set in a handsome, cynical countenance.

In the next few days she found no reason to alter her opinion that she had somehow stumbled into a dream. No greater contrast could have been found between her old life and her new. The fashionable house in Green Street was furnished in the latest Egyptian style, which her godmother confessed had cost the earth but had been well worth the expense. Did not Sylvie think it charming? Her ladyship herself had had the happy notion of lining the drawing room with crimson silk so that one might almost believe oneself in a tent in the desert, although one would not really wish to be in the desert at all, of course.

Sylvie forebore to point out that anything less like a tent in the desert she had yet to see, and allowed herself to be led from one room to the other, storing up details for Kendall.

She had been a little shy at first, but it was impossible to remain so when her ladyship made her laugh a dozen times a day with her vague pronouncements. Sylvie's experience had never included gentle, helpless women who got their own way by refusing to believe that everything would not happen exactly as they wished, and who broke into a flood of tears when crossed, only to be all smiles a moment later.

It did not take long, of course, for Sylvie to realize

that, however kind, Lady Bridlington was vain and more than a little silly, her mind given over almost wholly to pleasure. She seemed only to read the newspapers in order to discover which of her friends was going into the country, what great lord was expected to return to his town house, or who had become engaged to whom. And although she read whatever book was presently in fashion and was even able to quote five or six lines of Lord Byron's poetry, she was amazingly ignorant on the most elementary of political topics and frequently complained that she could not understand why the wretched war with France dragged on when she was sure everyone was tired of it.

But it was impossible to doubt her genuine desire to make up to her goddaughter for what she plainly saw as a dreadful life. And it was beyond Sylvie's ability to make her godmother see that she had been not so unhappy as occasionally bored and a little restless thinking she might never see more of the world than that particular corner of Cambridgeshire.

Those first few days passed in a whirlwind of fittings and shopping, scarcely giving Sylvie time to catch her breath. Only one thing occurred to mar the harmony, and that was on the first evening, when Sylvie made the acquaintance of her ladyship's only son.

Although Sir James said everything that was proper and was evidently very punctilious, Sylvie found it difficult to warm to him. After only one evening she began to understand why Lady Bridlington seemed to be forever talking of her son but seldom spent time in his company. He bore with her ladyship's chatter very well, but Sylvie suspected he was less than pleased by her own sudden appearance in their midst. However, he said nothing she might object to, and even condescended to sit conversing with her for some twenty minutes after dinner.

But for a young lady who had previously been able to count on the fingers of one hand the new gowns she had had in the last five years, everything was a heady experience, from choosing materials at the linen drapers to visiting the little modiste Lady Bridlington had told her about. Within two days, the first of the gowns was sent home; and when she saw herself transformed by a gown cut in the latest mode, her hair fashionably arranged by Lady Bridlington's own formidable dresser, Sylvie scarcely recognized herself, and her former life seemed a million miles away.

Lady Bridlington was complacently inclined to agree. The child was turning out very well indeed. And if she displayed a tendency to be too frank, her manners were pretty and, aside from a certain levity, exactly what her ladyship would have wished in a daughter of her own.

Sylvie would be a taking little thing, given the proper encouragement, and Lady Bridlington was sure she quite loved her already. And to think, St. Ives had thirty thousand a year if he had a penny!

In the meantime, it was necessary to be very careful, and particularly to see that no hint of scandal should attach to the child's name. If that were ever once to occur, not even all of the dowager's influence would be able to bring the thing off. St. Ives might be a rake, but he was a Staunton, and his mother had been a Desborough. He might be prevailed on to marry to prevent a scandal, but he would never do so once that scandal had already occurred.

That was why her ladyship had been so harsh when one of the maids had dared to be disrespectful. Luckily, no harm had been done, for the servant girl had most affectingly begged Miss Fairfield's pardon, pleading concern about an aged father who was ill and not expected to recover. Sylvie had shown a disconcerting tendency to inquire more closely into the matter, even inviting the maid to sit down and tell her all about it, but fortunately Mary had been too well trained to commit such a solecism, and she became unexpectedly devoted to the young miss after that and jealously guarded her right to help her dress and take up her morning chocolate.

Indeed, aside from a very few early incidents, all the servants seemed to look upon Miss Fairfield tolerantly, and Saltish, a high stickler, had even unbent sufficiently to be heard telling her the best place to go to obtain a particular book, and promising to send one of the footmen after it that afternoon.

All in all, things were going very well.

X

My Lord St. Ives was not finding things so much to his taste. He had left his grandmother's house bent on teaching Miss Fairfield a lesson, and with that purpose in mind had refrained from returning to find out how she was faring with his formidable grandparent. If he had derived a certain perverse pleasure in seeing her under that excellent lady's handling, it had been a high spot in an otherwise bleak week. He discovered that the Fagiani bored him; his usual haunts were devoid of amusement; and the recent turn of events with Fairfield's daughter had left him feeling disilllusioned and more jaded than he could have believed possible.

To top it all he had received a letter from Kitty, spread over two sheets, which cost him several shillings for the privilege to read which left him in little doubt as to where his duty lay. She had alternated betwen raptures over her dearest Nicky's agreeing to take her, the daring gowns she meant to have, and the apparently equal attractions of a Captain of Dragoon Guards with whom she was presently carrying on a clandestine and probably highly dangerous flirtation. Knowing Kitty, the danger, and not the Dragoon Captain, was the attraction.

In an excess of ill humor, St. Ives had screwed up the letter and thrown it into the fireplace. Damn them all, he thought savagely and went off in search of oblivion.

He was well on the way to finding it when he had the misfortune to encounter his uncle and Lord Rockingham outside of Boodle's. If St. Ives was fairly well on the go, Lord Timothy had reached the rollicking stage, and he hailed his nephew with joy. "Come in, come in, my boy! Rockingham and I were about to sample some of Brooks's

new shipment of burgundy. Didn't know you was back—
did you know he was back, Rockingham?—but damme if
I'm not glad to see you!"

"I can't say I share the pleasure," retorted St. Ives
with ill grace. "Hallo, Rockingham. Are you playing
nursemaid or will you join us in drowning our sorrows?"

My Lord Rockingham put up his brows, but as Lord
Timothy chose that moment to loudly discover an old
friend, nothing more was said until they were seated.
Then Rockingham observed somewhat dryly, "To what do
we owe this charming mood, St. Ives? One might almost
suppose you had already grown tired of the Fagiani. Or
have you been exchanging insults with Lambeth again?"

"The devil!" said St. Ives. "Who told you so?"

"My dear Nicky, I hardly know. One hears things. Ah,
Brooks, there you are. A bottle of brandy for my wild
young friend here, and Lord Timothy and I will try the
new burgundy you were telling us about."

As soon as the proprietor had taken his leave, St. Ives
said, "Damn you, Rockingham! Was anything said of a girl?"

"You alarm me, Nicky," sighed Rockingham. "You
positively alarm me. I had understood the Fagiani to be
the bone of contention between you. Surely there cannot be another so soon? Timothy, I begin to feel our age.
No, you young hothead," he added, "you will not succeed in quarreling with me, so quit glaring at me. Now
that I think of it, yes, I believe there was some mention
of an—er—young lady. Nameless, of course," he added
gently.

"You will oblige me by forgetting whatever you heard."

"Oh, nothing easier, dear boy. You know my wretched
memory." He glanced up. "But you should understand
there may be those who lack my convenient losses of
memory." He lifted his head then and added, "And here,
unless I miss my guess, is one of them. I collect we are
shortly to be accosted by still another member of the
family. Really, I wonder if I should withdraw. Well, Staunton? You see me surrounded by your relatives."

Michael Staunton smiled and shook hands with Rockingham. "How do you do, Lord Timothy?" he said. "I need
not remind Lord Rockingham that I can claim no relation-

ship with you." His eyes shifted and he added, "Well, St. Ives, I am glad to have a chance to speak with you. Will you grant me a few minutes?"

"You have nothing of a private nature to say to me," St. Ives replied shortly. "Say what you wish and be done with it!"

Staunton's pleasant countenance flushed slightly, but he said evenly, "As you wish. I understand you have consented at long last to have the Lady Catherine stay with you. I understand her viewpoint, but is that wise?"

"I see you have been busy, as usual, cousin!"

Staunton's fingers whitened on the back of Rockingham's chair, but he held his temper. "I find it hard to credit, but if you are indeed contemplating such a step, I beg you to reconsider. Laura is, I know, sometimes difficult, but you—surely you are the first to agree you are not the one to have the keeping of a young girl in your hands!"

"I will certainly put a spoke in your wheels, if that is what you fear," sneered St. Ives.

Staunton turned a dull shade of red. "I might have expected you to be unpleasant, St. Ives. I can only say I would be more reassured if I thought this sudden interest in your sister contained any other motive but spite. Gentlemen, I bid you good day." He bowed stiffly and was gone.

"Ah, *hostis honori invidia*," murmured Lord Rockingham inconsequentially.

Whether or not St. Ives was seriously alarmed at the hint of rumor he heard from Rockingham, the next morning he was extremely short with his valet, who bore his lordship's ill temper with his usual lack of expression. St. Ives presented himself at his grandmother's house at an unseasonably early hour, only to be informed by her butler that the young lady in question was no longer with them. She had, Horsham rather thought, although he could not be certain, left on the afternoon she arrived.

St. Ives stared at the man as if he had taken leave of his senses, then pushed past him and took the stairs two at a time to his grandmother's dressing room.

The dowager was awake and dressed, seated in an

upright chair and reading a letter from her voluminous correspondence. She put up her brows a little at her grandson's black countenance. "Ah, St. Ives," she said, "I see your manners are as disgraceful as ever. Have the goodness to close the door behind you."

He did as she bid, then turned and said with a cold edge to his voice that she had never heard before, "Very well, ma'am! What have you done with her?"

The dowager reached out a delicate hand for her walking stick. "What do you care? You wished to be rid of her, did you not?"

"Good God!" he said harshly. "I may have wished to be rid of her, but it was never my intention to thrust her alone and unprotected on the streets of London! Surely you could see that she was little more than a child."

"Can it be that you possess a conscience after all, St. Ives?"

"Have the goodness, ma'am, to tell me how long ago she left your house and what she may have told you! I must try to find her—if I am not already too late."

"I will accept that your concern does you credit, however belated," said the dowager, "and has no doubt overcome what few manners you possess. I certainly was given no reason to suppose you cared in the least what became of the girl. If I was wrong, I apologize, but I assure you I am not as lost to propriety as you seem to believe. You will find the girl in Green Street with her godmother, Lady Bridlington. But I will not answer for it whether she will be willing to receive you. She has, after all, little reason to thank you for the plight she presently finds herself in."

St. Ives did not appear gratified by the news that Miss Fairfield had been spared the fate he had so obviously envisioned. His eyes narrowed on his grandmother's face and without another word he turned on his heel and strode out, leaving the dowager to nod with faint satisfaction before returning to her letters.

St. Ives's temper was not improved by being obliged to spend the rest of the day seeking an audience with his suddenly elusive quarry in Green Street. The first two times he called he was informed by a footman that

her ladyship and Miss Fairfield were not at home; and
the third time, late in the afternoon, that her ladyship
was resting in her room and could not be disturbed.

When rudely informed that his lordship did not care if
Lady Bridlington never awakened again, and that he demanded to speak with Miss Fairfield and had every intention of remaining there until she came down, Saltish,
mistrusting the dangerous look in the earl's eyes, showed
him into a small saloon on the first floor.

Saltish found Sylvie on the second floor, engaged in
writing a letter. She started at his message, turning a
little pale, but thanked him quietly and rose at once to go
downstairs in a dignified manner that did her no harm in
that very proper gentleman's estimation.

Indeed, Saltish had been of two minds whether to
deliver the message at all. The whole household had
naturally been intrigued by the unexpected arrival of her
ladyship's unknown goddaughter, and Saltish had not failed
to remark Sir James's astonishment when he was informed
of the young lady's arrival. But it had not taken much
time for the butler to realize that, whatever her origins,
Miss Fairfield was a lady of quality, and he would treat
her accordingly, a circumstance that had nothing to do
with Lady Bridlington's pronouncements on the subject.
Miss Fairfield might have been reared in the country and
have little notion of how to go on in London, and her
father might have acquired an undesirable reputation, but
she was a lady for all that. She was not above giving a
kind word to those who served her, and she had developed quite a friendship with the butler, after that first
day, so that she had gotten into the habit of asking his
advice on a number of subjects, from the proper amount
to bestow in vails upon the servants to hints on the
normal routine of the household. She was not one who
was above herself, as the saying went.

But the appearance on the scene of my Lord St. Ives,
a young man of known and regrettable reputation, placed
a construction on events that Saltish, for one, was sorry
to see. He would even have made some excuse to
linger had not his lordship looked up as they came in and
demanded, "Well, what do you want?" leaving the butler
with no choice but to bow stiffly and withdraw.

Sylvie had been looking a little pale, but at that she put up her chin and said, "Yes, my lord? Did you wish to speak with me?"

St. Ives, expecting the same bedraggled creature, found himself confronted by a young woman in a morning dress of jonquil muslin trimmed and ruched with green ribbon at the neck and wrists, her soft curls cropped in the current mode and dressed *à la grecque.* The knowledge that Miss Fairfield had been busy outfitting herself in the first style of elegance did not seem to exercise a beneficial effect on his temper. He looked her up and down and said, "Well, ma'am! Very fine! But I would have thought you would have had the courtesy to inform me that you meant to leave my grandmother's protection."

"If I should have done so, I am sorry, my lord, but you made it more than plain that you would be glad to be rid of me."

"So that rankled, did it?" he said. "But surely not enough to make you forgo the very healthy profit you expect to realize from this adventure."

"My lord," she said, "I had thought—I had hoped you would have spoken with your grandmother. She must have explained that I have—have reconsidered my decision. I do not—that is, what I said that morning no longer—no longer applies. You have nothing to fear from me."

"What new game is this?" he demanded. "Do you wish me to believe you have experienced a sudden attack of conscience, Miss Fairfield? You will forgive me if I find it a little difficult to credit, under the circumstances. You made your character quite plain in my house, if it had not been made so the night before."

"No, my lord, you did that!" she retorted, angry once more. "You and my father made me the prize in a game of chance, between you, without ever considering what my feelings were or whether I might not be what you so obviously expected! I merely saw no reason to disabuse you. And I was glad when you were angry because it made you see, as nothing else could have, exactly what you had done! Now I think it is time for you to leave. I do not expect we will be obliged to meet again."

He stood observing her, a frown in his eyes, but some of the harshness had left his face. After a moment he said, "I think you'd better explain, Miss Fairfield. It almost seems I must have been right in my first impression of you after all."

When she raised her brows and made no answer, he added maliciously, "I thought you looked like a little brown sparrow."

She made no attempt to speak, and he swore. "Good God. I must have been drunker than I thought. But what in the name of all that's holy possessed you to come with me then, you little fool?"

"I may have been a l-little fool, but at least I wasn't bent on the worst sort of mischief!"

"Nor was I, Miss Fairfield," he said coldly. "How was I to know Fairfield possessed such a daughter? And neither your conduct in your home, or in my own, you must admit, gave me any cause to think differently."

"No, my lord," she admitted in a little voice. "But I was very angry. I may have behaved badly, but you—"

"You behaved like the veriest trollop, Miss Fairfield!"

She sighed. "Yes, my lord."

"I think you'd better tell me the whole, God help me! And I want the truth this time."

"I have told you already, my lord," she said unhappily. "You—you made me angry by thinking I must be—must be exactly like my father. And my father, too—well, I have never been particularly happy at home. After that night I thought anything would be preferable to remaining there another moment."

"You were wrong!" he said crudely.

"Yes, my lord. I can see that now. I thought it would be easy enough, once we had reached London, to slip away."

"God give me patience! And if it had not proved so easy, you naïve little fool, or if you had next encountered a man less drunk or more determined than I?"

"I have a gun," she said simply. "I would have used it if necessary."

He burst out laughing. "Oh, my God! I hardly know whether to be pleased or sorry the necessity did not arise. Am I to take it you know how to use this pistol of yours, Miss Fairfield?"

"Of course, my lord," she said, surprised. "Papa says it is my only accomplishment."

He grinned, but there was unexpected understanding in his eyes. "Makes your life miserable, does he?"

"Oh, not precisely miserable, my lord," she said. "And to be just, I think I am a great disappointment to him."

He shook his head again, as if in disbelief. "Good God, what a damnable mess. If you had no intention of wedding me—and I am beginning to think you are just naïve enough to be telling me the truth—what did you intend? To come to this godmother of yours?"

"No, my lord. I did not even remember her then. I had meant to go to my old nurse until I could decide what was to be done. I thought—I thought I should be able to find employment until my brother comes down from Oxford in the fall. I see now that it was very foolish, but I did not know that I would ever be obliged to explain it to you, or that your—your grandmother would become involved. I am sorry, my lord."

He raked his hand through his hair. "Foolish! If I had treated you in the way you deserved you would have been well served! Of all the idiotic, naïve, wanton stupidity—!"

She stiffened again. "Well, if you had not been drunk and bent upon ruining me, none of it might have happened!"

"It may surprise you to know, Miss Fairfield, that though I was certainly drunk, I was not bent on ruining you," he said. "I intended marriage."

She looked astonished. "You intended—?" Her cheeks flamed. "If you wish to be wed, my lord, I would suggest you go about it in the normal fashion! Or did you think Fairfield's daughter only fit to be won as if she were no more than the common trollop you called me?"

"If *you* wished to be wooed and won, Miss Fairfield," he retorted, "you should not have agreed to come with me! Well, it is a damnable tangle, and it is clear there is only one solution. We will have to be wed, and as soon as the thing can be decently accomplished, if we are to avoid a scandal."

"M-my lord?" she faltered, shocked to the core of her being.

He smiled unpleasantly. "Use the head I imagine you possess, Miss Fairfield! I will acquit you of attempting to blackmail me into marriage, but you have been gone from your home for more than three days, and a dozen fools know you left it in my company. What do you imagine will happen to your reputation once that story gets around?"

"If I am to believe you, I have no reputation already, my lord," she said. "Fortunately your grandmother is by no means as pessimistic as you. She thinks that no one will dare to gossip if she lets it be known that I was in her company from the beginning."

"Am I to take it you confessed the whole to my grandmother?

She smiled a little unwillingly at the memory. "I didn't have to, my lord. She guessed immediately, I think. Perhaps she does not operate under such a powerful prejudice as you do."

"Good God!" he said. "Well, if you had seen fit to confide in *me*, Miss Fairfield, instead of deliberately assuming the manners of an unprincipled and ill-mannered little doxy, we might have been able to pull off what my grandmother proposes. But at least three households of servants know it to be a lie. There's even some talk already."

She paled. "Nevertheless, I mean to try, my lord. It might be different if you really wished to marry me, or I you. But we don't even know each other. What sort of marriage would that be?"

"What has wishing got to do with it?" he said. "I've told you I was prepared to marry you; that should be enough for you. Even if we were capable of fooling every one else with such a naïve tale, do you think your father won't have a good deal to say on the subject?"

"Oh," she said, suddenly ashamed. "No, of course not. But if it is only my father who concerns you, I know enough to keep him quiet, my lord."

A glint of humor came into his eyes. "I may have misjudged you, Miss Fairfield. *Not* such a little sparrow after all, it would seem! But if you know enough to keep his tongue between his teeth when he is in his cups, you've more faith than I."

"Oh. No, my lord," she said again, acknowledging the truth of this. "He can never keep a secret after he's broached his second bottle. But if you made it worth his while?"

"My acquaintance with young girls just out of the school-room is admittedly slight, Miss Fairfield," he said, "but I begin to think you are going to be an experience for me. Do not hesitate to tell me if there are any more crimes you would like me to commit. We have already discussed blackmail and bribery, have we not?"

"Well, how was I to know you would object?" she said. "From your reputation there does not seem to be much you have not done already!"

"I did not say I objected, Miss Fairfield. I merely wished to know if you had anything else up your sleeve."

She laughed then. "Well, not unless you think you could contrive to shut up the others present that night. I must confess that has been worrying me."

"I intend to shut them up," he replied. "But the only way to do so is by informing them that you are shortly to become my wife."

"No, my lord. I have said that I do not aspire to be my Lady St. Ives."

"You may not aspire to it, Miss Fairfield, but you'll have me for all of that!" he said rudely. "Whatever you have heard about me, it is not my custom to ruin respectable females, particularly when they are naïve chits with less common sense than my little sister!"

"And if you were not bent on making a foolish and unnecessary quixotic gesture for your own incomprehensible reasons, my lord," she argued, "you would see that none of this concerns you any longer! You have pointed out that I am as much to blame as you are. Very well, I admit it, and I do not intend to compound my folly by contracting a marriage we must both regret. I have already told you that your grandmother and my godmother do not believe the situation to be so desperate. I think that is all that needs to be said on the subject."

He lost his temper then. "You will marry me, my girl, if I have to carry you kicking to the altar! And if you have any idea of leaving *this* household, I would advise you against it! I will not answer for my temper if you put me to the trouble of finding you again."

"Do you ever answer for your temper, my lord?"

He swore and strode to the door. "I will be out of
town for a few days. I will return on Friday morning to
take you driving in the park. It will be best for us to
be seen in one another's company as soon as possible.
In a month or so, as soon as we have satisfied the conventions, we will announce our betrothal."

"The spectacle of you satisfying the conventions must
naturally be an instructive one, my lord," she said, "but I
must decline your offer."

"I expect you to be ready on Friday!"

XI

On her way to change for dinner, Sylvie turned instead to
her godmother's door. She had raised her hand to knock
when the door opened and Crimping, her ladyship's dresser, appeared.

Crimping looked startled, but said "Oh, there you are,
miss. Her ladyship would like a word with you."

Then, before Sylvie could go in, she added, "I wonder
if I might speak to you first, miss?"

Sylvie halted, wondering what the dresser, who did not
like her, could want; but it seemed that Crimping merely
wished to recommend a niece of hers who was seeking
a position as a lady's maid.

Sylvie stared at Crimping. "You know I have no need
for a lady's maid! And surely it would be better to speak
to my godmother on such a subject?"

The dresser's expression remained unreadable. "Yes,
miss," she agreed, "but if your circumstances was to happen to change, I hope you would be kind enough to keep
my niece in mind. Now if you'll excuse me, miss?" She
curtsied and glided down the hall.

Sylvie tapped on her godmother's door.

Lady Bridlington, seated before her dressing table, was

engaged in pushing a great many rings on her plump fingers. "Oh, there you are, my dear," she said as Sylvie came in. "I fear you'll be late for dinner if you don't hurry and change, but Crimping has just been telling me that Lord St. Ives has been here! I had hoped—but that he would actually come so soon! Oh, my dear, you must tell me everything! What did he say?"

Sylvie stared at her godmother. "Ma'am, what do you mean? Did you *know* that St. Ives would feel honor-bound to offer for me once he learned the truth?"

Her ladyship clasped her hands together at the news. "Oh, my love!" she breathed. "Oh, it is what I dreamed would happen!"

Sylvie began to feel ill. "Ma'am, is that why you were kind to me? Because you believed I would wed St. Ives?"

"Oh, my dear, of course not! How could you think such a thing? But I saw how it must be, of course, and I could not be happier if you were my own daughter. You must know how fond of you I have become, and when I think how proud your Mama must be—! Oh, my love, and you can have no notion of all the caps that have been set at him over the years, all to no avail. I swear I could almost die laughing!"

"Ma'am! Surely you must have known I would refuse him?" cried Sylvie. "You talk of setting caps at him! Oh, don't you see, it would be a thousand times worse to marry him simply because he feels trapped into offering for me?"

Her ladyship looked suddenly like a child whose favorite treat was snatched just out of reach.

"Refused him?" she gasped. "You r-refused *St. Ives?*"

Then, because she was a kind woman at heart and must have seen that Sylvie was looking almost ill, she pulled herself together and took Sylvie's hands in hers. "Oh, my dear, of course you are upset! I daresay he was in a dreadful temper and handled the whole thing badly. But there, you are a sensible girl, I know, and will realize that what he says is right. You would be the Countess of St. Ives then and could do exactly as you wish. Was it not you who was so sensibly discussing finding a husband just a few days ago and saying you did not mean to be too particular? And now you have had the biggest prize in London dropped into your lap! There are a great many girls who would give all they possess to be in the position you are in, I can tell you."

"Oh, ma'am, you must know I was speaking of a marriage between equals. Not this—this polite form of blackmail. We both know he would never have looked at me had I not been forced on him. And you are wrong, he was not angry—or at least not after a while. But don't you see, that only makes it worse? How could I accept an offer of marriage knowing that both of us must be miserable?"

"Well, if we are to talk of only marrying when we are sure to be happy," said her ladyship, "then none of us would ever have married."

Sylvie smiled despite herself, and her ladyship went on, "People of our class do not commonly wed for love, my dear. I married my poor Wilfrid, not because I loved him—though I'm sure I soon learned to do so—for I had scarcely seen him half a dozen times before we were wed. I married him because my Papa thought he would make a good, sound husband and would be able to take care of me. As it turned out—but then, Papa could hardly have foreseen that, and he meant it only for the—but there! That is nothing to the point! What I mean to say is that you must not think St. Ives feels as you do, for he is a man of the world, my dear, and he knows well that such matters occur every day. No, you may depend on it that he has decided it is time he was settling down."

"I do not—do not know what St. Ives may be feeling —indeed, he behaved better than I expected, or had any right to demand—but I give you my word, ma'am, that nothing—*nothing*—would prevail upon me to accept such an offer from him."

Her ladyship glanced up at her. "Oh, my dear, it is no wonder you have taken him in dislike, for from anything I can tell, he behaved quite horridly to you. And you must not think that when her grace first disclosed the whole to me that I was not terribly shocked. I would have given much to have had him there to receive a piece of my mind—not that, from anything I have ever heard, he pays the least heed to anyone!" she added. "I told the dowager frankly that I thought that it was wicked, and so I do. Drunk he may have been, but you can't tell me he didn't do it merely to make mischief. But it would be foolish to repine too much upon what is only youthful high spirits, after all. Young men will be wild, my love, but I hope it does not mean they are *evil*. Why, I remember hearing tales of what my own dear Papa did when he was a boy, and he became so amazingly respectable that I often wished he was not quite so—but there, never mind! What I mean is that you have always lived a retired life, so you cannot be expected to understand that frequently the worst rakes make the most straitlaced husbands. It has always seemed the oddest thing to me, too, but so, I can assure you, it is. I could name a score of men right now who were positively wicked when they were young and now are the very patterns of respectability and have never given their wives a moment of unhappiness."

Sylvie was already a little ashamed of her impassioned outburst. "Indeed I do know that, ma'am," she said, "and I am sorry if I am behaving like a heroine in a romance. I know it must seem so to you. Nor do I dislike his lordship. But I am as much to blame as he, if not more. He was drunk, as you say, but he did not—he did not *constrain* me to accompany him. I went with him willingly because—oh, I do not expect you to understand. They made me so angry that they could treat me like that, Papa most of all. But I have been used all of my life to being unloved and unwanted. That sounds melodramatic, too, I know, but it is the truth, ma'am. Surely you would not wish that for me in the future as well?"

Her ladyship's face crumpled like a child's, and Sylvie said unhappily, "Oh, ma'am, I never meant to upset you! We need not speak of it anymore. Only tell me this, if you please. St. Ives seemed to think—is that what you and the dowager meant when you assured me that everything could be hushed up? That if it were known he was willing to marry me no one would dare to gossip?"

"Oh, my dear, we meant it for the best!" cried her ladyship pitifully. "You must believe that."

"There, don't cry, ma'am," said Sylvie. "I don't blame you. You were not to know. Am I correct in assuming there are registry offices in London that specialize in domestic employment?'

Lady Bridlington choked on a sob and turned pale. "Oh, my love, no!" she gasped, beyond her usual easy tears. "Oh, pray, do not even speak of it! You must believe that anything would be preferable! *Anything!* No, no," she babbled on desperately, "you do not know, how can you, how dreadfully unhappy you would be, away from your friends and family, and how dreary—yes *dreary!*—such a life is! And there is never any coming back once you have taken such a step! No, no, you think you were unhappy before, but at least you had your horses and your old friends and your freedom! Think how it will feel to be among strangers and constrained to be always calm and proper, and never have your soul to call your own again! Oh, my dear, it does not bear thinking of!"

Sylvie was indeed a little daunted, and her ladyship went on eagerly, "Yes, yes! Oh, and my dear, much worse! It is improper even to speak of it, I know, but you are a sensible girl, and you must know that things are not always as they seem—or how odious men can sometimes behave toward women they think are their inferiors. I trust you may never learn! But the stories I have heard—!"

"Oh, ma'am, I hope I shall not have to accept a job as a maidservant."

"My dear, believe me, you must on *no* account even consider becoming a maidservant! A governess is bad enough, but they are at least respectable and not considered servants, exactly. Although I am sure nothing could be worse!" she added tragically. "The only female I ever knew who was a governess ended by becoming a dreadful bluestocking and founding a select seminary for young ladies of quality. Although I believe it was well-thought-of, and a few of her old friends even sent their daughters to be educated there, naturally they did not receive her, and I believe she was quite unhappy, poor soul, whatever face she may have put upon the matter, and oh, my dear, to even think of preferring that to St. Ives!" she ended in a wail and burst into a storm of overwrought tears.

Sylvie took her godmother in her arms, soothing and

petting her until her tears subsided. Then she said, "Well, ma'am, as for founding a select seminary for young ladies of quality, although it would be an excellent notion, I am not at all clever, like Kendall, and I daresay I would be a total failure at it. Besides, I have discovered that I do not like women as well as men, so that I don't think it would do for me to be always surrounded by them. As for the rest, you are being nonsensical, you know. It would not be forever, and I promise that at the first sign that the master means to persecute me and thrust me out unprotected in the snow, I will pack my bags and return to you."

Her ladyship ignored this and eagerly latched onto her earlier statement. "I know quite what you mean, my love, for I have often thought how tired one grows of females after a while! And that is exactly why it would be far preferable to be married, even to a man one positively disliked, than to be required to spend the rest of one's life in the company of women and children. No, no, you are still upset, and it's no wonder," she ended a little desperately, "but you will soon see how right I am and how silly you were. And my dear, not that I mean it would weigh with you, precisely, but just to think of your having captured St. Ives, and how jealous everyone will be of you—! And, oh, my dear, how *proud* your Mama would be!"

"Oh, ma'am, I never meant to make you unhappy, when you have been so kind to me. Still, you must understand that I cannot accept his offer. I have already told him so. But I do not mean to do anything rash, and I hope I am still welcome to remain with you, at least until I can decide what is best to be done. Please, we will talk of it again later. I have not yet changed for dinner."

She fled before her ladyship could renew her arguments or her tears, but her mind was in a daze. The two scenes she had just endured had given her the beginnings of a headache, and she would have given anything to be allowed to remain in her room.

As it was, she was late downstairs, and her sorely tried spirits sank at the discovery that her ladyship was far too upset to be discreet and was even now pouring the whole into her son's willing ears.

Sylvie hesitated a little stiffly in the doorway, tempted to turn and go straight back upstairs, but to her surprise Sir James looked up, immediately detached himself from his Mama, and came forward to gravely offer her his arm.

He carefully saw her seated and said with considerable restraint, "Forgive me, Miss Fairfield. I know the subject my Mama has just been revealing to me must be a painful one, and I do not mean to intrude, but if you will permit me to say so, I can only honor you deeply for what I perceive to be a delicacy of scruples uncommon in one of your sex. My mother does not appear to understand the gravity of the situation, but it is clear to me that any woman of sensibility must find repugnant the very idea of marriage to such a one as my Lord St. Ives."

His mother, discovering that she had been harboring a viper in her bosom all these years, rounded on him with every appearance of fury, but he held up one hand and said deliberately, "Forgive me, Mama. I know what your feelings are on this subject, but I can only suppose the real affection you feel toward your goddaughter, and your natural desire to see her make an advantageous marriage, have led you a little astray. Only consider: the very reasons you put forward for Miss Fairfield's accepting his lordship's offer are those that must make any woman of sensibility recoil. He has wealth, he has position, I admit it; but what has he ever chosen to do with them? He seems to delight in defying every principle honored by decent Englishmen. He has been involved in more scandals than I care to recall; his name has been bandied about on the tongue of every gossipmonger in the country—is *that* what you would have Miss Fairfield ally herself with, ma'am? His temper, as no doubt Miss Fairfield can attest, is violent, and his whole behavior, from first to last in this unfortunate business, has been what any man of breeding would be ashamed to own. Indeed, Miss Fairfield," he added with unaccustomed warmth, "I did not at first wish my mother to befriend you, for even though I hope I am not insensitive to the plight of anyone less fortunate than myself, I could not approve of my mother's connection with anyone of your father's—er—reputation. But I can only say, after having become acquainted with you more closely, that I honor you most sincerely and will do whatever may lie in my power to aid you."

Having thus succeeded in alienating both members of his audience, he then conducted them most correctly into the dining room and proceeded to make a very good meal. He was the only one to do so. His mother turned her shoulder on her only son and refused every dish offered her. Sylvie, less impolite, tasted automatically whatever was on her plate, having discovered with surprise that, although she might say very much the same things about his infuriating lordship, she perversely resented James saying them.

When James was unwise enough to once more allude to the subject, she lifted her eyes and said, "You do me far too much honor, Sir James! His lordship's reputation does not weigh with me in the slightest. He may be a rake, but I have frequently thought that if I had been a man, I might have become one, too; for to be forever required to do something only because it is considered proper is something I have little patience with."

James looked startled, and fixed his heavy gaze upon her face. "I see," he said after a moment. "May I ask, then, Miss Fairfield, why you have refused his lordship's offer of marriage?"

"He does not care for me," she said simply. "What sort of marriage would we have built on such a foundation?"

Then she was angry to have said so much, for James seemed greatly moved, and was determined to honor her for what he insisted on calling her scruples. In the end she replied more than a little rudely that she did not wish to speak of it again, and she excused herself to go away to bed, only to meditate on the perverseness of a nature that might publicly renounce any desire to wed the wild young Earl of St. Ives and privately seemed inclined to dwell, with disturbing frequency, on the thought of a pair of brilliant blue eyes.

She had told James the truth. She did not condemn St. Ives because she discovered she had always longed to be like him. To be able to do what one wished without caring for anyone else; to live life to the fullest with

never a thought for tomorrow; *that* was what she had always wanted. For one brief magical moment, she had seen
what might have been.

She thought now a little recklessly that if he had suggested she become his mistress instead of his wife, she
might have accepted. But to be his wife—to drag him
down into the sort of sordid relationship her parents had
enjoyed—no. She had only to try to imagine that handsome, cynical creature bound for life to a woman who
was not of his class, and whom he despised, to realize
how impossible it was. The sad truth was that Prince
Charming had managed to find her after all, and had
seduced her, not with actions, but with a vision of what
it could mean to be loved by such a man. But, he had
not found Cinderella at all but a—what had he called
her?—a little brown sparrow. Well, princes did not marry
little brown sparrows, even in fairy tales, nor did they
live happily ever after. They were more likely to find
themselves a showy swan and break the poor little sparrow's heart.

Then she had to smile at her own absurdity. That's
enough nonsense for you, my girl, she told herself. You
knew from the beginning he was not for you. You would
be far better occupied in deciding what is to be done now.

But her future seemed dismally clear. Either she would
end up as governess to someone else's children; or, if
she were lucky, she would marry someone like James and
raise her own uninteresting offspring. She wondered why
a week ago either of those alternatives would have
seemed inviting.

XII

Being a woman of considerable strength of mind, Sylvie
had recovered her spirits by morning, and she set her-

self to discover what would be best to do next. With that in mind, she inquired of the butler the location of the most reputable of the registry offices for domestic servants.

Saltish was startled, but he gave her a few names, indicating the ones her ladyship used.

She purposely avoided those, out of kindness to her godmother, and armed with the directions Saltish had provided her she sallied bravely forth, for the first time on her own in the streets of London.

If her thoughts were still inclined to be a little dismal, she soon discovered that could not last long among the cheerful hubbub she found herself in. In the carriage with her ladyship, whisked from one dressmaker's establishment to another, she had seen little of London. And since she was healthy and curious, and untroubled by any of the airs that made walking such a chore for fashionable women, she soon began to enjoy herself immensely. She walked briskly along, taking in the sights and smells around her, and though she drew a few curious stares at first, she soon left the more fashionable streets, where the sight of an unattended young lady was cause for remark, and plowed into the more modest, and to her far more interesting, neighborhoods of less prosperous tradesmen and dressmakers and shops. It was still quite respectable, for she understood from Saltish that one didn't find the true slum areas until one ventured into the City, or near Covent Garden; but she liked the cheerful people she saw here better than the fashionably idle men and women she had left behind.

She found the registry office she was seeking without much trouble, though once she was obliged to inquire the way from an old gentleman in gaiters who was leaning against a shopwindow. That gentleman removed the pipe from his mouth with deliberation and looked her up and down before saying with mild scorn, "Well, missy, and what're ye doing out without yer Mam is what I'd like to know?"

That had made her laugh, of course, and after a moment his own eyes had crinkled engagingly and he had given her the directions she had asked and warned her not to go speaking to strangers, for she never knew what shiftless fellows she might encounter.

After this promising beginning, she met with little success at the registry office. The personage at the in-
quiries desk seemed to take a dim view of an elegantly
dressed young female inquiring about employment. And
when Sylvie disclosed a little of her circumstances to
make the woman believe she was indeed serious and
not running away from home, the gray-haired manageress
was very little more forthcoming. The opportunities for
suitable employment were limited for girls barely twenty years of age who, on their own admission, had no
experience and few skills.

When the subject of recommendations was raised,
Sylvie could only extricate herself with what remaining
dignity she had, for the only two women who might fur-
nish her with suitable references were unlikely to do so.

She retraced her steps and turned in the direction
of the dowager's elegant house in Arlington Street,
where her grace received her immediately in the private sitting room on the first floor.

As soon as Sylvie came in the dowager said, "Horsham
tells me you came quite alone, my dear. Never do such
a thing again. If Lady Bridlington cannot spare a maid to
accompany you, I will supply one myself."

Sylvie lifted her chin. "I assure you, I am quite capable
of walking three blocks by myself, ma'am. If this is what
fashionable London is like, I am glad I have never had any
ambition to figure in society!"

Her grace looked up and patted the sofa beside her.
"Ah, you are enraged. It becomes you, my dear. I think
we must contrive to keep you always a little angry."

That had made Sylvie laugh, of course, and her grace
added promptly, "But come and let me look at you." She
studied the simple but becoming primrose crepe morning
gown. "Ah, yes, quite proper. Sophia may be a scatter-
brain, but she has taste. Is it she who has put you so out of
countenance?"

Sylvie sighed and took the seat beside the dowager.
"Yes—I mean, no, of course not. She has been very
kind, much more than I deserve, but—St. Ives has been
to see me, ma'am," she ended a little desperately.

Her grace appeared to have no difficulty in following

this rapid change of topic. "So he's the one to put you in such a temper. What has that young scoundrel been up to now?"

"He has asked me to marry him."

The duchess gave a crack of laughter. "Has he? Then he has more gumption than I gave him credit for. What's there in that to put you in the glumps?"

"You must know that I refused him!"

Her grace appeared unperturbed. "Did you now? Can't stomach him for a husband, eh? I've no doubt you're right, my dear. He'd make the devil of one."

"Yes, your grace," agreed Sylvie a little dismally.

The dowager bit back a smile. "And Sophia and that son of hers are plaguing the life out of you. Well, I'll have a word with Sophia. If you won't have that graceless grandson of mine, there's an end to it. I can't say I blame you. We must find someone more to your liking."

"Yes, but ma'am, can you? St. Ives said that if I don't marry him we can't hope to shut up the gossip, and I—I quite see he may be right. There were a number of men there, and they all know I came away with him. They were drunk, of course, and, although *he* certainly remembered nothing of the night before, I cannot think we can depend upon them all being so obliging."

Her grace seemed to find this practical view of the matter rather amusing, but she only inquired, "So what do you intend to do now?"

"I don't know, ma'am," Sylvie admitted. "I had thought —that is, I meant to go back to my original plan of seeking employment, but after today I don't—I went to a registry office, you see, but they seemed to think—" She sighed then and ended simply, "I was hoping you could give me some advice, ma'am. That's why I came."

The dowager immediately demanded to be told the whole story and seemed to enjoy it hugely. But she said, "I find it an odd day when that scapegrace of a grandson of mine is to be regarded as an authority on manners!"

"I have said there will be no scandal, and I meant it. You just see that you don't go wandering all over London again like a gypsy, and leave me to take care of the rest. And let me hear no more of positions or of running away like a whipped dog. If you cannot face down my grandson, and a whole gaggle of gossiping old fools with him, then you're not the girl I thought you."

Sylvie smiled, but she could not resist saying, "Then you really think I need not worry? I am prepared to face down any number of gossiping fools, but I would not have my godmother hurt for the world by any scandal of my making."

The dowager answered her a little impatiently, and it seemed impossible after that to press her further. And since Horsham came in soon after with the intelligence that her grace's carriage was at the door to take Miss Fairfield home, Sylvie took her leave, a great deal more relieved than when she had come, and enjoyed the novel pleasure of traveling home in an old-fashioned town carriage with a ducal crest on the door.

When Horsham returned, the dowager said cryptically, "She'll do, Horsham. I had begun to think I was getting too old, but I wouldn't have missed this for anything! Fairfield's daughter, eh? Well, it's not what I'd have liked, but times are changing, and perhaps it will make up for that other, so long ago."

Horsham, who had been her friend for more than fifty years, bowed in perfect understanding. "Oh, yes, your grace, I believe so," he said serenely. He poured her a glass of her favorite claret and presented it on a silver tray.

My Lord St. Ives, attempting to run the fool Fairfield to earth, remained unaware of his grandmother's amusement at his expense. Despite his assurances to Sylvie, it galled him beyond measure to be obliged to pay off Fairfield; nor did he have any illusions about what the relationship would cost him, first to last. He wondered briefly if Miss Fairfield had any idea of the trouble she was likely to cause him.

Inquiry had elicited the information that Fairfield had ridden into Kent with a party of friends as soon as the races were over, but when St. Ives traced him there it was only to discover that his quarry had left on the previous day to return to Cambridgeshire, nursing a string of hunters.

St. Ives swore and retraced his route, hoping to overtake Fairfield before he reached home, but they must have missed each other somewhere on the road, for St. Ives reached Newmarket without discovering him.

Fairfield's door was opened by the same dour old woman who had been present on that fateful night, and it was plain she recognised him immediately, for she turned pale and cowered away from the door.

Irritated, he demanded to know when Fairfield was expected. She hesitated, then said, sullenly, "And what would ye be wanting with him? Shame on both of ye is what I say, for ruining an innocent girl! I don't say she done right, but the rest of ye are evil, drunken men, lords or no, and I just pray Miss Syllie'll see the evil of her ways before it's too late!"

Her face began to work then, and she scrubbed angrily at her eyes. "And that's all I've to say to ye! I don't know where t'master is, and I'd advise you not to let Blackmer know ye're here, for he was powerful fond of Miss Syllie, he was."

St. Ives was not accustomed to being called to account by slatternly servants, and the experience did little to improve his temper. He held his anger in check and told her to inform her master as soon as he arrived that Lord St. Ives would be awaiting him in the village inn.

She accepted the message with a sniff and closed the door in his face.

Nor was his ordeal by any means over. The village inn was not one accustomed to his patronage, and apart from possessing no private parlor for his use, and only a dark bedchamber over the yard, the taproom seemed to boast nothing but an inferior wine and the local home brew.

The landlord apologized profusely, explaining that they did not usually cater to the quality and offering to send young Bill over to Newmarket to fetch whatever his honor wished.

St. Ives, wishing he had gone to Newmarket instead, impatiently refused and requested a tankard of ale. It was quickly forthcoming, and an excellent meat pie as well, but he was then left with nothing to do but cool

his heels until Fairfield chose to show up. He could either
lounge in his room all day or sit in the taproom. He
chose the taproom.

It did not surprise him to learn from the landlord that
Fairfield was little regarded in the neighborhood. He
himself had seen the state of Fairfield's lands, and the
local people were hardly likely to approve of such waste
and profligacy; but by the time he had spent the better
part of the day listening to the local gossip, he was torn
between amusement and anger. He himself was subjected to cautious scrutiny, for it was clear that the village
was suspicious of anyone associated with the Hall. It occurred to St. Ives that he had seldom in his life been
obliged to do anything he did not want to do, and he was
not enjoying the experience.

Fairfield at last arrived, looking ill at ease. He had
been shocked by the news that St. Ives was waiting for
him and had evidently gone to considerable pains to find
him. He had no idea what St. Ives could want with him
now, but he instinctively distrusted the earl and would
have avoided the meeting if he had thought it possible.

Fairfield had not been having a particularly easy time
of it himself. Perhaps it was too much to say that his
conscience was bothering him, but he had been irritable
and jumpy since that night of folly, cursing Hinton roundly
for her impertinence and finding little pleasure in any
of his old pastimes. He had avoided Blackmer simply by
going into Kent without warning and leaving no word when
he might be expected back.

He told himself he had done the girl a favor, for she
was so stupid and Friday-faced she'd get a husband no
other way. But for once in his life he knew he was
lying to himself. He did not tell himself in so many words
that once it had been confirmed that St. Ives had no
intention of marrying the girl, he would have to do something, but that was what was in the back of his mind. He
would have to either do something or make a conscious
decision not to.

St. Ives glanced up when Fairfield came in, but he did
not rise. "It's about time you got here!" he said. "I am not
accustomed to being kept waiting, and I've wasted all the

time I intend to on this affair. I have your vouchers to the tune of some eight thousand pounds. I would like to know when you intend to reclaim them."

Fairfield was caught off guard. Of all the things he had expected, that had been the last. "My lord——?"

St. Ives's brows went up. "The matter is clear enough, I should have thought. I hold your vouchers and expect to be repaid."

Color invaded Fairfield's cheeks. "My lord, you force me to remind you of a certain wager!" he said. "I do not believe you can have forgotten it already."

"The wager, as I recall it," replied St. Ives coldly, "was to be everything I had won that night staked against your daughter. You lost the bet. Have I made myself clear?"

Fairfield was out of his depth. It had never occurred to him St. Ives would take this line. A cold sweat began to stand on his brow.

"If we are to talk of wagers, my lord, and notes of hand," he said, "I think you will find yourself at a disadvantage! I am not particularly proud of that night, but it was a bet, honorably entered into, and I have performed my part in it. You, on the other hand——you have taken my poor Sylvie away, but I have heard no talk of nuptials. What is it, have you used her for your own ends without meaning to honor your part of the bargain?" he added. "Perhaps we should be talking of breach of promise, my lord, instead of money owed!"

"If I thought you had a single spark of feeling for your daughter, I would not find you so completely disgusting," said St. Ives. "Yes, I have taken your daughter away, with your full approval, and I cannot discover that you have given a single thought to her fate."

Fairfield slumped into a chair. "Then you would be wrong, my lord," he said heavily. "I was drunk——I never meant——but it is too late now. I agreed. What else can I do?"

"You could behave like a man for once in your life and demand satisfaction for the supposed harm I have done your daughter! But then that is too much to expect, isn't it?"

"Oh, yes, I am aware of just how far that would take me," said Fairfield with a sneer. "How many people do you suppose would take the word of a defenseless young girl over that of the Earl of St. Ives? Oh, yes, I know the world well, my lord! Men such as you can do what they like with impunity, while it is the poor girls like my Sylvie—and people like myself, yes myself!—who suffer for it."

St. Ives turned away. "God, you are wholly despicable, do you know that? Your daughter is worth ten of you. At least she had the spirit to try to make me pay for the way I treated her. But you—! I don't have a high opinion of human nature, Fairfield, but I discover that even I am capable of being disgusted. Let us have an end to this. I will tear up your notes of hand in return for my own promise to wed your daughter. And you may consider yourself lucky I do not treat you in the way I would like!"

Fairfield had been sullen; now he began to turn ugly. "Not so fast, my young buck! Who are you to stand there talking of disgust, I'd like to know? You've ruined my poor Sylvie and now you try to cheat me as well. Well, my lord, I've a notion to see restitution made after all. The Countess of St. Ives. How would that suit you, eh?"

"It would not suit me at all, for I discover I've an aversion to the mere thought of allying my family with yours. But you may relieve your mind on one score. I have no intention of wedding your daughter. If I had ever done so, it would now be out of the question since she has already left my protection in favor of another's."

Fairfield's jaw dropped. "Sylvie?" he said incredulously. "My little Sylvie?" Then he was suddenly furious. "Well if that don't beat all! When she's lorded it over me all her life with her highty-tighty manners and her airs, just like her mother, damn her! Well, I'll settle with her later, but you've done me a favor by telling me, my lord. But that don't change the fact that you're the one that ruined her. It seems to me you've had the value of what you say I owe you."

"Eight thousand pounds worth?" inquired St. Ives incredulously. "Come, come, Fairfield, you put a high price on your daughter's—er—charms."

"If my Sylvie's gone to someone else, as you say, you're the one who drove her to it!"

"No, you are the one who drove her to it," said St. Ives, sick of the whole. "I should refuse, out of what few principles I possess, to enrich such a blackguard as you by so much as a penny, but I grow sick of the subject and even sicker of you. I'll give you ten thousand pounds on top of your notes of hand, in return for which I will expect my own note, as well as your signature on a document relinquishing any further claim you might feel you have on me. Well, is it a deal?"

Fairfield hesitated, his mind working quickly. In truth it was better than he had begun to believe he would get out of the deal, and if that bitch Sylvie had really made a fool of him and found another protector so soon, he washed his hands of her. He nodded.

St. Ives drew out his pocketbook and extracted the money, along with the crumpled vouchers. Then he looked up and deliberately replaced the vouchers. "You will understand I am a little hesitant to trust you," he said dryly. "You will receive these when I have my own note in hand. I will send my groom for it if you will write a letter to your housekeeper telling her where to find it."

Fairfield reddened, but he did as he was bid, suddenly as eager to be finished with the business as St. Ives. The earl offered no refreshments while they waited for Wicken to return from his errand, and he said nothing further, as if Fairfield were not in the room.

When Wicken returned with the paper, St. Ives looked at it briefly, then tore it once across and dropped it into the fireplace. Only then did he hand over Fairfield's own vouchers.

Fairfield received them sullenly and threw them into the fire without looking at them. St. Ives laughed nastily. "For one of your character, you show a touching faith in the honesty of others, Fairfield."

When Fairfield frowned, he added wearily, "You have nothing to fear from me. I can assure you I wish to have no further transactions of any nature with you."

Fairfield strode toward the door. Behind him, St. Ives said softly, "For your information, Fairfield, your daughter received no harm at my hands and is presently residing with her godmother—at no thanks to you. I might add she is shortly to become my wife.

"Even I balk at taking advantage of an innocent child who has done nothing worse than possess you for a father. But I give you my word, you will never set foot in any house of mine. Whether or not your daughter chooses to continue to acknowledge you is entirely her own affair, although I cannot imagine why she should. Now get out of here before I change my mind and give way to my better instincts as far as you are concerned."

He had not moved when the door opened again some five minutes later, and an aggressive voice said, "My Lord St. Ives?"

St. Ives glanced around, frowning, and encountered the hard stare of a burly figure whom he recognized immediately as a groom. His frown deepened for a brief moment, then cleared. "You must be Blackmer," he said. "Come in. I was expecting you."

The groom seemed a little startled, but he did not abandon his attitude. "Aye, and well you might be, my lord!"

St. Ives subjected him to a hard scrutiny, then he relaxed. "Come in and have a seat," he said. "Will you have ale or wine? I'm afraid it's all that's available."

After an astonished moment, Blackmer did as he was bid. "I'll have ale, and I thank you."

His lordship looked up and poured out two glasses.

St. Ives was brooding before the fire that night, having retired to his bedchamber to escape the constant stream of visitors to the taproom. He was making steady inroads into his second bottle of wine when he heard the sounds of a carriage arriving. He stirred slightly and poured himself another glass, only to have his door burst open unceremoniously a few minutes later. He started up, then dropped back into his seat and drained his glass. "Oh, it's you, is it?" he said. "What the devil are you still doing in this benighted place?"

Mr. Strickland came in imperturbably, brushing the raindrops from his elegant driving coat. "I thought you would be glad to see me, dear boy," he remarked. "Really, I wonder why I bother, particularly after I have gone to such effort to track you down. By the by," he asked, "what have you done with the girl?"

St. Ives laughed. "You will shortly be able to offer me your felicitations, Frederick."

Mr. Strickland seated himself and poured a glass of wine. "I thought she was a straitlaced little thing. Unusual in Fairfield's daughter, but there you have it."

St. Ives glanced up. "Then you had more judgment than I. It was left for my grandmother to discover the truth for me, damn her. Are you not going to say I told you so?"

"I never waste my time on forlorn hopes. I presume you are in the area settling with Fairfield? Now there I might be tempted to say I warned you, Nicky. I do not admire your choice in future relatives. But then I forget, you left me to pick up the pieces for you that night, didn't you, and you may not yet realize the full extent of your father-in-law's—er—charms."

"You are mistaken," said St. Ives. "I have just enjoyed an hour of his company." Then his eyes narrowed. "But am I to understand you *have* picked up the pieces?"

Mr. Strickland stretched his boots toward the fire and yawned. "And a most trying business I found it. I took certain—er—liberties in your name, but you should have no trouble with any of them. Except for Lambeth, of course, who seems to have gone underground somewhere. I must confess I did not make too great an effort to seek him out. You should be required to bear some of the unpleasantness after all, don't you think?"

St. Ives was still regarding him. "Your kindness is exceeded only by your officiousness, damn you!"

"But really, Nicky," protested Strickland, "since *my* intellect was not impaired at the time by a vast quantity of inferior wine, it was clear to me that once you had time to consider the matter, you would reach the conclusion you obviously have."

The earl's mouth twisted. "I wonder if I deserve such touching faith in my sense of honor," he said. "I was as likely to thrust her aside as callously as I have all the rest."

"Yes—why didn't you?"

"I don't know. Perhaps I thought to try a new role for a change!" Then his eyes narrowed on the flames in the grate and he laughed. "No, I do know. Because she was being so gallant about it, damn her, when she had every reason to throw my damnable conduct up in my teeth. Because, for a moment, she reminded me of Kitty. But you needn't credit me with any virtues. I find this marriage will suit me very well." He smiled then a little unwillingly. "Though I've a notion you've underestimated my betrothed. I wonder what next she has in mind for me."

XIII

Sylvie, the worst of her fears allayed, was merely enjoying herself. She was young and her spirits resilient; she was on her first visit to London, and she meant to make the most of it. Besides, it was impossible to worry too much about the future when one was for the first time in one's life dressed in the latest mode with nothing to do from morning to night but amuse oneself. And since the majority of her new gowns were yet to be delivered, frustrating Lady Bridlington in her ambition to present her goddaughter to as many of her acquaintances as possible, Sylvie found herself with a great deal of time on her hands.

It had not taken her long to discover that Lady Bridlington's notions of entertainment did not suit her own. Lady Bridlington rose at ten, had her breakfast in bed while she pored over her morning's post and the newspapers, then emerged from her bedchamber a little before noon, only to eat a light luncheon. In the afternoon she visited, or shopped, or went for a drive in the park until it was time to change for dinner. Then, if she had no engagement in the evening, she would sit chatting before the fire until a late hour, eating a great many sweetmeats.

Sylvie, after observing this delicate regimen for a few days, slipped away one afternoon while her ladyship was resting. She went for a brisk walk and returned pleasantly tired, having enjoyed herself immensely, but her ladyship was so shocked to think that Sylvie had gone out without even a maid to accompany her and read her such a stern lecture on how *fatal* it would be to give anyone reason to think her fast, that Sylvie thought it best not to risk further displeasure by repeating the exercise.

After that she ruthlessly dragged the housemaid Mary with her, and, armed with a guidebook, they toured the nearest sights. Mary was town-bred, and no walker, and she tended to dawdle in a way that Sylvie found extremely exasperating, but at least she was willing, and she was now devoted to Sylvie and bore good-naturedly with the antics of one she clearly considered kind but a little queer in the nob.

Her ladyship permitted these excursions reluctantly, for until the truant gowns were delivered there was little else she could do with the girl.

Returning later than usual from one such afternoon— involving a visit to Astley's Amphitheatre to see the show (which Lady Bridlington most certainly would *not* have approved of, had she known) and then exploring the mysteries of the Pantheon Bazaar—Sylvie was informed by Saltish that a young gentleman had called to see her and was even now waiting in the small saloon.

She had long since come to be on excellent terms with the butler, and she glanced at him with suddenly startled eyes, thinking it might be St. Ives. But Saltish calmly took her parcels and escorted her to the saloon door. She took a deep breath, patted her curls into place, her heart beating a little fast against her ribs, and entered the room.

At sight of the slender young man who looked up as she entered, she gave a glad cry and ran across the room.

The young man warded off her clutch at his lapels and said with brotherly indignation, "Hey, no, Syllie, this coat has got to last me another two terms!" Then he grinned at her and put an arm about her shoulders.

She made an effort to pull herself together. She was not usually weepy, but she hadn't realized until that moment exactly how homesick she had been. "I'm sorry! But oh, Kendall, I'm so glad you're here!"

His open countenance darkened a little. "I should rather think so! Here I come home after only a month or so to find you gone, Papa as touchy as a bear with a sore tooth, and some tearful tale from Hinton about drunken revels and orgies in the house! *Orgies*, Syllie?"

"Oh, Kendall, she didn't!" Sylvie said, impressed. "Do you think Hinton even knows what an orgy is?"

"A great deal more to the point, my girl," he said, "do you? And what the devil's been going on while I've been away?"

"But Kendall," she said remembering, "what are you doing home? It can't be term time yet."

"Oh, I've been rusticated," he said impatiently. "It's a great piece of nonsense, and damned inconvenient, too, because I'd just traced down an important fragment of Homer I need to complete my research."

Then at her astonished look, he had the grace to redden. "Oh, it was nothing, only for a fortnight. Chuffy insisted on sneaking out, and I thought I'd best go along and see he didn't get into trouble. He has no more sense than you do. Then of course we were locked out, and the bagwig caught us trying to rouse one of the other fellows, and the long and the short of it is we were both fined and sent home for a fortnight. Seeing as how when I was away in the summer you got into that scrape with old Barnley's gig and damned near broke your neck, I thought I'd best take a run home and see how you were doing." He fixed a piercing eye on her. "Up to your old tricks again, Syllie?"

"Yes. I mean no, of course not! You will understand when I explain what happened. But have you really been home? What—what is happening there?"

"I could get precious little out of father. He would only say you'd gone off with St. Ives and were going to marry him and I'd damn well keep my nose out of it if I knew what was good for me! What with Hinton talking of orgies and father ready to spit fire, let alone Blackmer treating me as if it were all my fault—! Is it the St. Ives I think it is, Syllie?" he asked incredulously.

"Yes, but that doesn't matter now! Is poor Joe dreadfully upset?" she said. "I wrote to him, yes and to Hinton, too. They should have known not to worry about me."

"Well of all the—! Good God, Syllie," he said. "What else are they to think when you go off in the middle of the night with a man like St. Ives?"

She could not resist grinning at him. "Well at least I didn't get myself rusticated! You know you're only upset because Blackmer has given you a rare combing, for otherwise you could have been home for three days without noticing I was gone."

"No, for I came to see you," he said. When she laughed he grinned sheepishly. "Well of course I would have noticed if you were gone, stupid. But perhaps I haven't given you enough attention. Blackmer said I hadn't, anyway."

"How could he say such a thing? Only last summer you took your nose out of your books long enough to notice that I had changed my hairstyle three months before."

He grinned. "Well, I have noticed you're looking different now. In fact, I almost didn't recognize you, you've grown so smart."

She paraded for him. "Yes, have I not? Indeed, you can have no notion. My walking dress is *à la hussar,* my boots are of French kid, my bonnet cost more than I used to spend for housekeeping in a quarter, and my hair is dressed *à l'anglaise.* Lady Bridlington says it is all the crack just now."

"Yes, but who the devil are all these people, and what are you doing here? I inquired at St. Ives's house—"

"Oh, Kendall, you didn't?" she interrupted, awed.

"I should say I did! And I meant to have the truth too, I can tell you. But the starched-up fool of a butler denied all knowledge of you, and just when I was getting really angry, he suggested I try the Dowager Duchess of Wraxham."

"Kendall!" she cried. "You don't mean you went there *too?* You have—you have unmanned me! I don't think I would have had the courage."

He grinned. "Yes, well, you might have had my place for the asking, I can tell you. I must say this for you, Syllie. You are moving in high circles these days. But who is Lady Bridlington, for God's sake?"

"She's my godmother, of course. I expect you may not know, but she was at school with Mama, and Hinton used to say she might invite me to stay with her someday. Well, she never did, of course, but when we were trying to think what I was to do, I remembered her. And she has been so kind."

When he only looked impatient, she told him everything that had occurred. He listened, his good-looking face growing darker, but when she finished, he looked up and said in some relief, "Well, it sounds as if everything may be all right, then. Only—must I—shall I call St. Ives out, Syllie?"

She went off into a peal of laughter.

"Well, I own I'd as lief not," he said, "for besides the fact that it's illegal, I have no doubt he's a devilish shot. But I will if you think I ought, for he's behaved damnably."

She grinned. "If it comes to that, *I* should be the one to call him out, stupid!"

"Oh, I know I could never hit the side of a barn," he admitted cheerfully. "You were always the better shot."

She sighed then. "Yes. Poor Papa. I fear we have both been a sad disappointment to him. I was never the daughter he wanted, and you always had your nose buried in some book. Perhaps it is no wonder he never—never cared for us."

Kendall's mouth tightened. "My God, Syllie, I knew he was a dashed loose screw, but I never dreamed he'd—"

"You didn't quarrel, did you?" she asked.

"Good God, I should rather think so!" Kendall said anxiously. "I've only put up with him all these years because of you, you know. I'm not dependent on him. My fees at Oxford were paid out of Mama's money, and Lord Summerhill has promised to help me when I'm through, and I daresay he wouldn't have minded if I spent all my holidays with him. No, I think this may have been a blessing after all, Syllie. If you can stay with this godmother of yours, I don't mind admitting I'll feel a great deal easier about you. You know you were never happy at home. But none of this explains what St. Ives has been doing at the Hall again?"

"At the—oh, Kendall, you don't mean he's been to see Papa again?" she breathed.

"Yes, and greased him handsomely in the fist, by the looks of it. Even I had the deuce of a time getting the story out of him."

She said blankly, "Then he is—I thought when he had had time to think it over he would see—" She flushed at Kendall's frown. "Well, I didn't tell you before, but St. Ives has—has offered marriage. It's all a great piece of nonsense, as I told him, and it makes me angry that he has gone back to Papa."

But Kendall was looking oddly relieved. "Well, that's all right, then! I didn't want to say anything before, but the whole thing's damned awkward, Syllie. If St. Ives has made an offer, then he sees too that it's the only thing to do."

"Well, everything *isn't* all right!" said Sylvie crossly. "And I never thought to hear you talking such fustian. Yes, *fustian!* Why should he be obliged to wed me, or I him, just because it would please everyone else? It's what I have no patience with!"

"Yes, but Syllie," Kendall pointed out, "I know you can't wish to marry him—from everything I've ever heard he's also a damned loosed screw—but it's not like you to refuse to face reality. Whatever this dowager says, there *is* likely to be talk. St. Ives is right. And what kind of man would he be if he left you to face it alone?"

She blushed a little, but said stubbornly, "No! I'd as soon go back home to Papa until you and I can live together as we'd planned. I will not make both St. Ives and myself miserable in a marriage we do not desire."

Kendall looked away, his face a trifle strained. "Yes, well, that was one of the reasons I went home to see you, Syllie. I've had a letter from Lord Summerhill, and he has promised to get me posted to Vienna in the fall. It will mean working like the devil to finish early, but it's more than I ever even hoped for. And it's not only that I dare not refuse him, when he has been so kind, Syllie;

but I would be a fool to pass up such an opportunity! Europe will be totally redrawn once Napoleon is defeated, and it's just a matter of time now! However small a part I might play in it," he said passionately, "such a chance will never come my way again in my lifetime! This is history of the like I'll never see again!"

She was conscious of a feeling of betrayal and was instantly ashamed of herself. Kendall had to make his own life, and hadn't she herself already decided it might be best to find an alternative to their plan? So she said, "Oh, Kendall, that's wonderful! I know how pleased you must be."

"I knew I could depend on you, once I had explained it, Syllie," he said in relief. "You can't conceive of how lucky I am to get the chance. I hardly dared hope—"

He went on in glowing terms for some minutes about the advantages of the offer, the particular problems the Congress faced, and what he foresaw would be the ultimate outcome. Then he seemed to realize that she was unexpectedly quiet, and he broke off. "I beg pardon for running on like that! The thing is, what are we to do with you?"

She knew there was no question of her going to Vienna with him, so she said gaily, "I did not mean to boast, but St. Ives is by no means the only string to my bow, you know. I have grown so grand that her ladyship thinks it very likely I will be able to attach some eligible gentleman to me. Then our plans would have been for nought, after all. I might even be in a position to do you a good turn someday."

Kendall looked relieved. "Yes, well, I'm all right, of course. But look here, I—I don't like leaving you just now, but I promised Lord Summerhill I'd go up for a week or so until I go back to school. You must promise to let me know if you're in trouble. I daresay this godmother of yours will know what to do much better than I, but you must write if you need me. Anyway, I could put off going to Vienna for a bit if I had to. It may be months before the Congress does anything more than preliminary skirmishing."

She was touched, and began to talk brightly of the treats Lady Bridlington had promised, the new gowns she possessed, and the novelty of living in a household with a score of servants to satisfy one's every need.

Kendall obviously had no patience with such a life, and he said he hoped Sylvie would not be infernally bored. He supposed he must do the pretty to her ladyship, though he'd as soon not. He then gave her a brotherly hug and took his leave, though his conscience did prompt him to add, "I say, Syllie, you are all right? You would tell me if you weren't?"

She smiled. "Yes, of course, stupid! I only wish you need not go so soon. But I don't doubt that Lord Summerhill has promised you some rare treat in the form of a treatise on Ethiopian government, or something."

Kendall grinned. "Much you would know about it! If I stop by to see Blackmer, I'll tell him you've become as grand as a duchess. That should please him. Although I should warn you that Hinton was talking darkly of those who get above themselves and tempt the wages of sin. But then she also said she trusted Mama would be watching over you, so perhaps she is prepared not to think too harshly of you."

Sylvie laughed and watched him limp through the door.

XIV

The next few days were rainy and cold, preventing Sylvie's usual excursions. She had begged repeatedly to be told some way in which she could help her godmother, for she was used to being busy, but in that well-run household it seemed there was nothing for her to do except go on an occasional errand or help Crimping with the mending.

One drizzly afternoon Sylvie was sighing over her forced inactivity when a quick step sounded in the hall and the door was thrown open without ceremony.

At the sight of a pair of rather stormy blue eyes and a handsome, willful countenance, she started violently and jabbed her needle into her finger.

St. Ives's expression relaxed a little, a gleam of wicked mockery in his eyes as she thrust the injured finger into her mouth. "The punishment of unpunctuality, Miss Fairfield!" he said. "Or had you forgotten I was to take you driving this afternoon?"

The room seemed full of his presence. He was wearing buckskins and a blue coat, his cravat so carelessly tied that on any other man it would have looked unkempt, and he smelled of the damp and the out-of-doors. It had been almost a week since she had seen him, and she had forgotten how much like a small boy he could look, despite his reputation.

She smiled at the thought but merely said calmly, "No, my lord."

"Does that mean no, you have not forgotten, or no, you are not coming?" he demanded. "I told you, did I not, that I would return on Friday to take you driving with me so that we could begin to be seen in one another's company?"

She set another inexpert stitch. "Yes, you told me, my lord. But if you had taken the trouble to ask me, I would have told you I had no intention of accompanying you."

He came to stand before her, looking down at her. "I warn you, Miss Fairfield, I am in no mood for more of your nonsense! My grandmother is plainly become senile, but if you had any more sense than my left boot you would spare yourself a great deal of unnecessary grief. And if you continue to behave like an outraged virgin, don't expect me to play the gentleman! Have I made myself clear?"

"I have long since given up expecting you to play the gentleman, my lord. But I begin to think it is a very good thing after all that you met me. It is clear that no one has ever crossed you in the whole of your life. It should prove a valuable experience for you."

"I am more than aware of your opinion of me, Miss Fairfield!"

She folded her mending and put it away. "Are you,

my lord? I doubt it. I am aware that you are considered vastly dangerous, but I merely find you overbearing, rude, and utterly spoiled."

He laughed harshly. "You hit hard, ma'am. Shall I tell you how I have been spoiled? The first years of my life were spent with a father who could not stand the sight of me and a mother who spent as little time in her home as she could manage. You see, Miss Fairfield, my mother, in a fit of pique over one of their many quarrels, encouraged my father in the belief I was another man's by-blow."

At her shocked expression, he said mockingly, "A pretty story is it not? My father acknowledged me because his pride would not allow him to do anything else, but he understandably did not like to be reminded of my existence. I doubt we exchanged above a dozen words before I was seven or eight years of age. Unfortunately, at that point it became apparent even to the meanest intelligence that for all those years my mother had been enjoying a particularly cruel jest at his expense. All of the Stauntons, you see, show a remarkable resemblence to one another."

"I see, my lord," she said quietly. "But surely your mother could see what it was doing to you?"

"Oh, I don't say that I blame her! My father was a cold, disagreeable man who made her life as miserable as he did mine. His friends had all warned him against the match, with some justice, I must admit. It was probably the only time in his life he allowed his emotions to rule his head, and I believe he spent the remainder of his life repenting it. My mother, you see, Miss Fairfield, *was* spoiled, and as willful and unfaithful as she was beautiful. Perhaps it was not her fault that the same qualities that had made my father fall desperately in love with her were those he most despised after their marriage. Mercifully, she was killed in a carriage accident when I was twelve. She was, of course, with another man at the time!"

"Were they eloping, my lord?"

He shrugged. "That was naturally what was thought, but I have always doubted it. My mother was nothing if not practical, Miss Fairfield, and her current lover had scarce-

ly a penny to scratch himself with. My father may have
had many faults, but he had at least the virtue of being
able to afford her expensive tastes."

She smiled. "She sounds fascinating. You must have
loved her very much."

"Oh, I don't doubt but what I worshiped her as a boy,"
he said, "but I soon learned that I had no chance of
competing against the other men in her life, and there
was never a lack of those."

"I don't suppose there would have been," she remarked, "but there is no use in condemning women like
that, you know. It is as if they needed more love than
the rest of us. I think my own mother must have been
a little like that. Not that she took lovers—or she may
have, but I was too young to remember."

His black mood seemed to be gone. "You are a strange
child, Sylvie. Did you love her?"

"I scarcely remember her—but no, I don't think so,"
she answered. "She was very pretty, and she always
smelled of violets. She used to tuck me into bed when
she was feeling happy, and her scent would remain behind her for hours afterward. But she and my father
quarreled incessantly, and she was often moody and un-
approachable, I think. I thought at the time that it was
my fault when she got into such moods, for she could
never bear to have us around her then." She smiled.
"I have never dared to admit it before because Hinton
and Blackmer were amazingly devoted to her, and
Kendall was older, but he does not remember as I do."

"Poor little Sylvie!" he said mockingly. "I don't doubt
you have felt guilty about it all these years. Well, there
is the difference between us."

"Perhaps," she said with a frown. "Papa did not love
her, you see, and she needed to have people around
her who loved her. Papa quickly consoled himself after
she died, and we even got on better without all the
tantrums and quarrels. It is very sad, I think, not to be
mourned when you die."

"You are a romantic, my dear! Very few of us are
mourned, you will find. My father quickly consoled himself too, only he was far too hypocritical to take mis-
tresses, so that he married, to do her justice, exactly the

sort of woman he should have married in the first place.
You will forgive me if I doubt either of them was capable
of living happily ever after."

"Oh, I thought—" For some reason she blushed. "I had
hoped that he had perhaps realized his mistake and grown
to love you."

He laughed. "Poor little sparrow! You *are* a romantic.
Will that soft heart of yours be wrung when I tell you
that he had long since discovered a more kindred spirit
in my cousin Michael, a most obedient little boy who did
not bear the dread taint of the Desboroughs? And soon
afterward my father had a daughter to gladden his heart
in his last years. He left a large inheritance to Kitty,
whatever remained unentailed to my cousin Michael, and
what he could not legally dispose of elsewhere to me,
with the proviso that I could go to the devil as fast as I
wished and restore the property and title to a true
Staunton."

"I see," she said, conceiving a vast hatred for the late
earl. "So that is exactly what you have been doing."

"Do not try to work me into your neat little theories
of black and white, my dear. I require a wife, not a
confessor!"

"You require neither, my lord."

He smiled silkily at her. "You are mistaken. The one
thing you seem unable to grasp, with your naïve nobility,
is that *I* am neither noble nor a romantic fool like you.
I entered into that wager precisely because I found
myself in need of a wife. And believe me, I have every
intention of holding you to your end of the bargain. It
has recently been brought home to me that my young
stepsister is enduring a life not much happier than my
own—or your—childhood was, and I require a wife so
that she may come and live with me. In addition, if I am
to confound my father as you seem to wish, I need an
heir. I see no reason why you should not suit my purposes as well as any other."

She flushed, and then was angry that his words had the
power to hurt her. "I can see that you care for nothing,
my lord," she said evenly. "But do you care so little that
you think a *Fairfield* a proper match for a Staunton? I
have no beauty to recommend me; you yourself have

already condemned my conduct; and I am more at home in the stables than the drawing room. If you have any doubts, you need only ask my father. I have neither conversation nor accomplishments. Is that what you desire for your wife?"

He ran his eyes over her in a manner that made her cheeks redden. "You have listened too long to your father, Miss Fairfield," he said. "Unlike him, I see you for what you are. You are a silly chit of a girl whose heart is altogether too warm and impulsive to be allowed loose on her own. You behave like a schoolgirl and seem to have rather less knowledge of the world. I don't doubt your godmother will soon change all that, more's the pity! but you are by no means plain. Indeed, you have improved a great deal more than I expected even in the short time since I saw you last. With the proper clothes and hairstyle you do very well, and as I thought when I first saw you, you have the most beautiful eyes I have ever seen."

She had been staring at him round-eyed, but at that she came to her senses. "Do you think I want Spanish coin from you, my lord?" she inquired scornfully.

He laughed. "If you call that flattery, my girl, you only prove what I have been saying. Most women, even my minx of a sister, would call that shabby praise indeed.

"Much more to the point," he added with a certain arrogance, "you seem to have a modicum of intelligence and a great deal of spirit. You even seem to have somehow escaped the prudery that afflicts most of the silly young fools today. If you will only stop opposing me, I don't doubt but what we shall do very well together."

"What you mean is that you will do very well, my lord. You have yet to tell me what I am to gain."

He frowned. "You have said you were not happy at home. I may not be the husband you would choose, but I can promise I won't interfere in your pleasure. I will settle a handsome allowance on you, and, saving only that I will require you to chaperone my sister until she marries —which will probably not be too long, for a sadder little baggage I've yet to see—I will ask little of you. You will have a house in London of your own, as well as various country estates to play chatelaine over to your heart's content. You will have an income to indulge whatever fancies you may possess, and once you have presented me with an heir, you may go your own way. I will engage not to interfere as long as you remain discreet."

The picture he painted chilled her to the bone. She knew just how long he would be content with such a bloodless marriage. "That prospect does not tempt me, my lord," she said dryly.

"No, I can see it don't suit with your romantic notions!" he retorted. "Had you dreamed of a knight riding to rescue a damsel in distress? Well, I fear I am no knight. I have made no secret of what I am, but if it is romance you crave, I am sure I can oblige you. I have a vast deal of experience, God knows, and you are appealing enough. You would prefer no doubt that I tell you that your eyes have the look of the sky before dawn, or of a startled fawn, and that a man is never certain whether they are gray or black or something in between. That there is something oddly bewitching in that grave, funny little face of yours with those straight, disapproving brows. Or that your lips, stern though they are, were made for kissing!"

"No," she said evenly. "For I know I am none of those things."

"Oh, my dear, you know little of men!" he said in amusement. "Have you not learned yet that there is enough woman in you to go to any man's head? Well, that will change soon enough, I have no doubt," he added. "But I may have the unlooked for pleasure of teaching you." He stared down at her, and then, prompted by his own particular devil, bent his head and kissed her.

She permitted it, standing rigidly. When he at last released her she stepped back and said, "Is that how you kiss your opera dancer, my lord?"

His brow drew swiftly together; then he laughed. "You have a sharp tongue, Sylvie. And no, Miss Innocence, it is not. What do you know of opera dancers anyway?"

"I should imagine the whole world knows of yours, my lord. You seem to have taken little enough pains to hide them."

"They need not concern you. You will be my wife—a position not without standing. And I promise you will not find me ungenerous."

"Is that before or after you have gratified the whims of whatever bird of paradise happens to be under your protection at the moment?" she asked. "No, I thank you. I may be naïve and a fool as you say, but I prefer to know that I have some value to my husband other than as a chaperone for his sister. I would also like to know I might expect some—loyalty, if not fidelity, from him. You do not know the meaning of the word, my lord."

His temper rose then. "You found it amusing to pretend to trap me into marriage, Miss Fairfield. Well, it is you who has been trapped! You'll marry me because you damn well have no choice! I have paid through the nose to shut up that father of yours, and I have quieted the rest of those fools on the strength of the fact that you are to become my wife. I have known not a moment's peace since I met you. I have had to endure a damned cheeky lecture from my grandmother; I have been subjected to impertinence by a bunch of foolish yokels; and I have been obliged to spend the better part of the week pursuing your father, suffering his insolence when I would like to ram his foul tongue down his oily throat!"

"You confuse me, my lord. Am I to marry you to save my reputation, or to salvage your pride?"

"Both!" he snapped.

"You have made a great many threats, my lord, most of them foolish, but you have not yet told me how you intend to wed me against my will, for you will do it no other way," she said. "I have listened to you, because in a way I thought I owed you that, but now you will listen to me. If you require a wife, choose one among your own kind and woo her like any other man. Or does the great Earl of St. Ives only take what he wants? Well, you shall not take me, and, I warn you, I will not be bullied."

His blue eyes were on her face. "I would not bet on that, Miss Fairfield," he said softly. "I would not bet on it if I were you."

He started toward the door, then halted and added impatiently, "You almost made me forget, I have a present for you. Outside."

He imperiously held out his hand to her and she weakly put her own in it, startled by this rapid about-face. His fingers closed over hers and he pulled her downstairs, saying curtly, "Never mind your coat. You will not be out long. I will put my greatcoat over your shoulders."

He stared down the gaping eyes of the butler, accepted his coat, and wrapped it around her shoulders. Then he pulled open the door and drew her outside.

She saw a man walking a horse up the street at that moment, and she froze. "Oh, my lord—" she faltered. "Blackmer—! *Cintra!*" She ran forward, dropping his coat unnoticed behind her, and threw her arms first around the groom, then around the big rangy animal.

His lordship retrieved the coat and walked forward, saying with a slightly rueful grin to the groom, "Well, you said it was what she wanted most."

She looked around, tears standing in her eyes. "Oh, Blackmer, you don't know how glad I am to see you! I hoped I might have a letter—but to actually see you!" She clasped his hand tightly in both of her own. "Tell me everything! How is Beauty and the foal—and Hinton— and when must you go back?"

The groom drew his hand away and said with a trace of embarrassment, "Now, Miss Syllie, it ain't proper for you to take on so, especially when you're looking as fine as fivepence, as I always knew you could. I've come to be your groom, which you might have knowed I would, but not before giving your Papa a piece of my mind, I can tell you."

She giggled a little. "Oh, poor Papa! What a great deal he seems to have been obliged to endure lately. Has he been dreadfully angry?"

"Proper boiled!" said Blackmer with great cheerfulness. "But don't you fret yourself no more about him. *He'll* learn soon enough, with neither of us there to see to things, but he don't need concern you no more."

St. Ives had been watching the pair of them, but now he stepped forward and put his coat once more about her shoulders. "I'm depending on you to see to it that your mistress doesn't get into trouble, Blackmer, which she seems to have a great tendency to do," he said. "Now she must get in out of the cold. Take the horse back to my stables until arrangements can be made to house you both at Lady Bridlington's."

"Yes, my lord," replied Blackmer.

She knew what a stickler Blackmer was, and that he had only remained with her father for her sake, and this ready acceptance of St. Ives's authority astonished her. When the groom had ridden away, she looked up and said, "I don't quite know how to thank you, my lord. It was most—"

He was holding the fronts of his coat together around her, so that she stood very close to him. He looked down at her, his old mocking expression in his eyes. "Sticks in your throat to be obliged to accept it from me, don't it?" he said.

She met his eyes. "No, my lord, I am far too happy to have them both with me."

He drew her closer for a moment before dropping his hands and saying in his usual tones, "Now in with you. I'll not have your death from pneumonia laid at my door."

She remained for a second, staring up at him. "My lord?" she said. "Did you mean the things you said in there?"

"I always mean what I say, Miss Fairfield," he retorted. "What specifically did you have in mind?"

She turned away. "Never mind."

"If you mean that I will not be bested by a chit of a girl with a vile temper and a damned sharp tongue in her head, yes I meant it," he said.

The cold was putting the color in her cheeks, and she felt oddly exhilarated, as if she had been running. "Then I think you do not yet know me, my lord!"

"No. But I will, little sparrow. And that's a promise."

XV

Lady Bridlington was still in bed when Sylvie sought her out early the next morning. Her ladyship had endured a trying week, with one thing and another, having had the prospect of St. Ives dangled temptingly before her face only to have it snatched out of reach at the last minute for a scruple she could not begin to comprehend. But she was a kind woman, and incapable of sustaining anger for very long.

"I'm glad you've come, my love, for there was something I particularly wanted to ask you," she said. "You'll never guess what I've received—now where did I put it? I know I had it in my hand just a moment ago—" She glanced up for the first time. "Well, you're looking cheerful for so early in the morning, I must say," she added, recalling her grievance.

Sylvie laughed and kissed her godmother's cheek. "Yes, and you are looking quite wastefully fetching yourself, dear ma'am! Is that ravishing confection meant to be a nightcap?"

Lady Bridlington could not resist glancing in the mirror beside her bed and preening just a little. "Yes. I must admit I am very pleased with it myself. I had begun to fear that Fanny was quite losing her touch, for the last two caps I had from her made me look positively ancient. Not that that is anything to marvel at," she added philosophically, "for I'm sure I'm getting on, but naturally one does not wish to have everyone know it. I hope you know what James was ranting about this morning, my love, for I could make neither head nor tail out of any of it! I could have sworn he said St. Ives had sent over a horse and groom for us to keep. If he hasn't room in his own stables it seems odd of him to expect *us* to house his animals for him."

Sylvie blushed. "Oh, ma'am, I beg your pardon; of course, I should have asked your permission first. My Lord St. Ives was only kind enough to bring me my own old groom and mount."

"Well, that explains it then," said her ladyship. "Though if you had only told me you wished to be mounted, I'm sure there would have been something suitable—did you say *St. Ives* brought them down for you?"

Sylvie's color increased. "Yes, ma'am."

Her ladyship's expression took on a look of guarded joy. "Oh, my love! Oh, does that mean you have—oh, I

knew you could not be so foolish when it had been explained—oh, I could not be happier!"

"No, I have not changed my mind, ma'am," said Sylvie.
"If you think I ought not to have allowed him to bring
Blackmer and Cintra to me, I am sorry. They are mine,
after all, and I don't think I could bear to send them
back now. But that is not what I wished to speak with
you about."

Her ladyship had sunk once more into gloom. "No,"
she said, "I don't doubt but what you only wished to
tell me some new scheme you have concocted that is
designed to put me into an early grave. And if it is
anything more to do with becoming a governess, I assure
you, you will be wasting your breath, for I will not listen
to a word of it!"

Sylvie laughed. "Oh, ma'am, I am sorry I am such a trial
to you. But if you will only help me once more, I promise
I will cease to plague you. Anyway, I have nearly
abandoned the scheme of becoming a governess. I daresay you were right, and it would not have suited me
after all. What I wanted to know is if you number any
widowers among your acquaintance?"

Her ladyship looked up, her face rigid. "No!" she said
flatly. "I will not allow you to become a governess to a
widower."

Sylvie's eyes began to twinkle mischievously. "Poor
ma'am! Of course I do not wish to become—but if you
know any widowers in need of a—No, no!" she said,
laughing. "I will not tease you any longer! Only I think I
have issued a—a sort of challenge to my Lord St. Ives—
at least it is clear he means to regard it as such. And it
occurred to me that if you knew any widowers, it might
be just what I was looking for."

As her ladyship turned pale and groped for her vinaigrette, Sylvie relented. "No, no, ma'am, it is not as bad
as that. Only he returned here yesterday and we—in
short, ma'am," she added with a certain martial light in
her eyes, "my Lord St. Ives is about to find himself
bested, for perhaps the first time in his life, and I promise
you it will do him a world of good! That is why I am in
need of a widower."

"I think I shall go mad," said her ladyship. "St. Ives

offers you what he has offered no other, and all you can think of is to turn it into a contest between you. I *shall* go mad. They will come and lock me up in Bedlam and throw away the key."

"No, of course they will not, ma'am," said Sylvie. "And I have not turned it into a contest—or if I have, I promise it will not rebound on you. Only if you do know of any widowers who are perhaps hanging out for a wife and are beyond the age of—of foolishness, I wish you would tell me."

"I do not know any widowers, and if I did they would not be hanging out for a wife!" said her ladyship. "Widowers—wealthy ones anyway—never hang out for a wife."

"Well, he does not have to be wealthy—at least not very. And I will settle for his not being a widower—though I confess I was rather taken with the idea," said Sylvie teasingly. "His poor motherless children looking to me for—all right, ma'am, I will be serious! But I meant it about the widower. It seems to me that my only option now *is* to marry, and as quickly as possible. And I thought a widower would not be likely to be too particular, or desire any untoward delay."

Her ladyship shook her head feebly. "I shall go mad! You talk of widowers when you might have had—" Abruptly she sat up and said with more spirit, "On second thought, it is clearly you who are deranged! I shouldn't wonder if you should not be locked up somewhere, for your own good."

"Well," said Sylvie, grinning, "if you don't know any widowers, I shall just have to find some. How would I go about that, ma'am?"

"Good God, Lady Castlereigh!" cried her ladyship. "You and your nonsense made me forget all about it, which only goes to show what a state I'm in!"

She was searching through her correspondence again, and Sylvie asked, "Why, is she likely to know many widowers?"

"I'm sure if there *were* any eligible widowers, Maria Castlereigh—no, of course not!" she snapped. "I've told you there aren't any, and I don't want to hear another word about it. Ah, here it is! How I could have forgotten

even for a moment, when I've received the most flattering invitation—not that I don't know whom we have to
thank for this, of course! Lady Castlereigh specifically asks
that I bring you, my love. There, see for yourself. My
charming young guest, she calls you. You should be vastly
flattered, my dear."

Sylvie quickly read the invitation and said with a faint
frown, "But this is for this evening! Surely she should have
given you more notice?"

"Yes, but you see she writes that it is quite an im-
promptu affair—just a few couples got together for dancing—and she apologizes for the shortness of the notice.
Not that I would regard it," added her ladyship frankly,
"for I was never before invited to her house, and well
she knows it. Mark my words, we have the dowager to
thank for this. Not that I'm sure I shouldn't decline now
—for everything's ruined," she added gloomily.

"No it's not," said Sylvie. "And I think we should go."

Her ladyship brightened. "Well, if you think—though I
don't know if I'll have the heart to enjoy myself. But
perhaps you are right, my love. Yes, I'm persuaded you
are," she added more cheerfully, "for you would meet a
great many people who might be of use to you, if they
only would."

She sat up, her gloom apparently forgotten. "Yes, yes,
but there is not a moment to be wasted! Where is
Crimping? She knows how I dislike lying about in the
mornings! You may hand me my dressing gown, my dear,
and then run away, for I've a thousand things to be done
if we are to be ready in time. On second thought, take
Mary and see if you can find a spray of roses to match
my purple silk. The rain has turned off and you will be
glad of a chance to get out of doors. But no dawdling,
mind, and none of your sight-seeing. That was all very
well, but now we've serious business to attend to. Oh,
and if you're going to be out, you may as well change
this library book for me. I'm sure I don't know why Mary
Williams recommended it, for I could scarce get through
ten pages. Oh, there you are, Crimping."

Sylvie went away to execute her ladyship's errands,
glad to have given her godmother's thoughts a more cheerful direction. But she herself was wishing she might re-

tract those few hasty words. She knew that she must begin to go into society, but she had never shown to advantage among people she did not know, and the thought of a great many fashionable people looking her over was not calculated to increase her confidence. Added to that was the ever-present fear that she would find herself face-to-face with one of the gentlemen who had been present that night at her father's house. Then she chided herself for being a coward and went in search of Mary.

Nevertheless, it was with considerably mixed feelings that she dressed for her first ball. Her ladyship had apparently overcome her own feelings, and she fussed around Sylvie and Crimping, who had been lent for the occasion, and only succeeded in increasing Sylvie's nervousness. Sylvie's hair was at first too severe and must be done over, then it was discovered that a pair of silk sandals had not been delivered after all, and peace was not restored until Crimping came up with the happy notion of miss wearing the jonquil crepe with the white satin slip, for she had never been sure (she said) that the pink did not make Miss Sylvie look a little sallow.

Sylvie could have hugged the forbidding maid, with whom she had been on the barest of terms, and she was obliged to admit with something like wonder that the results of all that labor had been well worth it. In the half-gown of jonquil over a slip of white satin, with pearl buttons down the front of the bodice and a pearl necklace lent by her ladyship about her throat, even she detected an elusive beauty in her reflection. Her soft brown curls had a ribbon of pale yellow threaded through them, and a shawl of the same shade was draped at the correct angle across her elbows. She knew she had never looked better.

Even Crimping seemed pleased, and her ladyship said happily, "Oh, my love, you look delightful! I must confess, when I first saw you I did not think we would be able to do the trick, but it just goes to show how wrong you can be! No one would know you for the same girl."

That made Sylvie laugh, but she could not resist saying, "I only hope you may be right, ma'am. I must confess that is a thought that has me in the quakes."

Her ladyship glanced quickly at a curious Crimping, and

Sylvie obediently abandoned the dangerous topic. She only wished she might dismiss it from her mind as easily.

Dinner had still to be gotten through, and an hour or more afterward before her ladyship had decreed it would be proper for them to start. But Lady Bridlington passed the time by describing to her in detail every person she was likely to meet, and upon whom it would be important to make a good impression. Even James, who had declined to accompany them, complimented them with heavy gallantry on their gowns and made a joke about hoping they would not be too exhausted from their coming "dissipation."

It was a fashionable half-past ten by the time they were at last set down before Lady Castlereigh's door in Grosvenor Street. There had been quite a crush of vehicles before them, and there were constant cries of "Make way for my lady's carriage!" The street was lighted up as if it were daytime, and Sylvie became so fascinated that she forgot a little of her nervousness. With tolerable composure, she allowed herself to be divested of her cloak by an impassive footman, and followed her godmother up the stairs to the first floor, trying not to crane her neck to stare at everything.

She was a little shy of meeting her hostess, but Lady Castlereigh, a tall, oddly dressed woman with a vague air and penetrating blue eyes, greeted Lady Bridlington graciously, saying, "So kind of you to come. London is thin of company just now, you know. I vow every year not to remain, but the least we can do is try to come up with some entertainment. And this must be Miss Fairfield? I am glad to make your acquaintance, my dear."

Sylvie murmured a reply, her color a little high, and became aware that her hostess was looking her over critically, a not unkind look in her eyes. "You must allow me to present you with an eligible partner, my dear," said her ladyship. She signaled with her fan as though she were conjuring up a spirit, and a tall, extremely thin man detached himself from a small group nearby. "My nephew, Horace," said Lady Castlereigh. "Ah, there you are, Horace. Sophia, you know my nephew, I believe? Miss Fairfield, may I present Mr. Epping? Now run along, children, for the set is just forming, and allow me to have a chat with Lady Bridlington."

To call Mr. Epping a child was stretching the matter, but he picked up his cue and bowed, offering Sylvie his arm. "If I may have the honor, Miss Fairfield?" he said.

She accompanied him onto the dance floor, praying she had not forgotten any steps, and she had to concentrate for the first few minutes until they came back to her.

Mr. Epping made one or two comments, to which she replied rather vaguely, and at last he observed, "It is now your turn to introduce a topic, I believe, Miss Fairfield."

She looked up, startled. "What? Oh, I'm sorry, but I have to mind my steps, you see. What did you say?"

He was taken aback ."Mind your—?"

"Yes, but I think I have the hang of it now. It is one two *three* four," she said in relief.

Mr. Epping was uncertain whether to be diverted or to write her off as a hopeless provincial. He chose to be diverted. "I see, Miss Fairfield!" he said, a faint twinkle in his eyes. "Congratulations. Do I understand this is your first visit to London?"

She made some unexceptionable answer, and after that, when the movements of the dance brought them together, they discussed various uninteresting topics. In truth, she was more interested in looking around than in making polite conversation, for if this were her hostess's idea of an informal get-together, she would like to have seen a formal one. More than thirty couples had taken to the floor, and perhaps as many more stood or sat around the room. The heat and the noise were already tremendous. She caught sight of Lady Bridlington conversing with a forbidding woman in a satin turban, and then Lady Castlereigh standing beside a vivacious blonde in red. Her eyes searched the faces in the throng with some trepidation, but she could find no face that was familiar to her, and she relaxed.

She was just observing the odd frowns of a forbidding matron in puce when she became aware that Mr. Epping had once more asked her a question. She flushed. "I beg your pardon, sir, I fear I was not attending. Would you tell me who is that odd woman in the corner, the one in the puce satin and the hid—and the purple shawl?"

Mr. Epping obediently put up his glass to see whom she meant. "Do you mean Mrs. Willingford, Miss Fairfield? She is certainly wearing a hideous shawl," he said, "but what has she done to draw your interest?"

She laughed. "Nothing. And that *is* what I meant to say, but it was most unkind of me. I was only curious because she has been trying to attract the eye of that lovely young girl in the pink gauze, and I think she is far from being pleased."

Mr. Epping, who had the reputation of being somewhat of a gossip, did not have to look to see whom she was talking about. "Ah, that is her daughter, Miss Amanda Willingford, no doubt. She is certainly lovely, and it is a good thing, for her Mama has five daughters to fire off, and she is only the second. The Willingfords are as poor as church mice, I fear, and no doubt her Mama is trying to catch her eye because she has allowed Mr. Luttrell to lead her out for the third time this evening."

"Why, what is wrong with Mr. Luttrell? Is he not respectable?"

"Oh yes, perfectly respectable. But not a penny of course. And worse—"

When he saw that she was looking wholly bewildered, he smiled. "He is a poet, Miss Fairfield."

She was astonished, and twisted around to obtain a second look at Mr. Luttrell. "What, in the style of Lord Byron?"

"Oh, no—though it would be better if he were, of course. Mr. Luttrell's poems are very classical, I believe, but I'm afraid they do not take. But are you not an admirer of our crowning light, Miss Fairfield?"

She smiled and said, "No, I found him sadly romantic, but I daresay that is because I have not the least sensibility, myself. Indeed, I could not help wondering if he were suffering from a stomach disorder or the like, which is what made him so gloomy."

Mr. Epping surprised those nearest them in the dance by giving a shout of laughter.

She said quickly, "I have no doubt I should not have

said that, and I beg you will not repeat it. Are you an admirer of Lord Byron's, Mr. Epping?"

"No, no, Miss Fairfield," he murmured. "Indeed, I have been longing to say much the same thing for months now, but have not plucked up the courage to admit I cannot understand a single thing the fellow says!"

Before they could say anything more, the dance ended, and he bowed and returned her to her godmother. "I hope I may have the honor of leading you out again before the evening is over, Miss Fairfield," he said with an unexpected twinkle. "I am longing to exchange opinions on our great portrait painter, Mr. Lawrence."

Lady Bridlington watched in amazement as he strolled off. "Why, my dear," she said, agog with curiosity and delight, "whatever have you been saying to Horace Epping? I have seldom seen him more animated! My dear, if he should take a liking to you, then you will be made, for no one has more influence—outside Mr. Brummel."

Sylvie looked surprised. "What, is he an arbiter of fashion? I would not have thought it, for he was not at all toplofty. I must confess I liked him."

"Liked him—?" repeated her ladyship faintly. Mr. Epping had ruined more than one hopeful young lady's career merely by uttering a condescending word, and he was known to despise the general run of young ladies. Indeed, Lady Bridlington had been quite in despair when Maria Castlereigh's evil genius had prompted her to offer her nephew as a partner. "Liked him—to be sure, my love," she said again.

Sylvie, uncaring whether or not she made a mark in society, was nevertheless feeling rather pleased. After the first few minutes she had not found her first London gentleman so forbidding after all, and if he were one of the high sticklers she had heard about, then they were not nearly so bad as she had feared.

She was grateful that she was not solicited for the next two sets, for it gave her an opportunity to observe. It was still very warm in the room, but she was excited by the music and the number of people, and she was busy storing up details to tell Blackmer. This was what he had always wanted for her, and she did not mean to forget anything to report of her first party.

After that she was introduced to a great many persons, and one or two glanced at her curiously. However, few were particularly interested in Lady Bridlington's unknown young guest, and she began to relax a little more. Then there was a slight stir by the door, and she looked up just in time to obtain a clear view of the Earl of St. Ives, looking very much at his ease and disturbingly handsome in a deep blue coat.

Hers were by no means the only eyes on his tall figure. It was a mistake to say that St. Ives's scandalous behavior had placed him beyond the pale of polite society, for it was still an age where few did not retain a secret admiration for a rake, and particularly such a handsome one. But St. Ives seldom chose to grace such functions with his presence, preferring no doubt the entertainment at one of the gambling hells or other.

He greeted Lady Castlereigh easily and stood conferring with her for some minutes. "Well, I have done as you asked, Nicky," she said in amusement. "Do you really mean to eat up that little mouse?"

He carried her hand to his lips and replied coolly, "Do you think she needs protection from me, Maria?"

"Yes," said her ladyship. "Or I would if I were not a woman. She seems to have kept poor Horace well enough entertained, at all events."

"Did she? You will excuse me, I know, Maria." He bowed, kissed her hand once more, and turned away. He stood in the center of the room for a moment, supremely unaware of the eyes upon him, and seemingly searching for someone among the crowd. Then he strolled purposefully forward, making more than one damsel's heart flutter in her breast and their mamas wonder how such a careless bearing and a dark, unsmiling countenance could contrive to be so handsome.

He came straight across the room and stood before Sylvie. "My dance, I believe, Miss Fairfield?" he said and held out his hand.

It was a move worthy of a master strategist, and she knew it. In one blow he had transformed her from Lady Bridlington's unimportant goddaughter into a figure for general speculation. Even Lady Bridlington was looking staggered. It was unusual enough for St. Ives to attend such an affair, and for him to single out a previously unnoticed young lady the moment he entered the room was food for the wildest gossip.

Sylvie had no choice and allowed him to lead her onto the floor. When the music began she lifted her chin and said, "Very well done, my lord! But do you imagine that will change my mind?"

"No!" he said, and surprised her by adding, "But you are increasing my awareness that you are a remarkable girl, Sylvie. You're a good sport—but then you don't like Spanish coin, do you?"

"Was that Spanish coin, my lord?"

"No. Oddly enough, it was not. You dance very well."

"I fear Mr. Epping might not agree with you," she said a little ruefully. "I learned from our vicar's sister, but I have had few opportunities to practice. And I fear I can only do the country-dances. Miss Hapwood did not approve of waltzing."

"Then you must learn. You will like it," he said.

"Will I, my lord? Then I must certainly learn, by all means."

When the figures of the dance brought them back together again, he asked if Blackmer and Cintra had settled in, and they talked easily of that for the remainder of the dance. Only when the music was ending did he bring the conversation back to a personal note. "Well," he said, "your move, I believe my dear."

She did not pretend to misunderstand him. "Do you think I will not have one, my lord?"

"No, I was sure you would," he said promptly.

She laughed then. "Well, I will admit you have delivered a—a 'facer,' if you like. Is that the right word? But I have no doubt I shall come about again."

When he grinned, she added, "Besides, I am not sure but what you haven't done me a service. A great many people are going to know who I am after tonight. Even now people are staring at us."

"Are they?" he said. "Then let us give them something to watch, by all means!" He bowed over her hand with practiced gallantry, unmistakable intimacy in his manner and in the way his fingers retained hers just a touch too long. Then he straightened and looked at her mockingly.

Her color was a little high despite herself, but she said coolly, "I have never doubted your experience, my lord, but I am neither one of your opera dancers nor one of the silly girls who fall at your feet like ripe plums if you deign to give them a glance. It seems you have enough of both already."

He laughed, but he was nettled. "Minx!" he said, and left her.

She watched him go, her expression unreadable. He nodded to several persons, carelessly drank a glass of champagne, and stopped to speak with a vivacious blonde.

That lady, with a knowing look, said, "Not quite in your usual style, Nicky."

"Oh, do you think not?" he asked.

Lady Jersey, her eyes on his face, said, "A word of advice because I love you. You'll catch cold at that, my dear. Fairfield's daughter, isn't she? Well, Fairfield's all to pieces, but by today's standards the family's an old one. However loose he may be, he'll not stand around while you trifle with his daughter." She cast a glance at the young lady in question and added with unaccustomed sympathy, "That one's not up to your weight, Nicky. Throw her back."

He too looked across at Miss Fairfield, now in earnest conversation with her godmother, and he grinned. "You can't know Miss Fairfield if you think that, Sally."

She was startled. "What game are you at, St. Ives?" she asked suspiciously.

He was still grinning. "Ask Miss Fairfield! She seems to be setting the rules."

Lady Jersey was beginning to look irritated. "I will," she said, "but I've a feeling I'll get no more out of her than I have out of you. Now go away, Nicky, for you've done enough damage for one night."

She watched him go as Miss Fairfield had done. Provoking boy! But he had always amused her, and he was so handsome. She would indeed have to make the acquaintance of the little Fairfield. It promised not to be such a dull winter after all.

For Sylvie, only one event stood out with any clarity after that. Her hand was sought for a number of dances, but none of her partners made any impression on her until she looked up to find a familiar, exquisitely dressed gentleman at her elbow.

She had not seen him in the room earlier, but she knew immediately that he had been present on that fatal night, and her heart seemed to stop.

He was watching her closely, a warning in his eyes. She looked up, unaware of the pleading in her own, and he shook his head slightly. Then he bowed and said with easy charm, "I have been trying to catch your godmother's eye all evening, to beg her to present me, Miss Fairfield, but I see I will have to risk your displeasure by taking it upon myself. I am Strickland, you know."

She only knew that he did not mean to denounce her, and some of her color came back. "I—how do you do?"

He smiled at her disapproval, "I am well acquainted with your godmother, and that acquaintance dared me to hope I might beg the honor of this dance, Miss Fairfield."

She rose obediently and was able to inform Lady Bridlington in a nearly normal voice that she would be taking part in the set just forming. Lady Bridlington looked up and, at the sight of her partner, smiled and nodded happily, leading Sylvie to suppose he must be a gentleman of some standing.

He, in turn, bowed charmingly to her ladyship, and said gaily, "You see how lost I am to all sense of propriety, my dear Lady Bridlington! I, despairing of your ever taking pity on me and making the proper introductions, have been reduced to sponsoring myself. That hurdle has now been cleared, and Miss Fairfield has kindly agreed to overlook my effrontery. It remains only for you to add your kind approval, and I shall think myself a very clever fellow."

Lady Bridlington laughed and fondly waved them away, turning back to her comfortable gossip.

Mr. Strickland led Sylvie onto the floor, taking his part gracefully, and smiling upon her quite kindly, but he said nothing until they had reached a point a little isolated from the remainder of the dancers. Then he remarked, "You know, I had a notion the other night that you were

not just in the common way, Miss Fairfield. I can see now
that I was unusually prescient."

Color flamed in her cheeks. "Indeed, sir?"

There was a great deal of shrewdness in his glance.
"Ah, and that was maladroit of me. I must beg your
pardon, Miss Fairfield. I meant it as a compliment. You
may have taken a dislike to me. People do. Think I'm
a frippery sort of a fellow, you know," he added, "but I
had hoped you would be able to forgive me for my part
in that evening."

"Your part?"

"St. Ives is a friend of mine," he explained.

"If St. Ives is a friend of yours, sir, then you should
have prevented what happened that night."

He looked around, fearful of being overheard, and then
sighed. "I know it, ma'am! It's been keeping me awake
o'nights. But the thing is, there's never any stopping St.
Ives when his devil's riding him."

Her expression softened. "Yes, I have discovered that
for myself. Was his devil riding him that night?" Mr.
Strickland began to look a little vague, and a sudden suspicion made her say, "I have often wondered—did Lord
Lambeth have anything to do with the wager that night,
by any chance? He was there I know."

"Good God, don't tell Nicky I told you, I beg you,
ma'am! He and Lambeth have been at each other's throats
for weeks over—" He coughed and quickly changed what
he had been about to say. "Over some stupid thing or another."

She smiled automatically, trying to adjust to this new
explanation. "I—but he was still drunk, sir," she reminded
him.

Mr. Strickland considered it for a moment. "Yes. But
I've seen him drunk, and I've seen him sober, Miss Fairfield, and St. Ives is only dangerous when he gets that
black mood upon him."

"I should have said my Lord St. Ives is dangerous whenever his will is crossed."

Strickland laughed. "I thought I should like you, Miss
Fairfield!"

She frowned up at him. She liked him too, for though
she could see why he gave the impression of being a

frippery sort of fellow, there was a great deal of intelligence in his eyes when he did not trouble to hide it behind his fashionable mask. It occurred to her that she might have found a valuable ally, if he were indeed a friend of St. Ives. "If that is true, Mr. Strickland, I hope you will—do you ride?"

He looked startled, but said gravely, "If the inducement is strong enough, Miss Fairfield. Am I to take it that you wish me to ride with you? Tomorrow, perhaps?"

"Oh, yes, please!" she said, glad of his ready understanding.

The dance ended then and he returned her to Lady Bridlington's side, then stayed chatting with her godmother for a moment. But as he excused himself, he was wondering in amusement what the girl could want of him. Ah yes, it certainly promised to be an entertaining winter after all.

XVI

St. Ives, in the meantime, did not return immediately to Mount Street, but sauntered down Saint James instead, though it was a chilly night, and looked in at one or another of his clubs. None of them seemed to please him, for he did not stay long at any, and it was past midnight when he seemed to find what he was looking for in Anthony's, one of the more discreet of the hells in Pall Mall Street. He strolled through the outer rooms and looked in at the inner rooms where the play was usually deeper. At one of these he halted.

At a word from someone, Lord Timothy Desborough looked up and waved a cheerful hand. He was not drunk, but he was well into his second bottle and decidedly jovial. "Hallo, dear boy. Come and join us," he called. "Though, I warn you, I'm devilish lucky tonight. Not to be beat. Told you it was only a matter of time till my luck changed."

"Indeed, my lord," said an amused gentleman at Lord Timothy's right. "We would all be in a quake, for he's won a fortune off us tonight, if we were not reassured by the knowledge that we shall win it all back again within a fortnight."

St. Ives laughed and went to observe the play, but he declined to take a hand, and his attention soon wandered. He observed several gentlemen playing *vingt-et-un* in a corner of the room, then said something to his uncle and walked leisurely across.

Lord Timothy, absently following his movements, frowned and put up his quizzing glass, then grunted. Lambeth, eh? Devil take the boy! If there was going to be trouble tonight, he'd best stay sober. He pushed away the bottle of burgundy at his elbow and called loudly for a pot of coffee, causing several of his companions to blink and one of them to go so far as to accuse him of meaning to keep a clear head while his luck was running, a suggestion Lord Timothy found so insulting he nearly forgot his pesky nephew in indignantly denying it.

At least one other gentleman in the room watched the events with almost as much interest as Lord Timothy. He observed St. Ives with slightly narrowed eyes until one of his companions said, "Here, Staunton, are you going to play or not? What are you so interested in—? Oh, I see! It's that damned cousin of yours! What's he up to now?"

Michael shrugged and turned back to his companions. "Nothing good, I have no doubt. Shall we continue, gentlemen?"

St. Ives, in the meantime, had reached his quarry. "Ah, Lambeth," he remarked softly. "I am delighted to see you returned safely."

Lambeth glanced up. He was not precisely afraid, but St. Ives's appearance had startled him, and he was aware of a sudden pounding in his heart. After a moment he said smoothly, "You do me too much honor, my lord! I had not thought to find you so concerned for my health."

"Naturally I would not wish any harm to befall you while

there remains a certain piece of—er—unfinished business between us."

Lambeth's palms began to sweat, but to his credit he did not betray any emotion. He had hated St. Ives for a long time now, and there was a certain relief in having it out. He had known St. Ives could not forgive him for that last affair. He even wondered what St. Ives had done with the chit, and then he rose, a hint of suppressed hatred in his eyes, and bowed. "I am at your service, my lord." He added, almost unwillingly, "I am glad it is to be over."

The men at Lambeth's table exchanged quick glances, and one said, "My lords! I beg you both, have a care to where you are!"

Neither appeared to have heard him. Lambeth stood staring at St. Ives, a grim excitement in his face, and St. Ives, watching him, said softly, "By God, I almost believe you would do it tonight. Has your hatred of me at last overcome your instinct for self-preservation, Lambeth? What a pity! I might have rid London of your presence at long last."

Lambeth, experiencing a strange jolt, realized it was not to be over after all. It was true that he hated St. Ives, but he himself no longer quite knew the reason. Jealousy of his wealth and his arrogant assurance, perhaps, coupled with the fact that St. Ives had more than once made Lambeth look a fool in public. He wondered what St. Ives could be up to now. "We shall never know, shall we, St. Ives?" he sneered. "What is it you want?"

St. Ives pretended surprise. "But I thought you knew. I believe you promised me, the last time we played, to pit your skill against mine again one day, did you not? Perhaps you would care to give me a rubber or two of piquet."

Lambeth frowned, his mind working. "Now, my lord?"

"But of course, now," said St. Ives. "Unless you have some objection?"

Lambeth was caught in a vicious predicament. For a number of reasons he welcomed the opportunity to play against St. Ives, but it could not have come at a worse time. He had been playing more than usually deeply lately, and that disastrous night at Fairfield's had not helped matters. He cursed St. Ives for choosing this moment, but he said, "I am at your disposal, of course! I must warn you that I consider piquet my game. Wheeling here can attest to that."

Wheeling, one of Lambeth's companions, said, "Oh, aye, he's devilish good at it! Best try another game, St. Ives. I think Lambeth must have played piquet in his cradle."

St. Ives merely bowed and indicated a table set a little apart on one side of the room.

Lambeth hesitated, then strolled over and seated himself. St. Ives stopped to speak a few words to a waiter, then himself came forward. In a moment the waiter appeared with a fresh pack of cards and a bottle and glasses. "A cognac Anthony keeps for me," said St. Ives. "You will join me?"

Lambeth accepted a glass and observed St. Ives surreptitiously. He did not really fear for the outcome of the game, for piquet required a cool head and an ability to suspend passion that he had reason to believe St. Ives lacked. But he distrusted St. Ives, and it would be disastrous to go down to him to anywhere near the tune that he had the last time they met.

Then, like the true gamester he was, he forced back the thought and watched as St. Ives picked up the pack and broke the seal, his dark face unreadable. Abandoning all discretion, Lambeth gave himself over to the pleasure of besting St. Ives. He cut the pack toward St. Ives and said almost gaily, "What stakes, my lord?"

St. Ives cut, and lost the first deal. He handed over the cards, his long fingers playing idly with the ribbon of his quizzing glass. "Why, what you will, Lambeth."

Lambeth began to deal the hand. "Then let us not waste your time or mine. Shall we say ten shillings the point?"

St. Ives agreed without a murmur. "Certainly, let us say that. But why not multiply the stakes?"

Lambeth glanced up quickly. "As you wish, my lord. Multiply by what?"

St. Ives shrugged. "Oh, to make it interesting, double. Pound points, a hundred pounds the rubber."

Lambeth's eyes narrowed slightly, for this was deep playing indeed. St. Ives must be very confident—or else very reckless. "Certainly, my lord. I care not how badly I fleece you, after all! Pound points it shall be."

The game opened quietly, no big hands being scored, each man bent on summing up his opponent. St. Ives, as Lambeth had suspected, proved to be an erratic player, taking unnecessary chances to take a pique and depending too heavily on the discard of his opponent. He seemed almost dissolute, his black locks disordered and his cravat loosened. He was drinking steadily and gave the appearance of being already more than half drunk. He played carelessly, and Lambeth wondered why he had insisted on playing tonight.

St. Ives lost the first rubber, though there was not much more than the hundred points in it for Lambeth. Lambeth, his doubts laid to rest, gathered up the cards. "I believe the luck was on my side that time," he remarked.

St. Ives shrugged and dealt the next hand, and they did not talk much after that. One or two men glanced over at them from time to time, but no one came to disturb their solitude. There were only the murmur of voices in the background and the occasional interruption of a waiter come to replace the brandy or supply fresh glasses.

But Lambeth, lulled thus early into a false security, began to suspect after the end of the first hour's play that St. Ives was far from being as erratic as he appeared. Once or twice he made a particularly brilliant pique, and once Lambeth had glimpsed a calculating expression in St. Ives's lazy blue eyes before his lids came down to hide them again. He was certainly drinking a great quantity, but Lambeth had reason to know that St. Ives drunk was at his most dangerous. He frowned and began to play more cautiously, pushing aside his glass and calling for a bottle of claret, feeling the need to keep a clear mind.

St. Ives's score was creeping up. Lambeth made a couple of stupid discards, allowing St. Ives to win a capot he should not have had, then he drained his glass and ran his hand irritably across his brow.

St. Ives called for another bottle, and while they waited for it Lambeth said, "You should not have had that last capot."

St. Ives stretched in his chair and yawned. "No, you should have held the club-guard. But I don't imagine it will happen again." ·

But for Lambeth the next hours were interminable. A small group had gathered to watch by now, and Lambeth became increasingly aware that he had met his match. His nerves were beginning to betray him; but he still refused to believe that St. Ives, with the amount of liquor he had consumed, could be keeping track of the discards. No, it was just St. Ives's damnable luck, and it could not continue. St. Ives played coolly, even recklessly, because to a man of his wealth it mattered little if he won or lost. Lambeth, aware that it must be apparent that his own play grew more cautious as St. Ives's score rose, cursed him bitterly, his hatred intensified.

For Lambeth, it mattered a great deal whether he won or lost. In fact, he might easily find himself facing ruin if the evening went heavily against him. He might have made an advantageous marriage, but his wife's fortune was not sufficient to withstand too many nights like the one spent at Fairfield's, and she had shown herself at their last meeting, like the true Cit she was, inclined to resent her money being squandered on gaming debts. Since her fortune was not yet in her hands, and therefore not in his, and would not be until she was thirty or gained the approval of her trustees, he dared not go too heavily into debt.

Then he forced himself to relax and wipe everything from his mind except the need to defeat St. Ives.

Lord Timothy, who had wandered into another room to try his newfound luck at the EO table, came back and stood observing for a few minutes. He watched St. Ives take a particularly difficult pique, and cried happily, "Piqued, repiqued, and capotted, by God!"

Lambeth tossed back his claret and said coldly, "I did not expect you to hold that spade, St. Ives. You are, I think, a very cool-headed player. It is unexpected in one of your—ah—temperament, my lord. I see I must take warning."

"Oh, aye, you'll not find a cooler player than St. Ives," agreed Lord Timothy. "How does it stand?"

"I fancy I have a slight advantage at this moment," drawled St. Ives. "But the evening is young yet, and Lambeth's luck began to change on that last hand. Do you care to continue, my lord?"

Lambeth found it impossible to draw back. His luck *had* started to change in that last hand, and it irked him beyond reason to be obliged to acknowledge defeat.

"Certainly, my lord, play on." He gathered the cards and began to shuffle them. "But you surprise me, my lord. I had thought to hear of your coming nuptials. Or have you had second thoughts? Not that I blame you, of course. If one can contrive to enjoy the—er—fruits of marriage without its obligations, one would be foolish to undertake it, wouldn't you say? Marriage is, after all, but cold comfort to a man on a long night!"

Several of the bystanders laughed, and one or two glanced at St. Ives, wondering what was behind the innuendo.

St. Ives retained his sprawled position. "You should certainly know, Lambeth," he said insultingly.

Someone snickered, and Lord Timothy glanced sharply at his nephew, but though Lambeth's face darkened with temper, he let it pass and after a moment the game continued.

In the next half hour it became clear to most observers that the game had subtly altered. St. Ives, as if he had only been trifling before, began to play brilliantly, a glint of something—it was hard to tell whether anger or excitement—in his blue eyes and a slight smile on his lips. He took advantage of every mistake his opponent made, scoring points on the slimmest of chances, and time and again tripped up his slower opponent by his choice of discards.

Lord Timothy, as if recognizing the signs of danger in his nephew, once bent to say something in an urgent undertone in St. Ives's ear, but he received only a lazy glance for his pains. He frowned, looking unusually irritable, then shrugged and accepted the entreaties of one or two of his friends to come and try a half hour with the dice cups.

Michael Staunton was not so wise. He, too, had come to observe the game, and after St. Ives had ruthlessly spoiled a major pique and succeeded in scoring a five-hundred-point rubber, he burst out, "St. Ives, for God's sake, have a care!"

Lambeth was indeed beginning to look nasty, but Staunton's voice had carried, and those present who were not already aware of the ongoing feud between Lambeth and St. Ives glanced over. A few, suspecting trouble, even hastily took their leave.

St. Ives glanced up at his cousin. "Again you interest yourself in my affairs, cousin!" he said shortly. "It would seem you grow a great deal too busy on my account."

Staunton indeed looked as if he regretted his outburst, and he would have spoken had not the proprietor, who had been watching the scene with growing apprehension, come up then. "My lords, I beg of you," he said, "have a care to what you are about! I desire to have no trouble here. I beg there will be none."

St. Ives said, with scarcely a glance at the proprietor, "And there will be none, if you take your fat carcass away! And by all means take my cousin here with you! Lambeth, I believe it is your deal."

Anthony stood wringing his hands in indecision, then sighed helplessly and went away. Staunton shook his head and strode off as well, drawing one or two sympathetic glances, but it was doubtful whether either of the two seated at the table even saw him go.

It was three o'clock, and nearly everyone else had grown tired and gone, except for the yawning waiters and Anthony, still hovering in the background, when Lambeth at last threw down his cards and said with scarcely disguised loathing, "Very well, I am done for! How much is it?"

St. Ives, without a flicker of expression, totaled the score. "I make it fifteen thousand."

Lambeth repeated it almost blankly. Then he looked up, his eyes suddenly focusing on St. Ives's curiously unweary countenance, and he said with a hint of violence, "I think you have achieved your objective, my lord! You did mean to goad me into losing more than I could afford to pay, did you not?"

"Oh, yes," said St. Ives negligently, pouring more brandy into his glass.

Lambeth resisted the impulse to fling the contents of his own glass into that sneering face. "Very well!" he grated. "What is it you want of me?"

St. Ives raised his black brows. "Why, I thought you knew. Your silence of course, my dear Lambeth."

Lambeth laughed suddenly. "What have you done with her? Bought her off, or merely foisted her onto someone else?"

St. Ives looked up, his expression no longer lazy. "The lady is shortly to become my wife. You are to forget all knowledge of that night, and if it should ever happen that you meet again—which I intend to take steps it does not—you will not betray by so much as a flicker of an eyelid that you meet for anything but the first time. Do I make myself clear?"

For once Lambeth was caught off guard. "Ah, but then your—er—betrothed and I are old friends," he said suggestively. "Didn't you know? You might even say that I—ah—was the first to discover her somewhat unexpected charms."

St. Ives, in one fluid movement, rose from his chair and grabbed Lambeth's cravat, jerking him up. Anthony started forward in alarm, and Lambeth was too startled to do more than gape, trying desperately to loosen the suddenly unmerciful constriction about his throat.

"You will not so much as speak my future wife's name again! Do I make myself clear?" St. Ives said softly. Then, as Anthony reached them, he thrust Lambeth away and sprawled again in his seat, swallowing a mouthful of brandy as if in need of something to take the bitter taste from his mouth.

Anthony was pleading with them to consider his position, but neither of them paid him the slightest heed.

Lambeth stood, breathing hard, one hand going automatically to straighten his mangled cravat, his eyes on St. Ives's face. After a moment he said, "And if I refuse?"

St. Ives glanced up. "I think you know the answer to

that. You will give me your word, in exchange for which
I will agree to forget all your present debts to me. At
this point I make it a little more than twenty-five thousand
pounds. I doubt that whatever enjoyment you would gain
by embarrassing me is worth so much."

Lambeth had recovered now. "You are mistaken!" he
said harshly. "God, how I hate you! And it would cause
you a great deal more than embarrassment, I think, particularly if you mean to marry the chit. I wonder why you
do mean to marry her. You could have gotten her for far
less if you'd a fancy for her. Fairfield wouldn't have been
difficult—if the price was right."

St. Ives straightened. "I have said you will leave her
out of this! However much you hate me, you are in no
position to lose such a sum to me. Your wife's trustees
may be inclined to look favorably on you at the moment,
but if you think they are likely to welcome this latest
debt, you do not know Sir Adrian. My grandmother, happily, does; and one word from her, on top of the information that you have managed to run through a good portion
of your wife's fortune in a little less than a year, will no
doubt make up his mind about the advisability of unwinding
the trust anytime before your wife reaches her thirtieth
birthday. How long is that? Five years?"

Lambeth knew himself defeated. He laughed and said
with loathing, "You are well informed, damn you! Obviously, you leave me no choice." Then his eyes narrowed.
"But you are wrong. I am not dissatisfied, you know. I
meant to ruin you, and I'm not sure I have not succeeded
beyond my wildest dreams. The thought of your marriage
to that chit will sustain me in my darker hours; and I have
a feeling it is a jest that will only grow sweeter as the
years pass. No, I am not dissatisfied! I wish you joy, and
I hope that she and that father of hers bleed you dry."

He rose and bowed. "And now, my lord, it has been a
long—and I hope you will forgive me—not particularly
pleasant evening. You can count on my compliance with
the terms of our—er—agreement. My compliments to
your betrothed."

XVII

Sylvie had a great many reasons to be grateful for the presence of the calm and steady Blackmer, but not the least of them, she discovered, was the measure of independence it gave her. Not even her godmother could object to an expedition made in the company of her groom, and it certainly made it easier to meet Mr. Strickland the next morning without a great many awkward explanations.

She had had little opportunity to speak to Blackmer yet, and, as they rode through the city in the early-morning cold, she said, "Oh, Joe, you can't know what it means to me to have you here. Are they making you comfortable?"

"Aye, they've done me well enough. Though I'm bound to own I don't think much of London stables, what I've seen of 'em," he said with a grin. *"Mews* they call 'em. More like cupboards if you ask me, but that's neither here nor there. Nor can I say I've taken a shine to Sir James's groom, particular. A smarmy kind of fool that don't ever say what he means." He spat expressively.

She gave a peal of laughter. "Oh, no, is he? He sounds exactly like James, who is very good and immensely proper, and sometimes I have to fight the temptation to stick a pin in him just to see if he'll deflate like a balloon."

"Aye, I suspected that was the way of it," said Blackmer. "He stepped out when I first came to make sure I wasn't going to contaminate his servants, most like, and he condescended to give me a word of warning that I was to take good care to see you came to no harm, or he'd know the reason why."

177

"Oh, no, he didn't! I can't imagine what possessed him, for he doesn't even like me, you know."

Blackmer switched the wad of tobacco in his mouth. "Officiousness, most like. He don't bother me, Miss Syllie."

She eyed him. "No—but I've been meaning to ask you. Why didn't you take offense when St. Ives told you the same thing?"

He scratched his head. "Well, I don't rightly know, Miss Syllie, and that's a fact. I don't deny that when he came up to the Hall I was in a fair way to forgetting myself, for I don't know when I've been so upset as when I learned you'd gone off with him. But when I went to see him, meaning to have the truth from him, he just looked at me and said straight out, 'Well, from what I can tell, you're the only master on the place, so if you've anything to say to me, say it!' Then he damned my soul to hell for letting you do such a harebrained thing—which I don't deny I deserve—and ended by offering me a drink."

He chewed reflectively. "I don't say he done right, and from what all I've heard he's a proper wild-un. But I can't help thinking, all in all, that I ain't sorry it happened. You can't tell me old Sir Prunes and Prisms back at Lady Bridlington's house won't see to it you're treated like a lady at last; and even though her ladyship's a bit like a mother hen that's got too many eggs to set, she's been kind to you and means to see you presented as you should be. I don't mind saying that when I saw you last night, looking so fine, it nearly made my heart burst." He grinned sheepishly. "Hinton says it's the work of the Lord, and while I don't go so far as to say that, I can at least sleep nights now, not wondering every minute what's to become of you."

She blinked back unaccustomed tears. "Oh, Joe. What would I do without you? But you—you *like* St. Ives, don't you?"

When he nodded, she couldn't help laughing. "Oh, I know. So do I. Isn't it ridiculous? Did he tell you I was to wed him?"

"Aye, he said so," said the groom. "I said happen I'd believe it when you told me yourself."

"Oh Joe!" she said again.

They had reached the park then, and no more was said, for Mr. Strickland greeted them on a showy gray. He complimented Sylvie on her seat, glanced at the groom curiously, then made her laugh by saying, "My congratulations, Miss Fairfield! I must confess I did not really expect to see you here after so late a night."

"Yes, but I am shockingly provincial. The truth is, there is nothing I like better than an early-morning gallop. But I think you couldn't quite believe I had been so impertinent as to ask you to meet me. I scarcely know how I dared it myself, only that you had been kind, and you seem fond of my Lord St. Ives."

"Miss Fairfield," he said, "I wonder if I might request that we use one of the lesser-known paths? I dare not think what would become of my reputation were I to be seen exercising at such an hour. *You* may be too new to London, but I fear I would never be able to live it down," he said comically.

She obediently turned her horse. "You are being nonsensical, I know. But tell me, does everyone—?" She hesitated. "Forgive me, but it sometimes seems that people in London care more for form than for substance."

"But of course, Miss Fairfield!" he said. "Take me, for example. I am noticed because I dress exquisitely and behave in a manner that any sensible English yeoman would think mad. I disdain exercise of any sort, I am bored, and I am often rude. But people copy me and look to me for advice. Do you think I would be in any way out of the ordinary if I were not precisely form without substance?"

She laughed. "Very well, sir! I can see that I shall have to study the picturesque. Shall I be rude or merely eccentric? Only I feel I should warn you, I doubt I have the courage to carry off too much eccentricity."

"Neither, Miss Fairfield," he said. "In fact, I think you may be the one exception to my rule. You have the makings of something far more interesting, and that is a truly natural personality."

"*I* do?" she asked in astonishment.

He smiled. "Yes, you, Miss Fairfield. You have a natural wit; you continually surprise one by saying exactly

what you think—something very rare in London, you may
believe me—and from what I can tell you have the
distinction of being the only female ever to cause my
poor friend St. Ives a moment's exertion. In fact, Miss
Fairfield, I predict a brilliant future for you!"

She had turned a little pink, but she met his eyes and
said, "I hope you are right, Mr. Strickland. For that is
precisely what I want."

"A brilliant future, Miss Fairfield?"

"Oh, I daresay your idea of a brilliant future is very
different from mine, sir. But what I desire is to—to
achieve a modicum of independence."

"And what do you think I can do to help, Miss Fairfield?" he inquired gravely.

She hesitated, then looked up mischievously. "Do you
know any widowers, Mr. Strickland?"

"Do you want one?"

She grinned. "Well, I do not have my heart set on a
widower, of course. Lady Bridlington says that in her experience widowers—at least wealthy ones—are never
hanging out for a wife."

He glanced quickly at her. "You are beginning to
interest me, Miss Fairfield! Forgive me, but the only
reason I can see why you might desire a husband is
because you oppose St. Ives's suit. Is he—er—aware of
your sentiments on the topic?"

"Mr. Strickland, you at least must know how disastrous
would be a marriage between us! Please believe that I
have no aspirations to be Lady St. Ives. Of course I have
told him so, repeatedly! But I think you know him well
enough to know what the merest hint of opposition does
to him. That is why I dared to hope you might be willing
to help me."

"I have no doubt such scruples are to your credit, Miss
Fairfield. But, forgive me, is there not perhaps a touch of
stubbornness on your own part as well? We are all agreed,
I think, that if a scandal is to be avoided you must marry
in the immediate future. St. Ives has shown himself not
only willing, but, as you say, determined, to wed you.
Surely, under the circumstances—?"

"He is determined now, Mr. Strickland," she said. "How
long do you think he would be content with such a match?"

"I begin to think you are a remarkable young woman, Miss Fairfield."

"It is not remarkable to be realistic, Mr. Strickland," she said. "You may even call it vanity, if you choose. I have no desire to compete with a succession of beautiful opera dancers, for we both know I must invariably lose."

He started to say something, then seemed to change his mind. "It would do no good, I suppose, to point out that the opera dancers mean nothing to him?"

"You are a good friend, Mr. Strickland," she said with a smile. "I think that too. When he finds someone he can love, he will give them up without a backward glance. Or, perhaps with only a few backward glances," she amended. "It would be unrealistic to expect him to reform too much all at once."

"Will you eat me, my child, if I say I think you are precisely what St. Ives needs?"

When she only smiled, he sighed. "Very well, but must it be a widower? You tempt me to offer myself as a suitable substitute. Opera dancers hold no lure for me, I promise you."

"No, no, only think how disillusioning it would be to see you brought to the level of other men, with grubby children pulling at your coattails?"

"The thought, I must confess, does strike a certain chill in me," he admitted. "Not that it would ever come to such a point. I feel sure my lifeless corpse would have been taken up from some frozen field long before the banns could be posted."

She frowned. "Oh, no. I must confess I had not thought of that. Is he likely to be very angry with you?"

"Yes, but we have already agreed, have we not, that we need not consider him! Only if he plants me a facer—which I fear is he apt to do, Miss Fairfield—and I am obliged to leave London in disgrace once it becomes known that Strickland had been engaging in a common brawl, I hope you will take pity on me and come visit me in my lonely exile."

"Yes, but you will not be obliged to leave town, you know! We need only put it about that you were set upon by footpads, and that you acquitted yourself quite nobly. Although," she said, "I do not think one would engage in fisticuffs precisely with footpads. But surely between us we can think of something."

He was amused at this betrayal of her knowledge of boxing cant. "Do you know, Miss Fairfield?" he murmured, "I have the oddest notion I shall rue the day I allowed you to embroil me in your schemes. I begin to think poor Nicky deserves you after all, for it is clear you have been sent as retribution from above. What am I to do if I discover any eligible widowers? Send them with a letter of introduction?"

"Oh, dear, it does sound cold-blooded, doesn't it," she said, "but there is no use my giving way to scruples now, or turning back over a mere lack of resolution. And if you persist in being so ungallant as to laugh at me, Mr. Strickland, I may change my mind and accept your offer, and then where would you be?"

"In the suds, Miss Fairfield!" he said. "It is plain I am no match for you."

Sylvie was well satisfied with her morning and I hoped she had found a friend. But she discovered that she was called upon to put the resolution she had boasted of to the test much sooner than she had anticipated.

She returned to Green Street to breakfast and was preparing to go out again on several errands for her godmother when James formally requested a few minutes of her time.

She was startled, for James rarely sought her out, but she allowed Saltish to take her pelisse and muff again, and she accompanied James into his study.

Once the door was shut behind them he took up a position before the fireplace and seemed uncertain of how to proceed. He stood looking at her for a moment, his manner so grave that she began to be alarmed. "What is it? Is something wrong with her ladyship?" she asked.

"As far as I am aware, Miss Fairfield, my mother enjoys her usual excellent health. I might add that when I saw her late last night she was in exceptionally high spirits."

She knew now why he was looking so grave, and could not help saying, "I see. But it was, after all, only one dance. Unwise, I agree." She smiled a little. "But then his lordship has never been noted for his wisdom."

"I wish I might share you lighthearted view of the matter, Miss Fairfield," James said, "but it seems clear that the Earl of St. Ives is indeed serious in his proposal of marriage. Might I inquire, Miss Fairfield, if you are still of the opinion that a marriage between you and his lordship is out of the question?"

"I have not changed my mind, sir," she said evenly.

He bowed. "I see. I would like to formally request then, Miss Fairfield, that you do me the honor of becoming my wife."

She could only stare at him in astonishment. "But you don't even *like* me!" she burst out.

"Believe me, Miss Fairfield," he said, "if I did not feel that we might find a modicum of mutuality—indeed, that we might look for a sanguinity not always to be found in marriages of our class, I would never have taken such a step, whatever the provocation."

"A modic—, yes, I see," she said weakly. "Is that what you desire in marriage?"

He looked surprised, then permitted himself a slight smile. "Ah, I can see I have startled you. In a normal situation I would myself consider that I have been too precipitate. One does not care to rush into a step of such magnitude. But I flatter myself that you are aware of my worth and that you must regard my suit favorably, even with gratitude, under the circumstances."

She sat staring at him stupidly. In her boastings that morning to Mr. Strickland, she had somehow never pictured James in the role of the unknown suitor. It was a respectable match; he was right that she could not afford to be too choosy; yet she discovered that when put to the test her resolution was not as strong as she had hoped.

"I—forgive me, but I don't know what to say! I had not gotten the impression that you—indeed, I would have said you disapproved of me," she said.

He put the tips of his fingers together and rocked a little on his heels. "I do not scruple to admit that I had grave doubts about my mother's befriending you, Miss Fairfield, but I am happy to say that you have shown yourself worthy of her regard. It is true that you possess a levity that betrays you at times into appearing more careless of convention than I could wish, but I do not hesitate to lay the fault on your upbringing, which has been disgraceful. In short, Miss Fairfield," he said indulgently, "I do not fear I shall ever have to blush for my wife. And I flatter myself that my own excellent example must correct any slight errors in your conduct in future."

"Such praise from you un—un*mans* me, sir," she said a little weakly. "May I request a little time before I give you my answer?"

"You will forgive me if I say that the sooner our engagement could be announced, the sooner we might both expect a cessation of attentions that must be as unwelcome to you as they are to me. I fail to see what there is to require any time on your part. I hope I am not overly vain, but I flatter myself—"

She interrupted before he could get that phrase out once more. "What is the real reason you have proposed? Is it because you desire to wed me, or merely because you wish to end the connection between Lord St. Ives and this household?"

He considered the question, then bowed his head. "Very well, Miss Fairfield, I will be frank with you. It was not my plan to marry at this time, nor would I normally look to the daughter of a man I can only consider an undesirable connection, but I think it best to put an end to the present situation and at the same time insure that your reputation remains unsullied by any breath of scandal. Once our betrothal is announced, not even my Lord St. Ives would dare to persist in his unwelcome and, I might add, impertinent attentions to you."

She smiled unwillingly. "I would not be so sure of that. You do not know my Lord St. Ives."

"I find no cause for amusement in the idea that he might persist in his attentions to a woman affianced to another, Miss Fairfield!"

"Even when it was he who had ruined her?" she inquired softly. Then, as James flushed, she smiled and shook her head. "Doesn't it tell you something about me, James, that I do understand his lordship, even though I disapprove of his quixotic gesture?"

"I think you allow your levity to betray you. If I did not know better, I would almost believe you were enjoying yourself in this disgraceful matter."

"That is just the point. You do not know me at all, James!" She grinned. "I think I *am* enjoying myself. Nothing ever happened to me before that was in any way an adventure, and I had begun to believe it never would. Did you never long for adventure, James? No, I can see you have not."

"You will forgive me if I find your present conduct as unbecoming as it is ill-advised!" said James stiffly. "I had thought you shared my sentiments. I can't believe that you only look upon this whole thing as an—an *adventure!* I begin to think you are right, Miss Fairfield. I do not know you. Indeed, it seems I have been grossly misled."

"I never attempted to mislead you, James. It was you who imputed your own motives to me."

"I can see that I gave you too much credit, Miss Fairfield. I should not have allowed myself to forget who your parent is!"

"That was unhandsome of you," she said cordially. "I have not cast aspersions on your character."

"You will allow me to hope you may not find yourself disappointed in your opinion of St. Ives!"

"No, I do not think I shall be disappointed. Enraged yes, but not disappointed. But you are wrong, for it is still not my intention to accept his offer."

"I hope when you find yourself with neither offer, you will not expect to look to me!"

"No, I would not come to you, James. And you should be grateful that I have prevented you from committing a grave error," she said. "Only think how unhappy you would have been to discover that I mean all the unconventional things I say!"

He bowed coldly. "I pray you will excuse me now, Miss Fairfield. I hope you will not have cause to regret this day's work. I can only say that I shall not."

She rose. "No, I shall not regret it. Indeed, you have taught me a valuable lesson, little though you know it. Pride—*insufferable* pride—is not the exclusive property of those with high rank. But I would advise you not to speak to your mother about this conversation."

"I assure you I wish only to forget it, Miss Fairfield!"

She laughed. "I am sorry to have made you so angry, but it is good to see that you can lose your temper. You ought to do it once a month, just to remind you that you are human like the rest of us! Good day, James. Thank you for a—a most interesting half hour. I see that there are some things I am not prepared to do, even for the pleasure of circumventing my Lord St. Ives! You have opened my eyes."

He held the door stiffly for her, a dark tide of color in his face. She sailed through and smiled at the patiently waiting Saltish. "Yes, now I am ready to go," she said. "It was nothing important after all. I expect to be back in time for luncheon."

XVIII

It might have done Sylvie a great deal of good to deflate James's pretensions, but, once she had time to consider, she was aware that she had refused an offer that would have enabled her to escape from St. Ives's web. Still, the thought of marriage to James was not to be borne, and she had every intention of forgetting the whole as soon as possible.

When she returned from her errands and saw St. Ives's curricle sweeping down the street behind a pair of chestnuts harnessed tandem-fashion, she willingly waited outside for him.

His groom jumped down and went quickly to the horses' heads, and then St. Ives himself climbed down. "Well, Miss Fairfield, have you recovered from last night's exertions?" he inquired.

"I do not consider dancing an exertion, my lord. Is that the newest way to drive—tandem?" she asked curiously.

"*I* do not follow fashions, Miss Fairfield. Nor would it be advisable for most drivers I know to try it."

She laughed. "That certainly puts me in my place!"

He stood looking down at her with an unexpectedly rueful smile. "It was, oddly enough, not my intention to put you in your place. Are you going in or out?"

"In," she said. "Did you come to see my godmother?"

"I came to see you, as you very well know," he said. "If you are not too cold, come for a drive."

She eyed the chestnuts longingly. "Well, all right, but I mustn't stay away too long. They are a beautiful pair, although I believe I prefer your grays."

He helped her up into his curricle. "A great many people prefer the grays, since they are the best team in London. But you will not find these too contemptible, I think."

She watched as he expertly rounded the corner. "No, they are not too contemptible," she agreed.

"Did you enjoy your success last night? I understand you kept both Horace Epping and Strickland tolerably well entertained. But a word of advice: if either is in your mind, you will have to look elsewhere. Both have been confirmed bachelors for years."

Her color rose a little. "I can see I shall have to cultivate your advice, my lord! It should save me a great deal of time."

"Has Bridlington proposed yet?" he asked. "He will, you know, if for no other reason than to prevent my tainted presence in his house."

She had to laugh. "Your conceit is only exceeded by your exaggeration of your own importance, my lord!"

"Am I wrong?"

"No, and for exactly the reason you said," she admitted. "But you have not asked what my answer was."

"No. I have no need to. You may be damnably stubborn, but you're no fool. Bridlington is an impertinent whipstraw —without the saving grace of being amusing."

"I am flattered, my lord," she said. "I thought you considered me every kind of a fool."

He grinned. "Only when I'm angry!"

She laughed, but shook her head. "By the by, why did you wish to see me, my lord? I know it was not to turn my head with flattery."

"To convince the world of my devotion, of course, Miss Fairfield!" he said. "It is well known that St. Ives never drives females about. That I have broken my own rule in your behalf must lend credence to the stories already circulating. Why did you consent to come?"

"I couldn't bear to miss an opportunity to drive tandem. Besides," she added, "I was angry with James. I knew nothing would more displease him than to know I had accepted an invitation from you."

He laughed and quirked an eyebrow at her. "No doubt! Did he tell you it was your duty to marry him to escape my debauched advances, or merely that any woman of sense must prefer his offer to the threat of scandal hanging over her head?"

"Both. But you misjudge him. I have his word for it that only his duty to protect his mother's goddaughter from your unwelcome attentions would prompt him to offer for one of my family."

"One had only to be acquainted with *his* father to realize how overrated respectability is," said St. Ives. "A more pompous, addlepated fool I've yet to meet. I hold no brief for your father, m'dear, but he has the virtue of being an open scoundrel. Between that and hypocritical old fools like Bridlington and my own father, I'll choose a scoundrel any day."

"Yes, but then you might be expected to," she pointed out.

"Oh, I'm not a scoundrel, my dear! Some might like to call me that to my face, but as long as I possess the title and the slightest portion of my fortune, they will not do so. It is the difference between your father and me. He has no money."

"You're very cynical, my lord," she said. "And there are a great many differences between you and my father. But at least you have never held my background against me."

"But then I might not be expected to!"

She laughed. "No, my lord, you are wrong. I have become perfectly aware of what it means to be a Staunton."

"I hope you do not mean to judge by me, Sylvie," he said. "No one would consider me an asset to my name, believe me!"

She shook her head. "I can see you will not be serious, my lord."

"I will be as serious as you like when you stop talking nonsense!" he retorted. "If I am to be praised for not behaving like a bigoted ass, you pay me no compliment!" He grinned down at her. "Besides, aren't we agreed I have no standards to maintain?"

"Does it give you pleasure to pretend that you are irreclaimable, my lord?"

He looked pained. "And that was the unkindest cut of all, my dear! I can bear to be called almost anything but a cock strutting on his own dunghill."

She laughed again. "It will do no good, I can see, to say that was not in the least what I meant! But where are we going?"

"Why? Does it matter?"

"No, only that if you are determined to be seen in my company, you might as well be of some use to me."

He put up his brows in amusement. "Where is it you wish to go?"

"Why, only to the House of Commons, my lord."

For the first time he was startled. "Good God! What the devil for?"

"Well, I was given to understand it is open to the public, but when Mary and I tried to gain admittance we were turned away at the door by a dreadful little door-keeper. And it occurred to me that he might not turn us away if you were to escort me."

"I imagine you didn't grease him in the fist," he said.

"Grease him in the—you mean *bribe* him?"

"Yes, Miss Innocence! And a handsome living he makes of it, I don't doubt. But you can't really wish to go to the House of Commons, you foolish child. I assure you nothing is duller."

"Certainly, I do," she corrected him, drawing on her gloves. "For I want to be able to write and tell Kendall all about it. I wish, of course, that Mr. Fox were still alive, for I would give a great deal to be able to hear one of his speeches, but I daresay it will be almost as good without him."

"What a strange child you are, Sylvie. What do you know of Mr. Fox?"

She put up her brows at his tone. "A good deal more than you, I shouldn't wonder. Kendall is a great admirer of his and has collected all of his speeches."

"Then you would be wrong!" he said. "Fox was a friend of mine. Probably the only politician I've ever known, as a matter of fact, that wasn't a damned insufferable prig—but then, no one of my uncle's set could ever be accused of that," he added. "A great deal else to their discredit, but never that."

"They may be prigs in your estimation," she said, stung, "but at least they are attempting to accomplish something with their lives."

He burst out laughing. "Most of which will only have to be undone tomorrow. But that was addressed to my account, I know. I am beginning to suspect you of being a bluestocking, my dear!"

"No," she said seriously, "for they are very bookish, and clever, and I have never been that. But I do think it an admirable thing to be a member of Parliament, however you may laugh, my lord."

"*I* am a member of Parliament," he pointed out wickedly.

"The House of Lords!" she said scornfully. "Do you even attend its sessions?"

He laughed again. "No, my little conscience, I don't. But I *will* take you to the Commons today if you have your heart set on it."

He was as good as his word, and he proved to be unexpectedly knowledgeable, pointing out the members and explaining some of the finer points of the debate. He took her to tea in the members' dining room and introduced her to several of the more prominent politicians, treating her indulgently, as if she were a child, or his younger sister, and she enjoyed the outing far more than she cared to admit.

Only when he left her on her godmother's front steps did their unexpected accord falter a little. He smiled, flicked her cheek with one finger, and said, "I will come for you at ten on Thursday morning to take you riding. I wish to see for myself that you are to be trusted on a horse in London."

She stiffened. "I do not believe I will be available at that hour, my lord."

His blue eyes frowned, and he did not pretend to misunderstand her. He started to say something, then grinned and took her hands. "Oh, very well! *Dearest* Sylvie, may I please have the pleasure of your company? I promise to take the greatest care of you and return you to your godmother uncorrupted and sound in limb. Does that satisfy you?"

She shook her head, but had to laugh. He grinned down at her for a moment, unmindful of Saltish, who had come to open the door; then he pinched her chin and was gone.

XIX

They did not need this latest expedition to fuel the gossip that was already rampant. By the morning after Lady Castlereigh's ball, almost everyone of note in London knew that St. Ives was up to another of his tricks. Few believed he could be serious, for those who had seen the object of his latest whim reported her scarcely pretty and very shy—and Fairfield's daughter? my dear—! People had come to expect almost anything from St. Ives over the years, but if he were so lost to what was due his position that he might contemplate such a misalliance, they knew that neither his grandmother nor his stepmother were likely to forget that a Staunton might look as high as he pleased for a bride. There were one or two high sticklers who would no longer countenance a match between their daughters and the wild young Earl of St. Ives, but the mothers who were ready to whistle such a fortune down the wind for the sake of principles were few and far between. Society had no illusions that if St. Ives ever chose to reform there were few doors that would remain closed to him.

Lord Timothy Desborough, one of the first to hear the tale, dismissed it with his usual insouciance, but when the opportunity arose, he ventured to drop a hint into his nephew's ear that it might be best to pay less attention to the lady in question.

The result of this sage counsel was perhaps not what Lord Timothy had anticipated. St. Ives had dropped in to see his uncle before going to one or another of his clubs, and he said with a grin, "All over town, is it?"

Timothy frowned at him. "You'll catch cold at that, m'boy. You've not asked my advice—"

"You're right, but when did that ever stop you?"

"Stick to the bits of muslin, that's my advice! This one ain't in your line, is she? Nothing but a chit of a girl, by the sound of it. She'll have you in a parson's mousetrap before you know what's happening if you don't take care."

"I take it you speak from experience, uncle? You begin to interest me after all."

"Lord, yes!" admitted Timothy with a grin. "Before your time, that one was, but she was a devilish taking little thing. Met her at Bath before Prinny had made Brighton all the rage. I was dancing attendance on Mama while she drank the waters, so what was I to do to fill the time but fall in love? If m'mother hadn't taken a pet and decided the waters weren't fit to drink, it might have been all over for me. But she was a beauty, which this chit of yours ain't, by all accounts. Fairfield's daughter, too. I don't like the fellow, but the family's respectable enough. You can't trifle with chits of that sort without creating a scandal."

St. Ives's mouth twisted mockingly. "Hold it, you go too fast for me, Timothy. Are you concerned that I shall be forced into marriage or that I'll ruin the girl's reputation?"

"Both," said his lordship.

"You seem convinced that I am unable to handle my own affairs," he remarked. "I wonder where you obtained this touching faith in your own perspicacity, uncle?"

"Aye, I know you when the devil's in you," Lord Timothy said, unimpressed. "Just have a care, is all I say. I've already warned you, you'll go too far one of these days. By the by, how'd you make out with Lambeth the other night?"

"I achieved what I was after," replied his nephew.

Timothy frowned. "I suppose it would do no good to warn you any more in that direction?" he said. "Only keep that fool of a cousin of yours quiet! If you've got to carry on a feud with Lambeth, it don't help to have him calling attention to it with his bungled attempts to interfere."

St. Ives's eyes came up, then he looked away again. "Yes, I seem to have a surfeit of busybody relatives," he said. "But you may set your mind at rest, Timothy. I know exactly what I am doing."

The second of St. Ives's family to receive news of his latest flirt received it with less equanimity. Lady St. Ives would have been inclined to take it all in light part—or merely by complaining bitterly to her intimates that she was constantly being greeted by gossip concerning her stepson—had she not received a letter that led her to place a more serious construction upon the whole.

Her old friend, Lady Yoxall, had written to say that she had been present at Lady Castlereigh's that night, and, although she did not like to disturb her dear Laura unnecessarily, she was by no means as certain as the rest of London appeared to be that St. Ives was merely amusing himself. St. Ives might be merely *flirting* (such a dreadful modern habit, of course), but she prided herself on being a very good judge of human nature, and she did not think that that was what was in the mind of any of the parties involved. It seemed more likely that Lady Castlereigh had invited the girl expressly at his lordship's request, for that lady had been most kind to the girl and had even presented Mr. Epping to her. Certainly Lady Castlereigh had never been an intimate of that silly Bridlington woman, and as for St. Ives, he had come to the party only to dance with the girl, for he could not have been in the room above five minutes before he sought her out, and he made no attempt to remain for even one dance with anyone else.

And, although it was not commonly known, Lady Yoxall had reason to believe that the old dowager duchess approved of the girl, for Mrs. Burwell had actually seen the young lady in question leaving the dowager's house in the duchess's own carriage. She hoped that her dear friend would not think she was being presumptuous, but she felt she would not rest comfortably until she knew Lady St. Ives was aware of what was happening. She remained hers, affectionately, etc., etc.

Laura was moved to bestir herself to the point of setting forth for London for the second time in a month. It might be expected that she would have welcomed the news of her stepson's possible coming nuptials, but anyone who suspected that did not know her ladyship. Her motives for wanting St. Ives to marry were wholly selfish and not a little spiteful. His dissolute life was a convenient sin to throw up at him when all else failed her. After all, he had a duty to his name to beget an heir, and his failure to marry was all of a piece with his failure to conform to any other canon of decent behavior.

But the news that he might actually be contemplating such a step, and to such a partner, stunned her ladyship. If she had ever stopped to consider the question, she would have been hard put to say what kind of girl she desired her stepson to marry. She had no matchmaking instincts; she was not forever attempting to pair him off with the daughter of one of her friends or the other; and she had even been known to say that she would not do any young lady with whom she was acquainted such a disservice. St. Ives would prove the worst of husbands for a gently bred girl with even a modicum of decorum. But Fairfield's daugher—! She might have been moved now and again to say that he might as well choose his bride from the class of women he frequented, since no decent girl would have him, but the thought of a Staunton allying himself with any but an equally old and honored name filled her with repugnance. The Fairfield's were the merest commoners—the baronetcy was only second generation, after all—and the present baronet had been rolled up for years and was little more than a hanger-on among that set of gentlemen who seemed to care little about whom they mixed with in their pursuit of sport and pleasure. She would not put it past St. Ives to marry just to spite her, but if he thought he was going to marry this girl without her having a great deal to say on the subject, he was very much mistaken.

She therefore descended bag and baggage upon her parents and subsequently enjoyed a comfortable evening closeted with her mother and abusing her stepson's manners and morals before sallying forth to Mount Street the next morning.

She found St. Ives over a late breakfast as usual, looking rather disheveled, with the morning *Post* propped up against the coffeepot before him. He looked up, then returned to his paper once more, saying only, "You wasted little time, I see. Will you have something to eat, or merely coffee?"

His calm acceptance of her presence seriously alarmed her. It had not occurred to her that he actually intended to marry Fairfield's daughter, and she said with unaccustomed meekness, "Coffee, please," and accepted the seat he pulled out for her.

He poured her a cup and handed it to her. "Well, do you not wish to know if I mean to wed Sylvie Fairfield? That is why you came, is it not?"

She turned pale at this directness, discovering she no longer wished to know. It had not struck her until this moment that were St. Ives to wed she would become the dowager countess, and the Priory would have a new mistress. For one second she was paralyzed with fear. It caused her to laugh, in a manner very unlike herself, and say playfully, "I should deserve your contempt if I had no more sense than to place credence in a story anyone must know for sheer nonsense. But if Kitty is to make her come-out this spring, it is time I was thinking of gowns, so I brought her in for fittings with Mama's dressmaker."

He looked at her. "Kitty will have her coming out this spring only if Miss Fairfield, after we are wed, consents to have my chit of a little sister living with us."

Lady St. Ives, for once in her life, was bereft of words. "You cannot—," she gasped. "Even *you* would not—! No! It is unthinkable! I will not permit it! And if you are so foolish as to contract such an alliance, I give you my word mine is one foot that will never cross your threshold! No, nor will I permit Kitty to do so! I am still somebody, I hope, and I would advise you to think well before you undertake such a step!"

Then she realized she had gone too far. His expression was so still she was alarmed despite herself. He spoke then as if she were a child or someone who was hard of hearing. "You will receive my wife, and you will do so with every appearance of complaisance, or I can promise you will regret it every day for the rest of your life. Need I remind you that it is Kitty's generous allowance that has allowed you to live so handsomely; that I am the one who pays for your servants and provides you with horses and carriages. You would never set foot in another house of mine for as long as I live: that includes this one, the Priory, and the house in Bath where you presently reside so comfortably. I have allowed you a great deal of latitude and put up with your petty complaints and sly innuendos, but I give you my word, Laura, if I ever discover that you have made a single derogatory remark about Miss Fairfield, or given any of those overfed, overpampered excuses for women that you call friends so much as an indication that you are not completely delighted with my bride, you will find out exactly how much of an enemy I can be!"

She stared at him, her mouth a little open. She had never heard that tone of voice from him before. If he were suddenly to estrange himself from her, she would be the one to suffer, and she knew it. Without his financial support and the use of his houses she could manage to live, for her jointure was a generous one; but she had always thought of that money as a nest egg, and she had been required to touch very little of it. She doubted whether she could support herself in the manner to which she had become accustomed.

As for St. Ives marrying and absolving himself in the eyes of the world (for she had no illusions about that, particularly if he had the approval of the dowager duchess), it did not bear thinking of. She did not wish to give up her role as the outraged and injured victim of his depravity. No, the marriage must be stopped, no matter the cost!

St. Ives said now, very softly, before any half-formed plans could take shape in her mind, "I would think carefully, ma'am, before you decide to war with me."

For a moment she looked old and rather pitiful, but it was a weakness she permitted herself only briefly. She regained control and stood up, every inch the grande

dame. "I suppose you expect me to wish you joy in your
coming nuptials! And I suppose it is no more than I could
expect from you, after all! You will forgive me if I do
not feel well enough to call upon your—prospective
bride—before the wedding. I trust you will let me know
when it is to be?"

His eyes were hard. "No, I will not subject her to
that ordeal until it is absolutely necessary," he said. "But
I will expect you to pay her every observance once the
engagement has been formally announced. I *trust* your
health will be sufficiently recovered by then. And since
you have, by your harebrained dash to town, placed
exactly the construction on the affair you were most
anxious to avoid, I also trust you will remember what I
have said."

He had unobtrusively pulled the bell by his side, and
he looked up now and added smoothly, "Ah, yes, Chelmsford, her ladyship is just leaving. Please show her out."

Chelmsford quickly hid a smile and bowed respectfully
to her ladyship. "Yes, my lord. This way, your ladyship."

Lady St. Ives, bright spots of humiliation in her cheeks,
strode out of the room followed by the butler, who hadn't
found himself so much in charity with his lordship for
years.

The third of St. Ives's relatives to receive the news
took it, like Lord Timothy, with a grain of salt, but after
careful consideration he, too, was moved to see for
himself exactly what was behind it. Michael Staunton was
enjoying a leisurely breakfast in one of his clubs when
a young gentleman of cherubic countenance burst in on
him. "I say, Michael," said Lord Somercote cheerfully,
seating himself and blithely taking a sausage from his
friend's plate. "Better look to your interests. It seems
as if St. Ives may throw in the towel at long last."

It could be supposed that the conduct of his cousin had
caused him a great deal of embarrassment over the
years, but Michael had seldom been known to complain
publicly. Indeed, his interference the other night had
been very unlike him, and had caused one or two thoughtful persons to place a more serious construction on the
feud between St. Ives and Lambeth than they had pre-

viously been inclined to do. Michael had even confessed
to a friend that he had behaved stupidly and succeeded
only in calling attention to the very thing he wished
to avoid.

He received the news calmly, saying only, "It is certainly too early for you to be in your cups, Chuffy, so I
can only suppose you have either got the story wrong,
or my cousin is once more playing off one of his tricks.
Even St. Ives would not wed one of his fly-by-nights, and,
since that is the only class of female he consorts with,
I do not think I am likely to hear of his betrothal any
time soon."

"Aye, well, that's where you're wrong!" said Lord
Somercote. "It's all over town that St. Ives is pursuing
a chit who is staying with Lady Bridlington, and bets are
already being placed in White's on whether he's going
to be caught at last."

"One of his flirts!" said Michael indifferently.

"*You* may call it that!" retorted his lordship. He grinned
suddenly. "Fact is, I did myself. But I'm damned if I've
ever seen St. Ives set up a schoolroom chit—with no
more than passable looks and less conversation—as his
latest flirt! Fact!" At Michael's sudden frown, he added,
"Saw her myself this morning. Well enough, I suppose,
if you like little brown mouses with big disapproving dark
eyes, but Lord, whenever did St. Ives? If he ain't serious,
what's he up to then, for he's taken no pains to hide it
from the world. Went to Lady Castlereigh's the other
evening seemingly for no other reason than to stand up
once with her, and he took her riding in the park this
morning. Mind you, *I* don't say he'll come up to scratch
at last, but a great many others are beginning to say it."

Michael betrayed no more interest in the subject,
merely recommending his young friend to go soak his
head until he was sober and continuing to eat his breakfast with unimpaired calm. Lord Somercote, disgusted,
went away to find a livelier audience.

Once he was gone, however, Michael bethought himself of an invitation to Lady Wolverhampton's rout that
evening. He had planned to forgo it, but now he thought
he might have a look-in after all. Lady Wolverhampton
was a great friend of Lady Castlereigh.

BOOK TWO

XX

Thus it was that Lady Wolverhampton, envisioning only a modest little party, found herself with a social triumph on her hands. Long before Lady Wolverhampton had left her place at the entrance to her ballroom, it was clear that the evening was to be accorded the highest accolade: people complaining that it was a dreadful crush, with scarcely room to breath.

That a great many people had come merely to see St. Ives's latest flirt mattered not at all to Lady Wolverhampton. Indeed, she could have embraced that erratic young peer, and she made a point of being extremely kind to Lady Bridlington's young protégée. She did not suppose she would be actually lucky enough to obtain St. Ives's presence as well, for though she had certainly sent him a card, they had never had more than a nodding acquaintance and he had never accepted one of her invitations. But she was a practical woman, and she did not mean to be too greedy. It was enough that the *haut ton* was filling her house, drinking quantities of the expensive champagne she had hurriedly ordered in place of the inferior vintage she had intended before it became clear that her modest little party was likely to be transformed into the event of the season.

The center of all this had, surprisingly, turned out to be a rather ordinary young woman of no particular beauty and a shy, if not unpleasing, manner. She was certainly no toast, but she had a natural dignity that was appealing, and she did not put on any airs. Miss Fairfield thanked Lady Wolverhampton most properly for inviting her and said when asked that she had never been farther than Cambridgeshire before, and yes, she was certainly enjoying her stay in London. Lady Bridlington had been so kind to have her, and she had met a great many others who had been equally kind.

Lady Wolverhampton had not expected to find St. Ives's latest flirt a shy little mouthful, and she found herself inclined to revise her earlier opinion that St. Ives was merely amusing himself again. Fairfield's daughter, eh? Well, well, it could be worse, after all; and no one was likely to forget that Lady Wolverhampton was one of the first hostesses to obtain Miss Fairfield's presence.

Lady Wolverhampton was not the only one present that evening who was inclined to place a more serious construction on the matter after laying eyes on Miss Fairfield. Most found little to praise in her, aside from a certain graveness of manner, but oddly enough this seemed only to confirm them in the belief that St. Ives must be serious at last. However, there were a discerning few who, after making Miss Fairfield's acquaintance, pronounced her a young girl with more than the usual wit and a certain quiet charm that was as refreshing as it was unexpected.

Mr. Horace Epping was among the latter. He danced with Sylvie early in the evening, and he ventured to say, as they took their places, "Well, Miss Fairfield, I really did not know when we met that you were so soon to become famous."

"*In*famous is the word I believe you are seeking, sir."

He laughed. "Poor Miss Fairfield! Do you dislike it?"

"Not at all," she lied. "You must know I have come in for a great deal of attention I would certainly not otherwise have had. I must be grateful for his lordship's attentions, however brief they may prove to be."

Mr. Epping found himself unexpectedly relieved that she did not seem to nurse improbable ambitions in that direction, but he was more curious than ever to know what was behind the mystery. "You remind me once more of your good sense, Miss Fairfield," he said, "but your opinion that St. Ives is merely amusing himself is no longer universally shared, I believe." Then he surprised himself still more by saying, "If you had been the usual little beauty with more hair than wit, Miss Fairfield, no one would have been in the least amazed by St. Ives's interest. But you are not in his typical style, you know."

"You mean because I am plain and a nobody, they believe St. Ives must be serious?" she asked in amusement.

He liked her better than ever. "You will forgive me, Miss Fairfield. A great many people will say you are plain because they do not see beyond their own noses, but if St. Ives has been able to see that you are an unexpectedly lovely young woman, then I like him the better for it. I had not previously believed him capable of so much discernment."

"I think I have never had a compliment I value more, Mr. Epping," she said. "Thank you."

His eyes began to twinkle. "Unless I am much mistaken, you are going to be receiving a great many compliments in the future, Miss Fairfield. Whatever people may think of you, I have a feeling they will not be indifferent. It is, perhaps, a gift worth far more than mere beauty."

The dance ended then and he took her back to her godmother, saying with a grin, "And still I have not discovered what you think of our Mr. Lawrence. You must take pity and promise me another dance before you are quite besieged, or I fear I shall not sleep a wink tonight."

If Sylvie was not precisely besieged, she had the satisfaction of dancing with a great many gentlemen after that. And if she was unaware that any of them were widowers, she thought that a few went away with a different opinion of her than what they came with.

For her own part she could not say that she was having any success in her plans. The days were slipping past, and though she had met a great many gentlemen, none had made more than a fleeting impression on her. She was aware that she was viewing each as if through St. Ives's mocking blue eyes, and she became furious with herself and with him. It did no good to remind herself that she was in no position to be too fussy. Yet she could not envision spending the rest of her life with any of the gentlemen she had met so far.

She knew she was being ridiculous, for any strange man must seem unlikely at first; but she was also honest enough to admit that no man could hope to compete with St. Ives. If she allowed his specter to stand between her and every man she met, she might as well admit defeat.

She was standing with her godmother after the first supper interval before they went back into the ballroom, when she became aware that she was being observed by a tall, grave young man who looked faintly familiar, and for a moment she was visited by her old nightmare that he might have been one of those present that night at her father's house. But when she colored and lifted her chin, he came forward immediately.

Lady Bridlington's attention had been diverted by two old acquaintances, and he was able to say with a very charming smile, "I beg your pardon, ma'am! That was inexcusable of me I know, but you see, you had been pointed out to me, and I fear I was startled enough to forget my manners." He grinned and shook his head. "Ah, and I fear that must make it even worse! I can only attempt to recover myself by pointing out that we—we share a mutual acquaintance. I am St. Ives's cousin, you know, Michael Staunton."

She knew now why he looked familiar, for there was indeed a resemblance between the two. She colored a little. "I see. Am I to understand it was his lordship who pointed me out to you?"

"No, of course it was not! I should perhaps warn you that my cousin and I are not often on the best of terms."

"Then you merely came to satisfy yourself as to whether the rumors are true or not?"

He spread out his hands. "I ask you, Miss Fairfield, is that fair? Is that right? I have already apologized for my clumsiness! Must I go away again in abject disgrace?"

She laughed then, unexpectedly liking his open countenance and easy manners. "No, Mr. Staunton, and I apologize! It is only that I—"

He gave her his charming smile, and she found herself responding.

"Knowing my cousin, ma'am, I can imagine. Shall I compound my impertinence by saying that now that I have met you, I no longer credit the rumors?"

"You *are* frank, Mr. Staunton."

His eyes twinkled down at her. "I shall risk being thought disrespectful toward the head of my family by saying that I don't believe St. Ives can have met with any encouragement on your part. If I could believe that my cousin had the good taste to prefer you to his usual style of female, I would be very happy, I assure you."

She looked at him curiously, and when he requested the pleasure of the next two dances, she willingly agreed. Now that she had the opportunity to observe him, the resemblance between him and his more vital cousin was slight. Michael Staunton seemed to possess an openness and a hint of humor in his eyes that St. Ives lacked. And if he was far from being as handsome as St. Ives, he was also less arrogant, and that fact did him no particular disservice in her eyes. She wondered if this were the cousin St. Ives had spoken of. He looked precisely the sort of solid, well-mannered young man an old and proud gentleman might prefer to his own wild son.

Having led her out on the floor, Mr. Staunton smiled down at her. "Having begun so badly, ma'am, I hardly know where to go now. I scarcely dared hope you would consent to dance with me. I am not usually so maladroit, I assure you."

"That is certainly a dilemma, sir," she agreed. "No doubt the correct topic at this point in our acquaintance should be either the heat in the ballroom or the great number of persons present."

He laughed. "Yes, it is very warm, and Lady Wolverhampton always packs far too many persons into her rooms, and I think you are laughing at me, Miss Fairfield! On second thought, you are right. We should not neglect any of the steps if our acquaintanceship is to continue."

She was a little startled. "Is our acquaintance to continue, Mr. Staunton?"

He met her eyes. "I hope so, Miss Fairfield. It is up to you to tell me that I have not given you a complete disgust of me."

She was thrown a little off guard by his candor. She liked him, but she was not certain if he could possibly be as serious as he sounded. After a moment she said, "No, of course not, Mr. Staunton. But your own frankness encourages me to hope I might adopt a similar attitude. Something his lordship once said led me to believe—did you perhaps grow up with your cousin?"

"Yes, but I was never up to his lead. I am the elder by a few years, but I must confess I seldom succeeded in having the slightest influence on my wild young cousin."

She smiled. "I doubt that few people have ever had much influence on his lordship. Do you live in London?"

"Part of the year only, Miss Fairfield. I have estates in Berkshire that occupy more of my time than I would sometimes like. Do I understand this is your first visit to the City?"

After that they talked easily on a variety of topics without referring to St. Ives again. She thought he showed himself to be a man of both sense and considerable understanding, and her liking for him grew. When the dance ended, he thanked her with a warmth in his eyes that told her he was not merely being polite, and when he requested the privilege of waiting upon her and her godmother in the morning to make sure they had recovered from the night's exertions, she assented readily.

He did not remain long with her after that, but bowed and made his way through the crowds, smiling at someone here, stopping there to say a word or two to someone else. She watched him thoughtfully, not quite aware she was doing so, until a mocking voice at her elbow said, "Very touching! I see my cousin concerns himself in my affairs, as usual!"

She had not expected to see St. Ives, but she should have learned by now not to predict his actions. "I had rather thought your cousin was interesting himself in his own affairs, my lord."

His eyes narrowed. "A word of advice, my dear! You would be wise not to look in that direction."

"And you are being nonsensical, my lord," she said,

"I only met Mr. Staunton for the first time this evening; although I must confess that I liked him and will readily meet him again."

"Come! I want to talk to you!" he said, taking her by the wrist. He ignored the stares they were attracting and led her across the room to the door of the ballroom.

Short of creating a worse scene, she saw no way to prevent him. She allowed herself to be drawn out into the hall, her temper rising. The butler and a couple of lackeys looked up, but St. Ives ignored them in his usual arrogant fashion, and he had nearly drawn her into a little room opposite the staircase when there was a sudden commotion below them on the stairs.

A stout gentleman of indeterminate years, accompanied by two other gentlemen, was coming up the steps. It could be seen that all three had a great deal to drink, for they were arguing loudly about something. One of the gentlemen said, "Tell you what, let's go to Anthony's. You like Anthony's. Nothing but a bunch of flats to be found here."

The stout gentleman said, "Devil take it, think I don't know it's flat here! I've come to see that chit of my nephew's and I ain't leaving until I've done so! Where's the—oh, there you are!" he said, catching sight of the butler rapidly bearing down on them. "Take our hats and coats, there's a good fellow. No need to worry about invitations. Know Lady Wolverhampton well. Not the least bit of trouble in the world."

St. Ives, with an expression of disgust, released Sylvie's wrist and strode forward. The stout gentleman, catching sight of him, blinked and said happily, "Nicky, just the fellow I want! Come to see this chit of yours. These pudding-hearted fellows would have nabbled off if I had let them!"

St. Ives looked grim, and one of the gentlemen accompanying Lord Timothy tugged at the other's sleeve and whispered something in his ear. The other, in what he apparently imagined to be a whisper, pulled away and said drunkenly, "Good God! Even St. Ives wouldn't call out his uncle, you fool!"

St. Ives said in a dangerous voice, "I am honored by your confidence, Mainwaring. Now get Timothy the hell out of here before he brings the whole ballroom out upon us!"

But Lord Timothy had spied Sylvie and was making his erratic way forward. He executed an exquisite bow and said punctiliously, "Delighted to make your acquaintance, my dear. I am Desborough, you know." He halted abruptly then and leaned to peer at her in the dim light.

"Good God!" he said, sobering fast. "*You* can't be that chit of—"

"If you call her that 'chit of St. Ives' once more, you old fool, I *will* call you out!" St. Ives said savagely.

Timothy ignored this and said sternly, "Am I to take it this *is* Miss Fairfield?"

"You may take it any way you like!" snapped St. Ives.

Sylvie intervened then. "Yes, my lord, I am Sylvie Fairfield," she said evenly.

"Then the cat's in the cream now, dear boy," said Lord Timothy. "You'll have to marry her."

"I have every intention of marrying her!" answered St. Ives in a goaded voice. "But it was not my intention to announce it to every gossip gathered in this house!"

"Good Lord, no! Send in a notice to the *Gazette*, that's what you want to do, dear boy. There's been enough gossip already."

Sylvie, allowing the tension of the evening to get the better of her at last, most regrettably giggled, bringing both pairs of eyes back to her. St. Ives, fast losing patience with all of them, said, "And that's enough out of you, my girl!"

"No it ain't!" retorted Lord Timothy. "You needn't think you can run roughshod over the girl. If he tries it, my dear, he'll have me to answer to, and so I promise you. Now, if you will permit me, I will call on you soon to offer my formal felicitations. Know Lady Bridlington well, you know. My dear." He kissed her hand gracefully and, gathering his companions, sailed out with unimpaired dignity.

"Oh, my God!" said St. Ives in disgust. His grip on her wrist tightened. "We'd best go before some other fool descends on us."

Sylvie, still tending to levity, said, "You needn't think

you can run roughshod over me anymore, my lord! I have only to tell your uncle!"

"You'll need more than his protection if you don't take care, you wretched child!" he said. "What the devil am I going to do with you?"

"Leave me to my own devices!"

He stood looking down at her, a strange expression in his eyes. "When you have no more devices than a babe in arms? I think not, little sparrow. And I am no longer certain I would if I could."

When she only gaped up at him, his mood changed again and he said, very much in his old manner, "You are coming to the Priory over Christmas. We will announce our betrothal then."

"I fear I must decline this offered treat, my lord. I have said I will not marry you; nor will I come to your house."

"I thought you would say that. That is why I took the precaution of enlisting your godmother's support while you flirted with my cousin!" he said. "Superior tactics, my dear! You really didn't suppose your godmother would miss the opportunity to spend the holidays at an earl's principal seat, did you?"

"It ill becomes you to sneer at my godmother, my lord."

"I don't sneer at her. I merely use her folly to gain my own ends."

She suddenly felt very tired. "I think it is time we returned to the ballroom, my lord."

"You are an ungrateful girl!" he said. "I have not exerted myself much in my life to be kind; practically never, before I met you. But you do nothing but throw it back in my face."

She could not help smiling a little. "I was not aware that it was *kindness* you had in mind, my lord."

He shrugged. "Apparently I was mistaken. But I am not so blind that I have not seen you are homesick. I thought you would enjoy the Priory."

She was astonished, but he had already turned away. She followed him back into the ballroom, thinking she would never understand him.

And when, much later that night, she at last fell asleep,

it was only to dream that St. Ives and his cousin were each pulling her between them while Lady Bridlington and the dowager duchess took sides in the background, urging her to choose, and Mr. Epping called out to her that both only wanted her because she was plain.

XXI

When St. Ives called for her the next morning, he was in his usual mood, half teasing and half mocking. He rode up on a beautiful chestnut and said to Blackmer, "Has she adjusted to the traffic yet?"

The groom grinned. "Oh, you don't need to bother your head about Miss Syllie—Miss Sylvie, I *should* say, o'course!" he amended properly. "I ain't—not since she was five and I threw her on her first pony. I've seen many a man that wasn't up to her lead, and that's a fact. At home to a peg in the saddle she is, your lordship."

St. Ives turned to observe her then, her small gloved hands very capable on the reins. "Do you drive?" he asked curiously.

Her color had risen under his scrutiny, but she smiled and shook her head. "No—at least nothing but the farm gig, and I don't consider that. You, I have no doubt, are a member of the Four Horse Club. I confess that has always been an ambition of mine."

He grinned at her. "Well, I don't promise to get you elected to the FHC, but I'll teach you to drive a four-in-hand if you like. Not in London, however. We will have to wait until you come to the Priory at Christmas."

She had been pink with pleasure at the prospect, but she said politely then, "Yes, of course, my lord. I shall look forward to it—when I come to the Priory."

She spurred forward, leaving them both behind, offering St. Ives an excellent opportunity to observe exactly how much at home to a peg in the saddle she really was.

Blackmer grinned and remarked, "Happen you've more of a fight on your hands than you think, my lord."

St. Ives looked at him for a moment, then rode after her, vouchsafing the groom no answer.

Despite this inauspicious beginning, those who were energetic enough to have been present in the park at that unfashionable hour were treated to a fascinating spectacle. St. Ives rode attentively beside her for the better part of an hour, and she did not give the appearance of being at all shy with him. Indeed, the observer would have said that she kept him well entertained, for several schoolroom parties, as well as old Mrs. Billingshurst, who each morning was driven once around the park at that precise hour, heard him give a shout of laughter at one point, to which Miss Fairfield tossed her head and replied something before riding on. Yes, it had proved a most profitable morning, and it did not take long for this latest tidbit to reach the public's ears.

Sylvie, happily unaware of this, was enjoying herself. The sun was shining down on them, making the park, with its bare trees, sparkle in a way that reminded her of home. A brisk breeze put the color into her cheeks and whipped a stray strand of hair or two free from its confining hat; and St. Ives was an excellent rider.

"I had meant to thank you before now, my lord. Because of you I find myself so forward with the world I can promise you I am feeling quite wealthy."

He looked startled, and she grinned. "Perhaps I should express my thanks to your trainer." When he still looked puzzled, she said demurely, "Blackmer put a pound on your mare, Little Incognita, for me. I had forgotten about it, but he brought my winnings when he came, and they will come in very handy."

It was this remark that produced the shout of laughter that had so startled old Mrs. Billingshurst.

"Little wretch!" he said.

She laughed. "Yes, but it is far less indelicate of me to mention it than it was of you to name her that. *That* must certainly shock any woman of sensibility. Was she named for the highflier you took from Lord Lambeth?"

His smile disappeared. "Who told you of that?"

She frowned at his change of tone. "Why, it hardly matters, does it? It is only that I hope she was a very beautiful female."

His expression relaxed. "She is!" he said. "And you are a minx. By the way, how well do you know Lambeth?"

"I had thought that any acquaintance with my Lord Lambeth is to know him too well," she said, and then she deliberately changed the subject and the remainder of the ride passed on amicable terms.

When he had seen her into the house in Green Street again, St. Ives walked back down the steps and eyed Blackmer who was standing at the horses' heads. "What happened between Miss Fairfield and Lambeth?" he demanded.

Blackmer spat. "Nothing much," he said. Then, at St. Ives's expression, he relented. "That don't mean it couldn't have, though, if Hinton hadn't happened to be nearby."

St. Ives began to look grim. "Did that sort of thing happen much?"

"No, nor it shouldn't've happened that time," admitted Blackmer, "if I hadn't been caught unawares. We usually took good care to see she didn't come next or nigh 'em when her Papa had guests."

St. Ives's blue eyes were suddenly hard. "It appears I have more to place at Fairfield's door than I had yet believed. You will oblige me by seeing to it that neither he nor Lambeth approach her again without my knowledge."

If he thought the order strange coming from one of my lord's reputation, Blackmer did not reveal it. "You've no cause to doubt me, my lord."

St. Ives, himself conscious of the incongruity in the situation, grinned then a little ruefully. "And you've every cause to doubt me."

"Mayhap, my lord," said Blackmer. "And mayhap not. And it was me told her about the filly you took away from Lord Lambeth. I'll bid you good day, my lord."

Sylvie had, in the meantime, discovered that she had an unexpected visitor. Saltish informed her as soon as she came in that Lady Catherine Staunton had called to see her and was even now waiting in the blue saloon.

Sylvie was startled, but she went in without stopping to put off her riding habit.

A young girl was seated on the sofa turning through the pages of a periodical, but at sight of Sylvie her blue eyes widened and she jumped to her feet and said ingenuously, "But are—*you* cannot be Miss Fairfield?"

Sylvie, uncertain of what she had expected herself, could not help but be amused by this artless speech. She came forward and held out her hand. "Yes, I am Sylvie Fairfield. It was—it was very kind of you to call on me, but where is your Mama, or your maid? I have been in London only a short time, I know, but even I have learned that you should not have come alone. Have you come to see for yourself what all the gossip is about?"

"Yes," said Lady Catherine. "But if you are indeed going to marry Nicky, and I think you must be, for even Mama fears it is true, then I am very glad after all! I must say, when I asked St. Ives to choose someone we could both like, I never thought he would really do so, for he seldom does anything to please anyone but himself. I had quite made up my mind that he meant to have Julia Horneby after all. But I can see that I wronged him," she added handsomely, "and I shall have to tell him that I very much approve of his choice!"

"Thank you," murmured Sylvie, feeling it was expected of her. "But did you ask St. Ives to marry, then?"

"Oh, yes," said Lady Catherine. "For Mama has promised I may make my come-out this spring. Only from the circumstance of Mama and St. Ives being unable to abide each other, so that he is often amazingly rude to her and will never stay in the same house with her, and Mama being determined that I should make my bow from Nicky's house, which even I can see is quite ridiculous, for he bought it himself after all, since Papa hated to be obliged to come to London." She gave a seraphic smile. "At any rate, I decided it would be much better for Nicky to marry instead of merely finding some dreadful woman to chaperone me, as he meant to at first! But I never really expected he would do it," she added, "for he is odiously selfish and has a very bad temper, you know."

Sylvie, feeling as if the interview was not turning out

quite as she had expected, said in a bemused voice, "Yes, I know."

It was not hard to see that this lovely young girl and St. Ives were related; although they did not much physically resemble each other, there was a similarity, if only in the imperious angle of the head and the self-assurance in the blue eyes. In truth, Sylvie had never given much thought to St. Ives's sister, believing her safely in Bath, although she had wondered whether Lady Catherine would be inclined to resent her brother's intended marriage to a girl scarcely three years older than herself and of a very different family. But this confiding young creature betrayed no trace of resentment, or shyness; and Sylvie could not help noticing that all St. Ives's relatives bore an unmistakable self-assurance she very much envied.

She said now, "But you must not believe all you hear, you know, Lady Catherine. I know his lordship's name has been—been linked with mine in the last weeks, but no more than it has with many other young ladies in the past. I myself do not think that St. Ives is at all desirous of settling down just yet."

Lady Catherine seemed a little daunted, but Sylvie suspected she was never cast down for long, for almost immediately she brightened. "Yes, but Mama did not in the least mind his name being linked with all those others, which only goes to show that she did not believe him serious. And I do not think the rest were in the *least* respectable, for she would never speak of them to me. But now she is in a dreadful rage, and they have had a worse quarrel than all the rest, which I must own is not the least consistent of her, for she has been saying for years that if St. Ives would only marry she could be happy at last!"

"Does not the fact that your Mama is so angry show you how ineligible would be a match between your brother and myself?"

Lady Catherine dimpled. "No, for St. Ives is not the least respectable, you know! He cares no more for such nonsense than I do. I think it is enormously romantic, and I must say I would never have expected it of him. Is he very much in love with you?" she added wistfully.

Sylvie smiled. "No, of course he is not, no more than I am with him! We are—we are friends, that is all. He has been kind to me because of my mother, who was a friend of his mother."

"Well, it is certainly odd," said Lady Catherine with an unexpectedly knowing twinkle, "for I have never known St. Ives to have a *friend* like you before. And he is never kind unless it suits his purposes. Besides, even I know that if he does not intend marriage, it is very wrong of him to pay such pointed court to you—or for you to encourage him!" she added. "Do you not wish to marry him then?"

"I—! You don't understand!" cried Sylvie, losing every advantage of her three years' seniority. "We would not —we could never make each other in the least happy."

"I expect you mean by that that you do not think he would make you happy," said Lady Catherine wisely. "You may be right, but do you know, I have long observed that former rakes make the most *interesting* husbands. They may stray a little—what Grandmama Wraxham calls their bits of muslin, you know—but at least they are never boring. And worthy men almost invariably are. Papa was, you know. I don't remember him very well, but Mama is forever telling me how good he was, and what a high stickler, which makes me think he must have been a dead bore. It is no wonder he disapproved of Nicky so much. I must say, however angry I may sometimes be with St. Ives for making me stay in Bath with Mama when I am so unhappy there, he is never boring. Indeed, I have quite made up my mind to marry a rake myself, for I do not think I could bear to be tied to a prosy old fool for the rest of my life."

Sylvie could not help being struck by this truth, but she was forced back onto her last defense. "But I do not think that St. Ives has the least desire to be wed."

Lady Catherine laughed. "I don't suppose any gentleman ever *really* desires to be wed!" she said naughtily. "Indeed, I have often thought how marvelous it must be to be able to do exactly as you like, without ever having to worry about chaperones, or propriety, or people saying you are fast. I would give almost *anything* to be a man. But since I am not, I mean to marry very soon, for at least when you are a married woman you may do as you like."

Sylvie had to laugh at this simple philosophy. "Do you mean to marry straightaway, then? Surely you are very young."

"I am nearly eighteen. I think that is quite old enough. How old are you?" asked Lady Catherine.

"By your standards, very much on the shelf, I'm afraid. I am twenty."

"And this is your first season?" asked Lady Catherine in astonishment.

"Yes, I—you see, I have always lived at home and kept house for my father," said Sylvie. "But then Lady Bridlington, who is my godmother, wrote and—and invited me to come and visit her for a while."

"And then you met St. Ives!"

"Yes, and then I met St. Ives."

Lady Catherine frowned unexpectedly, her eyes going to Sylvie's face. "Grandmama Wraxham says I have no notion of discretion, and I very much fear she is right," she said. "It has just occurred to me—you are not angry because I said that I had asked Nicky to marry, are you? Because you must not regard it, you know. I never had the least expectation he would really do so—in fact, he told me he wouldn't! He said he would be—be damned before he would marry to suit either my wishes or Mama's. Surely, you did not think he intended only a—a marriage of convenience because of me, did you?"

Sylvie hesitated, then decided to be truthful. "Yes, I did think it," she said gently. "You are—that is—something he said once made me think he has become concerned about you, and also that he thinks it is time he had an—an heir."

Lady Catherine looked astonished. *"Nicky?"* she squeaked. "No, no, I think he must have been hoaxing you! I do not say he does not dislike Michael, for they have been at loggerheads for as long as I can remember, but Mama has been trying for years to make Nicky realize he must have an heir, and he will only laugh and say he has no need of brats in his own image."

Sylvie frowned suddenly. "I collect—do you refer to

Michael Staunton?" she asked a little diffidently. "Surely he can not be your brother's heir?"

"Oh, lord yes!" said Lady Catherine. "Have you met Michael? He used to be quite my favorite cousin, you know. In fact, I had nearly made up my mind to marry him, for Mama approves of him, and I daresay it would be a very good match. But now I think I would prefer someone more romantic—a soldier perhaps!" She dimpled. "I am *very* partial to soldiers, for they all look so splendid in their uniforms, don't you think? We had the Eleventh Foot stationed in Bath, and they gave the drollest parties. In fact, if Mama had persisted in making me remain in Bath, I daresay I would have gotten engaged to one or another of them, for I am *very* rich, you know, and considered an excellent *parti*. But now everything has turned out for the best, for I would much prefer to have my London season first. I mean to break a great many hearts."

Sylvie laughed. "If you mean to break a great many hearts, surely it would be better for you to plan to have at least *two* seasons before you settle down to be a married lady?"

Lady Catherine grinned engagingly. "Yes, well I have thought of that, and if you marry Nicky and I know I shan't have to go back to that dreadful place again, I might consider it." Then she caught sight of the time and jumped to her feet. "Oh, no, it cannot be so late already! I was to return a book for Mama—that is how I managed to get out alone today," she added with a twinkle, "for Mama has one of her migraines and cannot be disturbed. She *always* has a migraine when she is angry! Anyway, I told Lizzie—that's my maid, you know—that I was going to meet one of my friends, and we would walk together to the library. I wish I might come and see you again, but Mama wants to return to Bath tomorrow. Only say that you will at least consider what I have said," she added. "If you feel you cannot like St. Ives, I will understand, but it would make things so much better if you would marry him and make him respectable again!"

Sylvie said, without much hope of being attended to, "I do not dislike St. Ives, I promise you. It is only—only that I do not feel we should suit."

"Yes, but all of my friends think he is enormously romantic," said Lady Catherine. "Not that I mean to suggest that it would weigh with you, exactly, but he is considered a splendid match, you know. There, I do not mean to tease you anymore!" she added. "I hope I may see you again, and I am *too* learning discretion, for I will not even say that I hope it will be when I dance at your wedding! Only there is very little time, you know, if you are to have a honeymoon before the season begins!"

She had indeed brought a book with her, and as Sylvie laughed, she picked it up and went quickly to the door. Sylvie started then, remembering herself, and said, "No, no, you must not go out alone again. I dare not go with you myself or I will be late for lunch, but—oh, I know!" she said. "Blackmer will escort you. He is my groom, and a very old friend of mine. Can you wait just five minutes longer until he can be sent for? Yes, indeed I rang, Saltish," she added as the butler entered. "Will you be so kind as to send for Blackmer to escort Lady Catherine home? Thank you."

Lady Catherine proved she could be discreet upon occasion, for she chatted animatedly in front of the butler on a variety of light topics, then allowed Blackmer to take her book and escort her down the front steps, saying only, at the last minute, "And you won't forget, will you?"

She favored Blackmer with such a sunny smile that Sylvie had no doubt she would have wrapped that crusty old groom around her smallest finger before they had progressed two blocks.

Sylvie stood observing them for a moment, then shook her head and went away to change her dress. St. Ives might have genuine cause for concern about his sister, she thought. She had been amused by that young damsel, but she could see that Lady Catherine was precocious for a girl just seventeen. Indeed, some of the things she had let slip made Sylvie think that Lady St. Ives had very little control over her, and unless something were done soon Lady Catherine might really elope with one of her officers. If she had been truthful, and Sylvie had no reason to doubt her, Lady Catherine was possessed of a considerable fortune, and that, coupled with a lively disposition and a Mama who kept too tight a rein on her without in the least managing to curtail her activities, meant that she ran the very real danger of being snapped up by some unscrupulous fortune hunter, which was doubtless what St. Ives feared.

Sylvie had no way of knowing how deep was St. Ives's affection for his sister, of course, but his remark that Kitty was enduring a life not much happier than his—or her—own childhood, made her believe that he would at least care if Lady Catherine were made unhappy. She had liked Kitty too, and she did not wish to see her come to any harm, but St. Ives had been far more practical when he had proposed to hire some woman to chaperone her. If he had offered her that position, instead of asking her to be his wife, she would have jumped at the chance.

When she met Mr. Staunton again a few days later, she could not resist broaching the subject to him. She and Lady Bridlington had been bidden to a Mrs. Fitzhugh's drum, and Michael came over to them almost as soon as they entered the room.

He had paid a correct call of twenty minutes' duration the day after Lady Wolverhampton's ball, but she had not seen him since. When he led her out to the set just forming, she said, "I have been hoping to see you again. I would like to ask you a question."

He gave a mock sigh. "And I flattered myself you might merely have been glad to see me for my own sake—as I was you. I came tonight in that hope. But if the only service I may render you is to answer a question, you must know I will do so."

She smiled, but chose her words with care. "Lady St. Ives—is she very displeased with the—the current rumors regarding her stepson and myself?"

He smiled down at her ruefully. "I wish I might withdraw my promise, Miss Fairfield! She is—how may I say this without sounding as if I agree with her?—Lady St. Ives is a very proud woman, and she holds the Staunton name in almost unnatural respect. It is frequently so, I understand, with women who marry into better families than their own. I do not wish to seem to encourage you in that direction, but in fairness to my cousin, I must say that he is unlikely to allow her opinion to weigh with him."

She liked him better for his reply. "You sound as if you do not approve of such—such unequal marriages, Mr. Staunton," she said. "You must not think I disagree with you, but, forgive me, you are a Staunton as well. Do you hold the name in that same degree of respect?"

He shrugged and said gently, "I am a Staunton, Miss Fairfield. I am not St. Ives."

"You are his heir."

He grimaced. "I set little store by that, I can assure you. My cousin is still a young man."

"Yes, of course. I should not have mentioned it. I met your cousin, Lady Catherine, a few days ago, and I must confess I did not know what to make of her."

"Kitty is a minx," Michael said. "I do not wish to involve you in my family squabbles, but my aunt is not perhaps the best person to bring up such a lively girl. I wish—but never mind! It does no good for me to talk of it, for I can merely observe and disapprove. I have no influence."

"I do not understand exactly how Lady Catherine is placed, but I found her charming. I have heard—both of them speak of the possibility that Lord St. Ives might take her to live with him. Do you think that is likely to happen?"

"I can only hope not," he said with a shrug. "The only person less qualified than my aunt to have the care of Kitty is St. Ives. He has seldom been bothered about her since my uncle died, though he was made her guardian. I am sorry to see Kitty unhappy in Bath, but at least she can get into less mischief there and would not come under St. Ives's influence. But forgive me, I did not mean to go on forever about my family matters. Tell me instead how you have been occupying yourself since last I saw you. I wished to call again but feared to make a nuisance of myself."

She assured him he could never do that and followed his lead in changing the subject, but her mind kept returning to it. She thought Michael might be right about Kitty. Then she reminded herself that it was none of her concern.

XXII

During the next week, Sylvie saw nothing of St. Ives, but Michael Staunton called twice more, once to sit with Lady Bridlington and herself, and again to take her for a drive in the park. She found him easy to talk to, and she began to think of the possibility of receiving an offer from him. This time she knew what her answer must be. She was not in love with Michael, but she liked him very well, and she thought that theirs could be a happy marriage.

Michael himself seemed to make no secret of his preference for her company, and though his conduct was always circumspect, she knew that more than a few people were observing the seemingly developing triangle with interest. Fortunately, Lady Bridlington, who could never resist a personable young man, had so far managed to close her eyes to his increasing attentions, and she said frequently that he was most kind, and so charming! Nothing to compare to his cousin, of course, for she declared St. Ives had quite won her heart, but there was something about grave young men with excellent manners that was irresistible.

Sylvie was thinking about that with a smile one brisk afternoon as she changed a book for her godmother at Hookham's library. Mary had been dispatched to find a length of blonde lace her ladyship was trying to match, and Sylvie was in no hurry to regain her chaperone, enjoying her uncustomary freedom and the bright November day. She had just tucked the book into her muff and decided not to wait for Mary when a voice at her elbow said, "Ah, I thought I recognized you, Miss Fairfield. Have you grown so high and mighty you will not acknowledge an old friend?"

She turned to stare into the face of Lord Lambeth. "You have never been a friend of mine, my lord," she said. "Now pray let me pass. I am to meet my maid in a few minutes and am already late."

He smiled. "Ah, well done, my dear! Almost to the manner born! Quite a change from the ill-favored chit who hobnobbed with grooms and stablelads, eh? I must confess I did not recognize you. But then, when I stole a kiss on the staircase, little did I know that you would turn out so well. I hope there need be no hard feelings between us. I had even spared a thought that you might find it in you to be grateful to me. It was not my intention to do you a good turn, at the time, but one never knows what will occur, does one?"

She was suddenly too angry to guard her tongue. "I know precisely what you intended, my lord!" she said. "It is exactly what I might have expected from a man who would force himself on an 'ill-favored chit' simply because she only had grooms and stablelads to protect her. But if you thought to defeat St. Ives by such a despicable trick, you are a bigger fool than I thought you, and I had not believed that possible!"

"I apologize for the 'ill-favored,' my dear," he said silkily. "I meant no offense. And really, the joke is on me, you know, for I never guessed that you would turn out to possess so many—er—resources. But then you are Fairfield's daughter, are you not? I have often wondered exactly how you prevailed upon St. Ives to consent to marriage, for I'll swear that was not in his mind, but then, it is all one to me, and I congratulate you most heartily. He will be ruined all the same, and I do not begrudge whatever you may manage to salvage from the situation. I had no idea you were so clever when we were—er—hobnobbing on the staircase. I might even have been more insistent in my attentions. But then, doubtless you were wise. Even St. Ives might have balked at the idea of—er—damaged goods. My congratulations, my dear!"

She would have walked past without another word had not her arm been taken in a tight grip, preventing her from leaving. Then St. Ives's voice came from behind her. "Yes, you have miscalculated, Lambeth, perhaps more than you know. But take a very good look at her now, for you will never get this close again. Have I made myself perfectly clear?"

St. Ives did not wait for an answer, but, mindful of the stares they were beginning to attract, marched her briskly away, his grip on her arm not relaxing.

When she tried to pull away, he said from between his teeth, "Oh no you don't, my girl! Is there no end of the troubles you cause me? I would like to have knocked his filthy teeth down his throat."

"I wish you had," she said. "Why didn't you?"

"Because, my bloodthirsty little innocent, I have been stupid enough to carry on a public and very senseless feud with your friend, and I will not have you involved. I thought I had succeeded in preventing precisely this sort of impertinence, but I see I was mistaken. I may have to do something about my Lord Lambeth after all."

"He is not my friend, and I am already involved," she said. "Why does he hate you so? Surely not merely over an opera dancer?"

He stood looking down at her for a moment, his expression unreadable. "You are an odd child, Sylvie. But it need not concern you. Only he is not to approach you again, is that understood?"

She was faintly troubled. "I do not fear him, and I am seldom alone. But I think he would willingly do you a mischief if he could."

"He may try. He will not succeed. And you should not be alone now, either. Where is your maid, or Blackmer?"

She had to smile a little. "I am going to meet my maid, and I had not thought to hear you preach propriety, my lord."

"You see what you have brought me to. I think for the present it is best if you put up with such propriety. But if you come to the Priory, you may come and go as you like."

Her color rose. "If that is an invitation, my lord, it is an improvement over our last discussion on this subject. But I still think it would be most unwise of me to—to avail myself of your hospitality under the circumstances."

He smiled down at her, his blue eyes oddly softened.

"Yes, I know you do. But that is because you are too stubborn to own that you would like to come. I will even allow you to drive my grays if you behave yourself."

She laughed. "That is certainly an inducement, I own!"

"More than you know. I am known to hold female drivers in contempt, and I may even lose my groom into the bargain once he discovers I am contemplating entrusting his precious grays into your care!"

"Yes, but Wicken would never willingly leave your service, and you are safe on the other point because you have carefully planned it to take place in the country, so no one need ever know," she pointed out. "Indeed, it develops that is no inducement at all, so you are defeated, my lord!"

He grinned, but merely said, "Blackmer is to tell me if Lambeth tries to approach you again. I must go or I will be late. And do not fight my battles for me, little one."

"No, my lord," she said. "That would be very foolish of me."

Mr. Strickland, who happened to have been one of the interested spectators of this scene, strolled round to his friend's house that evening and found his lordship still at the dinner table. He accepted a plate from Chelmsford, with whom he was on very good terms; graciously approved several slices of rare roast beef and a mushroom fricassee; and remarked calmly, as the butler withdrew, "Your Miss Fairfield never ceases to amaze me, dear boy. By the by, has she found her widower yet?"

St. Ives glanced up with a grin. "A widower, eh? Yes, I thought she was up to something of the sort. Did she enlist your help, Frederick?"

Mr. Strickland merely said, "Oh, I have it on her authority that she is not absolutely determined upon a widower. Your charm must be slipping, dear boy! I had not thought Staunton such a one for the ladies, but he looks to cut you out if you don't take care."

St. Ives eyes hardened. "Yes, it appears I underestimated him. Damn his impertinence!"

Sylvie received an unexpected visit from Kendall a few days later. He called one afternoon while she was out and waited rather impatiently for her return. When she came in, he limped forward. "I was about to give you up, m'dear! Old Sobersides out there said he didn't know where you had gone."

He looked at her with slightly raised brows and added with a grin, "I must say you've become extremely modish. I scarcely recognized you."

She laughed, and at that moment Lady Bridlington burst in on them, saying in her vague way, "Oh, there you are, my dear. Were you able to get my book for me? Oh, but I beg your pardon, I didn't know you had a visitor—"

When Kendall had been made known to her, she looked him over and then set herself to be kind to her goddaughter's brother, with the result that he and Sylvie were allowed little time alone. Her ladyship sat with them almost all the afternoon, graciously drawing Kendall out and entertaining him with stories of how smart his sister had become, the number of beaux she could boast, and the fact that they were to spend the Christmas season at the Earl of St. Ives's country seat, Ellison Priory, one of the more famous houses in the country. But doubtless dear Sylvie had already told him all about that, for her ladyship was sure it must be very exciting to a young girl in her first season.

She invited Kendall to stay to dinner, saying that he must consider her house his home for as long as he liked, but this he politely declined to do, barely managing to conceal his growing boredom. She added archly that she was sure the dowager duchess of Wraxham would be more than happy to include him in the forthcoming party, once the position was made clear to her, and that doubtless he could make many useful contacts, for she understood he was hoping for a political career.

He declined this too, saying with relief that he had been asked to spend the time with his patron and did not like to refuse him. After that, Lady Bridlington at last took herself off, stopping only to remind her goddaughter that there remained but an hour to dinner, and they were engaged to Mrs. Weston that evening, but she knew Sylvie and her brother must have a great deal to talk about, and she would not intrude any longer.

Kendall escorted her to the door and shut it firmly

behind her before she could remember just one more thing to remind her dear Sylvie. Then he came back into the room and said with a frown, "Good God! What a fool she is, Syllie! It's no wonder you're looking fagged to death with that woman forever nagging at you."

Sylvie grinned. "And I was just thinking myself in particular bloom, too. She is not very wise, I know, but so kind I can not hold it against her. But I am sorry you cannot join us at Christmas. At least—I have not quite decided whether to accept the dowager's invitation, but I was hoping we might spend the holidays together."

"I think I'd end up murdering your godmother, m'dear!" said Kendall. "But what is behind this invitation? Does it mean you've changed your mind about accepting St. Ives's offer?"

"No, of course not. Only I would like to go to the Priory, and—but never mind!" she said lightly. "Tell me what you have been doing instead."

So he told her of his stay with Lord Summerhill and how they might be able to depart for Vienna as early as August, for Lord Summerhill did not believe the fighting could go on much longer. After Wellington's victories on the Peninsula, everyone expected him to soon be in France, and then it would just be a matter of a mopping-up exercise. Then the real work would begin.

"Yes indeed!" she said, teasing him. "I'm sure Lord Wellington himself would be the first to say that without the politicians he could never have gotten so far."

Kendall grinned. "No, to hear Summerhill talk, Wellington's damned angry, and he blames the mismanagement of the war on the Home Office. Anyway, I didn't come to bore on about that. The thing is," he said, "I had a talk with Summerhill, and he seems to agree with me that you should marry St. Ives. He thinks it's merely female scruples on your part. I never knew you to engage in female scruples, Syllie, but I've given it some thought, and the more I think about it the more I think you mightn't do very well together, you know. He's as horse-mad as you are, by all accounts, and it would be a very different life from what I could give you, m'dear. And if you're thinking he's disliked, it seems from Summerhill that it's quite the contrary. He says most of the

women in London are half in love with him. Why are
you so set against him, Sylvie? It's not because of me,
is it? You must know I never set much store by that
plan to set up housekeeping together."

She smiled up at him, but her smile somehow went
awry. "Because I'm more than half in love with him myself, *stupid!*"

"I had begun to suspect something of the kind," he
said. Then he grinned. "And you needn't look so amazed.
I know you think so, but I'm not blind, m'dear. I suspected
the last time there was more to it than you were letting
on. Is he unkind to you?"

"No, he has been remarkably kind—when he isn't
losing his temper," she said. "I think—I think he even
likes me a little now. I don't expect you to understand,
but I couldn't bear to see him grow tired of me, as he
has of all the rest." She shook her head then and said
with determined lightness, "But you are way behind the
times, you know! I have already received another offer
for my hand. Indeed, you would not credit how popular
I've become."

Kendall was diverted, and he immediately demanded
to be told the story. He laughed a good deal at her portrait of James. "Good God, Syllie, I should think you would
refuse him! What a saphead!"

"Oh, no, how can you say so! I have it on his own
authority that anyone must recognize his worth!"

He turned serious again. "Yes, well, there is no question of you marrying him. But Syllie, I wanted to say
that I'm not particularly proud of the way I behaved last
time. And if I have to give up going to Vienna for the
moment, there is no question about it, of course."

"I've always known that. Will you look in and see Blackmer before you go? He would be very hurt if you don't."

He promised to do so and prepared to take his leave
when the door burst open a second time and Lady
Catherine danced in, followed by a rather stunned Saltish.

"I mustn't stay, for I only slipped out while Mama was
lying down on her bed," she said gaily. *"Such* a time of it
we've had, and all because of you, you know, and I
wouldn't have missed any of it for the world! They've had
a bigger row than all the rest, and Nicky has told Mama

that she has no more notion than a baby would of how to control a seventeen year old, that even he could do a better job of it, and that I am to come and live with him after all, for if Mama wished to see me married to the first fortune hunter I was silly enough to imagine myself in love with, she was going in the right way about it! Of course," she dimpled, "I was not supposed to be listening, but I'm glad I did, for I learned something else, too. I am to go to Somerset over Christmas, for Nicky said it was time I began to go into company a little and learn to behave myself, and Grandmama Wraxham will be there to chaperone me and see that I don't get into any more scrapes."

She came to a halt then, eyeing Kendall. "Oh! I didn't realize you had company. I'm sorry to have burst in on you that way."

Sylvie made the introductions, unable to help noticing that Kendall was a little dazed by Lady Catherine's vivacious beauty.

Kitty held out her hand. "You are Miss Fairfield's brother, then? Why, that means you will be a sort of brother of mine, too. Do you not live in London?"

Kendall looked like someone coming up for a deep breath. "No, I have just come down for a short while," he told her a little shyly. "I am at Oxford presently, you know."

"Are you?" said Kitty politely. "I think if I were a man I would much prefer to join the army than to spend my time poring over stuffy old books."

Kendall stiffened. "I possess a limp which, unfortunately, makes that impossible," he said.

Kitty did not seem embarrassed. "Do you?" she said. "They say Lord Byron has a limp, though I have never seen him myself. Anyway, he is enormously romantic, so I shouldn't think having a limp would matter much. Have you read *Childe Harold?* Mama would not allow me, but I did anyway, of course, and I thought it was simply beautiful, and so sad!"

To Sylvie's surprise, Lady Catherine seemed to have the key to putting Kendall at his ease, which few people had ever done, for he said contemptuously, very much as

he would have to Sylvie herself, "Byron! A second-rate
poet whom you silly women have turned into a god! Now
if you had read Catullus or Livy—!"

Lady Catherine seemed inclined to want to argue the
matter, and they discussed it hotly for several minutes,
fast reaching excellent terms, until Kitty guiltily remembered the time. "Oh, dear, Mama will be in such a pet!"
she said in comical dread. She gave Kendall an alluring
smile that made him swallow suddenly and become once
more tongue-tied. "Oh, how glad I will be to have you
both in the family! I never had so much fun before, or
anyone to talk to, you know. And I can hardly wait until
next week. St. Ives says he will take me down himself,
in his curricle, and everything would be perfect if I did
not have to leave early, for Mama has promised I will
spend some time with my Grandmama Conyngham. But
never mind, it does no good to think of that now. Will
you be coming down too, Mr. Fairfield?"

When Kendall declined, Kitty shrugged prettily and said
it was too bad, but doubtless there would be plenty of
time later for them to get to know one another, and he.
must certainly come to her coming-out party. She smiled
sunnily at them both and went away, promising that she
and Sylvie would have some famous cozes once they were
in Somerset.

The both stared after her, Sylvie bemused, and Kendall looking as if he had been struck by a thunderbolt.
At last Sylvie said gently, "She is very beautiful, is she
not? I think she's a sad minx, but I must confess I like her."

Kendall drew an unsteady breath and reverted more
or less to normal. "Yes," he said, "but you're right, she's
not for the likes of us. Is St. Ives like that too?"

She hesitated. "I—yes, in a way, he is. Oh, not quite
so impetuous, or confiding, but with that same charm, when
he cares to exert it."

"Look here," Kendall said abruptly. "It's just occurred
to me. Lord Summerhill was telling me that St. Ives's
house is only a couple of hours ride from his. I might
ride over one day, if you'd like."

"Oh, yes," she said, brightening, and they left it at that,
both oddly loath to continue the conversation.

XXIII

Sylvie did not see St. Ives for nearly a week after the episode with Lambeth, but Michael found an excuse to call nearly every day, either with a book she had expressed an interest in on a tidbit of gossip he knew Lady Bridlington would enjoy.

Sylvie no longer doubted his intentions, and she told herself she was happy. Michael would make her a good, kind husband, and if her mind was traitorously inclined to dwell on problems that were not her own, such as what might happen to Kitty, or if St. Ives would ever find the right wife for him, or did he mean to do something foolish about Lambeth, no one else ever need know.

One evening she and Lady Bridlington attended a rout at a Mrs. Preston's house, and Michael, as had become his custom, found an excuse to join them almost as soon as they entered the room. They talked of indifferent subjects for a few moments, and then, when her ladyship's attention was distracted, Sylvie said, "Forgive me. You once said it would not be wise for Kitty—the Lady Catherine—to live with her brother. Do you still believe that?"

Michael smiled. "Kitty is not my problem, thank God. I know you are fond of her, as I am myself, but I think you are well enough acquainted with St. Ives to realize he has not the patience—not to mention his other faults —to control a highly spirited young girl."

"Do you dislike St. Ives?" she asked.

"I was very jealous of him as a child, of course," he said with the openness she most liked in him, "but now I like to think I am a little wiser and can see that he is rather to be pitied. He has never cared for anyone, you see."

"But he has—he has told me something of his childhood. Surely that must stand as his excuse?"

Michael looked unexpectedly stern. "Forgive me, but my cousin needs no excuse, Miss Fairfield! My uncle endured more than should be demanded of any man, first with St. Ives's mother, then with my lord himself. I do not know what he has told you—something base, no doubt! —but my uncle took me in when I was homeless and never once made me to feel an outsider or unwanted. It was left to my cousin to do that!"

He seemed to remember himself then, and he flushed a little. "I usually try to contain myself concerning my cousin, but I was very fond of my uncle. I do not like to see him the object of St. Ives's vile innuendo."

She was more than a little troubled. She did not think St. Ives had been lying to her, but she knew that most people would be more inclined to accept Michael's version. She merely said, "Yes, I can see you were fond of your uncle. But I am sorry there is—unpleasantness between you and my Lord St. Ives."

"I fear there will always be that," Michael said, "but I hope you will not let it disturb you. If you have indeed been listening to my cousin, I am only surprised you have consented to see me at all. He has always felt that I influenced his father in the matter of his will. I hope I need not tell you that I did not, though I can understand my uncle's thinking. Even as a boy, St. Ives was wild and profligate. Money means nothing to him, as it meant nothing to his mother. However, the feeling between us is not helped by the circumstance of my being my cousin's heir—something you yourself mentioned. He will not believe that I am content with what is mine, but I neither anticipate nor wish to step into St. Ives's shoes. Believe me."

"And I do not anticipate stepping out of them! Since it would appear that we understand each other tolerably well, accept a word of advice. You would do well not to aspire to what is mine. Anything that is mine!" came St. Ives's voice behind them.

Sylvie had whirled angrily, but Michael merely smiled and held up a hand. "Do not distress yourself, my dear. St. Ives is right. We understand each other tolerably well.

May I call on you in the morning, when you are—free?"
He bowed, nodded to St. Ives, and walked away.

St. Ives was obviously in a foul mood, and he said
as soon as Michael was gone, "And a word of advice to
you as well, my girl! If you value my cousin, you will not
encourage him in that direction!"

"You are both rude and impertinent, my lord! I have
given you no reason to assume that tone with me or to
think you have any sort of claim on me."

He swore. "You have given me whatever I choose to
claim! I have been more than patient with you, by God!
You have been trouble since the first day I met you!
But understand this: you will marry me if I have to drag
you kicking to the altar, and I will not be made a laughing-
stock by you or by my cousin! Have I made myself
clear?"

Her cheeks were scarlet. "More than clear, my lord.
Does my behavior not suit your notions of propriety?"

He laughed harshly. "What I choose to do has no
bearing on what I will tolerate from you, and you would
do well to remember it."

"Why yes! I have already become an object for every
gossip and tattlemonger in London! Doubtless *that* meets
with your approval, but my innocent friendship with your
cousin does not! You have a strange system of values, my
lord!"

"If you have become an object of gossip, my dear, it
should please that romantic little streak of yours to know
that you are the heroine of the piece," he said insolently.
"Your reputation has remained untarnished precisely because I have seen to it that your name has been linked
with mine by every tattlemonger in London, as you say.
How long do you think any of those fools who were at
your father's that night would have kept quiet otherwise?"

She looked away. "I don't know, my lord. Perhaps not
long, and if so, I must be grateful to you. But if you would
use your head you must see that what I am doing is the
only way out for both of us."

"I am not a procurer, my girl!" he snapped. "And I
will not tolerate your name being linked with my cousin's,

either now or after we are wed! And do not throw my own reputation up in my face as you are longing to do. I may care little what people may choose to say about me, but you will find me less complaisant about what is said of my wife."

"Caesar's wife must be above reproach?"

"You may choose to put it so!"

"Then it would seem you have changed your mind, my lord. I thought I need only be discreet."

His brows drew together. "You will find that I know how to protect my own. If you thought to find me ready to play the part of a cuckold, believe me, you have seriously miscalculated."

She was so startled she could only stare. "You are ridiculous, my lord! You do not want me, but you will keep any other from having me. Do you mean to extend me the same courtesy?"

"Damn you!" he said under his breath. "I have known not a moment's peace since I met you! You are naïve, stubborn, intractable, and ill-tempered; and I would be better off saddled with my brat of a little sister than you! But I meant exactly what I said. I advise you not to forget it!"

XXIV

By morning, Sylvie had recovered from St. Ives's unexpected outburst; nonetheless, she was very troubled. The only possible explanation for it was the rivalry between the cousins, but the knowledge did not bring her any peace.

Michael's revelations the night before had had just a tinge of jealousy in them, however he denied it; and St. Ives plainly disliked his cousin. But it made her position

B-12314-9

impossible. She had determined to wed Michael, for now
she did not doubt that he meant to offer for her, but to
do so must only flame the enmity between the two men.
She did not credit St. Ives's wild threats, but she knew it
would cause an open rift between the cousins.

But it was there already, she argued with herself. She
would be doing nothing but momentarily creating a new
quarrel that must be forgotten in time. If St. Ives had
cared for her, things would be different—but he did not,
and where there was no affection there could be no
jealousy.

But she was confused and unhappy, and when Michael
arrived that morning she wished suddenly she need not
decide anything right away.

Michael made no mention of the night before, for
which she was grateful, and they talked on indifferent
subjects for some time. There was a warmth in his eyes
that was not to be denied, and at any other time she
would have welcomed it. Now she only wished that she
might postpone his inevitable declaration.

Then Michael looked up with his grave smile, as if
aware of her preoccupation, and said, "But the reason I
called—or rather, one of the lesser reasons—was to inquire whether you and Lady Bridlington mean to join the
party at the Priory over Christmas."

She was surprised, for she thought he must disapprove,
but she said with perfect truth, "I think—that is, it has
not been decided yet, but I think my godmother wishes
to go. Why do you ask?"

He grinned. "I have a selfish motive, Miss Fairfield!
For some reason I am to be included in the party, and
I hoped I might see you there." Then he shrugged and
added, "But I do my cousin an injustice. He has been kind
enough to let me regard the Priory as my home for many
years. I do not wish you to think I allow my feelings to
interfere with my sense of justice."

"No, I know you would not do that. Do I understand
that the dowager has consented to be his lordship's
hostess?" She smiled a little. "I had not thought her so
energetic, or obliging."

He laughed. "Yes, and it is perhaps to her I owe my
own invitation. If it means I may enjoy your company

uninterrupted for some weeks, I must be even more grateful."

He hesitated, then said quietly, "In fact, Miss Fairfield, you must know—or rather I believe you must be aware by now that there is nothing I would like better than to enjoy your company for the rest of my life. I ask—beg!—that you do me the honor of becoming my wife."

He was right. She had known, and she had never made any attempt to check the growing friendship between them. She had thought she knew her own mind, but now she would have put it off if she could. "Mr. Staunton—Michael, I will not pretend I am unaware of your feelings. I had even thought I knew my answer. There, you will think me more than conceited."

He smiled, but it did not reach his eyes, and he was regarding her gravely. After a moment she went on. "I do not know whether I intended—whether I meant to tell you the whole at that time or not. I hope I did. But there are reasons you can know nothing about that make me hesitate to give you the answer I had intended."

"My cousin?" he asked.

She looked up without surprise. "Yes, among other things. I have long suspected you must know more than you revealed."

"I know a little—and have guessed a little more. Forgive me, but I know your father, you see—and my cousin!" he said frankly. "It is partly that knowledge that makes me dare to speak now, when you have not had enough time to come to know me as I would wish. I believe there must be some reason why you would be on such terms with St. Ives as you appear to be. Forgive me," he said again, "but I must speak. If there is such a reason—and I do not ask what it is—I beg you will consider my offer seriously in favor of—whatever offer St. Ives may have made. Has he indeed proposed marriage?"

She nodded, and he said only, "I see. I am, perhaps, a little surprised. It has gone further than I suspected. In the face of that, I must seem to have little to offer, but I do offer it because I have learned to care for you a great deal."

She was more than touched. "You have shown yourself, as always," she said simply, "kinder than I deserve. I do not know what to say."

"Then say nothing—yet. It was never my intention to rush you. I think you know I will willingly wait as long as it takes. We will go to the Priory, and you may have time to learn to know me before you give me the answer I hope for."

"Yes," she said gratefully. "And I promise you I will not make you to wait too long. I must seem inexcusably missish not to know my own mind."

He smiled. "No. I would never accuse you of that." He hesitated, then to her surprise took her hand and raised it to his lips.

It was at that precise moment that Saltish announced in his most expressionless voice, "My Lord St. Ives."

She gasped and snatched her hand away, and then she was angry with herself for appearing so guilty. But Michael only straightened calmly and eyed his cousin, saying with a certain note of satisfaction, "Well, St. Ives! I was just leaving. You have a clear field—for the moment."

St. Ives stood observing him, but as soon as Michael had bowed and taken his leave, he rapped out, "I thought I had made myself clear on the subject of my cousin!"

She discovered she was trembling a little, for no reason she could explain. "Do you desire me to believe you are jealous, my lord?" she asked evenly. "You will not succeed. There can be no jealousy where there is no—affection."

He gave a cynical laugh. "You overestimate yourself, Miss Fairfield! Not even you could contrive to make me jealous of my cousin Michael."

She was hurt, and she struck back, "No, for you have no heart! I am well aware of it."

"And I suppose Cousin Michael does?"

"Yes! If you are interested, he has asked me to marry him, and I have said I would consider it."

He stood staring at her. "Has he indeed?" he said softly at last. "It seems Cousin Michael is full of surprises these days. Then you may tell him this for me, Miss Fairfield: I can promise you, you would find yourself widowed within a short space of being a bride. I really thought I had broken my cousin of the habit of coveting what is mine."

She pressed her hands to her burning cheeks. "You *are* jealous!" she cried. "Oh, not of me, but of *him* because your father preferred him to you! Oh, God, I wish I might never see another Staunton for as long as I live!"

"You tempt me to grant your wish, Miss Fairfield! You have caused me nothing but trouble from the day we met! But understand this! I have gone to a great deal of trouble to make people believe I am about to wed you, and by God I will do so!"

She laughed without humor. "Whose reputation are we saving, my lord, yours or mine?"

He cocked a black eyebrow at her in one of his lightning changes of mood and said, "Both, damn you! No, little sparrow, we are stuck with each other now, for good or ill. I am tempted to say ill, for you're an ungrateful little baggage with manners as bad as my own. But I begin to believe that at least I shall never be bored."

"You must be grateful you will never be given the chance to find out, my lord."

His mood shifted again, and he smiled grimly down at her. "Rid yourself of the notion you will wed Michael, my dear. You will not! I have just spoken to Lady Bridlington, and she assures me you set forward for Somerset a week from today."

He turned to leave, then appeared to think better of it, for he mockingly grasped the hand he had seen his cousin so recently holding. He stared down at it for a moment while she regarded him stiffly, her color high; then he deliberately bent and pressed his lips to the inside of hei wrist in an intimate gesture that reduced to nothing Michael's earlier respectful salute. St. Ives must have felt the jolt of her pulse against his lips, for he straightened negligently, laughed, and walked out.

Sylvie called on the dowager the next morning, for she was badly in need of advice, but it soon became clear that she had chosen a bad time. The dowager was engaged in superintending the packing of her baggage, for she was to go into Somerset a few days early, and

she had little time to spare. She lent only half an ear
to Sylvie's tale, interrupting now and then to issue a sharp
order to one of the maids or to the dresser engaged in
filling the numerous open trunks and portmanteaus, or to
send a footman after one item or another.

The dowager, it appeared, still traveled in the old
manner. Despite the fact that she was going to her grandson's house, she packed a good many of her clothes, a
number of pictures, her own bedding and pillows, her
favorite chair, a supply of her own special tea, and two
enormous jewel casks.

Sylvie, unable to contain herself, burst out in astonishment, "But ma'am, how long do you mean to be away?"

The dowager looked around distractedly from where
she was directing a search through a pile of linen for
a shawl she had decided she would need immediately
and could not be packed, and she said vaguely, "A month.
Or I daresay less—I don't know why I let the wretched
boy talk me into it anyway, for I'm never comfortable
away from home."

"Indeed, ma'am, you need not go on my account. I
would far rather remain in London, I promise you!"

The dowager glanced around sharply and seemed to
draw her mind back to her young guest with an effort,
for she said more kindly, "Nonsense, my dear. I am just
being crotchety, which is the only prerogative of my
age, believe me. Now what's this you've been telling
me about not wanting to go to the Priory? And what
were you saying about St. Ives and Michael Staunton?"

Sylvie obediently repeated what she had been trying
to tell the dowager for the last half hour. She had not
meant to confide so much, but it was such a relief to
talk that she found herself spilling out the whole tangle.

It was a very garbled tale, and she had the feeling
that the dowager knew most of it already. But her grace
did look surprised at one point and said rather dryly, "So
James Bridlington made you an offer, did he? Well, well!
Sophia wouldn't be pleased about it, but it's more than I
expected of him, dull young dog that he is. Never mind.
I said we'd make a fascinating woman out of you, didn't
I? You've got those two young cousins, including my grandson, at daggers drawn over you. You've managed to obtain

an offer from a young man that from all I can tell has never before looked farther than his own nose, and from everything I hear you've got both Horace Epping and Frederick Strickland showing a decided partiality for your company over far more beautiful young ladies. Not a bad piece of work for—what is it?—two months?"

Sylvie blushed. "It embarrasses me very much to have you talk that way, ma'am!"

The dowager grinned, but only said, "But what of Michael Staunton? Is he more to your taste than that graceless grandson of mine?"

Sylvie looked up. "I don't know, ma'am," she said. "I was hoping you could perhaps guide me. I like him—and I will not deceive you—I had decided to accept his offer. Now I don't know. I don't want to be the cause of any more trouble between them."

The dowager considered her words for a moment. "Well, I'm sure I can't guide you! I know nothing against young Michael—he's no relative of mine, of course, and I scarcely know him. He's well enough thought of, I believe." Then she seemed to lose patience. "Oh, get along with you, girl! I've no time to spend chitchatting away the afternoon! As for not coming to the Priory, let me hear no more on the subject. It's all settled, and I won't have you upsetting my plans at this late date. There, I said I was being crotchety, didn't I?" she added with perfect truth. "Now come and kiss me and then go away, and don't do anything foolish until I've more time to listen to your silly tales."

It was plain the dowager was preoccupied and in no mood for confidences, so Sylvie did as she was bid, kissing the dowager's soft wrinkled cheek rather shyly and receiving an affectionate pat from that formidable dame before the dowager turned her attention to the task at hand, apparently forgetting her guest in the debate that arose about whether she should take one or two of the hams she was fond of having for luncheon, and perhaps a dozen bottles of her favorite claret, for she could not be certain St. Ives would have it in his cellars. She would have to remember to have him lay some down for just such emergencies.

Sylvie escaped, only to encounter St. Ives in the hall,

still in his greatcoat. She halted, a little embarrassed after
their stormy parting the day before, but he seemed to
have forgotten it, for he grinned and said, "Wise girl!
Are you escaping before my grandmother can inveigle
you into helping with her packing?"

She could not help laughing at that and was able to
say almost naturally, "No, I rather think she found me
bothersome, and I have been requested to run away.
Does she always travel like that?"

"Oh, yes, invariably. I once saw her set forward for a
hundred-mile journey with no less than three coaches
loaded with whatever household furniture and bric-a-brac
she was certain she could not do without for even a
fortnight. She always travels with her own couriers and
outriders, and she will break her journey at least once
for the night on the short trip into Somerset, and then
she will complain incessantly about the dampness and will
have her own food set before her although she's been
staying at the same inn for at least forty years."

"Yes, well when I left her," she agreed mischievously,
"they were debating whether she should take her own
hams with her, as well as a dozen bottles of wine, for
fear the Priory will not be adequately provisioned."

"It will do no good, I suppose, to remind her that the
Priory cellars were so well stocked with smuggled goods
by my hypocritical father and grandfather that even
Timothy couldn't get through it in a lifetime," he said. "Or
that my housekeeper has been fretting herself to death
—and me with her, I might add—by writing to me every
other day with something else she feels sure she should
have on hand that is obtainable only in London. Or that
I have dispatched my chef, at a great deal of incon-
venience, because my housekeeper does not feel the
Priory cook can do justice to the occasion?"

She looked shyly down at him from where she stood on
the stairs. "It would seem you have been to a good deal
of trouble, my lord. Do you entertain frequently at the
Priory?"

"No, almost never," he answered coolly. "Oh, I have
taken a party of friends down now and again. And not
what you are thinking, so wipe that scandalized expression

off your face!" he added. "If you think Blackmer is straightlaced, you should see *my* old retainers, most of whom were brought there under my pious sire." He looked up and said with a twisted smile, "But I have never made an effort to retrieve my reputation before, and I am finding it a damned nuisance!"

"Are you trying to retrieve your reputation, my lord? If so, I am glad, for Kitty's sake as well as your own."

"It's not for Kitty's sake I'm doing it!" he said. He glanced up again and added unexpectedly, "Are you required elsewhere, or do you have time to go for a drive with me?"

"But you were about to visit your grandmother, were you not?"

"Yes, but I can see I will not be welcome. Besides, I have an aversion to performing errands she has far too many servants to do already. And, if you're a good girl, I might even give you your first driving lesson."

Suddenly she had no desire to refuse. To be bowling through the cold afternoon in one of his racing curricles, when few others would be in the park, was suddenly what she wanted to do above all things.

St. Ives's curricle had not yet been put away, and she willingly accepted his hand and allowed herself to be handed up beside his groom. She smiled at Wicken, and he grinned respectfully and tipped his hat before relinquishing his place to St. Ives and glancing inquiringly up at him.

St. Ives hesitated, then looked at Sylvie. "Yes, Wicken, you may come. I do not wish to offend either of your sensibilities by being seen driving Miss Fairfield without any sign of a chaperone. I am to teach her to drive—if she behaves herself."

Wicken seemed dubious, but he obediently climbed up behind them and they set off. It was a cold day, but the sun was warm, and it was pleasant to be driven through the streets of London. St. Ives, for some reason of his own, did not head toward the park, and when she glanced questioningly at him, he only replied briefly, "I cannot teach you while all the biddies in the park are watching us. I assure you it would be considered far more

improper than for you to be seen driving alone with me.
We will go a little way out of town, where you can do
no damage if the horses get away from you."

He seemed in an unexpectedly tolerant mood, as he
had sometimes shown himself with her, and she was content to ride along beside him, enjoying the speed and the
sharp wind. They said little, but when he had driven along
the road toward Richmond and had reached a clear
stretch of road, he pulled up and gave the reins into her
hands, saying, "You said you had driven a gig before, did
you not? Well, it is very much the same principle. Only
don't let the chestnuts have their heads or you'll end us
all up in the ditch."

He showed her how to loop the reins around her
fingers, and Wicken, swallowing the comment that rose to
his lips at the thought of St. Ives allowing a female to
drive his horses, sat back to enjoy the spectacle.

Although Sylvie had never handled such a spirited pair
and thus had a little difficulty with them in the beginning,
Wicken soon saw with a certain wonder that Miss Fairfield caught on amazingly quickly. St. Ives lounged beside her giving her a lazy word of instruction now and
then; still, Wicken knew that he would take instant control if she appeared to be getting into difficulty. But it
was not long before the groom had relaxed as well, already anticipating telling his cronies about this particular
episode.

Wicken was not unaware of the progress of the affair
between St. Ives and Miss Fairfield, but he had kept
his opinions to himself. Watching her now, however, he
began to think the match might do very well after all,
particularly if it meant that St. Ives intended to look to
his responsibilities at last, as it seemed. Wicken had been
informed about the coming house party at the Priory, and,
if he was glad to see the old house opened up for
guests again, he was wise enough not to say so. But it
was apparent that even more changes were afoot. St.
Ives had begun to go into society again, and he did not
come home in the wee hours of the morning from one
of his gambling hells or another more than once or twice
in a week now. He had begun at long last to put his
affairs in order, even spending several days with his bailiff

to see exactly where he stood. There was talk of Lady Catherine coming to stay with them in the spring, and furthermore, Wicken had learned that his lordship had—with a gift of an expensive diamond necklace—paid off that highly polished piece of nature who had caused so much recent trouble. In Wicken's experience, that could easily mean that St. Ives had grown tired of her and found another charming barque of frailty to take under his protection, but somehow the groom did not think so this time. No, it looked as though St. Ives were serious at last, and Wicken, for one, did not think it had happened a moment too soon.

Miss Fairfield, unaware of the favor she had won from at least one of his lordship's servants, was creditably acquitting herself with the ribbons. After a mile or so St. Ives had stopped observing her quite so closely, and she thrilled that he was not totally displeased with her. He even said, after observing her skill in negotiating a tricky curve in the road, "That must have been some gig, little one."

She blushed. "Yes, but you had already taken the edge off them, you know. They are a beautiful pair. Do you ever race them?"

Wicken stifled a gasp at this negligent summing up of a very well-known team, but St. Ives said with commendable restraint, "Yes, I race them on occasion."

"These are very fine," she said, "but I still prefer the grays. I must admit you drive very well."

The most notable whip in London meekly accepted this mild praise and showed her how to catch the thong of her whip. She practiced it, delighted with the new trick, and said impulsively, "Oh, how pleasant this is. I wish I were a man! To be able to do just as you wish, without asking permission of anyone or worrying about what people will say about you! I sometimes think I would give anything for such freedom."

"Would you?" he said in some amusement. "You are a strange child, little sparrow."

She considered it. "No, I don't think so. Kitty said something much the same to me—I mean, of course, Lady Catherine," she amended. "I told you she had come to see me. Indeed, she is the reason I thought of it, for she said she had always longed to be a man, but that she meant to do the next best thing and marry quickly, so no one would be able to tell her what to do."

He put up his brows. "Since no one has ever been able to tell her what to do, I fail to see what she was complaining about. Particularly since Kitty can get almost anything she wants by exploiting the gender she claims to despise. My little sister, in case you hadn't noticed, is a shameless flirt. Anyway," he added, "I should think I am an excellent example of what happens to men who do exactly as they wish with no regard for what people will say, and I know what you think of me."

She glanced at him out of the corner of her eye, but said calmly, "You are mistaken, my lord. Anyway, the only really disreputable thing I have yet heard laid to your credit was the Lady Colchester affair."

Wicken's eyes started a little, but St. Ives did not appear disturbed. "But then such tales are hardly likely to be repeated to a mere chit of a girl," he said. "And who the devil told you of that old tale anyway?"

"The point is, someone did tell me of it. And since it seems to have been considered such a dreadful scandal, it just proves that they would probably have told me worse things, if they existed."

"It was bad enough," he said.

"Was it? How old were you, my lord? Eighteen, nineteen?"

"Your own age, twenty!" he said.

The slight characteristic frown appeared between her brows. "Well, then, I would say you were certainly precocious, but then if I was informed correctly, Lady Colchester was some years older, and she was probably far more to blame than you, my lord," she said matter-of-factly.

Wicken had to stifle an involuntary laugh, and St. Ives grinned reluctantly at this rather novel view of a matter that had set the seal on his reputation. "I own she was the instigator of our—er—relationship, but I was by no means unwilling, and she was not my first affair in that line, only the most prominent. No, Sylvie, I make no excuses for my conduct. Here, it is time we were getting back."

She willingly surrendered the reins to him, saying, "I

should hope you would make no excuses, my lord! And if you had had a father who had a grain of sense instead of treating you as if you were some kind of—of leper all your life, then the whole sorry business might have been avoided. Or at least that poor man's death and all the scandal. Though with a wife like that," she added, "I'm not at all certain he wasn't better off! Whatever happened to her, by the way?"

Wicken was regarding her with new respect, but St. Ives only said lazily, "I don't know. She ran off with some more gullible fool—or shall we say more a gentleman—than I, and I believe they were living in Vienna. I assure you I am not in the practice of keeping up with my previous inamoratas."

He sounded very cynical, and Wicken said, before he could prevent himself, "My lord!"

St. Ives glanced around, but Sylvie said quickly, "Wicken means, I expect, my lord, that it was improper of you to say that. But certainly no more improper than my asking you about your—your former affairs. I beg your pardon! I don't know what came over me, only that I had been wondering and it just seemed to pop out."

He grinned. "And does not that, at least, convince you that you would do better to accept my offer, Sylvie? What do you think my precious cousin would think if he could know you as I know you?"

She stiffened immediately, all her pleasure in the afternoon gone. "I do not know, my lord," she admitted in a low voice. "Perhaps it would shock him, as you say. But I am not sure I do not prefer that than to know that you care for nobody and perhaps never will."

"Then you have very bad taste, my girl!" he said rudely. "And you are a fool! My cousin is not the man for you, and if you cannot see that then I have no patience with you!"

"And you are that man, my lord?"

For answer he gave an impatient exclamation under his breath and whipped up his horses.

They said little after that, and when he saw her to her door in Green Street and she thanked him for her lesson, he merely shrugged and turned away. She watched him go, regretting that her afternoon had been

spoiled, but thinking it was perhaps better if it were
their last.

XXV

The dowager duchess, perhaps because she had been a
notable hostess for many years and did not mean to
lower her standards at this late date, had procured a
number of eminent personages for the house party. The
assembled guests were to include my Lord Rockingham,
Lord Timothy Desborough, Lady Jersey, the Countess
Lieven, a Mr. and Mrs. Beckworth and their daughter,
Lord Alvanley, the Lady Catherine Staunton, and—
whether out of a kindness to Miss Fairfield, or because it
amused the dowager to add a certain piquancy to the
party—two people who had come to be considered Miss
Fairfield's particular admirers, Mr. Strickland and Mr.
Michael Staunton.

Sylvie and Lady Bridlington arrived at the Priory almost
at dusk on a blustery December afternoon after an un-
eventful journey that was broken only by Lady Bridlington's prattle and the occasional spatter of rain against the
carriage windows. It was too dark to see much of the
park they drove through, and though the house was alight
from top to bottom, there was little time to admire it
before they were whisked inside out of the weather.

They were greeted by a tall, spare woman dressed
in a slightly outmoded manner who came forward and
shook hands with them, saying, "Ah, I needn't ask! You
must be that girl of St. Ives's! I am his aunt, you know,
Venetia Desborough. I am afraid Mama is upstairs resting
just now, but she asked that I show you to your rooms and
make sure you are comfortable. I am sure you will wish
to rest before dinner; the journey is always so tiring!
And you must be Lady Bridlington," she continued in that

same brisk manner. "I remember you from before you were married, of course. You did very well for yourself, though they do say Bridlington left you in a sad state. But then, that was something you could not have been able to foresee, for none of us can tell what the future may hold—which is perhaps why I never chose to get married myself. Lacked the courage, no doubt—and who can say which of us was right."

Lady Bridlington, thrown out of countenance by these remarks, murmured something and trailed after their hostess, who had turned to stride up the stairs. Sylvie, uncertain whether to be amused or embarrassed, gave her godmother a reassuring smile and followed them both, wondering if all of St. Ives's relatives were not a little mad. They were all certainly outspoken, with that peculiar faculty of the well-bred for thinking they might do or say exactly as they liked. They might amuse her, but she was never quite sure what to make of any of them. Only Michael Staunton seemed to have escaped in some way, and she was suddenly very glad he was to make one of the party.

Lady Venetia showed Lady Bridlington to her room first, then walked on down the corridor a little way, saying, "And your room is just down the hall, Miss Fairfield." She opened the door to a charming room, frankly watching as Sylvie thanked her and went in, and she added as if to herself, "Yes, I begin to see what Mama meant. You may do very well for St. Ives after all. Have a nice rest, my dear."

Sylvie did not go to bed, for traveling had only bored instead of tired her, and as soon as she had supervised Mary's unpacking her things, she went down the hall and tapped gently on Lady Bridlington's door. Lady Bridlington was stretched out on her bed, but she was not asleep, and she beckoned happily to Sylvie to come in. "My dear, did you ever see the like!" she said. "They say there are a hundred rooms, and I daresay as many servants. But what did you think of Lady Venetia? I declare, she was always odd, for I remember her when she was a girl, of course, but I swear she has grown positively Gothic. Was ever anything more amusing? I was ready to sink, but I'm sure she means no harm, and I don't doubt that she gets a great deal of it from her Mama, of course."

Sylvie came into the room, automatically beginning to straighten a pile of shawls Crimping had left. "Yes, but they are all so amusing, you know, that I cannot help liking them," she said. "Did she never marry, then?"

Lady Bridlington, who seemed to be amazingly well informed on the exact relationship and fortune of almost everyone in either the Desborough or the Staunton families, proceeded to entertain her with an authoritative rundown on every member of either side, living or dead, for the past hundred years.

Sylvie listened, intrigued, and when Lady Bridlington seemed to have run down, she asked, "and did you know St. Ives's mother, ma'am."

Her ladyship tittered. "Oh, my dear, we all knew Ariel! In many ways he is very like her, you know; it fairly gives me a turn, now and then. Some expression, or those remarkable eyes of his, so like hers. I don't believe I've ever seen a more beautiful woman, but she was sadly unsteady. There was an affair with—well, never mind, it doesn't matter, after all—that was before she married St. Ives, and it nearly ruined her. When she took it into her head to marry St. Ives, there were a great many who predicted it would never work. They were so different, and, although I knew nothing against the man, I thought him rather proud and cold, and he was much older of course. As it turned out, everyone was right. The marriage was never a happy one, though they kept up appearances, but I'm sure they seldom met after that first year or so. Not that she didn't manage to keep herself well enough entertained!" added her ladyship. "But there, she's been dead for these twenty years or more, and there's no sense in raking up old scandals. Only I have often thought it hardly surprising that St. Ives should behave as he does, for I believe it is in his blood."

Sylvie said softly, almost to herself, "Yes, he said once that he had adored his mother. I wish I might have known her."

"Did he? Well, it's hardly surprising, I suppose, for a great many men made fools of themselves over her.

She was quite irresistible, and it's no wonder if the
dowager has a soft spot for Ariel's son." She looked up
and added, "And if you are thinking that he will lead you
a similar life, my dear," she said, "he well may do so!
But to my mind I am not sure it will not be worth it.
And you would do as well to wink at anything you may
find out, for you won't hold him with tears and threats.
Many's the time I thought of leaving poor Wilfrid." She
shrugged her plump shoulders. "But then where would I
have been. No, no, my love; men, even the best of
them, which I don't say St. Ives is, are inclined to stray
now and again."

Sylvie was a little shocked, not at what her ladyship had
said, but at this intimation that Sir Wilfrid, whom she had
always pictured to be exactly like James, should have displayed any peccadilloes. "But ma'am, surely you cannot
mean Sir Wilfrid—? I—I mean, you always speak so fondly of him, and I had naturally thought that you must have
been very happy in your marriage."

Lady Bridlington dabbed at her eyes with a wispy edge
of handkerchief. "It does no good to speak of it, and only
makes me unhappy, even now, but the truth is, I learned
soon after we were married that Sir Wilfrid was keeping
a mistress. It was while I was increasing with James, and
it almost broke my heart. But my mother told me that
in his day even my Papa had strayed, and I had always
thought Papa—but never mind! Mama said women will
never be able to understand it, but they would do well
to ignore it, for they cannot change it. And so, even
when he set up that little vulgar chit in Chelsea—but
there, I'm sure we need not go into that," she added
hastily, remembering herself. "But I hope you will always
remember it, as I have done, for you will be much
happier, my love."

Sylvie smiled fondly at her, knowing what it must have
cost her to be so frank. "I do not believe my own mother
could have been kinder to me, ma'am," she said. "In
fact, I know she would not have been, for whatever
Blackmer says, I don't think she possessed much patience.
I will always be grateful to you."

Lady Bridlington smiled mistily up at her and squeezed
her hand. Then Crimping came in to finish the unpacking

and help her mistress dress for dinner, and Sylvie went
away to her own room.

The rest of the party had assembled by the time they
came downstairs, and if Sylvie felt a little shy at first,
she was not allowed to remain so for long. Most of those
present were both interesting and amusing, and if they
were also rather eccentric, like the dowager herself, it
certainly made for a lively evening. Lady Catherine had
arrived the day before with her brother, and she smiled
happily as Sylvie came in, quickly changing her seat and
whispering with a giggle that Lady Jersey was wearing a
positively indecent gown, and furthermore, she was sure
she had damped her petticoats, and did Sylvie think Kitty
would be able to get away with it if she tried?

Michael chose to remain by her side for most of the
evening in a manner a little reminiscent of a dog with
a bone, but St. Ives, for once, was behaving impeccably,
and he merely observed them with a faint lift of his
black brows and devoted himself to flirting with Lady
Jersey.

Sylvie would not have exchanged more than a dozen
words with St. Ives all evening had she not discovered
that she had forgotten her reticule downstairs and gone
back to find it. It took her some time to locate it, for it
had fallen behind a sofa cushion, and when she was once
more ready to go upstairs, everyone else was gone and
only St. Ives stood at the foot of the stairs.

He smiled down at her and said mockingly, "Well,
Sylvie? I hope you appreciate the effort I have been
put to on your behalf. Dreadful, is it not."

She colored, but made no answer, and after a moment
he laughed and stepped aside to allow her to climb the
stairs to her room. She thought he stood looking up at her,
but she did not look back.

The first week drifted pleasantly by, devoted to hunting when the weather was fair or less strenuous exer-
cises when it was not. St. Ives proved himself an excellent if rather careless host, mounting his guests from
his superb stables and generally seeing that whatever
they desired was made available, though he did not seem
to put himself much out and relied mostly on his excellent
staff.

Sylvie had half dreaded trouble, but she did not find it. She enjoyed Michael's company, became even fonder of Kitty, whose lively chatter was a constant source of amusement, and each day passed more rapidly than the one before. She, who had never before known the amusements of a well-chosen house party, thought she had never laughed so much in her life. Mr. Strickland was his usual charming self, Lord Timothy was an irresistible old roué, and the rest of the assembled party seemed chosen for their wit and conversation. And since Michael had kindly given her time to make up her mind, she grasped at that brief respite with both hands.

St. Ives watched her growing friendship with his cousin with a cynical expression, but he made no attempt to interfere. Sylvie was torn between relief that he had perhaps seen reason at last and the most unworthy feeling that he had abandoned her. For his unwonted reserve did not extend to at least two of his guests—the worldly Lady Jersey and the Countess Lieven—with whom he appeared to be on excellent terms. He flirted shamelessly with both of them, and it could not be said that he received any discouragement.

Sylvie told herself that the less she saw of him the better it would be for her peace of mind, and that she was glad if he seemed to have relinquished her to his cousin with every appearance of complaisance.

But to see him on terms of intimacy with two such fashionable and lovely women gave her a pang that she knew was as ridiculous as it was painful. She could never hope to compete with such women. They were of his world, and it brought home to her, as nothing else could have, exactly what she was letting herself in for by marrying Michael. It was ridiculous to suppose she and St. Ives would never meet, and therefore she would be forced to watch him flirting with one beautiful woman after another, or, worse, marrying one of them, as he must inevitably do. She was not sure it would not be better to go back to her father after all, for then at least she might reasonably expect never to see St. Ives again.

But she did not allow herself to dwell too often on such gloomy thoughts, and she soon found herself on excellent terms with most of the party. Lady Jersey entertained

her with stories about Lord Alvanley and told how
hostesses always stationed a servant outside his door
when he was a guest because of his well-known habit of
throwing his bedroom candle on the floor and smothering
it with a pillow when he was ready for bed. Though
Sylvie laughed, Countess Lieven said it was quite true.
She herself had been present when he had nearly set
someone's house afire, and they had all been roused in
the middle of the night by a shrieking housemaid who
smelled the smoke. Fortunately he had only singed the
carpet in his bedchamber, and everyone had gone calmly
back to bed.

Only one event occurred to mar that first week. Sylvie
entered a room only to overhear Lady Jersey and
Countess Lieven talking on a sofa by the window. Lady
Jersey was saying, "I thought she would be quite impossible, but I rather like the child, I must confess."

Countess Lieven said, "Yes, but the family, I understand, is very bad?"

"Oh, impossible, my dear! But when did St. Ives ever
care for that! Not that it does any good talking, for the
thing is as good as done. What do you think? Shall we
make the rest of them angry with us and send them
vouchers to Almack's when they are wed?"

"Oh, when they are wed," the countess said indifferently.

Sylvie, her cheeks burning, had whisked herself out of
the room and run upstairs.

Christmas came, and brought Sylvie an expensive Indian shawl from her godmother, and, somewhat to her
distress, a lovely pearl and sapphire brooch from the
dowager. When she tried to protest, the dowager said
gruffly, "Hmph, as if I can't choose to give away a piece
of my own jewelry when I want. I don't know what the
world's coming to! A trumpery piece, and I'll hear no
more about it."

Sylvie kissed her cheek and went away, feeling very
much as the serpent must have in the Garden of Eden.
Luckily, the event was soon replaced in her mind by the
unexpected arrival of Kendall, who had ridden over to
see her as he had promised and had even remembered

to bring her a present in the form of a book of poetry she suspected he himself despised.

She was so pleased she could have cried, but she only hugged him and asked how long he could stay and if he could possibly remain to dinner. This he was unable to do, saying that he must get back, for he meant to leave for Oxford the next morning to do a little catching up, and he still had nearly a two-hour ride before him that day. But he entertained her with a tale of an obscure book on Homer he had discovered in Lord Summerhill's library, and told her of the political talks he had enjoyed with Lord Summerhill till all hours each evening, and she teased him a little on sparing a day from such dizzy delights to ride over to see her.

They had been sitting together for nearly an hour when the door behind them opened without warning and St. Ives strode in. He halted at the sight of Kendall, his black brows up. Then he said, "And this, I presume, is the long-lost brother. How touching. Have you come to call me to task at last, or am I indulging myself in too much optimism?"

Sylvie was furious, and Kendall turned a slow, unbecoming red and lurched to his feet, stammering in his haste. "S-Sylvie does not need me to interfere. She can take care of herself."

St. Ives's lips curled. "Can she? You will forgive me if I suggest she has done a very poor job to date! But I'm glad you're here, whatever the reason. I want to talk to you!"

He turned and strode out, holding the door behind him, and after a moment Kendall glanced at her briefly and followed, his mouth unnaturally grim.

She was angry enough that she would have gone along and demanded to be admitted if they meant to discuss her, but just then Lady Catherine came in. Kitty stared curiously as Kendall and her brother disappeared into St. Ives's study, but then she began to tell Sylvie in excited terms of the horse that St. Ives had promised to buy her. She was in raptures, for her Mama had never consented to her having one before, and St. Ives had promised to let her choose it, subject only to his own veto, as soon as they returned to London.

St. Ives and Kendall were closeted together for more than half an hour, and when they emerged she could not tell from either's expression what had occurred, or if they had quarreled. She had feared the worst, but though Kendall was looking defiant, he was also a little chastened, and with Kitty present it was impossible to say anything.

Kitty jumped to her feet in her impulsive way and cried, "Mr. Fairfield! How glad I am you could come! Will you be able to stay long?"

Kendall answered her readily, if rather stiffly, but Kitty soon had him laughing at her nonsense. St. Ives stood observing, but did not take part in the conversation, and Sylvie was too upset to absorb much of what was said. Kendall left soon after, Kitty having extracted a promise that he would come to see her in London and that he must keep the date of her party free. It was clear that Kitty had little idea of the effect she could have on an inexperienced, impressionable young man.

Sylvie was able to have only a brief private word with Kendall as she walked him to his horse. She searched his face, and he met her look, saying in answer to her unspoken question, "He raked me over the coals, damn him! And I'd feel a good deal better if he weren't so damnably right!" He hesitated then and after a moment said with difficulty, "We have used you shamefully—father and I—only I never meant to, Syllie, I hope you know that. I've no right to interfere now in whatever you decide to do, only promise me you won't make too hasty a decision about—about that other fellow you were telling me about."

She frowned at him in surprise, but they had reached his horse by then, and Kendall greeted Blackmer with evident signs of relief. They stood chatting for several minutes, and as Kendall pulled himself into the saddle, he looked at the groom and to the surprise of both said stiffly, "I don't think I've ever told you how grateful I am for all you've done for Sylvie—for both of us—over the years, Blackmer. I know I need not ask you to continue to look after her, but I just wanted to say that I—I feel better knowing she's got you." He looked down at the old groom for a moment, then gave Sylvie a funny little salute with his crop, and rode away.

Blackmer stared after him for a moment, then he turned back. "Will you be wanting Cintra this afternoon, Miss Syllie? He could use the exercise."

She turned to him gratefully. "Oh, yes, Joe. That is exactly what I need. But Kendall's right, you know. I don't know what I should do without you!"

XXVI

The second week passed almost as uneventfully as the first. Sylvie made the acquaintance of Lord Rockingham and found him rather enigmatic, with a dry, biting wit she could not help but find amusing. Something Kitty had let slip made her think St. Ives's stepmama blamed Lord Rockingham for a good deal of St. Ives's more unfortunate propensities, but Sylvie found nothing, other than an immense cynicism, to object to in him. He and the dowager were on excellent terms, and he spent a good deal of his time playing cards or gossiping with her grace, or flirting dispassionately with either Lady Jersey or the Countess Lieven, both of whom seemed to know exactly what to make of him.

Sylvie knew he had observed her in his own rather bored way, but what he thought of her she could not tell, though he was not unkind to her. Only once, when he had come into a room to find her in close conversation with Michael, did he raise his thin brows and murmur provocatively, " 'O! beware, my lord, of jealousy; It is the green-eyed monster which doth mock the meat it feeds on.' "

Sylvie flushed scarlet, and Michael looked thunderous for a moment, but Lord Rockingham had strode unconcernedly on.

At the end of the second week, Kitty reluctantly departed to rejoin her mother and maternal grandparents, and Sylvie was obliged to own that the house party grew a little flat after that. Miss Beckworth's conversation could not take the place of Kitty's chatter, and Sylvie began to feel a little restless, despite the congenial company.

Michael, as if sensing her mood, invited her to accompany him one morning for a ride. She went willingly, for she had had little exercise for the past weeks and was grateful to him for the thought. The day was unexpectedly fine, and they rode as far as the nearest village, though Cintra had fidgeted at first from being cooped up for so long. Michael looked grave and inquired gently if she would not do better with a more ladylike mount, which had put her back up a little. But to his credit he said no more, and they enjoyed a leisurely canter.

They had reached the village and were riding side by side in its narrow main street, Cintra jibbing at the noise in the streets and objecting to the presence of the skittish young gray Michael was riding. Sylvie turned in annoyance to try to control the black's unusual antics, when she caught a brief glimpse at the other end of the street of a raking bay she thought she knew too well. She started, forgetting Cintra, but the rider had his back to her, and she could not be certain.

She rudely interrupted whatever Michael had been saying. "Isn't that Lord Lambeth there?" she demanded.

Michael halted and turned to look, his expression grave. "Yes, I believe so. I recognize that big bay of his. What business can he have in the area, I wonder?"

The same thought had occurred to her, and she bit her lip and looked away. It was possible that Lambeth had a house in the neighborhood, or was visiting friends, but the sight of him had set up an unpleasant train of thought in her mind. After a moment she said, "I don't know— but I suppose it would be useless to warn St. Ives! He will not accept that Lord Lambeth is a dangerous man."

Michael stared at her. "You think he means trouble?" he asked quietly.

She turned, startled, for she had not thought anyone else might share her concern. Michael added rather deliberately then, "I, too, distrust the man, but you are right, I fear. It would be useless to try to make my cousin see reason on that subject. I have already tried— to my regret—and received only his contempt for my clumsy efforts."

There was a natural question in her eyes, but he did not enlighten her further, and suddenly he seemed as eager to return to the Priory as she.

They said little more on the ride home. She was more than a little troubled, and to have her fears in some part confirmed by the level-headed Michael did nothing to allay her unease, but she knew it would be useless to broach the subject with St. Ives.

However, she might have tried had something far more immediate not driven all thought of Lambeth away from her mind.

She and Lady Bridlington had gone up together after dinner, her godmother chattering on as usual, and as they reached her door, Lady Bridlington ended whatever she had been saying by breathing in awe, "And the necklace, my dear! Five thousand pounds if it's worth a penny! What I couldn't find to do with five thousand pounds! But I daresay it's chicken feed to her."

Sylvie had no idea what the object of this discussion had been, but she was startled at her godmother's tone. "Ma'am, you are funning, I know. Surely you have everything you could want? Your fine house—your clothes— the carriage?"

Lady Bridlington sighed comically. "Oh, my dear, I don't suppose anyone ever has everything they want, but I'm quite sure I don't. What with James going on forever about being obliged to retrench and pulling long faces about the least little extravagance, I was really desperately unhappy until you came. But there, that only shows what a comfort you've been to me, for I haven't thought of all that in weeks!"

Sylvie had halted and said miserably, "Oh, ma'am! When I think of the charge I must have been—all those clothes! Oh, if only you had told me! How *could* you think I would wish you to spend so much if you could not afford it! I'm sure I didn't need a quarter so many dresses."

"Why, what a piece of nonsense," said her ladyship warmly. "As if I would ever begrudge a penny spent on

you! I've never been so happy in my life since you
came. Why, if it hadn't been for James being particularly
provoking just at that time, I would have insisted on paying
for everything myself and never counted the cost, for you
must know how fond I've become of you, almost as if you
were my own daughter."

But Sylvie had turned alarmingly pale, and she said
now, in a voice her ladyship had never heard from her,
"Ma'am—you—I think you'd better tell me exactly what
that means."

Lady Bridlington perceived too late that she had been
guilty of an indiscretion, and she attempted to recover
herself. "Why, I'm sure I haven't the least idea what
you're talking of, my love," she said faintly. "You know
how my tongue runs on! I wonder you can think so little
of me as to even suggest you have been a charge upon
me!"

Sylvie said in the same voice, "No, ma'am. I don't mean
to be put off. You said—you implied—that you had not
paid for everything yourself. If that is so, I must know
who has."

Lady Bridlington lapsed into her easy tears. "Why, if
I'd known you would make such a fuss, I never would
have told you," she said petulantly. "You will say I should
not have allowed it, and perhaps I should not have, but
with things in such a state and James forever pulling long
faces, when her grace kindly offered to frank you, it
seemed the very answer. I don't see what there is to
upset you so, for it makes no difference whether I pay
the bills or the dowager does—except that she can afford
them a great deal better than I can!" she added with
inarguable logic. "Why, my dear, I'm sure I couldn't have
afforded *half* the things we have purchased, and it would
have been such a shame, for you have turned out better
than I ever dreamed, and as for that fur-lined cape—"

Sylvie had been keeping a tight rein on herself, but
now she said a little wildly, "Ma'am, you had no right—!
How *could* you think I would consent to allow her grace
—oh, can't you see what an impossible position you have
placed me in? No, no, it was bad enough when I thought
that you—but to know that she has been allowed to dis-
charge all of my debts, that she—oh, it is unbearable! I

must repay her, every penny, if it takes me the rest of my life!"

"*Repay* her?" goggled her ladyship. "When I'm sure she hardly regards the expense?"

"Of course I must repay her! I only wish I had known before I allowed you to order those last things. They must be sent back, every one of them. Except for the green gauze, for I'm afraid I've already worn that. And as for the cape—well, I have worn it too, but perhaps I can manage to sell it and get back a part of the money it must have cost."

"Send them back? *Sell* your cape?" cried her ladyship, almost beside herself. "When the whole world knows you are soon to be her granddaughter-in-law?"

Sylvie had been pacing a little in her agitation, but at that she turned, her face very still. "Yes, the whole world knows it ma'am," she said in a low voice, "because you conspired with St. Ives to make them think it! No, do not bother denying it! You may have done it out of kindness—I no longer know," she added wearily, "but it was not kindness to allow me to become so heavily indebted to her grace that I must be unable to repay her—as you must have known I would. I—oh, but it does no good talking. Please leave me, ma'am, I have said too much already, and I am not certain I can guard my tongue."

Lady Bridlington, in a flood of tears, could not leave it at that, and she followed Sylvie into her bedchamber, trying brokenly to explain why she had seen nothing wrong, since her grace's own grandson had been responsible for the plight Sylvie had found herself in, and she had never dreamed Sylvie could object. But her remarks seemed to fall on deaf ears, and when she realized what Sylvie was doing, her tears left her and she began to grow indignant. For Sylvie, ignoring her, had ruthlessly roused Mary, dozing by the fire in her room, and was ordering the packing of all the new gowns that had just arrived from the dressmaker's.

Mary, almost as startled as her ladyship, gaped and said naïvely, "What, never all of them, miss! And that green one was so becoming, too." But she began to do as she was ordered.

Lady Bridlington, shocked by a display of scruples she

could only find incomprehensible, and aware that she had erred badly in allowing Sylvie to learn of the dowager's part in the affair, tried again to make her listen to reason, but only succeeded in making Sylvie round on her at last.

"Nothing you can say will do any good, ma'am! You refused to believe it when I told you I would not marry St. Ives, even when I tried to make you see how unhappy such a marriage would make me. You conspired with him to make me the object for every gossipmonger in the city. You have refused to believe that I can know my own mind, or that I will not weakly give in because you and his grandmother think I should. And this is what comes of it. Well, I shall marry Michael Staunton because I have no choice, but I am not sure I can ever forgive you, ma'am. Now please go away before I say anything else I will regret."

"Michael—? Marry Michael?" gasped her ladyship, her mouth opening and closing in shock. "You cannot be serious! Marry Michael *Staunton* when you might have St. Ives? And when I have told everyone you will—"

But when Sylvie ignored her and went on folding dresses and directing Mary which to bring out of the closet, her ladyship shook her head in bewilderment and went away, her face crumpled.

Sylvie herself gained very little sleep that night, but she was downstairs early the next morning and went in deliberate search of St. Ives. She found him alone in the breakfast room and said without preamble, "My lord, may I have a word with you?"

"As many as you like, Miss Fairfield, but not, judging from your expression, where we may be interrupted at any moment. I have been meaning to suggest another driving lesson, but you have been—er—otherwise engaged. Will that satisfy you?"

She hesitated, then said, "Yes, my lord. I would like to go now, if you are quite finished with your breakfast."

He was already in buckskins and top boots, but she had to go upstairs to change into her habit, which she did as quickly as her trembling fingers would allow.

His curricle was waiting at the door, with Wicken standing at the grays' heads, but St. Ives did not invite the groom to accompany them this time.

It was a cold day, with a hint of snow in the air, and she had not dressed warmly enough, but she hardly regarded it. She waited until they were out of sight of the house, too preoccupied to appreciate the skill with which St. Ives took the first nervous fidgets out of his horses, and she only looked up with a start when he said, "Very well, what is it I am supposed to have done now, little sparrow?"

The use of that name almost overcame her, but she turned and said, "My lord—I have just—why did you not tell me that your grandmother was paying my bills?"

He frowned, his black brows coming together, but he said coolly, "For the simple reason that I did not know it."

"You did not—Oh, is that true, my lord? I thought—"

"Did you think my money had paid for the very gown you stood up in, my dear?"

She was too oddly relieved to dissemble. "Yes, I did think it. I don't—Oh, you don't know what I have—but it makes it no better, of course. Did you really have no idea that she had all the bills sent to her?"

"Whatever else you may think of me, my dear," he drawled, "I am not in the habit of lying. But why does it matter so much to you? At worst, it would only be a trifle premature."

She scarcely heard him, hardly knowing why she was almost giddy with relief. How could she explain what she had felt at the thought that St. Ives might have paid for even her smallest toothbrush?

He was still watching her closely, and he said now in a harsh voice, "Do you really hate me as much as that, Sylvie?"

They had had little opportunity to talk in the last weeks. She had not wanted to be forced into a tête-à-tête, but now it was of paramount importance to her to make him understand.

"I do not hate you—I don't think I ever hated you." She gave a little smile. "It is rather you, I think, who must despise me. You said I have been nothing but trouble to you. But—but please believe that I had no idea it was your grandmother who was paying for me. I mean to pay her back, every penny."

She was near tears, but St. Ives, for answer, swore violently and wheeled his grays. When they reached the Priory once more he set her down at the front door, saying curtly, "You will have to do without your lesson after all! Tell my grandmother I will not be in to luncheon." He drove off at such a speed he narrowly missed Wicken, who had come from the back of the house at the sound of the curricle returning.

Wicken leaped back, then glanced at Sylvie who sighed and said faintly, "I fear—I fear I have made him angry. Will he be all right?"

Wicken shrugged and removed the straw from his mouth. "Aye, miss, you don't need to worry about him. It's those grays I wouldn't vouch for!"

St. Ives did not return to luncheon, and her godmother had barricaded herself in her room, too unwell to see anyone except her dresser, and it was, all in all, a dreadful day. St. Ives did reappear at dinner, but he seemed in a brittle mood and drank a good deal more than he had been doing of late. And things were not helped when they received unexpected guests after dinner, among whom was Julia Horneby.

Sylvie was bound to own that Mrs. Horneby was indeed lovely. She came in on a puff of cold air, and in the ensuing greetings and introductions, she soon found an excuse to change her seat for one nearer St. Ives. She had apologized prettily to the dowager for breaking in on them, saying they had been to a party in the neighborhood and she could not resist looking in. She was very gay and a little provocative, and very sure of herself, and Sylvie could not read the expression in St. Ives's eyes as he greeted her. They certainly sat in close conversation for some time, while the rest of the talk became general, and Sylvie knew a stab of pain at the sight of that black head so close to Julia Horneby's golden one. She told herself dully that this was the wife St. Ives should have—and perhaps would have when this brief episode were over, if Kitty could be believed. She sighed and tried to listen to whatever it was that Lady Jersey was saying to her.

She would have been even less happy if she could have heard Julia Horneby's conversation. Julia smiled and said archly, "My dear, you would not credit the stories we've been getting. I vow I have not laughed so much in years. Is that your little brown mouse?" She nodded toward the corner where Sylvie was conversing with Mr. Strickland and Lady Jersey.

St. Ives did not turn his head. "Hello Julia," he drawled. "Is this where you have been hiding yourself?"

She was a little piqued that he greeted her so casually, but she smiled and said lightly, "Yes, dreadfully dull, is it not? But Quinby would come here." She was a widow and made her home with her inattentive, rather effeminate brother. "Did you miss me?"

He merely raised his brows and turned to look at her at last. "Did you think I would?"

She frowned, but made an effort to ignore his ill humor. "But you have not answered me!" she said in a teasing voice. "Is that your little mouse? It is unkind of you to make her the object of your gallantry, you know, Nicky. Do you think she will understand when you grow tired of this game and amuse yourself elsewhere?"

He turned to look toward the corner where Sylvie sat, and he frowned abruptly at the sight of Michael Staunton now occupying the seat next to her. "And if it is not a game?" he said cruelly.

She was startled, for she did not understand his mood or the brooding way in which he was observing Miss Fairfield. She had heard the story almost a month ago and had not known whether to credit it or not. Her first sight this evening of Miss Fairfield had reassured her, but it had been a shock to discover that the girl made one at a party at his house. She mistrusted St. Ives in this mood, but then she could tell he had been drinking, and perhaps that explained it.

So she said with a little laugh, "I think you mean to make me jealous! If not, I could almost find it in my heart to feel sorry for the poor child. Not quite in your usual class, is she, my dear?"

He smiled then and withdrew his gaze from his cousin and Miss Fairfield, saying, "No, she has rather less knowledge of the world than Kitty does. That is certainly not in my class—or yours, my dear!"

She was less pleased at the comparison, but he turned to her then and began to flirt so outrageously, very much in his old manner, that she was once again reassured.

Michael, observing the studious way in which Sylvie avoided looking in St. Ives's direction, finally said, "I did not know Julia Horneby was to be in Somerset. But then I have not seen her in London for nearly two months."

Sylvie, feeling as if some response was required of her, said evenly, "She is certainly very beautiful. Is she —do I understand she is a widow?"

He answered her indifferently, observing her with a faint frown. She was not unaware of his scrutiny, and she made an effort to school her features to betray nothing. She had made up her mind during the interminable hours of that day to tell Michael she would accept his offer. She believed, or hoped, he would understand when she explained to him that she must pay back every penny the dowager had expended upon her and that she hoped he would not begrudge the cost; if he did, she would do whatever was necessary, even to selling Cintra.

Something in her face must have betrayed her, for Michael ran his hands across his eyes and said roughly, "It gives you pain to see them together, doesn't it? No, do not attempt to deny it! I can see it in your eyes."

"You are mistaken. It is nothing to do with me whom his lordship converses with."

Michael flushed and said in a low voice, "You think I am mad! Indeed, I think I may be going mad. You love him. I can see it every time you look at him. Cannot you see that he will only make you unhappy? If not with Julia, then with someone else? God, is he to have everything, as usual?"

She said now, unhappily, "Forgive me, but I think there is a jealousy there, however you deny it, that makes you say these things."

But he seemed to be past hearing, for he said raggedly, "God, you do not attempt to deny it! I have been patient, thinking—but you are in love with him! Do you think he will ever return that regard? Or is it merely that you think his possessions will compensate for the nights you spend alone?"

It was unforgivable of him to speak so, but she knew he was upset, and she said quietly, "I will try to forget you said that. Now excuse me, but I have a headache and I am going to my room."

She rose, but before she could make good her escape someone addressed a remark to her. She answered woodenly, she scarcely knew what, but she had missed her chance, for then Lord Alvanley, perhaps a little bored with the evening, suggested they might have some music and asked her if she played.

She shook her head and said truthfully that she did not. The only other young lady present, Miss Beckworth, flushed painfully, but her Mama was quick to point out that she was sure dear Charlotte would indulge them if they cared to ask her.

Charlotte, looking ill, took her place at the pianoforte, giving Sylvie a terrified glance. Mrs. Beckworth seated herself near St. Ives's chair and said in a bright voice, "She is very shy, you know, but her music master tells me she has quite an ear. But then, you young gentlemen are not often fond of music—or at least drawing-room music!" she added archly.

St. Ives observed her contemptuously, then turned his back and resumed his conversation with Julia Horneby. Sylvie, watching this scene, told herself she despised him for his arrogance, and set herself to encourage poor Charlotte, whose playing was adequate, if uninspired.

Nearly everyone applauded her first piece, and her Mama begged her to play another and was kindly if not enthusiastically seconded, only Sylvie being close enough to hear Lady Jersey murmur, "Have you ever seen a more insipid girl? Does her Mama really think to interest St. Ives?"

Whatever her Mama thought, when the second piece was through, she said proudly, "There, was that not well done, my lord? The piece is particularly difficult, I understand."

St. Ives turned his blue eye upon her. "You relieve my mind, ma'am!" he said. "I only wish it had been impossible."

Sylvie slipped blindly from the room.

If the previously pleasant house party seemed to have turned into a nightmare, there was more to come. Most of the guests left the following day, and there descended on the gathering the usual malaise of a party where half the members had departed and at least three of those remaining were in most unconvivial moods. Lady Bridlington remained in her room, suffering, her maid said, from a bad cold; Lord St. Ives put in no appearance at all at breakfast; and Michael looked at her reproachfully when she came in, and he made no effort to speak to her.

Sylvie slipped away to the stables in midmorning and spent a comforting hour with Blackmer and Cintra. She returned feeling a little better, only to have the misfortune to encounter Michael in the hall.

He hesitated as she came in and looked as if he meant to go on upstairs, but after a minute he changed his mind and came forward, saying in his grave way, "I am glad of this opportunity to speak with you. I must beg your pardon for what I said last night. I spoke out of jealousy—without weighing my words, but it hardly matters why I said the things I did. All that matters is whether you can find it in you to forgive me, and say that I have not destroyed everything between us. *Is* that possible?"

He must have seen the answer in her face, for he gave a funny little half smile and said with a shrug, "Ah, I can see it is not."

She hardly knew when she had reached the decision, or what she meant to do now. She only knew she could not become a tool to be used against St. Ives, and she said, very gently, "I am sorry, Michael. It would not have worked, you know. Indeed, you do not realize it now, but you will come to thank me, someday. I have saved you from more than you know."

His mouth twisted. "Have you?" Then he smiled and added, "May I at least wish you joy in the relationship you are so obviously about to enter? I should have remembered that St. Ives always gets what he wants."

She would have liked to disabuse him of the idea that she was going to marry St. Ives, but before she could say anything more, St. Ives himself came up behind her and said smoothly, "But then, Michael, I have warned you before about desiring what is mine, have I not?"

Suddenly it was as if she were no longer there. Both of them had forgotten her existence. "Yes," Michael ground out at last. "You always cared more for victory than for actual possession, didn't you, St. Ives?"

"Perhaps. But once won, I keep what is mine, and you would do well not to forget it."

Michael's lips thinned and his face was no longer handsome. "My uncle was right!" he said contemptuously. "You are your mother all over again! Do you think the world does not know you for what you are, even as your father did?"

St. Ives laughed, as if deliberately taunting him. "Nevertheless, the victory is mine, as you said yourself."

Sylvie could endure no more. *"Stop it!"* she cried. "You are both of you disgusting. Despicable! I will not be a pawn to be maneuvered by either of you! And do not speak to me of love again!" she added when Michael would have spoken. "I am not convinced you know the meaning of the word. And I would not marry either of you if it meant starving to death first!" And she pushed past them both and ran up the stairs.

The dowager, observing this scene from the doorway of the library, waited until Michael had stalked off. "You're a fool, St. Ives!" she said then. "You've bungled the affair badly. I expected better of you."

St. Ives turned to look at her, apparently unsurprised by her presence. "I know exactly what I am doing," he said.

She gave a short laugh. "Do you? You'll lose her if you don't watch out. I told you she wasn't one of your namby-pamby misses!"

Unexpectedly, his face softened. "I hope you are wrong, ma'am," he said. "I sincerely hope you are wrong."

XXVII

Sylvie had recovered from a stormy bout of weeping by the next morning, but she would have liked nothing better than to return to London immediately. However, when she stopped in to see her godmother, it seemed that Lady Bridlington was genuinely ill. Crimping went so far as to request that a doctor be sent for, since her ladyship was feverish and susceptible to a chill. Sylvie's heart sank, for it meant there was no chance of leaving the Priory anytime soon, but she sent kind messages through Crimping and promised to tend to the matter of the doctor.

But she should have known that Michael would not cause her any more pain. When they met at the breakfast table, he looked at her steadily, wished her good morning, and returned his attention to his breakfast. He shortly made some excuse to spend the day elsewhere and left the house.

She did not see St. Ives until dinnertime, and then she thought there was only a suppressed air of expectancy about him, as if he were waiting for something that would amuse him.

To her surprise, he came to sit beside her after dinner. He smiled at her in his careless way and said under his breath, "Smile, little sparrow, or they will think I have been beating you. I have brought you in for a great deal of unpleasantness, I know, but I give you my word I will not let any of this touch you. When no announcement is forthcoming of our marriage, it will soon be believed that I was only amusing myself after all, and you will be rather pitied than blamed. If that is not to your taste, you may with my blessing tell anyone you choose that you had

266

never any intention of wedding me. It is little enough I can do for you, and no one will disbelieve it, God knows," he said. "As for that other matter, you may safely leave that to me as well. I will find some way of hushing up whatever gossip there may be, and I will see that your father causes you no trouble. You should be able to continue to live with your godmother, for I believe she is genuinely fond of you. Perhaps in time you may even forget your painful experiences with a rake."

She resisted the impulse to smile sadly at him, thinking that, after all, he was the naïve one. "Thank you. I believe you meant it for the best, my lord."

He shrugged. "Did I? I wonder. But never mind. Did you mean it when you refused Michael, too? Or was that just your famous temper again."

She thought she owed him that much, at least. "No, my lord, I meant it."

He shrugged again, but she thought, absurdly, that he looked a little relieved. "I see. May I ask then what you plan to do?"

"I don't know, my lord," she said. "It no longer seems of such importance, anyway. I think I may even return home until Kendall and I are able to do as we originally planned. He has been offered a post in Vienna with Lord Summerhill, did you know? I will not be able to go there with him, of course, but when he returns I don't doubt we can work something out."

A brief smile came into his eyes. "What, no widowers?"

She laughed at that. "No, my lord, I think I have abandoned that particular ambition. But I am—am sorry about Kitty. Will she still have her coming out?"

"You might rather be sorry for me! Kitty will survive being thwarted for once in her life."

"Will you, my lord?" she asked with a smile.

"Yes, little witch, I will. Is your godmother very ill? Would you prefer to return to London without her?"

This was a new St. Ives, and one she had infinitely less defense against, but she merely shook her head and said, "No, my lord, I would not leave her. She is not, I hope, very ill. The doctor was here to see her today, and he reports a mild case of influenza."

Someone addressed a remark to him then and he got up, leaving her to come to terms with a strong instinct to burst into tears.

The dowager contracted Lady Bridlington's chill next and took to her bed with a mild fever. She took it badly, blaming Lady Bridlington for being so foolish as to bring it into the house and threatening to refuse admittance to the doctor if he should dare to show his face. But she looked frailer, somehow, and older, when Sylvie looked in to see her, and oddly naked without her elegant gowns and profusion of jewels.

Sylvie felt a great wave of affection for her. "Well, at all events, you look a great deal better than my poor godmamma, ma'am."

"Hmph!" said her grace. "I look what I am, a crotchety old woman, but I might have depended on Sophia Bridlington to take on as if she were dying over a cold in the head. And what have you been up to that you look like death warmed over? Quarreling with my grandson again, no doubt, and both of you saying a great many silly things you shouldn't have!"

Sylvie smiled. "We have been quarreling, ma'am, but I hope it is for the last time. As soon as my godmother is well enough to travel, we will be returning to London. But I want you to know that I—I have appreciated all you have done for me. And I would not have approved of your being obliged to pay for me had I known about it, but I am grateful for that too. I hope you know I mean to pay you back."

Her grace snorted. "Well, you're a fool, of course, but that's nothing new!"

"No, your grace. But you knew that from the beginning."

The dowager grinned reluctantly. "Aye, you've spirit. If you want the truth, I'm sorry you won't have St. Ives. You might have been the making of him. I made a mistake, all those years ago, in letting Ariel marry his father, and I was hoping you might in some way rectify it. But if you won't, you won't, and there's an end to it. And if that godmother gives you any trouble, remember you'll always have a home with me if you want it."

Then, as if ashamed of her brief weakness, she added gruffly, "Now go along with you! And tell that woman of mine I want a glass of claret, and I won't have any nonsense from her."

Sylvie was touched, but she merely kissed the dowager's old cheek and said, "I am sorry, too, ma'am, for I can't think of anything nicer than having you as a grandmother. I will never forget you, and I hope someday to be exactly like you. But St. Ives will find a young lady who will be precisely the granddaughter-in-law you could have wished, and I shall dance at their wedding."

The dowager watched her leave. From the looks of it, Sylvie had made up her mind. In love with him too, little fool, and bent on being noble.

Sylvie, in the meantime, paid another dutiful visit to her godmother, but the doctor was there and her ladyship was inclined to be fretful. She promised to return later, and then, feeling oddly at a loose end, she slipped out of the house to go for a walk.

To her disgust, her thoughts seemed inclined to dwell on melancholy reflections, and she soon gave up any idea of making constructive plans for her future and merely walked to exhaust herself, seeking a release in the physical exercise. It was a cold day, with frost in the air, but if she walked quickly she was able to keep warm. The ground was wet, and she had failed to change her shoes, so she kept to the road that led to the rear of the house, staying on its dryer cinder surface.

She walked farther than she had intended, and by the time she was tired enough to have gained a certain measure of peace, she discovered she had come several miles. It would soon be dark, and though she was not particularly daunted by the thought of the long walk back through the gathering twilight, it was getting colder as well, and if she were too late someone might begin to worry about her. Something she remembered one of the maids saying made her think that the road she was following curved around to meet the main lane to the house, so she walked on.

And indeed, within five or ten minutes of brisk walking she came in sight of the main road leading directly through the park, although the Priory itself was not yet visible. The main road was flanked by trees, and a little copse lay between her and it; however, the two roads did not actually meet for some yards off. Weary and more than ready to put off her wet shoes, she chose the shorter route and began to mount the little rise, beginning to hurry a little. She was almost to the road when the sound of hoofbeats reached her, and within a very few seconds St. Ives had come into view on the main road.

She thought to hail him, but there remained considerable constraint between them, and he would only be bound to offer her his seat, so she did not. From the reason of the slightly higher ground she stood on, he had not yet seen her, and he was unlikely to unless he happened to be searching the copse.

For a brief second she had an excellent view of him, then a curve in the road took him out of her sight, and she stood patiently, waiting for him to reappear. At that instant there was the sound of a gun fired within fairly close range. The sound didn't alarm her. Someone might have taken a shotgun out from the house, or perhaps there were poachers about, particularly since St. Ives had not occupied the Priory in so long. But she doubted that St. Ives would take a calm view of the idea.

Then his chestnut rounded the bend into view again, and she started, for one dreadful second unable to believe her eyes. The saddle was empty, the reins hanging slack, and the chestnut badly frightened. St. Ives might have taken a toss; even the best riders did so at one time or another, *but he would never let go of the reins!*

Then she had picked up her skirts and was running, frantically, desperately, across the uneven ground, slipping in the mud, aware of nothing but a growing horror as she repeated numbly to herself, "Oh, God, he can't be dead. He can't be dead!"

When she first caught sight of him sprawled in the road so horribly still, the terror was so palpable in her mouth and lungs that she could scarcely breathe. He was lying on his side, halfway off the road, and the chestnut, once its initial fear had passed, had returned to crop peacefully nearby. Sylvie scrambled down to the road, scarcely noticing the branches that tore at her skirt and hair or the rocks that slid under her feet.

She dropped beside him and with trembling fingers unfastened his greatcoat and thrust her hand against his shirtfront, sickeningly aware of the spreading stain beneath her fingers. At first she could discover no heartbeat, and she thrust her cheek against his chest, straining for the faintest indication of a pulse.

All she could hear was the frenzied pounding of her own heart in her ears, but then she became aware that his chest was stirring and she felt the strong regular beating of his heart against her cheek. For a moment she was too overcome with relief to do anything but remain there, her cheek against his stained shirtfront, while the tears slipped unnoticed down her face. Then she roused herself and quickly stripped off his cravat and began to unfasten his shirt.

She had just laid bare a nasty wound in the fleshy part of his left shoulder, that, though bad enough, was perhaps not as bad as she had first feared, when his hand came up and weakly grasped her wrist. "I've got a bullet in my shoulder, you idiotic girl; I'm not dead yet. I had no idea you would shed any tears over me."

She had not been aware that she was still crying, but she looked up now, too relieved that he was conscious to care about anything. He was very pale, but there was a trace of his old mocking expression. She folded his neckcloth and attempted to staunch the bleeding. "No, you're not dead—yet, but I told you someone would try to murder you someday," she said as calmly as she could. "Now hold this."

He laughed, albeit weakly, then winced at the pain it caused him, but he obediently put up a hand and pressed the cravat as she directed. "I'm not that easy to kill. Now please, help me up."

She had taken the handkerchief from his pocket as well as her own handkerchief, and she added both to the wad she was pressing against the bleeding wound. She was recovering a little now from her first terror. "On no account, my lord. It is, as you said, merely a shoulder wound. I feared at first—but you are losing a lot of blood,

and I must contrive to stop the bleeding as much as
possible, then fetch help from the house. Have you another handkerchief?"

"Greatcoat pocket, I think," he said.

She found it and added it to the wad of blood-soaked
linen at his shoulder, her hands shaking only slightly.

He watched her with amusement. "I told you I'm not
dead yet, you silly child. Now help me up."

She ignored him, concentrating on her handiwork. "I
fear I am going to have to find something to bind this
with or I will never succeed in stopping the bleeding.
If you could manage to hold this here again—? Yes, only
firmer, and try not to move."

With a grimace he pressed his hand to the bandage
on his shoulder, then watched as she stood and unself-
consciously raised her skirt and ripped the flounce from
the bottom of her petticoat. It was a good three inches
wide, she knew, and should make an admirable bandage.
Immediately she sank beside him again and began
winding the long strip of muslin tightly about his shoulder.
She was hampered by his tight-fitting coat, but she dared
not take the time or run the risk of jarring him further
by trying to remove it.

He was still watching her, and he murmured a little
maliciously, "I see you don't faint at the sight of blood!"
He winced as she tied off the bandage, but he kept his
eyes on her face.

She ignored that too, intent on her task. The makeshift bandage was immediately crimson, but the bleeding
seemed to have slowed a little, and she dared not
waste more time. She must bring help before he became too weak from loss of blood or developed a chill
from lying on the frozen ground.

"Now, my lord, I must go for help. I will put my
cloak about you so you will not get too cold, and I won't
be gone much above five or ten minutes. Promise you
won't try to move, or you'll only make the bleeding begin
again."

He swore and struggled to get up, grunting a little at
the effort it cost him. She tried desperately to prevent
him, but he only swore again and said, "I warn you, girl,

if you leave me I'll get back on my own! Now *help me up, I said!"*

She thought it best not to argue with him for the moment, and she put her arm under his shoulders to help him sit up. He grew even paler, but when he had managed to sit up he said, panting slightly, "Good! Now help me to my feet."

"My lord—!" she cried. Then something in his closed face made her bite back the rest of her words and do as he asked. She knelt beside him, taking as much of his weight as she could, and prayed that the bandage would not break loose again. He lurched heavily to his feet, swaying and leaning against her, the sweat standing in great drops on his brow, but he managed to stay erect. "Now," he said, his voice growing thick, "do you think you could contrive to help me mount?"

She was almost as pale as he was. "You'll kill yourself!" she cried. "Is that what you want?"

He swayed unsteadily toward the chestnut that was still standing docilely nearby, reins down.

She had no choice but to help him, but she said fiercely under her breath, "If you must kill yourself, I'll bring him to you! Can you manage to stand while I catch him?"

He laughed again, but it was a bare ghost of a sound, and it was clear it was all he could do to remain on his feet while she went cautiously toward the animal. The horse offered no resistance, and she grasped his bridle and pulled him around so St. Ives could mount.

This he managed to do, but only after several attempts, and by the time he finally sat swaying in the saddle, she could see where the bleeding had broken out again. She was past any emotion now, and only said furiously, "You won't last half a mile! I will have to come up before you."

She looked around desperately for a mounting block, and, spying a tree trunk nearby, led the chestnut over and managed to get a leg up. Unmindful of her skirts, she swung her leg over the saddle in front of St. Ives, taking the bridle from his slack grasp.

They made slow progress. St. Ives was soon leaning

heavily against her, and she thought with renewed fear
that he must have lost a great deal of blood. She supported
him as best she could, terrified he would fall at any
moment. She thought he had lost consciousness again, for
he was dreadfully heavy against her back, but when they
finally came in sight of the house, his hand came up to
grasp the reins above hers and he said in her ear, "Go
around to the stables! Find Wicken."

His words were beginning to slur, and she did as he
asked, infected by something of the same urgency she
sensed in him. She was rewarded by a soft, "Good girl!"
before he relaxed once more against her, his hand
falling away.

She came in sight of the stables, waiting until she was
sure no one was in the yard; then she headed to the
back, meaning to go in search of Wicken or Blackmer.
She had almost slipped from the saddle, having to trust
fate to keep St. Ives up a little longer, when she spied
Wicken's sturdy figure coming around the corner of the
building.

She could have cried in relief. Indeed, had she not
been otherwise occupied, she thought she must have
thrown her arms around that gentleman, for he started,
then apparently grasped the situation at a glance and
came forward quickly, saying only, "Aye, I thought I recognized the chestnut's gait."

He asked no questions, merely reaching up to steady
St. Ives while she slipped to the ground. Wicken must
have been extremely strong, for he managed to ease
St. Ives's tall figure from the saddle and support him
while she ran quickly to his other side.

"Oh, Wicken, thank God you're here!" she said. "He
won't let me fetch help. Please help me get him into
the house before he loses more blood!"

St. Ives had roused himself a little, and he shook his
head and said, "Wicken—good! Must get—must get to my
room. No one see me. Back stairs—you know the way.
Must have lost too much blood, damn it! Can't think
straight—"

"No, my lord," said Wicken in a soothing voice. "You
just leave it to me and miss here to see all's right. Come
along, there's a good lad." He seemed to find nothing

incongruous in addressing the notorious rake St. Ives as a good lad, and Sylvie was too scared to notice it, but a glint of mockery appeared briefly in St. Ives's blue eyes before he gave himself over to the unbelievable difficulty of merely walking the few yards to the house.

Though St. Ives made a valiant effort to maintain his own weight, his feet were dragging badly, and when they got him to the house, Sylvie stopped, panting, and said, "It's no use! I must get help. We'll never manage to get him up to his room."

But St. Ives said, "No. I'm all right! Just let me—let me get my breath. It's not much farther—"

When she frantically sought guidance from Wicken, the groom only said, "Best do as he says, miss." She sighed and admitted defeat, and in a moment they resumed their slow progress, her anger and fear giving her the strength to support her share of his weight.

They encountered no one, but by the time they had reached his room he was barely conscious, and her mind could scarcely function. Wicken supported him while she thrust open his bedchamber door, and between them they got him inside and into a chair.

He was dreadfully pale, his dark locks were untidy curls on his forehead, and his face was drenched in sweat. The bleeding had begun again, and she wasted no more time. "Help me get him out of his coat," she said to Wicken, "then you'd better go down and see to the blood in the house and put the chestnut away. If he will kill himself, we'd better do what we can to help him."

The first of these tasks proved easier said than done. St. Ives had rallied slightly, but it was evident he had exhausted his strength and could do little to help them.

They had gotten him to lean forward in his chair, Sylvie kneeling at his feet with her arms around him to support him, when the door opened behind them. Sylvie gasped and turned to stare into the face of a rather weary man in black whom she had never seen before. He quickly shut the door behind him. Wicken was looking grim, and his lordship, lifting his head, said indistinctly, "It's you, is it? Well, you'd better stop gaping—and come—and help. That is if you don't faint at the—sight of blood!"

The man certainly looked pale, and he swallowed a

few times, but then he seemed to rise to the demands put upon him and he came forward, saying expressionlessly, "Certainly, my lord." He seemed to have taken in the situation at a glance and found it in his province, for he added, "If you will permit me, ma'am, I think I might manage to get his coat off without undue damage. If you, Wicken, would be so good as to support him—thus —ah, very good! I will endeavor to slip both arms out of his coat and waistcoat at the same time." As he spoke, he moved deftly, and though he blanched a little at the quantity of blood on St. Ives's shirtfront and pants, not to mention Miss Fairfield's gown and Wicken's coat, he said only, "And now, I perceive, you will wish him placed in his bed? If I might assist Wicken in that task, I believe it may be accomplished without too much jarring."

Wicken eyed him, but did his bidding, and between them they lifted St. Ives while Sylvie hurried to turn down the covers. St. Ives, relaxing with a sigh against his pillow, said between his teeth, "Well, Manley? I thought you—hated me!"

"I should think it would be best for you not to exhaust yourself by talking, my lord," said the valet without emotion. He had knelt to remove St. Ives's top boots, a task he accomplished as deftly as the last, though he clucked a little over the mud and bloodstains on them. He set them gently aside and added in that same unhurried tone, "I perceive, ma'am, that the ball may still be lodged in his lordship's shoulder. Shall I arrange to have a doctor sent for immediately?"

She had been anxiously checking the fate of her makeshift bandage, but she looked up to say thankfully, "Oh, yes, please! But first, if you will lift his feet, Wicken, I believe we can get him under the covers. Those pillows —oh, yes, thank you! Now I think—"

"No doctor," interrupted St. Ives.

Wicken looked wary, but my lord's valet said in his calm way, "I perceive that you do not understand how much blood you have lost, my lord. You are very weak. Unless the bullet is withdrawn and the bleeding stanched, you are in danger of losing your life."

St. Ives swore. "I know how much—blood I've lost, you

—fool! Wicken can get the bullet out. D'you think I'm so easily murdered? No doctor, I say."

Wicken was looking grim, but the two servants stood there helplessly, neither prepared to take the initiative against his lordship's direct order. Sylvie hesitated a moment, then came forward and said as calmly as she could manage, "Your valet is right, my lord. You have lost a good deal of blood. You must permit us to send for the doctor."

St. Ives had closed his eyes, and his face was dangerously pale against the white pillows, but he opened his eyes at that and reached up to grasp her wrist with his hard fingers. "What, are you still here?" he asked. "Go away, there's a good girl. But first—I want your word you'll—hold your tongue! I won't have this—blabbed of." He collapsed a little against his pillows, as if the effort had been too much for him, but he added after a moment, "But I needn't worry—I know I can rely on you, Sylvie."

She flushed a little, aware of the interested observation of the others, but said soothingly, "Yes, yes, my lord, only you must consent to have a doctor look at you."

He grimaced, and his grip tightened on her wrist. "They'll only draw more blood, little fool! I've—lost enough already. And don't speak to me—as if I'm a—witless child. D'you think it was—poachers at that time?" He was breathing very hard, and there was a bright, almost feverish light in his eyes. "You—said someone would—murder me someday—and you were—more right than you knew. Someone—nearly did!"

The blood sang in her ears, and she thought she was going to faint. She was nearly as pale as he, but she managed to keep a tight grip upon her emotions and only said in a very low voice, "Lambeth, my lord?"

He gave a short bark of laughter. "Or, barring him—some other! I don't—lack for enemies, my girl. Now I'll have your word. No doctor."

"Why?" she cried.

"Because—you little fool—if there is a hue and—cry raised, it will drive him away."

"Good! That is exactly what I want to happen!"

He smiled unwillingly. "And I'll be a sitting duck. No thank—you! I prefer to call—my own tune."

She stared at him. It was a desperate game, and her heart cried out to have nothing to do with it. But she knew he was right. If it were Lambeth, they had no proof. Once a hue and cry was raised he would only be very sure not to fail the next time. It would be impossible to be on guard every minute against a stray bullet or a convenient attack by footpads.

She hesitated, then said to the groom, "Can you get the bullet out, Wicken?"

"I can, miss—but that don't mean I should!" said Wicken.

She turned back, encountered St. Ives's eyes fixed on her face, and admitted defeat. "I don't—all right, my lord. But I don't promise I won't change my mind if I see the first sign of infection or danger!"

St. Ives had closed his eyes again, satisfied, and after a moment she straightened, the urgency of the situation allowing her no time to dwell on her decision. "Wicken, you had best go and see to the chestnut, and remove any blood we may have left on the saddle or on the stairs. And take care that no one catches you. Manley— is it?" At his nod, she continued, "Manley and I will endeavor to get him out of his clothes and keep the bleeding checked as much as possible until you return. Have— have Blackmer see to the chestnut if you need. We will need hot water, something to—to cleanse the wound, and a great deal of lint. Do you think you could manage to procure them as well?"

"I will engage myself to obtain those items, and some basilicum powder, if you wish me to, ma'am," interjected the valet.

She nodded gratefully and turned back to St. Ives. His grip on her wrist had slackened and his eyes were closed, as if he had used up the last of his strength, but he said now, in a voice that brooked no argument, "No, not you! You're a good girl, but I don't need you. Tell Manley— brandy, too. Must keep my wits about me!"

She looked up, but Wicken said quietly, for her ears alone, "I think he's right, miss. I fear he'll need it if I'm to get that bullet out. It'd be better still if we could manage to knock him up."

St. Ives's eyes remained closed, but he laughed weakly. "I've a harder head than that, old fool! Now don't—

let the chestnut stand any longer." His fingers relaxed their hold on her wrist and he sighed and turned his head on the pillow.

Wicken went quickly out the door.

St. Ives, if not completely unconscious, had certainly used up the last of his strength, for he did not stir again as the remainder of his shirt was cut away from his shoulder and chest and an added strip fastened to the blood-soaked bandage around his wound. Only when Sylvie, gratefully making use of the basin of water Manley held, began to sponge away the dried blood from his chest and arms did he stir a little. He opened his eyes and stared at her as if he did not recognize her, then he shook his head as if to clear it and said thickly, "Told you—go—shouldn't be here—"

"No, my lord," she said, placing the cool cloth against his brow. He sighed and closed his eyes again and allowed her to sponge his face.

His pulse was weak and erratic, his breathing heavy, and he did not move again when she gently pulled the covers over him and took her place beside the bed in a chair Manley provided for her. She prayed she had not made the wrong decision, but surely Wicken would tell her if he thought the task beyond him.

Manley went to fetch the required supplies, promising to arouse no suspicion, and Wicken had not yet returned, so that for the moment she was alone with St. Ives. She sat rigidly beside him, her emotions so tightly in check that her face felt stiff from the effort not to cry, her hands gripped so tightly together that the knuckles showed white. She was not conscious of her tousled hair, or that her gown was nearly as bloodstained as St. Ives's clothes, or that there was a smear of mud on her cheek. Nor did the knowledge penetrate her brain that she must have given herself away forever by the strained white-ness of her face and the way her hands trembled so pitifully if she did not keep them locked together.

But Wicken, when he returned a few minutes later, gave her a sharp glance. "His lordship's right, miss. There's no need for you to remain. Forgive me, but you don't look at all the thing, if you don't mind my saying so. Perhaps you'd best go and lie down for a bit."

"No, Wicken, thank you." She managed to smile. "I don't *think* I'll disgrace myself by fainting on you, but I mean to stay. Did you—were you able to get the chestnut stabled without anyone seeing you?"

"Aye, miss. I've wiped off most of the blood too, leastways that around the stables and some smudges on the banister. I had to hide the saddle, of course, until I have a chance to clean it, and I don't doubt you left a trail leading all the way to the house."

She swallowed. "Yes. Do—do you think you could contrive to cover that as well, when you get a chance?"

He nodded, then glanced at the pale figure of his lordship. "This is a damnable business!" he burst out. "I don't know how you come to find him, but I thank God you did! Did you see anything?"

"No, nothing. I—I heard the shot, but I thought it must be—poachers, or someone out with a shotgun from the house. Then I—found him—and I'm afraid I was too upset to try to discover where the shot came from."

She lifted her eyes to the groom's face. He made no attempt to conceal the frown in his eyes, and she remembered the way he had spoken to his lordship on that wild night so long ago. It was clear he was very attached to St. Ives, and she hesitated only a second before adding, "It *is* a damnable business, Wicken. What do you know of Lord Lambeth?"

"Have you reason to believe he's in the neighborhood, miss?"

"Yes, for I saw him myself in the village just a few days ago," she said. "I am well aware that he is—one of those enemies his lordship spoke of. Is he, in your opinion, capable of—murder?"

Wicken spread his hands in a helpless gesture. "I don't know, miss. I'd not relish meeting him on a dark night if he had something against me, but that's just my own prejudice."

She shivered. "No, nor would I. And it was clear to me that he hates St. Ives. But it's all so stupid!" she cried a little wildly, losing some of her control. "Surely he would not *kill* him over an opera dancer who meant nothing to either of them!"

The groom observed her, his eyes revealing little of

what he was thinking. "If you'll excuse me saying so," he said gruffly, "very little means much to his lordship, miss."

"I know, Wicken," she said sadly. "You are—you are very fond of him, aren't you?"

He hesitated, his expression softening. "Yes, miss. I think you are too, if you don't mind my saying so."

It was not said disrespectfully; but it didn't even matter. They were only two people united in a common bond. "Yes, Wicken, I am too," she admitted. "Will he—will he be all right?"

Wicken grinned. "He's harder to kill than that, miss, as I should know. He'll be all right, don't you worry none."

"Thank you, Wicken. I don't know what I'd have done without you."

Both of them heard the soft knock at the door at the same time, and the groom went swiftly forward to prevent the entrance of any unheralded person, but it was only Manley, who came in his own calm way bearing a covered tray upon which rested a decanter and one glass. He set the tray down and removed the cloth, revealing a basin of warm water, a neat roll of lint, and a packet of basilicum powder.

Wicken eyed it approvingly, without sparing a glance for the valet, and rolling up his sleeves he set to work. He poured a generous measure of brandy, then from somewhere produced a long, wicked-looking knife, as well as a pair of tweezers from his lordship's own dressing table.

It all seemed dreadfully primitive to her. Wicken glanced up and said matter-of-factly, "He may not need the brandy after all, but it won't hurt to get it down him just the same. Manley?" The valet came forward from where he had been building up the fire and laying out a number of towels, and Wicken added quietly, "Will you be all right, miss?"

"Yes, I think so. What can I do?"

"I don't doubt but what I'll open up the bleeding again. If you would, miss, you could hold the basin for me while Manley keeps his lordship still."

She nodded. He observed her closely for a moment, as if to reassure himself, then turned away, apparently satisfied.

Between them they managed to lift St. Ives enough to pour some brandy between his lips. He choked a little, then stirred and opened his eyes. "What the—?" he said weakly. Then his eyes seemed to focus. "Oh, you're at that, are you?" he said, slurring his words. "I'm not quite dead yet, you know." He shook off the valet's hand and managed to grasp the glass in his right hand and swallow the brandy, ignoring the relief in his groom's eyes. "You'd best get on with it. No wait!" he said, rousing himself. "Where's—yes, I thought I saw you! She's not to stay, Wicken, do you understand? Get her out of here!"

Wicken frowned, but Sylvie said coolly, "Wicken needs my help, my lord. For once it is you who will take orders. You have insisted that no doctor be called, and I have consented, very much against my better judgment. But unless you stop behaving like a spoiled schoolboy, I will send for the doctor immediately."

The valet's expression remained unreadable, but Wicken's eyes began to twinkle. St. Ives gave a short laugh, then winced. "Egad, I think you would! Very well. You seem—for the moment—to have the upper hand—"

She could scarcely keep the relief from her voice. "Yes, my lord, I do." She paled as Wicken began unwinding the bloodstained bandages, but she came forward to hold the basin ready.

The wound Wicken laid bare once more was ugly, the blood still seeping listlessly. It seemed to have missed his heart by only a few inches. St. Ives grimaced as the last cloth was pulled away, and Wicken glanced up and said, "I fear this will hurt a trifle, my lord."

St. Ives did not open his eyes. "It's going to hurt—damnably—and well you know it!" he said. "You may as well—get it over with!"

The groom, drawing a quick breath, went about his task. After a moment he announced, "The bullet seems to have missed any vital organ, and I do not think the lung has been punctured. You were fortunate, my lord."

His lordship thanked him in a goaded voice, his eyes tight shut and his expression forbidding. His whole body stiffened, and she tensed with him, and then mercifully he lost consciousness. Wicken did not look up, but said as if for her benefit, "Aye, that's sent him off. Doubtless it's for the best. It's a nasty business. The bullet's in deep."

She nodded weakly. Then the groom exclaimed in satisfaction, and in another moment he had extracted the bullet.

Now that it was over, her head was swimming, and she knew an ignominious desire to be sick, but she held on to her fast-vanishing control while Wicken sponged the wound, dusted it with basilicum powder, and wrapped it tightly once more. St. Ives lay as if dead, only the faint rise and fall of his chest betraying that he still breathed, his black locks in wet curls on his forehead and the towels surrounding the bed stained heavily with his blood.

She stood, lacking the will to tear her eyes from that horrible crimson pile, until Wicken, glancing up from where he had been putting away his instruments, came forward and almost thrust her into a chair and put a glass of brandy in her hand.

She took it, ashamed of her sudden weakness, and drank, the glass clattering against her teeth, her hands shaking so. Manley, too, poured himself a generous measure and swallowed it quickly.

Wicken forebore to make any comment and only said gruffly, "He'll do well enough, I think, miss. But we'd best decide what's to be done now."

She made an immense effort to think. She glanced at the clock and could scarcely believe it was only six o'clock. "Yes, yes, of course," she said. "I don't—" She shook her head. "I don't quite know how we are to keep this quiet—but we must make an effort to do so. He must not be left alone, of course—but I fear I'd better change my gown and go downstairs, for I have been gone all afternoon. Manley, will you sit with his lordship? Wicken —Wicken had best return to the stables, or he may arouse suspicion. I think—I'm afraid I dare not miss dinner, but I will return to see how he is after I change for dinner, and I will—I will contrive to get away as soon as possible after the tea tray is brought in. Wicken, I don't —will it be possible for you to come back after dark and relieve Manley?"

At his nod she shook her head again as if to clear it and said uncertainly, "I will inform them at dinner that he has—has accepted an invitation to dine with friends in the neighborhood. It will certainly be thought a little odd, but his reputation is such that no one will be much concerned. Oh, I just thought! How glad I am that Julia Horneby and her friends called the other evening. Perhaps it will not be thought so remarkable if they think he has gone there. I only hope—but never mind. We will deal with that if it comes up.

"Use Blackmer in any way you think necessary, and tell him as much as you have to. And tomorrow—tomorrow we shall just have to think of something else," she concluded helplessly.

Wicken was regarding her with considerable respect, and the valet bowed gravely. She did not know how she was to manage after today, and she felt more than unequal to the task before her, or even to so simple a thing as going downstairs and chatting at dinner. She was still feeling oddly light-headed, and was aware of a pang at the thought of being obliged to leave St. Ives's side, but he was relying on her, and so were Wicken and Manley, to keep up the pretense that nothing was wrong. There was at least comfort in knowing that if she had sent for a doctor, she would scarcely have been allowed to nurse him herself. She looked at his still figure, then went quickly out of the room, not seeing the look exchanged by the two servants.

XXVIII

She went to change her dress before she went down for tea, not ringing for her maid, and she thrust her soiled gown as far back in the cupboard as she could. She would have time to dispose of it later. Then she rearranged her hair with trembling fingers, took a deep breath, and went to tap on her godmother's door.

Lady Bridlington was awake, but it was clear she was inclined to be querulous. Sylvie had seen little of her since their quarrel over finances, and her ladyship was still looking ill and very sorry for herself.

As Sylvie came in she said, "Oh, there you are. Crimping said you were not in your room, and no one seemed to know where you had gone."

Sylvie managed to say, "I am sorry, ma'am, I went for a long walk. Did you wish me for something in particular?"

"No, no!" said her ladyship. "Only I am feeling so badly, and I thought you might have looked in after luncheon. I am almost of a mind to go home, for my dear Dr. Broadie knows just what to do for my cough, and I'm sure there's no point in remaining here any longer. What I shall say to the dowager I dread to think! When I think of the fortune—as well as the title—you've whistled down the wind, all for a set of foolish principles, I could scream with vexation, and likely I shall be carried off by a fever, for it's all of a piece with the rest."

Sylvie did not feel equal to one of her ladyship's bouts of tears. It had never occurred to her that her godmother might wish to go home at this point. She said, praying her voice was steady, "But do you think you should travel, ma'am? I should have thought you were far too unwell, and you know how queasy you get on long journeys."

Her ladyship said, "Yes, but if you are to marry Michael Staunton, I'm sure it hardly matters! Indeed, we might have stayed in London."

Sylvie took a deep breath. "Ma'am, I think you should know I have refused Mr. Staunton's offer."

"You refused him?" cried her ladyship. "Oh, my dearest child! Not that it was not a most acceptable offer, of course, and I do feel deeply for the poor boy, but it would never have done, you know! Oh, my dear, you can't know how happy this makes me! And we will not speak of that other—no, no! It was only the thought of your throwing yourself away—but we need not go into that again. I'm sure I am feeling better already. But there, I am being selfish keeping you here with me. You run along downstairs and enjoy yourself. Perhaps you will look in on me again in the morning?"

Sylvie kissed her godmother, knowing that she had

revived all of her hopes and ambitions. But now at least her ladyship would be devising excuses to linger at the Priory.

When she came downstairs she found the dowager ensconced in her favorite chair, despite the advice of her physician. She had been conversing with Mr. Strickland, but at sight of Sylvie she said, "There you are! Come and talk to me, for I'm bored stiff."

Michael Staunton was standing brooding by the fireplace. He glanced up as she came in, but she ignored him and went willingly across to sit beside the dowager. "I am very glad to see you recovered so quickly, ma'am," she said, "but are you sure you should be up?"

"I would have been down sooner if that dratted Friday-faced physicker had left me in peace," said her grace.

Lady Venetia merely smiled from her place on the sofa and said, "Now, Mama, you know you're only upset because he said you shouldn't be drinking quite so much wine at your age. But then I daresay he didn't know about the oysters you ordered sent up to you last night."

Her grace gave a bark of laughter, but her mood seemed to have improved, for she patted Sylvie's hand and said, "Now tell me what you've been up to, my dear? Have you enjoyed your stay here?"

"Oh, yes, ma'am," said Sylvie. "It was very kind of you to invite me. I—does the doctor mean to visit you again any time soon?"

"No! I told him I wouldn't have him in the door if he showed his face here again! At my age I don't intend to be mauled about by some sanctimonious old bloodletter."

Sylvie sighed and changed the subject. They conversed desultorily after that, her grace maintaining the bulk of the conversation, which mainly involved the minute tracing of the relationship of a distant cousin she and Lady Jersey had discovered they had in common. Lady Jersey maintained her part in the discussion good-naturedly while the dowager thoroughly enjoyed herself by abusing a good many of that lady's illustrious forebears.

After the first few minutes, Sylvie ceased to pay attention, but after a while Mr. Strickland said, "I hope you are not coming down with the general indisposition, Miss Fairfield?"

She started. "What? Oh, no. No, of course not." She was blushing a little, but said only, "Why do you ask?"

He shrugged. "Merely that you were inquiring after the doctor, and I had not thought, listening to her grace, that his charm was such to invite a second visit."

She smiled. "You are doing him a grave injustice, for I thought him a very kind man. I was merely a little concerned about my godmother."

He was observing her with slightly raised brows, but he forebore to make any further comment, and she was soon able to escape upstairs again before dinner. She had lingered a little behind the others, not wishing to join the general movement upstairs, but before she could follow, Michael had come up quietly behind her and said in a low voice, "My dear ma'am—you are pale. Is something amiss?"

His manner was so much what it had been in the past that she relaxed a little and said quickly, "No, no, it is only that I think I walked a bit too far and am tired."

His eyes searched her face. "You are looking tired, but I think it is perhaps something more than that. Have you quarreled with St. Ives again?"

She smiled. "No, for I have not seen him all day, you know. I believe—that is, I think I heard his valet telling the butler that St. Ives had gone to dine with friends tonight. Which reminds me, we must go up soon and change or we shall be late." She put her hand lightly on the banister and would have walked up had not his own hand come out to detain her.

She looked around quickly. He was still regarding her intently, and he said now, "Miss Fairfield—Sylvie—dare I hope that we may continue as friends, even if there can never be anything more between us? I perceive that you are—shortly to become my cousin's wife. We shall be related then, you know, and I would not like to think we couldn't at least meet—as friends."

She scarcely heard what he said, wishing only that she might hurry, and she said a little disjointedly, "I do not regard what happened before, I assure you. I hope we shall always be able to meet as friends. I am sorry, I must go!"

He watched her hurry up the stairs, a bitter twist to his mouth.

She changed as quickly as she could, hurrying Mary and stopping to do little more than drag a comb through her curls and take up a reticule. Mary gaped when Sylvie said she did not care which gown she wore, only hurry, hurry!, and the girl seemed to be all thumbs at fastening the tiny buttons up the back, but at last Sylvie was ready. She looked out the door to avoid meeting anyone, then darted down the hall and down the next corridor to the wing in which St. Ives's room was located, hardly knowing what she should say should anyone find her there.

Luckily no one did, and she opened the door and slipped into his room, only to come up short at the sight that met her eyes. St. Ives was sitting up in bed, attempting to rise, while Wicken remonstrated with him and Manley stood by, disapproval patent on his face.

St. Ives glanced up as the door opened, but at the sight of her said only, "Oh, it's you, is it? Go away again, there's a good girl! And take this fool with you!'"

She advanced quickly into the room. He was still very pale, and there was a feverish glint in his eyes, but he looked more himself. "My lord!" she said. "You should not be up. What can you be thinking of?"

"I am thinking of getting dressed for dinner, my dear," he retorted. "If I may be left in peace to do so."

"This is foolishness, my lord. You are hardly strong enough to sit up in bed, and if you managed to get downstairs, you would only contrive to break open your wound again. You need not worry. I shall inform them downstairs that you have ridden into the village to dine with friends. I'm sure no one will question it too closely. We are only lucky Mrs. Horneby is known to be in the neighborhood. Now pray get back into bed before you make yourself worse."

He thrust back his blankets. "Manley, lay out my blue coat; it is not as tight as the others. You will have to tie my cravat for me, but I should be able to manage the rest with your help."

Manley cast a furtive glance at Sylvie. St. Ives saw it, and his lips curled dangerously. "You take your orders from me, I believe! Now do as I say!"

"No, Manley," she said quietly. "You will not go down-stairs tonight, my lord."

For a long moment he looked at her, then his brows rose. "May I know how you propose to prevent me, my dear Miss Fairfield?"

"Certainly, my lord," she said. "By forbidding your servants to help you."

His eyes narrowed. "By forbidding my—" He looked her up and down. "May I remind you that you are not yet my wife, Miss Fairfield? My servants take their orders from no one but me."

"No, nor am I likely to be your wife since it is clear you are determined to kill yourself, my lord."

He closed his eyes. "It is the veriest scratch! I have no intention of killing myself, you idiotic girl."

"No, my lord, it is not the veriest scratch," she said. "Wicken and Manley and I have been to a great deal of trouble this afternoon to prevent you from dying, and we do not mean to see our handiwork undone by some stupid notion you have taken into your head. My lord will be getting back into bed, Manley."

"Yes, ma'am," said the valet, and he moved forward to replace the coverlet.

St. Ives swore under his breath, and there was a brief moment when both servants waited to see what he would do next. They had both had a taste of his temper when his will was thwarted.

What his lordship did was to subside weakly but with ill grace back onto his pillow and say in a goaded voice, "I had no idea you were such a termagant, my girl!"

"No, my lord," she said calmly.

She had come forward to reassure herself that his wound had not begun to bleed again, and as she bent over him she saw that he was watching her with an ex-pression in his eyes she could not read. She met his look, her color slightly heightened.

"You are a good girl, Sylvie," he said softly. "But you needn't think you have won, you know."

"No, my lord," she said. "I am certain you will be just as headstrong as ever tomorrow."

He gave a short laugh. But when she would have moved away from him, he put out his right hand and stopped her. She was startled and stared down at him for a moment. He was frowning slightly, and he studied her, his eyes looking feverish, then he surprised her by bringing her hand to his lips.

It was so unlike him she jumped and turned scarlet.

"I begin to think you are quite a girl, little sparrow," he said. "I did not mean to lose my temper with you."

She pulled her hand away and said quickly, "No, my lord. I do not consider it. You are very weak."

He sighed and closed his eyes. "Yes, damnably weak! But I need no excuse to lose my temper."

As she moved away to confer in a low voice with Wicken, St. Ives opened his eyes again and said, "I am very grateful to you, child, but you are not to come here again. Wicken, is that understood?"

Neither of them bothered even to acknowledge this command, but it was clear that Miss Fairfield had risen considerably in the eyes of his lordship's two servants. Wicken promised her that he would keep his lordship in bed if he had to remove his clothes to do it, and Manley hurried across the room in his dignified way to open the door for her. She smiled gratefully at both of them and said, "Yes, I must depend on you, for I dare not be absent from dinner. I will look in again as soon as I can get away."

It was a little after ten when she was able to escape upstairs and return to his lordship's room. The evening had passed uneventfully, her grace merely grunting at the intelligence that St. Ives had dined in the village with friends. But Mr. Strickland glanced rather sharply at Sylvie before resuming his lighthearted conversation with Lady Jersey. Michael appeared more than ordinarily subdued, but she had no time to regard him, and she had taken the first opportunity to plead fatigue from her long walk and go up to bed.

When she entered St. Ives's bedchamber, only a few candles were burning, placed away from the huge bed so that they would not disturb his lordship, and Wicken and Manley were engaged in a desultory game of cards near the fire. She quickly hid a smile, for it had been clear to her almost from the first that there was a rivalry between the two servants. And certainly it was beneath my lord's valet to stoop to playing cards with his head groom, no matter that the same groom had been with his lordship since he had been in shortcoats.

They both rose when she came in, and Wicken said, "Aye, miss, he's sleeping now. He's a touch feverish, but that's only to be expected, and he seems to be resting comfortably enough. I took the precaution of putting some laudanum in his wine, so we can hope he'll sleep the night through."

She thanked him and went to look at St. Ives. He was still very pale, and when she placed a hand against his brow, it was hot to the touch. He stirred, but did not waken, and she could not resist the compulsion to smooth back the curls from his forehead. He looked very different from the arrogant rake of her earliest acquaintance, his mouth softened, and her heart stirred, but she only looked up and said, "Yes, he seems to be sleeping easily. You had best be returning to the stables, hadn't you, Wicken, before you are missed? I fear Manley will have to sit up with his lordship tonight."

"Yes, miss," agreed Wicken. He struggled with his conscience and added after a moment, "But I don't doubt but what Mr. Manley will know well enough what to do if his lordship should waken. I have requested that he rouse me if my lord shows signs of restiveness."

"Oh, yes, I am sure Manley will know what to do," she said. "You have both of you been wonderful, and I have complete faith in you. I dare not stay any longer, but I will look in again early in the morning."

Manley held the door for her and she flitted down the dimly lighted passage to her own room. Mary, as was her custom, was sitting up waiting for her, and Sylvie wished that she might dismiss her and only put off her dress in case she was needed in the night. But that might arouse too much suspicion, so she allowed herself to be undressed and her hair to be brushed and plaited for the night."

When Mary had gone she climbed into bed, but she left a lamp burning on her bedside table. She had not thought to sleep, but the events of the day had been so overwhelming that she knew little more from the moment her head touched the pillow until much later, when there was a quiet tapping on her door.

She was awake instantly, and for a moment could not think where she was or who could be at the door. Her lamp was still burning, but the fire had died down and it was very late. Then, as memory returned, she started up, thrust on her wrapper, and went to open the door, her hands trembling.

Manley, still fully clothed, stood in the hallway, and before he could speak Sylvie said, "Is he worse? I will come," and she closed the door behind her.

Manley led the way to his lordship's bedchamber, saying nothing until they had reached its safety, and then there was no need for words. St. Ives was tossing on the bed, the covers half off his shoulders and his cheeks flushed.

"How long has he been like this, Manley?"

"An hour, miss. He woke up and complained that he was thirsty and that his bandage was chafing him. Since that time he has been very restive, and I fear he will break open his wound again."

"Yes. Have you given him any more laudanum?"

"I have endeavored to do so, yes, ma'am," said the valet with dignity. "I fear that my efforts were met with singular unsuccess. He knocked the glass from my hand and made a number of exceedingly frank remarks about my touch and my countenance. I did not think it wise to provoke him further."

She smiled, but said, "Will you mix up another glass, and I will try to get him to swallow it. If he is no better by morning, I fear we shall have to send for the doctor no matter what he wishes."

She moved to the bed while the valet prepared the medicine. St. Ives looked alarmingly ill, and when she put her hand on his forehead it was burning. He opened his eyes, looked up at her a little blankly, and said, "Oh, it's you, is it? Just keep that fool Manley away from me."

He seemed to have forgotten his earlier prohibition on her presence, and she said soothingly now, "Yes, my lord. I will tend to you myself. You will not object, I hope, if I smooth your pillows and make you a litle more comfortable?"

He had closed his eyes again, so she slipped her arm under his head and raised him just enough to turn his pillow. When she laid him back, she realized that he was watching her, and though her color was a little high she completed her task and pulled the covers around him again. "Very wifely!" he remarked, then closed his eyes, as if the effort to speak had been too much for him. But he did sigh a little at the coolness of the pillow and seem to rest more comfortably.

When Manley brought the glass she said, "My lord, you must rouse yourself a little to drink this, and then you will feel much more the thing."

His eyes opened again. "You drink it, Miss Fairfield! You may have taken over the ordering of my servants, but you have not yet taken over the ordering of me."

She stood regarding him calmly. "Unless you drink this, my lord, I will send Wicken to fetch the doctor at once. If you are minded to behave stupidly, I will wash my hands of you, and everyone will know you were stupid enough to allow yourself to be shot by Lord Lambeth."

"So you know about that, do you?" he muttered briefly, wincing at the pain it caused him. "You think it is my *pride*—?" His eyelids came down abruptly. "Of course you do. Oh, very well! Give me the stuff, girl, and let me hear no more about it."

He would have taken the glass from her, but he was too weak, and after a moment she seated herself beside him on the bed and helped him drink it. He swallowed it in a gulp, then relaxed on the pillows, saying, "You think you—have the—upper hand, don't you?"

"Yes, my lord, I do. You must know I find it most gratifying to have the tables turned for once."

He grinned weakly. "You had best enjoy it while you can. I don't mean to be petticoat-led."

She ignored his words as she dipped a cloth in cool water and placed it over his brow. "Forgive me, my lord, but I cannot discover that you have ever been led. It might perhaps have been better if you had been."

Feverish but oddly intent, his blue eyes studied her

face in the dim light. "Ah, the prim and proper Miss Fairfield! I am well aware that you disapprove of me, but as I recall you were neither prim nor proper this afternoon. Is it possible you would not be glad to see me come by my just desserts?"

"If you are going to talk nonsense, my lord, I will leave you."

"No, don't go!" he said. "I want to talk to you."

She gently sponged his face and shoulders. "I will stay, but you are in no frame to be talking, my lord."

"No!" he said in frustration. "It's that damned laudanum. I can't think, and I must think! I must——"

"It is all being attended to, my lord," she said. "There is nothing for you to concern yourself with. I have done exactly as you wish."

He gave the ghost of a smile. "Yes, I believe you have. I begin to think I don't deserve you, Sylvie . . ." His eyelids drooped and he was asleep again.

She looked around at Manley, who had been observing the whole. "Go to bed, Manley. I will watch his lordship for the remainder of the night. You will need your strength tomorrow if we are to keep him from doing anything foolish."

"Begging your pardon, miss," corrected Manley, "but it is you who will prevent him from doing anything foolish. Good night, miss. I will be just next door if you should need me."

She sat in a deep chair next to the bed, rousing once or twice to replace the coverlet he threw off or build up the fire, but he did not awaken again. Much later, when the candles began to gutter in their sockets, her own lids drooped and she slept.

Something woke her almost at first light. She was very stiff, and she uncurled her limbs painfully, then glanced toward the bed. St. Ives was lying there watching her.

He smiled, an oddly intimate gesture so early in the morning, and remarked inconsequentially, "You are very pretty when you sleep. Don't you wear a nightcap?"

Color swept her cheeks, and she put a hand to her tousled curls and the soft brown braid that had fallen forward over her shoulder. He continued to watch her until she broke the strangeness of the moment by rising and saying in her cool voice, "How are you feeling this morning, my lord?"

He frowned impatiently. "I told you I was not so easily killed. I am stupidly weak, but I'll survive."

She put her hand on his brow and found it feverish but by no means as hot as the night before, and he seemed to be himself again. "The fever is down, thank goodness. But you have lost a good deal of blood, which is why you are so weak. How does your shoulder feel?"

"It hurts like the devil!" He reached up suddenly to capture her hand and hold it in his good one, turning it over as if to study it. Then his eyes lifted. "I think I'm very much in your debt, Sylvie. You very probably saved my life."

"I am almost certain I did, my lord," she said. When a corner of his mouth quirked, she added, "You may not be so lucky the next time."

He frowned quickly. "I don't remember a great deal, but I've a notion I said a lot of foolish nonsense last night. You need not regard it."

"I think your words were certainly dangerous, my lord, since you forbade us to have a doctor look at you, but you will forgive me if I disagree that they were foolish."

He was watching her closely. "What else did I say?"

"That you wanted no one to know of the—er—attempt on your life."

He swore. "I must have been worse off than I knew. Sylvie, I don't want you involved in this. You are to forget what has occurred."

She met his eyes. "I have a long memory, my lord."

He grinned. "I don't doubt that you do. Whatever you saw—or think your saw—you were mistaken. It was an accident—a poacher."

"You may tell others whatever ridiculous story you choose," she said, "but do me the credit of having a little intelligence! Poachers do not commonly operate in the middle of the afternoon, nor do they deliberately fire across a public road!"

"Nevertheless," he said, "I want you to return to your room and forget everything."

She sighed. "I am already involved, my lord. And if you persist in your determination to keep this—incident —from the world, you most certainly will need my help."

"You have no more sense than a newborn pup," he said, "and are about as much trouble! You haven't the least notion of what you're getting yourself into. Have you, for a beginning, given a thought to the consequences should you be found in my bedchamber at this hour dressed as you are?"

She blushed. "I fear I have consorted with you for so long that I have lost whatever sense of propriety I may have had. It seems to me that that is the least of our worries."

His face softened. "I thought you had grown tired of adventure and had opted for safety. Was it not you who told me only a few days ago that you meant to go back to your father, despite everything you had been through to get away?"

She seemed all of a sudden to have a little trouble with her breathing, but she never knew what she would have answered, for Manley walked in at that moment, and she managed to say with creditable calm, "Good morning, Manley. His lordship is better this morning, as you can see."

Manley wished them a polite good-morning, his expression revealing nothing, as usual, and he inquired respectfully if his lordship felt up to eating breakfast.

"No, you fool, I don't want any breakfast!" St. Ives said. "But I do want some coffee, and then I wish to be shaved. Go and see to it and don't come back until I send for you!"

Manley bowed, quite used to his lordship's temper, but Sylvie said, "No, my lord, I must go now. It would be useless, I suppose, to remind you that you hardly need to shave."

"Don't go yet. I must talk to you."

She hesitated. She had not quite lost that earlier breathless feeling, and she felt a treacherous weakening in her knees at the warmth of his glance. "My lord, I—"

He put up his black brows. "You said yourself that I am going to need your help."

She was defeated, as he knew she would be. "But I must not stay long," she said quickly, then broke off as he continued to stare at her, and she became all too aware of her own dishabille and his bare wide shoulders and the black stubble on his chin.

Her color mounted, but after a moment she went on as calmly as she could. "I have given it considerable thought, my lord, and I think it would be best if we were to put it about that you have succumbed to the influenza in the household."

"I have told you this is no more than the veriest scratch. I will be up again in no time. But I meant what I said. I don't want you involved."

She looked down at her clasped hands, weighing her words. "My lord—if the culprit is indeed Lord Lambeth, I do not believe he will stop at anything."

"I suspected that was what was in your mind," he said. "You know nothing of what you are talking about, and, I am telling you, you are not to meddle."

She looked up, a little angry then. "I know that he hates you and that he has already tried to do you a mischief! I know that he was in the area as late as last Wednesday."

He was surprised. "Ah, that explains it, then," he murmured almost to himself. "I must confess I had—nevertheless, you are not to interfere. I am immensely grateful for your help, but you are to stay out of it."

"And see him succeed the next time?" she cried.

"He will not succeed the next time, little sparrow, that I promise you. Has no one told you I was born to be hanged?"

She turned away. "I do not find that amusing, my lord!" Then she shrugged stiffly. "But I don't know what you think I will do, or even can do! If you are determined to kill yourself it is nothing to do with me." She sighed then, and added, "But I will not ask any more questions if you will give me your word that you will at least not try to get up today."

"If you insist, I will freely admit that I am damnably weak and want only to sleep for the next week. And you are a darling!" he added in a voice that was very unlike his usual mocking drawl.

She started, uncertain whether he could be serious or was still a little delirious, and the violent color invaded

her cheeks. He laughed softly, but then Wicken tapped
and stuck his head round the door, and she said, "Oh,
Wicken. Come in. We have determined that Manley shall
inform her grace that his lordship has succumbed to the
influenza. He returned very late last night, and woke
feeling feverish this morning, but he refuses to have the
doctor to maul him about. Do you think they will believe
that?"

Wicken grinned. "If they know his lordship, they will.
He ain't often ill, but I've seldom seen a worse patient,
even when he was a little nipperkin. Her grace, at
least, won't find anything out of the ordinary in that."

St. Ives remarked silkily, "If you are quite finished
discussing my reprehensible past and settling my immediate future, you will listen to me, both of you! You may put
it about that I am ill if you choose; it is as good an excuse
as any, I suppose. But I will emerge exactly when it
suits me, and neither of you will prevent me. And wipe
that grin off your face, Wicken. I am aware that you
believe the reins have shifted, but try me too far and
you will find out just exactly how mistaken you are. And
as for you, little one, it is clear that whatever man is
unlucky enough to wed you will need to beat you regular-
ly. Now go away so I may be shaved."

She went willingly, aware that it was growing late.
Wicken held the door for her, and as soon as she was
gone, he turned back into the room and said cheekily,
"May I wish your lordship every happiness?"

St. Ives met his look for a long moment and did not
pretend to misunderstand him. Then he grinned. "You
may." He closed his eyes. "And Wicken? Thank you."

The groom smiled to himself and went away to find the
valet.

Sylvie, despite her promise to St. Ives, dressed as
quickly as possible and went quietly downstairs, letting
herself out of the house and making her way to the
stables. Few of the household were awake yet, but she
knew Blackmer was an early riser, and she found him
currying Cintra and whistling tunelessly under his breath.

He looked up as she came in, and his eyes narrowed
slightly, but he went on with his task while she stroked

Cintra's black nose lovingly and gave him a carrot. After a moment she said, "Did you notice anything—out of the ordinary in the stables last night, Joe?"

He stopped whistling. "Well, now, not so's you'd notice. I was sleepin' heavier than I knew."

"Oh, that's good. I want you to do something for me. You can take Cintra if you wish. I saw Lambeth in the village this week when Michael Staunton and I went for a ride. Joe, do you think you could hang around the village and find out where he's staying and then—follow him?"

The groom shot her a quick look, leading her to suspect he knew more than he was saying. "It would be possible. I doubt he remembers me—but I remember him, right enough."

"Good," she said. "I can't tell you any more, but if— if he should happen to meet my Lord St. Ives, or—or behave in any way suspiciously, you are to get word to me immediately. Whatever happens, don't let him near St. Ives! His lordship's life may depend on it."

He glanced at her again, then appeared to become absorbed in his task, and after a moment she went back to the house.

When she went downstairs the second time that morning, she was just in time to see Manley in the hall conferring with the butler. He bowed at the sight of her, but betrayed no recognition, and ended by murmuring, "You will inform her grace then, as soon as she comes down?" He glided smoothly back up the stairs while the butler held the morning room door open for her, and she thought again as she went in what an excellent man the valet was.

Her grace was not an early riser, and she invariably breakfasted lightly on tea and toast in bed, but it was evident that she had received the tidings by the time she joined the rest of the party. She came in, saying gruffly, "Hmph! It seems St. Ives has been so foolish as to contract the prevailing influenza. I don't know what he expects us to do kicking our heels around here for ever."

Sylvie had to hide a smile, but Michael looked up, startled. Though Mr. Strickland's expression did not change, he too looked rather thoughtful before he returned to the *Morning Post,* which was brought in from London each day.

Lady Jersey said everything that was polite and wondered if they should not all go away and leave her grace in peace, but the dowager said that she supposed she'd better not leave if the wretched boy was ill, and if she had to stay buried in the country when everyone knew she hated it, she needed all the diversion she could get.

Lady Jersey looked amused. "Then of course I would not think of leaving you! Poor Nicky. I've never known him to be ill. I presume he has had the doctor to him?"

"At least he's shown some sense there," said her grace. "His valet says he won't have one near him."

Sylvie relaxed a little, then discovered Mr. Strickland's intelligent eyes fixed on her face. No one else offered to leave, and Sylvie could only be grateful that her godmother's illness made it out of the question that they should depart just yet. She felt a little mean, but Lady Bridlington's illness also made it unlikely that anyone would question her comings and goings, which would no doubt make things a great deal easier.

Indeed, although she dared not remain too long with him at any one time, she was able to slip away frequently during the day to check on his lordship's progress. He was still inclined to be feverish, and he seemed to have forgotten his earlier intention to get up, for he slept most of the day.

In fact, she did not see him awake until just before she went to bed that night, when she looked in on him for the last time. He was propped up on his pillows, and Manley was spooning some broth into his mouth. She would have backed out again had he not looked up and seen her. "How are the mighty fallen!" he murmured. "That's enough, Manley, take the pap away."

She came in then and said calmly, "I am persuaded you would do better to eat it all, your lordship, if you are to get your strength back quickly."

"You may be persuaded, my girl, but that is because you have not tasted the stuff! The least you could do is come and feed me yourself. I've no doubt your touch is a great deal gentler than Manley's here."

She smiled, but came forward and took the bowl from Manley, who slipped quietly out of the room. She took his place beside St. Ives and carefully ladled up a spoonful of broth. He swallowed it obediently, the gleam still in his eyes, and she said, after he took a second mouthful, "But how are you feeling, my lord? I looked in on you several times during the day, but you were always asleep."

He swallowed another mouthful of broth. "I know you did, for I was not always asleep. You are a good girl, Sylvie. What is happening belowstairs?"

She transferred another spoonful to his mouth. "Nothing out of the ordinary. Her grace is irritated with you for contracting the influenza when you have dragged her into the country, but a sense of duty prevents her from returning to London as she is longing to do."

He grinned, and she added, "Lady Jersey offered to take herself off her grace's hands, but your grandmother graciously declined, saying she'd certainly no intention of being left here to cool her heels alone. I am only grateful that my godmother's illness puts it out of the question for us to leave, for she, I'm afraid, has got the influenza and seems to be laid quite low with it."

He raised his brows mockingly. "I should be grateful I've nothing more than a hole in my shoulder, no doubt. That's enough now. If I must eat that revolting stuff, I don't have to swim in it. Pour me a glass of wine, there's a good girl."

She hesitated, but put aside the bowl and did as he asked. He smiled at her and took the glass in his good hand, then swore as the red liquid splashed onto the coverlet. "Damnation! I feel like an infant!"

She made no comment, but took the glass from him and helped him drink.

"It seems for the moment you still have the upper hand, Sylvie. What are the rest of them doing?"

She replaced the glass on the bedside table and said, "I fear your house party has devolved into a very dull affair, my lord. I believe Mr. Strickland rode over to visit friends of his in the neighborhood, and your Grandmama and Lady Jersey were together all afternoon in the small saloon. I do not know precisely what they were discussing, but I believe it involved a great deal of ripping to shreds the reputations of most of their acquaintances."

"You've a malicious tongue, m'dear! But you're probably right. What about my cousin? Has he renewed his attention to you yet? He will, you know."

She stiffened. "I do not expect you to see the value of your cousin, my lord, but he has been—has been more than kind. Mr. Staunton is, above all things, a gentleman."

"Which I am not! My cousin is a fool, but I do not expect *you* to see that. He was not the man for you."

"So you said before, my lord," she said evenly. "I must go. Will you be able to sleep again?"

"Will you come and soothe my fevered brow if I don't?" he teased. "On second thought, don't. You are very fetching in your nightgear, but I think you'd better not come in the night again, little one."

She smiled and went to the door. "I imagine you have paid the same compliment time out of mind to one or another of your light-skirts, my lord," she said serenely, "which somewhat tends to lessen the compliment to me. And you needn't tell me I should not use that word, for I am very well aware of it. Good night, my lord."

He laughed, then swore as he jarred his shoulder.

At almost the same moment, in a private parlor in the village inn, a man swore and said violently, "You fool, you have bungled the whole badly! What am I paying you for?"

His companion, a rather nondescript gentleman dressed in black, shrugged. "I did as you asked me, my lord. It is a difficult business. But I do not despair of seeing the desired—er—results."

Lambeth grimaced impatiently. "I hope you are not mistaken. Everything depends on you."

"So I apprehend, my lord," said the other.

XXIX

The next morning Blackmer reported to Sylvie that Lambeth was indeed still in the neighborhood, staying with friends, but that he had as yet betrayed no outwardly suspicious actions. He had gone into the village the night before for a drink or two at the only inn, but he had returned shortly after ten and was presently, with a party of friends, ridden into Bath. Blackmer himself had passed a rather uncomfortable night in a nearby farmhouse.

She looked guilty. "Oh, dear. I did not mean—that is—I did ask you not to lose him, but I daresay he can do nothing until his lordship is up and about again. Poor Joe. Are you very angry with me?"

Blackmer grinned and gave it as his opinion that he had never made the acquaintance of a Bow Street runner, but they had all his sympathy. She laughed. "Yes, well, perhaps if you were just to keep an eye on him during the *daytime.*"

He left then, and though Mr. Strickland was in the hall when the groom let himself out of the house, that vague gentleman merely looked at Blackmer absently before climbing the stairs to his room.

That day passed uneventfully too. St. Ives was still weak and slept a great deal, though he was able to sit propped up now. When she tapped on his door after she had changed for dinner, it was to find Mr. Strickland seated beside his friend's bed, talking easily.

She looked quickly from one to the other, for St. Ives's bandaged shoulder was very much in evidence, but St. Ives merely said, "Come in, now that you're here! It is useless to try to be discreet. Frederick here has been poking his nose in where it don't belong, as usual!"

"Now really, Nicky," Mr. Strickland protested. "Coming

303

it too brown, you know. If I hadn't known you for *quite* so many years, I might have swallowed the tale of your having taken to your bed with the influenza. But since I do know you, dear boy, there was nothing for it but to come and see what mischief you were up to now. My compliments, Miss Fairfield," he added, rising and bowing gracefully. "I wasn't yet aware that you were mixed up in this, but, judging from our acquaintance to date, I should not have doubted it. Nicky, if you really must go about getting yourself shot by—er, poachers, wasn't it?—I do wish you'd have the grace to wait until I'm out of the neighborhood. You know how I dislike getting involved in anything that smacks of poor *ton*."

Sylvie laughed as she came into the room, oddly relieved to find that Mr. Strickland knew. She thought him a shrewd man and hoped he might be able to help her make St. Ives see reason.

But St. Ives merely said, "Well, as long as you're here, you'd best make yourself useful. I'm finding it damnably dull being laid up by the heels, and since Miss Fairfield's sense of propriety will not allow her to do anything more than flit in and out when she thinks I'm asleep, you can keep me company. There should be a deck of cards somewhere about. I suppose you want to maul me as usual, Miss Fairfield?"

"No. Wicken told me he changed your bandage this morning and was quite satisfied with the progress of your wound. I merely looked in to see if there was anything you required before I went down to dinner."

"I'd wash my hands of the churlish fellow if I were you, Miss Fairfield," said Mr. Strickland. "It's plain his ingratitude knows no bounds. Now if you would promise to minister to me, I might even consider it compensation enough for suffering such a wound, however much I faint at the sight of blood."

She laughed, and St. Ives looked at her with an intimacy that brought the color to her cheeks. He said softly, "You know I am not ungrateful, don't you, little sparrow?"

"No, you are not ungrateful," she said. "But more than your gratitude I would prefer your assurances that you do not mean to do something stupid."

Mr. Strickland had not missed the exchange of looks. "Those of us who are his friends have long since given up expecting him not to do something stupid, ma'am," he said, "but we console ourselves with the knowledge that he has the devil's own luck."

She looked up. "Even the devil's own luck may run out someday, sir. But if you mean to stay with his lordship, I am grateful. I hope I may rely on you to prevent any immediate foolishness."

Mr. Strickland sighed. "Yes, I was afraid you would, ma'am. I will do my poor best, but I feel I must warn you my hopes are not high. More than likely he—or you—" he added, "will only manage to embroil me in something I'd much prefer not to know anything about. As a matter of fact, the more I think about it, the more I'm convinced that any sane man would leave for London immediately."

She laughed again and took her leave of them, and as soon as the door had closed behind her, Strickland said, "I tell you Nicky, if I were a marrying man—and I weren't afraid she'd exhaust me in a fortnight—I don't know but what I'd have her myself."

"Oh, no you wouldn't," said his lordship.

His friend regarded him with considerable amusement. "Like that, is it?"

St. Ives's reluctant grin appeared. "I believe I told you once she'd never give me a moment's peace. It's worse than I thought. I've got a dreadful notion she'll have me reformed and so respectable even you will acknowledge me, Frederick; and the damnable thing about it is, I've a strong feeling I'm going to enjoy it."

"Aye, you've got it bad," said his friend. "If I weren't so sure it will be the making of you, I'd even find it in me to feel sorry for you."

St. Ives grinned, but after a moment stirred and said in his old manner, "I am growing weary of this game, Frederick. I would like you to put aside your natural prejudices and pay a visit to my Lord Lambeth for me."

Strickland looked up sharply. "I thought it would not be long until you had embroiled me in your plans. I only hope Lord Lambeth is properly appreciative of the honor I do him."

"He won't be, but I give you my word it is the last thing I will ask of you. You may even return to—but no, I would prefer that you remained a little longer, to see that Miss Fairfield does not get into mischief. But on my honor I will not make you do anything you don't want to do."

Mr. Strickland regarded him. "I thought I was to be keeping *you* out of mischief. Of the two, I'm not sure I don't prefer you. I have the strongest suspicion that your Miss Fairfield is even more dangerous."

Mr. Strickland was sitting indolently in St. Ives's room the following morning while St. Ives endured being shaved by his valet. Strickland looked up and said suddenly, "Nicky, I feel certain you must have made the acquaintance of Miss Fairfield's groom. A rather stocky fellow with grizzled hair?"

St. Ives frowned. Mr. Strickland had pulled a snuffbox from his pocket and sat regarding it for a moment. "By the by, how do you like this snuffbox?" he added.

"Very pretty," said his lordship. "What about it?"

Mr. Strickland looked surprised. "Why, nothing. Bought it in town at Randle's. Thought you might like to see—oh! you mean the groom! It occurred to me that he seemed quite devoted to her—old retainer and all that—but it looks very much like he's been turned off. Seems always to be hanging about the village, and I saw him myself when I went to pay a visit to your—er—friend. Just thought I'd mention it."

St. Ives swore at a twinge of pain. "Ah, I think Miss Fairfield must be at it again! Unless I very much miss my guess, that is for my protection."

"Yes, that's what I thought," grinned his friend.

Blackmer, unaware that he had been discovered, continued to report to Sylvie, but he had little to tell her aside from Mr. Strickland's unexpected visit. She looked a little troubled at that, suspecting St. Ives was behind it, but, short of accosting Mr. Strickland, she did not know how to discover what they planned, and she was soon to discover that she had a more immediate worry to contend with.

Mr. Strickland was lounging in St. Ives's room, as had become his habit, while St. Ives was grunting and trying to adjust his bandage to where it did not chafe his shoulder unmercifully, when Strickland observed, "That cousin of yours has been asking questions, by the way. Doesn't believe any more than I did that you're suffering from the influenza."

St. Ives looked up. "I think it is perhaps time that I experienced a sudden recovery, Frederick. I've endured more than enough of your company. Ring for Manley. I believe I will go down to dinner tonight."

The result was that Sylvie was conversing with Mr. Strickland in the drawing room before dinner when the dowager said shortly, "Hmph! It's about time you were emerging! Sit down. You look like death."

Sylvie had no need to look around to know who it was, and she turned pale and glanced accusingly at Mr. Strickland, who merely murmured, "I assure you I did all I could!"

St. Ives was certainly looking drawn, as his grandmother had so unkindly pointed out, but there was a gleam of amusement in his blue eyes and he deliberately raised his grandmother's hand to his lips before doing as she said and sinking into a chair.

Lady Jersey patted his hand. "Poor love, you do look bad. Did you suffer very much?"

"Only from boredom!" he replied. "Frederick here braved the disease to keep me company, with the result that I had to leave my bed to seek escape. Well, cousin! Are you still here?"

Michael's mouth tightened, but he answered civilly, and the dowager, watching them, interrupted, "I won't have you two squabbling tonight. Give me your arm to go into dinner, St. Ives—though it's a question of who will be supporting whom! I'm famished."

St. Ives grinned wickedly down at her. "Ah, but you are always hungry, Grandmama. It is one of the things I most like about you."

She was in no way disturbed by this speech, and the rest trailed them into the dining room.

Afterward, Sylvie was never sure how she got through that interminable dinner, except that she was consumed

by such a blazing anger at his stupidity that she was able
to watch St. Ives's ordeal with scarcely a twinge. He
seemed to be in an outrageous mood, and he kept them
all laughing and flirted shamelessly with Lady Jersey. But
she could see the strain in his eyes before his lids came
down to hide them, and he was favoring his left shoulder
and using his left hand as little as possible. She saw
Michael watching him with a faint frown, and she wondered if he had somehow guessed something; but she was
too distraught to pursue the thought.

St. Ives was certainly drinking a great quantity of wine,
and by the time dinner was over his eyes were overly
bright and he was beginning to look feverish again. She
thought surely then he must excuse himself, but she had
reckoned without his stubbornness and his pride. He returned with them to the drawing room and sat conversing
in one corner with Lady Jersey, while the dowager com-
mandeered Michael and Mr. Strickland to play a game of
three-handed whist.

Sylvie had sat staring at the same page in her book for
a good quarter of an hour when the drawing-room doors
opened unexpectedly, and the butler announced, "Sir
Quinby and Mrs. Horneby."

After that, the evening assumed the proportions of a
nightmare, for Julia Horneby attached herself to St. Ives,
who made no noticeable objections, and her brother, a
somewhat vapid young man who looked as if he had been
drinking too much, soon came to sit at Sylvie's side, she
supposed because she was the only unattached young lady
in the room. He made tedious conversation, which she
scarcely even pretended to listen to. Indeed, long after-
wards she imagined that he must have thought her the
stupidest woman in England. If so, he did not reveal it, or
else he was not fond of intelligent women, for he remained by her side almost the whole evening, and would
perhaps have stayed forever had not Michael come to
her rescue, saying in his quiet way, "If you would excuse
Miss Fairfield for a few moments, Quinby, I have something to show her that she has been asking me about.
Miss Fairfield?"

She gave him a grateful look, and when they had
walked a little way apart, he said, "You were beginning

to look a little glassy-eyed, my dear. Quinby is a dreadful bore."

"Indeed, I am forever in your debt," she said.

"I only wish it were true," he said. "No, I do not mean to say anything more. But I have seen very little of you lately. I hope you have not been avoiding me?"

She managed to leave the impression that she had been spending a good deal of time with her godmother, though her conscience bothered her, since she had scarcely spared a thought to the poor lady; but he immediately asked after her health, and they were able to move on to a safer topic. They had been conversing for several minutes when Michael, his eyes wandering to where St. Ives stood bending his head to hear something Julia Horneby was saying in his ear, exclaimed abruptly, "St. Ives! You have cut yourself!"

Sylvie's heart stopped. St. Ives must have broken open his wound, for there was a smear of crimson on his left cuff and Sylvie, looking more sharply than the rest, could detect a telltale stain on the sleeve of his dark blue coat.

He too looked down at his cuff and said carelessly, "I must have done so at dinner. It is nothing."

He turned back to his companion, but Michael was continuing to look at him intently, and she could see that his grandmother, too, had broken off her conversation to look over at her grandson with suddenly sharp eyes.

Sylvie was hardly aware of any conscious volition; she only knew he must be got out of the room. She said something to Michael, she had no idea what, and rudely left him, unaware of either having crossed the room, or of Michael's eyes upon her.

When she reached St. Ives's side, Julia Horneby looked up, and it was plain she welcomed this interruption no more than she had the intelligence that Sylvie was still in residence at the Priory. However, Sylvie scarcely saw the woman, and she spoke in a voice she was not sure was her own. "My lord, I think it is more than time you returned to your bed. You are barely recovered from your illness, and it was foolish to remain so long."

She had not considered how intimate her words sounded until she saw the narrowed eyes of Julia Horneby and the interested gaze of that inveterate gossip, Lady Jersey. She continued a little desperately, "Your grand-mother specifically bade me see that you did not tire yourself too much. I am sure Mrs. Horneby and her brother will excuse you when they realize you have been ill."

The dowager seemed amused, but she did not contra-dict Sylvie's statement, and St. Ives was looking at her with a wicked gleam in his eyes. There was nothing to do but brazen it through now.

St. Ives must have seen the crimson stain on his cuff growing worse, for after a moment he smiled down at her, ignoring the rest of those present, and with a foolish-ly quixotic gesture offered her his left arm. He had scarcely used it all night, and she knew how much the gesture must have cost him, but she took his arm, although now she was near tears, and she tried to support it against her side as well as she could without being too obvious.

She could feel his arm trembling beneath her fingers, but even so he bowed to the company and murmured, "Very well, my sweet torment. I am clearly destined to live under the cat's-paw after we are wed."

There was a moment of silence, and Julia Horneby's eyes narrowed as she looked from one to the other. Then the dowager came to their assistance. "That's enough, St. Ives!" she said sharply. "Your engagement to Miss Fairfield has not been publicly announced, and I will not have you blurting it out in your usual indiscreet fashion. There, my dear," she added in a softer tone, "take him away and see that he does not come down again until he is completely recovered. If he thinks I want the rest of the house infected, he is sadly mistaken."

Sylvie walked as steadily as she could toward the door, but St. Ives must have been weaker than she had thought, for he was bathed in sweat and did not seem to be able to move quickly. Strickland opened the door for them, giving her an approving look that warmed her, and she was aware that they all stared after them in varying emotions. But none of it mattered except getting St. Ives back to bed.

As soon as the drawing-room door had closed behind them, he sighed. "One moment, little one, until I can get my breath. I'm weaker than I knew."

"Yes, and I should wash my hands of you!" she whispered furiously. "You have broken your wound open again, and if you do not suffer a recurrence of fever it will be more than you deserve. I think I was never so angry in my life! I hope you are proud of yourself, for it was nothing but pride that made you attempt to prove that you do not suffer as the rest of us! Did you find it *amusing* tonight, risking your life after we have tried so hard to keep you alive? Well, I did not, my lord, and I hope you have proved whatever it was you wanted to, for I do not think I will ever forgive you for as long as I live!"

He was leaning heavily against the banisters, his breathing rapid. "No, little one, and I apologize." He smiled at her. "But are you sure that is all you are angry about?"

Her anger deflated, and she was suddenly very weary. She looked up at him in genuine blankness for a moment, then she smiled faintly. "Oh. I fear that was more my fault than yours, for I didn't stop to realize how—how wifely I would sound. But I find I have grown so used to having your name linked with mine that it no longer has the power to shock me. I—I think I must have lived around you too long."

St. Ives smiled, but it was plain his thoughts were elsewhere. "Well, that's set the cat among the pigeons," he said. "If I'm right—*if* I'm right—Damnation!" he said in sudden frustration. "If I'm to play the game through, I need my strength, and I'm so weak now I can't even climb these stairs without your help."

"It would be useless to warn you that this is hardly a game," she said. "One attempt on your life has been made already. I believe he will stop at nothing now, my lord."

"I begin to think you are right, little sparrow. He will stop at nothing, now."

She could have cried in frustration and fear, but he was still leaning heavily against the banister, and she must try to get him back to bed. She dared not think what damage he had done by this foolish escapade, and she did not know whether he had the strength to make it up the stairs, even with her help.

She was just wondering if she would not have to return and seek Mr. Strickland's help, when Manley melted out of the shadows. "I anticipated you might need some help, ma'am. I regret this happening, but I fear his lordship was—er—most determined."

"I know, Manley. I am only glad to see you. He has managed to break open his wound again, I fear."

St. Ives looked up and said with a twisted grin, "Yes, I know, Manley. And wipe that smirk off that pallbearer's face of yours! I admit I would be grateful for an arm up the stairs."

But before they had reached his bedchamber, St. Ives required more than an arm, and when he sank on his bed with a grunt, it was clear he was nearly done in. "Damn it, damn it!" he said. Then he grinned. "What, are you still here, Sylvie? Go away, there's a good girl. Manley, I very much fear we shall have to sacrifice this coat. And don't say I told you so, for you did, damn you!"

"Yes, sir," Manley said. "I had anticipated that eventuality. It is a pity, but then there was always a slight droop in the left shoulder—just the merest hint, for in general Weston is not to be faulted. But then it can't be helped, and we can order a new one as soon as we return to London."

St. Ives closed his eyes. "It is plain I am going to have to increase the already exorbitant fee I pay you. But I warn you, if I hear one more word on the subject of this coat I will not be responsible for my actions. Now get me into bed, for I've a number of things to do in the morning, and I shall need all my wits about me."

Sylvie had not wished to call attention to herself while the valet was engaged in cutting St. Ives's coat from his shoulders, but now she came forward and cast an eye over the blood down his lordship's sleeve. "Well, my lord, if you were attempting to prove to us how brave you are, you have succeeded, but there will be no repeat of this incident until I am convinced you stand in no further danger. I give you my word, I will go to your grandmother with the whole tale and see that a doctor is brought in to examine you if you persist in this folly. Now Manley and I will change your bandage. I fear it is going to hurt, but you have no one but yourself to blame. I can only hope you have not caused any lasting injury."

He submitted, too weary to protest, and though the wound had begun to bleed sluggishly, the damage could have been much worse. She bandaged the shoulder tightly again, maintaining a frozen silence.

Only when she would have risen to go away did his hand come out to clasp her wrist. "Termagant!" he said. "I promise you won't rule the roost after we're married." Then he sighed, and his eyes flickered shut again.

She stood looking down at him, then could not resist reaching out and brushing his curls away from his brow. He did not stir, and after a while she went away. Manley, busy cleaning up the bloody bandages they had stripped from St. Ives's wound, pretended not to notice the tears in her eyes.

Whether her edict had any effect, or whether St. Ives himself realized he was still too weak to do much more than lie propped up against his pillows and sleep, he seemed content to remain in his room for the next few days. Manley had dutifully reported downstairs that his lordship's rising too early had brought on a recurrence of his chill, and no one had challenged the story. Michael was clearly bitter, and he made no attempt to more than greet Sylvie politely. She was sorry to have hurt him, but it was impossible to tell him the truth, and she had more pressing matters to worry about.

She had challenged Mr. Strickland with St. Ives's plans, but he professed ignorance, adding with such truthfulness that she could not doubt him, "My dear, whenever did St. Ives reveal what he planned to do? And you had best leave it to him, you know. I know that sounds like hard advice, but I have learned from painful experience that there is nothing for it but to trust him to see himself out of any tight corner he may get himself into."

This was naturally not an attitude designed to appeal to her, and she was aware of being a little angry with him, but he looked so languid in his immaculate gray coat and ridiculously high shirt points that she finally turned away in disgust.

As soon as she had left, Mr. Strickland, looking much less languid, went to St. Ives's room. "I fear I have come down considerably in Miss Fairfield's estimation," he said. "Really, Nicky, I have frequently wondered why I put up with you, but never more than in the last week."

St. Ives was up and dressed, except for his coat, and was exercising his stiff arm. The thick bandage was plainly visible beneath his shirt, and it was doubtful if he could get a coat on. "Never mind, Frederick! Console yourself with the knowledge that you may soon relinquish all your care to another and may wash your hands of me."

Mr. Strickland grinned. "It is the only thing sustaining me," he admitted. Then he looked up, abandoning his affectations for the moment. "I just hope I am not doing the wrong thing. She's right, you know. The damned fellow's dangerous."

Sylvie found her fears somewhat lulled during the next few days. St. Ives seemed content to remain in his room, and she, abandoning all discretion, spent most of those days with him and Mr. Strickland. Her godmother was still confined to bed, the dowager and Lady Jersey were usually closeted together, and Michael seemed to have no desire for her company.

And they were, strangely, almost halcyon days. Mr. Strickland was amusing, St. Ives in an oddly contented mood, and somehow the hours flew by, though she was never afterward able to remember what they had done to pass the time. She should not have been in his room, she should have felt guilty about abandoning her godmother, and she had long ago decided to spend as little time in St. Ives's company as possible, but none of these things mattered now. In the deepest recesses of her mind was a paralyzing fear; but in those few days of joy, she blossomed out, with St. Ives's eyes resting intimately upon her whenever she looked his way, and Mr. Strickland treating her as if he had always known her.

She could see it in her mirror each morning before she rushed to see St. Ives again. It was a process that had been begun when she first left home, but only here, with the fear of St. Ives's death never far from her mind, was it completed at last. They were not so lost to propriety that she took her meals upstairs, but she thought she would even have gone that far. The real world seemed far away to her, and even the others in the house took on only a marginal reality, ceasing to exist as soon as she left them.

Her grace showed herself unexpectedly vague about where Sylvie spent her time and asked no questions, though once or twice Sylvie found the dowager staring at her in something like triumph. But it was left to Lady Jersey to say one evening, "Why, my dear, what's happened? You're absolutely radiant!"

Lady Jersey apologized then, but they had all known exactly what she meant.

Only when Sylvie came one morning into St. Ives's room and found him up and dressed did the bubble burst. Manley was there, putting the last touches to his cravat.

He turned to smile at her, the expression in his eyes almost a caress, but he only said, "Frederick will no doubt blanch at the sight of it, Manley, but it will have to do. And now, the coat."

Manley held his coat and he eased into it, grimacing at its tightness.

She had remained where she was, lacking the power to move, knowing it was futile to protest. His wound was by no means healed, nor had he regained all his strength, but she could not hold time back any longer. The world had caught up with them after all.

"The bandage is bulging slightly under his arm, Manley. See if you can rearrange it."

Manley did as she asked, and St. Ives's eyes met hers. He looked at her for a long moment, then said softly, "Good girl. I knew I could count on you."

She could not answer because she was suddenly deathly afraid.

Then the moment was gone. St. Ives viewed himself with a frown, then nodded and strolled toward the door, and she had no choice but to go with him downstairs.

He was greeted teasingly by Lady Jersey and rather mildly by his grandmother, who said, "Well, you've decided to grace us with your company at last, have you?"

He laughed and kissed her hand, which made her glance up at him searchingly before adding, "Well, at least we'll have a fourth for whist now. Frederick Strickland's too frippery a fellow to keep his mind on the cards. His grandfather was the same, I remember."

Mr. Strickland meekly accepted this censure. "Yes, ma'am, you cannot deny I grace a drawing room as few others. I cannot vouch for my esteemed grandparent, who is unhappily deceased, but to spend hours poring over a pack of silly cards does not provide enough—er—scope for my other talents."

Her grace's bark of laughter sounded. "Aye, you always were an impudent rascal, but you're amusing enough, I'll grant you that."

Mr. Strickland happened to catch Sylvie's eye, but he managed to retain his aplomb and bowed exquisitely in the dowager's direction. "You are too kind, ma'am. I can but do my poor best."

Michael Staunton, who had been sitting on a sofa a little apart conversing with Lady Venetia, went to stand beside his cousin. St. Ives was in the act of pouring himself a glass of wine, holding the glass in his left hand and pouring with his right, and Michael looked at him for a moment and then said evenly, "Well, St. Ives, I am glad to see you recovered. I think it is time I was returning to London. I waited only until I could take my leave of you."

St. Ives set the decanter down. "As you wish. When will you be leaving?"

"Tomorrow," said Michael stiffly. "I must thank you for inviting me. It has been a most—enlightening time."

St. Ives raised his glass to his lips.

After a moment Michael said, "I perceive that—congratulations are shortly in order!" His smile was bitter. "I hope you will understand if I fail to offer them to you. I am sure the words would stick in my throat." He looked away and laughed. "You always did have everything, and you valued none of it."

St. Ives looked down from his superior height, and at that moment the difference between them had never been more obvious: the carelessly handsome rake and the grave, stocky figure at his side who was almost a sun-bleached portrait of the first. "Yes," St. Ives remarked. "You always hated me, didn't you?"

"No, rather pitied you. Everything you possess should

have been mine. Even your father saw it. Do you think of that night, I wonder? That if it had been legally possible, it all would have been mine? But this is pointless. I do not expect we shall meet again."

"Yes, it is pointless," agreed St. Ives. "You will not believe me, but I never hated you, you know."

Michael gave a bitter laugh and turned away.

St. Ives watched him, then put his hands carelessly in his pockets and leaned against the mantel. After a moment, Lady Jersey called him over to settle some argument that had sprung up between her and Strickland. As he came forward, a paper that had been in his pocket fluttered to the ground, but he did not look back, and no one else seemed to have noticed it.

Only Michael saw it, glanced at St. Ives, who was laughing over something with Lady Jersey, and bent to pick it up. He looked at it briefly, but it was apparent his mind was elsewhere, for he carelessly pocketed it instead of restoring it to his lordship.

Some time later Michael pulled it out of his pocket, as if he had forgotten it. He read it, frowned, then abruptly left the room, the paper left unnoticed on the small drum table beside him.

Upstairs, at approximately the same time, Mr. Strickland was futilely attempting to remonstrate with his lordship. St. Ives was being eased out of his coat by the ever-present Manley, and it could not be said he was paying much attention to his friend. He looked up to interrupt at last. "Frederick, if you are still boring away on that same uninteresting topic I wish you would go away. Yes, Manley, thank you. You may now oblige me by finding Wicken and sending him to me. Then I will not require you further tonight."

Mr. Strickland said, "Damn it Nicky, the man's dangerous! At least let me come with you."

St. Ives smiled. "What, Frederick, is this a new leaf you are turning over? I scarcely recognize you. I wonder what possible use you think you could be to me?"

"If you insist on being such a damned fool, I'll be a witness to your murder!" Strickland said. "Have you thought what I'm to tell Miss Fairfield when you succeed in getting yourself killed?"

"Ah, I thought there must be some reason for this flattering show of concern. You need only disclaim any knowledge —you're such a frippery fellow she will easily believe that."

"I've tried that," Strickland said, "and what's more, she didn't believe it! And even if she did, I come off looking like a complete fool!"

"Yes, but Frederick," pointed out his friend, "there can be nothing new in that. You have for years, you know."

Strickland sighed in disgust. "I might have known you'd not take this seriously. I've half a mind to rouse whatever authorities there may be in this godforsaken place and be damned to you!"

"I have something very different in mind for you," said his lordship. "You are to keep Miss Fairfield occupied."

Mr. Strickland shook his head. "I take everything back! I might have known you would reserve the most dangerous task for me. If she gets wind of this, my life will be worth nothing. I've a strong mind to remain in my bed tomorrow with the prevalent influenza. In fact, I feel feverish already."

St. Ives scarcely heard him. He was smiling a little and he said now, almost to himself, "Yes, it will not be easy. I wonder what she thinks she has next up her sleeve?"

XXX

But Sylvie had nothing up her sleeve, and she was relying heavily on Blackmer. She had received regular reports, and though he was finding his present employment tedious, Blackmer could tell her with confidence that Lord Lambeth had made no trips that might be considered questionable. To all intents and purposes he was in the neighborhood on business, though he was staying with friends, and he daily received a gentleman of sober mien who looked like an accountant or a lawyer. The rest of the time he hunted with his host or took a shotgun out for some sport, but never had they strayed anywhere near the boundaries of the Priory.

She did not know what to make of it. Lambeth must be perfectly aware that his first attempt had failed, but he continued to linger in the neighborhood, seemingly without a care in the world.

She knew that St. Ives couldn't be relied on not to do something as foolish as it was dangerous, but it had never occurred to her that things would reach a head so quickly, or that she would be given no time to prepare. And that was why she was so very shocked the next morning when she came down to breakfast a little earlier than usual, went into the drawing room to look for a book she had left there, and found a note on one of the tables, where a maid had obviously put it for safekeeping. It showed her clearly how much she had underestimated his lordship.

She had not meant even to read it, of course. Only she picked it up to see whom it might belong to, and the words seemed to leap up at her. There was no thought of propriety after that, and she was reading it hastily and unconsciously. Lambeth had written to agree to meet St. Ives as requested at eight o'clock on Wednesday morning in a woods near the main road leading to the Priory. God in heaven, what could he be thinking of? Surely he could not have called Lambeth out? But there was no mention of seconds. She read it hurriedly again to make sure.

No, no mention of seconds, only that vague threat implied in the words. And if it hadn't been for some maid finding the note where St. Ives had carelessly dropped it, no one would ever have known about it.

But there was no time. The meeting was for today, *right now!* for it was already after eight, and she had no idea what she should do. St. Ives would never forgive her if she roused the household, and besides, that would take too much time. Even to find Wicken would take far too long, and there was no time, no time! The sudden memory of Blackmer steadied her a little. Good, careful Joe! Surely he would be able to prevent an ambush, which was what she feared most or at the very least warn St. Ives. Yes, yes, she must cling to that thought, for without it was only cold terror.

But then all rational thought left her, and she grabbed

a cloak and let herself out of the house. Then she was running, with nothing in her mind but that she must get there before it was too late.

Mr. Strickland, unaware that his quarry had eluded him, was at that moment coming down to breakfast.

Also at that moment, or perhaps a little earlier, St. Ives was carelessly leaning against a tree trunk, his hands in his pocket. He was still a trifle pale, and any sudden movement jarred his injured shoulder, but if he was aware that he was in no shape to meet anyone, he did not reveal it. He stood looking around, as if he had not seen the world too many times at that hour—which he had not. Then he straightened slightly at some noise, too faint to be recognized, which told him that he was not alone.

He heard nothing more, but he had already learned all he needed to know. He pushed himself away from the tree and said almost wearily, "All right, the game is over. Lambeth is at this moment on his way back to London with, I trust, a very reliable escort in the guise of my darling but misguided Miss Fairfield's groom. And my own groom is at this moment right behind you. I have said the game is up."

There was silence for a long moment, then a sharp sound of a twig snapping, and a man stepped into the clearing, his eyes steady and the pistol he held negligently pointed toward the ground.

Sylvie reached the clearing half an hour later. It was empty and there was no sign of any recent occupancy. She clung, panting, to a tree, bewildered and terrified, and tried to make sense of it. There must be some sign. In her worst nightmares there had been St. Ives's lifeless body, but never this peaceful clearing where the sun shone weakly through the bare branches in the early-morning cold. Where were they, and where was Blackmer?

Suddenly it was as if the cobwebs had been lifted from her mind and a thousand pieces fitted together that she had been too blind—or too foolish—to grasp. Without another glance at the empty clearing she turned and ran back the way she came, her fears magnified a thousandfold.

She had nearly reached the house again, unmindful of the

stitch in her side or the fact that her hair was tumbling down her back, when there was the report of a gun being fired inside the house. She gasped, the last bit of color leaving her face, and covered the last few yards as if on wings. She burst into the house, nearly colliding with the butler who was coming from the back of the hall with a startled expression on his face, and she went instinctively toward the closed doors of St. Ives's study, hardly daring to think what she would find.

She thrust open the doors, and at the sight of St. Ives pocketing a small pistol, a gleam in his eyes, and Frederick Strickland lounging against the fireplace inspecting a playing card with a neat hole through its center, she swayed briefly where she stood, and for the first time in her life fainted dead away.

When consciousness intruded once more, she was lying on the sofa in the fierce grip of a pair of masculine arms, and Strickland was saying, "Damn it, Nicky, don't smother the poor girl!"

"She's coming round now," said St. Ives in relief. "Get me some brandy! This is your fault, you know, you fool, for I told you I could shoot the pips out of a card with it." As her eyelids stirred he added lovingly, "Yes, that's my girl, Sylvie. Only drink this and I promise you will feel more the thing."

But her memory returned and she struggled to sit up, pushing away the brandy and saying, "Oh, thank God I am not too late! You don't understand! I didn't either until just a few minutes ago, when I realized that Blackmer hadn't come to—oh, don't you *see?*" she cried. "It's not Lambeth at all—it never has been, only I was too blind to see it! *He* has no wish to see you dead! Oh, the opera dancer, but he must have known you would have dozens more of those in your life! Only one man would benefit from your death—! Oh, you must see! Michael, your heir!"

St. Ives was smiling at her with such warm approval in his eyes she scarcely recognized him for the same cynical rake.

"Yes, my darling, I know. Now drink this like a good girl."

"You *know*—?" she gasped. "And yet you let me go on

believing it was Lambeth, and even set poor Blackmer on to watch him—and—oh, oh, *damn you!*" she cried and promptly burst into tears.

Mr. Strickland stared in horror at this unprecedented display of emotion from the usually unflappable Miss Fairfield, but St. Ives, with great presence of mind, thrust the brandy glass into Strickland's hand, seated himself on the couch, and pulled her into his arms, letting her cry against his chest and pressing kisses upon her tousled hair and whatever portion of her face he could reach. "Yes, I know, my darling; I had really meant to spare you this," he said ruefully. "Now stop crying, there's a good girl, so that I can kiss you properly."

His words finally penetrated, for she hiccuped, her sobs abating. "Oh, what are you doing? You must not—your *shoulder*, my lord!"

He turned up her tear-stained face and kissed her lightly on her mouth. She colored frantically, more important matters for the moment forgotten, and cried, "Oh, you should not—what are you—? you *must* not!"

"I hope you do not mean that I must not kiss you until we are married, Sylvie, for I have a dreadful suspicion that my grandmother, ably abetted by your godmother, is already planning an enormous affair in Saint George's, which we shall both of us hate, but dare not refuse, since they are, in a way, responsible for my discovering the one girl in the world I cannot live without."

She had ceased trying to escape from his arms by now and was staring up at him as if she could never take in enough of his face. But at his words she corrected involuntarily, "But they had nothing to do with it. It was your own drunken temper."

His shoulders shook slightly, and he kissed her swiftly again. "Yes, my darling, but if you had not had a temper to match, I might have married you off to some poor unsuspecting fool, and think how dull both our lives would have been."

She had snuggled back against his shoulder, and now she shyly raised his hand to her cheek, both of them apparently having forgotten the presence of Strickland. "You would not have regretted it, for you would have gone on having one mistress after another and creating a great many scandals. And I would not have known, for I had not yet learned how—how exciting life can be."

He was looking down at her with so much love in his eyes that she caught her breath, suddenly dazzled, but he only said, "My sympathies are with the unknown gentleman! It is clear no one but I can handle you, and I begin to wonder if even I know what I am letting myself in for. Incidentally, little love, I thank you for setting Blackmer on to watch Lambeth. He turned out to be very much a help. But I fear he is unsuspectingly on his way to London. We will have to make it up to him when he discovers that Lambeth is merely returning home after managing to convince his wife's trustees to relinquish her fortune."

She sat up as much as his arms would permit her and said in a troubled voice, "Then I was right? I thought I must be, but I did not want to believe it."

St. Ives pressed a quick kiss on her hair. "I fear that you were being used, my love. My cousin may have grown fond of you, but I believe his ardor was prompted by the knowledge that were I to wed, his position as my heir would become extremely shaky. You see, my father encouraged him in the belief that I was bound to meet an early end—probably at the hands of some jealous husband," he added, "and I must confess I have done little to discourage him in that belief. It must have come as quite a shock to him when you appeared on the scene as my future bride."

"Yes," she said, "I had begun to suspect that he—that he might be using me to get back at you. Poor Michael." She went on, intent on her train of thought, "But if you suspected him, why did you persist in encouraging him to believe we were to marry?"

"Because, my sweet, at first it was only a suspicion. I had, after all, fallen head over ears in love with you myself, when you had no more conduct than a baby and were hopelessly shy around everyone else and only became natural with your old groom or when you were too angry to remember to hold your tongue."

"You did not!" she cried heatedly. "You only thought I would d-do as well as the n-next!"

"Well, perhaps not just then," he conceded. "But soon enough to ruin my peace of mind. But that is beside the point. As I say, I suspected Michael, but I had no proof.

Only that my father had most unfairly inculcated in my cousin a belief that he was far more worthy of succeeding into my father's shoes than I. I don't doubt but what he was right. The problem was I was already in those shoes and had no intention of stepping out of them. He must have consoled himself with the thought that I would not wear them too long, until he really began to believe that I meant to marry at last and beget an heir. And since I was foolish enough to publicly carry on a feud with Lambeth, my dear cousin decided to neatly place the blame for my untimely demise upon my known enemy. Or at least the most vocal of my enemies," he amended with a grin. "That is where you came in, Sylvie. Having already convinced him that his determined pursuit had failed and thus prompting him to a last desperate attempt to prevent my marriage, you then happened along on the scene, as it were, and prevented him from completing his handiwork. You also made it possible, with your admirable presence of mind, for me to hush up the whole."

"You—you thought even then that it was *Michael* who had tried to kill you?"

He shrugged. "As I said, I suspected it. If you'll remember, you had just made it clear to him that you would not marry him. Although *I* might suspect that it was only your famous temper that prompted your outburst, Michael did not know you so well and could only assume that the lure of my possessions had tipped the scale in my favor at last."

"No," she said in a very low voice. "He knew I loved you."

He kissed her swiftly again. "Did he? How very interesting. I can only wonder why you revealed to him what you had steadfastly refused to admit to me. But we will return to that later. For whatever reason, he thought he had lost, so there was no other choice than to eliminate me before the marriage could take place, for once it had done so he could never be certain I had not already begotten an heir." He watched her blush again. "And since he was rightly convinced that my death would be small loss to the world, he undertook the task with a determination I never suspected he had in him. If he had ever evinced such single-mindedness as a boy, I was not aware of it. But then, understandably, we did not get on well."

She shuddered. "Oh, do not joke about it! When I think of you lying there—!"

"It must have been a shock to him when he discovered that not only had he failed, but that no hue and cry was ever raised. He was, I presume, perfectly aware that Lambeth was in the neighborhood."

"Yes," she said bitterly. "Because I pointed it out to him."

"But he couldn't be certain how long Lambeth would remain. And though he knew that my case of influenza was a ruse, he dared not take any further step unless Lambeth could also have access to me. I must confess I was growing nearly as tired of the game as he must have been, and I decided to hurry it up a bit by enlisting Lambeth's aid. Frederick was kind enough to undertake that little task for me. Lambeth may hate me, but hardly enough to take the blame for my death at someone else's hands, and since he had already finished up his own business here, he consented to depart for London after performing one slight service for me.

"It only remained for me to 'accidentally' drop the note Lambeth had written agreeing to meet me, so that Michael would find it. If my suspicions were correct, Michael would see it as a heaven-sent opportunity to finish the job." He grimaced. "I must admit I thought I had covered every angle. You had helped by setting Blackmer on to dog Lambeth's heels, thus providing a convenient alibi for Lambeth—something Michael was not slow to realize the significance of—and Frederick here was to accomplish the simple task of keeping you occupied on the fatal morning. Obviously something went wrong, for you found out. I had meant to spare you that."

"I read the note too," she said simply.

He swore suddenly. "Damnation! It is clear I am not so clever as I had thought. Michael must have seen it as a valuable piece of evidence against Lambeth! Full marks to Cousin Michael."

"What will become of him?" she asked quietly.

He shrugged. "I must confess I do not particularly care, so long as I am not obliged to see him. He has sufficient money. I think he may mean to emigrate to America. I don't doubt he'll do extremely well there, and may even end up as one of their presidents, for he was always a plausible devil."

"While you," she said, "were always naughty and defiant and ferociously proud against the great injustice that was done you. I wish I might have known you as a little boy."

"When I was a little boy, my love," he said, picking up her hand and kissing the palm, "you were an infant in arms. And by the time you were old enough to know anything, I was already well embarked on my first scandalous affair. But I have every intention for you to be my last. I have asked you too many times to be my wife, but this time—"

"No, my lord," she interrupted, her whole face transformed. "You have never *asked* me."

He laughed. "Termagant!"

She felt suddenly breathless, but before she could reply, the door had opened behind them, and her grace was saying disapprovingly, "Whatever do you mean by shooting off fire arms in the house, St. Ives? I could scarcely credit my ears! You have only to thank the fact that my nerves are made of iron, or I don't doubt I should have gone off into strong palpitations."

She was observing with her bright dark eyes the interesting spectacle of Miss Fairfield seated on her grandson's knees with his arms firmly around her. "But never mind that! What are you going to do with this silly chit of yours? You cannot go around living in one another's pockets as you have been, especially with a gossip like Sally Jersey in the house! You will have to marry the girl."

St. Ives was observing the interesting color that fluctuated in his beloved's face. He said softly, "No, I do not have to marry her, Grandmama. I am going to do so because I am damned sure I cannot live without her. Now go away, and take Frederick here with you. I have just discovered I have some—er—unfinished business to take care of."

His grandmother only said, "Hmph, if you have been carrying on like this the whole time, I should have thought you could have done without him long ago. In *my* day— but never mind! I daresay it hasn't changed so very much after all."

Mr. Strickland offered her grace his arm, but before they could make good their escape, there was a commotion in the hall, and a familiar voice could be heard saying "Never mind announcing us. In here, you say? Is m'mother up, by the way? I've brought Lady Catherine with me, as you can see."

For the first time St. Ives appeared startled. "Oh, my God!"

The butler could be heard protesting weakly, and then the doors burst open once more and Lord Timothy strolled in, still in a dashing roquelaure that made him look like a boat in full sail, a dancing Kitty by his side. His eyes took in the spectacle before him, but he only said, "Well, well, this scamp of yours persuaded me to bring her down, St. Ives, since I was on my way to Bath anyway. That was before I had been obliged to endure a number of hours cooped up in a carriage with her. You have my sympathy. Hallo, Mother, Strickland," he added, and sauntered over to pour himself a glass of wine.

Sylvie's cheeks were once more burning, and she had succeeded in jumping to her feet this time. But Kitty was regarding them in delight, ignoring Lord Timothy, and she burst out now, "Oh, are you going to marry after all? I thought—"

St. Ives's patience was nearly at an end. "If I might have a moment of peace in a household that seems suddenly to have been turned into a lunatic asylum, I will endeavor to satisfy you all by proposing to my future bride!"

Kitty seemed uncowed, and Lord Timothy refilled his glass and said, "Slipping, dear boy! I should have thought you'd done that weeks ago. D'you mean you ain't even proposed to the chit yet?"

"I have been trying to overcome the clumsy attempts by my entire family to convince Miss Fairfield that no sane person would marry into such a family!" he said. "Frederick, I will be eternally in your debt if you will rid me of the presence of my relatives. Thank you, I knew I might rely on you. You are a prince among fellows."

Frederick laughed and unexpectedly kissed his hand to Sylvie before saying easily, "Come along, Timothy, I've been meaning to tell you that I've discovered an interesting champagne in Nicky's cellars. I can't tell when it was laid down, but it's damned good. Doesn't seem to have lost any of its fizz."

"Yes," said St. Ives cordially, "why don't you go and open a dozen bottles? Only save one for us is all I ask."

Lord Timothy was quite willing to go and sample Strickland's find, and Strickland was unexpectedly aided in his task by Kitty, who had been standing staring in a rather bemused way. She roused herself now and said impishly, "Yes, Grandmama Wraxham, let us go away too, for if they are to be married in time to do me any good, Nicky must certainly propose without delay. Did I tell you that Mama has come down with the influenza? It is the oddest thing, for she is almost never ill, but it meant she did not wish to have me around plaguing her, and Grandmama Conyngham becomes inclined to vapors if she is obliged to be around me too much, for she says I am never still. So when I discovered dear Lord Timothy was planning to come this way, I prevailed upon him. I hope you don't mind?" She twinkled at Sylvie and added over her shoulder as she shepherded the dowager out, "*Quite* the best husbands, I think!"

When the door had closed at last, St. Ives turned to Sylvie and said with barely disguised impatience, "And now, my little love!"

She looked up at him without shyness. "How much they make me laugh! I never knew people could be like that!"

He merely looked at her, and after a little the smile faded from her lips and she blushed, surprised by the ardor she could read in his eyes. "I don't—are you *quite* sure you wish to marry me?" she asked in a breathless voice.

He swept her into his arms again and kissed her so fiercely she lost any desire to awaken him to a sense of his own folly. When he at last loosened his hold, she stared up at him. "Oh! Is *that* how you kiss your opera dancer?"

He burst out laughing. "Oh, little sparrow! No, that is not the way I kiss my opera dancer! That is the way I kiss the silly girl who has turned my life upside down."

She smiled mistily up at him, but said seriously, "Lady Bridlington warned me that—that gentlemen do not look upon these things as females do. If you ever—feel the need for another opera dancer, I will try to understand. I do not mean to tie you down."

He kissed her again. "Then you are far more generous than I, my darling, for I intend to tie you thoroughly down! If you ever feel the need for diversions, I promise I will strangle you. And if I ever feel the need for an opera dancer again, I will come and tell you and you can be my opera dancer."

"Oh, shall I like that?" she asked shyly.

He smiled into her eyes. "You shall like it very much, for you, little one, are as big a rake as I am."

"Yes, I know," she said. "I do not know how I came to be so, for Kendall is not at all, you know. But I do not think anything shocks me very much. Even that night, when I consented to come away with you, I think I was hoping to have an adventure at last. Will we—Lady Bridlington said reformed rakes are sometimes the strictest of husbands. You do not mean to—to reform *too* much, do you?" she asked mischievously.

"Not before we have grandchildren, at least," he promised gravely. She laughed and lovingly smoothed a black curl from his forehead, making no effort to hide the expression in her eyes.

A long while later she stirred in his arms and said, "How well it has all worked out! Now Kitty can have her coming out after all."

"No," said my lord firmly, tickling a curl at her ear.

"No? But Kitty will be so disappointed!"

"Then let her be disappointed," he said. "I have no intention of spending my honeymoon playing duenna to my brat of a little sister. I am taking you into Italy, instead. Kitty can make her come-out next year."

"Oh," she breathed. "Oh, yes, I should like that above all things."

"Oh, not above *all* things," he murmured wickedly, and brought her hand up to his lips.

ABOUT THE AUTHOR

DAWN LINDSEY is a young native Oklahoman. Since college she has worked in advertising and public relations, primarily for several major zoos; and did a brief stint as a marketing analyst for a small California bank before writing her first novel two years ago. She and her husband presently live in San Francisco. This is her second novel.

A Special Preview of
a compelling opening section from

A COWARD FOR THEM ALL

The tumultuous saga of a proud
Irish-American family

by

James Kavanaugh

John Patrick Jr., called Jack, was born in Chicago in 1926 and Grandma Kate was happier than anyone had seen her in years. Three days before his delivery she had dreamed of mice running over an empty cake pan, but despite the fearful omen, Jack's broad shoulders and almost orange hair on a large Irish head reassured her. John Patrick bragged of a triple-threat quarterback at Notre Dame, and Margaret thanked God and Saint Anthony, but she was further distressed the night before Jack's baptism when she herself dreamed of an old man in a long coat standing on a highway in the moonlight. However, she dismissed the disturbing portent when the priest washed Jack's soul clean of sin. John Patrick Maguire could not stop smiling.

Margaret recalled the awesome signs a few months later when a bloated Kate dropped dead of a second stroke.

Over the protests of the Irish matriarchy, Johnny Muller draped his wife in a white silk dress and placed in her hands, along with her rosary, the sack of soil Michael O'Brien had given her the day before she sailed from Ireland. More than forty years had passed since Michael had made his promise: "The land is all yours. It won't be long now."

John Patrick received notice of a promotion to manage a new office of the Audit Bureau in Kirkwood, Michigan. His superiors agreed that marriage and a young son had settled the wild, gifted Irishman into a new maturity. It was a rare compliment to a Maguire, and Daniel, his father, stayed drunk for three days in celebration.

Margaret was delighted to leave Chicago. A smiling John Patrick bought drinks at a South Side speakeasy and promised to return only when he could pay cash for all of Marshall Fields. They left late in 1927 with their Tin Lizzie and a stocky year-old-Jack, who had his father's red hair and Margaret's light blue eyes.

Kirkwood, a prosperous town of forty thousand in southwestern Michigan, was a strange, angry setting for Margaret Ann, daughter of Kate and grandchild of Michael O'Brien. Neither she nor John Patrick had ever known the sordid religious bigotry of a small midwestern town.

Kirkwood was a Dutch Protestant stronghold, and the young Maguires arrived there when Alfred E. Smith, "the Happy Warrior," was running for president, the first Catholic ever to do so. Assuredly, Kirkwood was no extension of Chicago's South Side. There were no First Ward politics or illegal hooch at the Knights of Columbus, no boisterous White Sox games and Irish camaraderie that battled niggers and insulted Polacks. Almost overnight, the Maguires were the "niggers," and the pride of John Patrick's promotion was turned to bitterness. Three times they were unceremoniously refused access to Dutch neighborhoods. They finally rented a small frame house, purchased simple oak furniture, and unloaded Jack's crib. Margaret sprinkled the rooms with holy water as John Patrick struggled with boxes. They were crushed to see anti-Catholic cartoons splashed in the *Kirkwood Gazette,* depicting Al Smith welcoming an owl-eyed, salami-nosed pope to the White House. Crosses were burned in front of Saint Raphael's gabled brick rectory, and crude jokes about lusty nuns conceiving priests' fat babies in drunken orgies—Smith favored the repeal of Prohibition—drew lunchtime laughs in the Victory Cafe and in John Patrick's office.

It was a rude awakening for a proud Irishman and his shy wife who had known only the security of a giant city where twenty percent of its three million inhabitants were Irish Catholic.

John Patrick had come to Kirkwood with the dreams of a young businessman on the way up, and his dreams were magnified when he surveyed the dozen young women who seemed delighted by the handsome charm of their new manager. Although the fierce bigotry against Catholics outraged him, he tried to ignore the snide attacks, only snarling back when the remarks were too crude to tolerate. . . .

Although a few hundred Irish had settled in Kirkwood almost a century before, the Dutch had come in greater numbers with much more money and the finer skills of successful artisans and experienced farmers. They also possessed a historic hatred of Catholics that was born of Europe's religious wars and the fury of the bloody Spanish Inquisitions. These same Dutch Reformed had emigrated to Kirkwood, bought its rich black land, built it up to its present prosperity, and even named it in honor of God as a "church in the woods."

It was no wooded church to John Patrick Maguire, but a concrete coliseum where he was daily fed to mocking lions who soon learned to circle him at a safe distance. The Dutch believed Tammany Hall to be a papal plot, and they despised Franklin Roosevelt as a turncoat for supporting Smith against Herbert Hoover. But even when Hoover won the 1928 election and the Dutch of Kirkwood rejoiced, John Patrick knew that his own Irish victory was only a matter of time. He knew it especially when he watched his fearless infant son gleefully raise his fat fists to battle his own father. Then John Patrick lovingly buried Jack in awkward arms and told the boy his favorite story again and again until he kissed his beautiful son good night.

Margaret was apparently content to bathe her infant with hymns to Mary and the baby Jesus, and she nursed him for over a year until he bit her breast fiercely a third time. She knew little of angry politics, yet she shared John Patrick's bitter pain, especially when neighbors shunned her or suddenly talked in Dutch and laughed together in the grocery store at her pregnant belly when Jack was not yet a year and a half old. Remarkably, she reported none of this humiliation to her husband, sharing it only with God in whispered aspirations all day long and during the daily six o'clock mass she attended at Saint Raphael's. She begged heaven's forgiveness for not entering the convent, not convinced that an ambitious, handsome husband and a healthy son had released her from God's wrath.

Early in 1928, a great shame came to Saint Raphael's parish in Kirkwood. The soft-spoken and kindly Irish pastor, an uncomplicated farmer from rural Sligo, was shot to death at the dinner table by a crazed monk from Europe. The *Chicago Tribune* reported it as an unspeakable tragedy, but the *Kirkwood Gazette* kept the scandal alive with a disgusting prurience that delighted the Calvanist bigots.

Was it a love triangle with a nun? An illegitimate baby in the rectory basement? A Vatican assassination? All the historic crimes of Rome and its infamous popes were recalled, and wild-eyed ex-priests appeared in Dutch Reformed pulpits to recount in sordid detail the horrors of Roman Catholicism.

The Irish community was numb and embarrassed, and the Saint Raphael parish became divided: hostile cliques wanted vengeance, and passive groups prayed to ignore the new persecution. School attendance dropped, Catholics were denied jobs and publicly ridiculed, students left the seminary. Margaret cried for an entire week and she was terrified to go to the grocery store. John Patrick read the *Kirkwood Gazette* to shreds and swore bitterly at each new accusation. When his regional supervisor at the Audit Bureau, J. R. Harris, a tight-jawed WASP with thin lips and rimless glasses, hinted at a drunken orgy, John Patrick felt the blood rush to his head and had to leave Harris's office lest he break his jaw.

The scandal could have destroyed Saint Raphael's parish had not the bishop of Detroit, the archdiocesan seat for Kirkwood, appointed James Michael Doyle as pastor six weeks after the tragedy. A stocky Irish American with a booming voice and dark brown eyes glaring under bushy black hair, Doyle whipped the parish back into shape within two months. The parish council was fired, the ushers disbanded, the ladies guild terminated; James Michael Doyle was to be consulted about everything from altar boys to the menu at the Saint Patrick's Day banquet. Pockets of resistance were threatened with excommunication and wiped out; the editor of the local paper was threatened with legal action as well as receiving anonymous phone calls in a thick Irish brogue predicting a long stay in the hospital. James Doyle himself invaded a luncheon meeting of Dutch Reformed ministers and promised an all-out war if "God's more peaceful ways are not observed." His muscular body rippled defiance and commanded such respect that he was finally applauded when he quoted Jeremiah.

Almost overnight, the parish had its pride back. The high school football team got new emerald green uniforms and were informed that any missed blocks or "gutless" tackles would be dealt with in the rectory office. Sports, always significant, now became a religious crusade. James Michael Doyle conducted pep rallies personally. During the half time of a game Saint Raphael's was losing to Bay Harbor Central 6–0, he slapped a star halfback, knocked two powerful tackles over a locker room bench, and watched his team win 27–6. The team was undefeated the very first year, and schools twice the size were not only defeated but humiliated. John Patrick roared his approval from the sidelines with Jack on his lap. Even Margaret, on the brim of delivery, cheered her support. The *Kirkwood Gazette* called the team the Fighting Irish, after Notre Dame, and gave the games more space than was given to a mediocre Kirkwood Central, three times the size. When the Fighting Irish humbled Central 42–7 and four Dutchmen were carried from the field, a special mass of thanksgiving was offered by James Doyle. John Patrick smiled proudly at J. R. Harris and thereafter ignored his pompous initials, calling him "Jimmy boy" in front of the office staff.

Nor did it end with the football team. Ushers began dressing in tuxedos. A new statue of Saint Patrick with bishop's miter and green robes was placed in a special grotto, and evergreens were planted around the church. School attendance shot up. James Doyle preached eloquently that his parishioners were engaged in a holy war to save civilization, just as the Irish monks had done ten centuries before. The pastor soon became a legendary hero—even among the men.

Irish men traditionally were not fond of priests. Too many men remembered the stories of the famine when the priests had upheld England's right to tax the peasants to death. In the eighteenth century, priests had been persecuted heroes who defied English law to say their masses in caves and secret glens, protected by thick Irish shoulders bearing clubs, but when the clergy were reprieved in 1829 and permitted to conduct their services, a fearful new conservatism scarred their ranks. Most, as in Clare, supported landlords' rights from the very pulpits, and the brooding Irishmen would never forget. Even as they tipped their hats, begged a blessing, or permitted their own sons to enter the seminary, they cursed under their breath.

The women were more tolerant, almost obsequious, not because they truly loved the clergy, but because they recognized them as the only real defense against the total chauvinism of their oppressed and angry husbands. The women knew instinctively that the Holy Mother Church was a matriarchy as fierce and domineering as their own real control of the family. They well understood the clerical arrogance, and they also knew that the priests ate and drank better than most parishioners. They saw the expensive clothes and vestments, the lavish episcopal dinners, the extravagant rectories and cars, the vanity and selfishness. But they also saw the true shepherd who would give his life for the flock, who cared about the poor and gave his every waking hour to console the sick and lonely. They knew his devotion came from God himself, and they kissed his hand or the hem of his cassock in genuine love. They felt his tenderness and understanding in the confessional, his compassion at times of tragedy and death. He was the same priest who had defied the landlords, blessed the people's defiance, and died with his flock in the Great Famine of 1845. There probably was no finer or nobler love among the Irish than that lavished on such a priest.

James Michael Doyle did not know that kind of love. His was the respect given to a leader in war. Even the men knew they could not survive without him, and his powerful word became law. No one was to date a non-Catholic; every child was to attend a parochial school; and a boy who didn't go out for football needed a doctor's exemption or congenital blindness. Anyone who hadn't voted for Al Smith was in serious danger of excommunication.

There were twelve babies christened James Michael that very first year, and to have a vocation to the priesthood, always an honor, was suddenly a mark of divine preeminence. Even to be appointed an usher was an invitation into a sacred oligarchy controlled personally by James Doyle. In such an environment, John Patrick became an exemplary Catholic and a bellowing threat to every careless referee who officiated at a Saint Raphael game. He was James Doyle's kind of man, and at the baptism of his second son, James Michael Maguire, John Patrick was asked to be an usher. Of course he accepted, and he doubled his weekly donations. Only Margaret knew that he had never actively practiced his faith before he met her.

James Michael Maguire was born at the end of 1928 at the edge of the Depression, and he was the opposite of Jack. A small baby with no Maguire traits, he had light brown hair and serious, almost frightened eyes that gradually became hazel. He seemed docile and unprotesting from birth. He seldom cried. A week before his delivery, Margaret felt a shadow fall across her face, and a strange black bird stared at her from a cherry tree close to the house. Nor did it move when she emptied the garbage. She was afraid to mention it to John Patrick, and she rejoiced when the delivery was an easy one and the new baby seemed reasonably healthy. But James Michael Maguire was an anomaly, and even a two-year-old Jack, freckled and boisterous, twice slapped him in his crib and had to be restrained from tormenting Jim when he first began to crawl.

John Patrick made light of it. "It's the Maguire blood. Jimmy will learn to defend himself."

Actually John Patrick was thrilled with both sons, wrestling for hours with the feisty, oversized Jack and patiently teaching a tentative Jimmy to fight back. Jack was the powerful exemplar of what it meant to be a Maguire, and James Michael was expected to measure up. There were subtle signs even in infancy that he would withdraw from the impossible contest, but John Patrick was too happy to notice. Margaret, too, was never happier, fussing endlessly over the children and preparing her husband's favorite roasts with mashed potatoes and thick, rich gravy the way Johnny Muller had instructed her. Baking bread and Parker House rolls and apple slices with white frosting, and trying as best she could to satisfy her husband's strong sexual appetite although she didn't understand it and was embarrassed when he fondled her enlarged breasts while she was nursing Jimmy.

Curiously, in the early years, when success at work absorbed him and the joy of children was a novelty, her very shyness about sex excited him. He was satisfied to be the aggressor, charming her little girl's fears, and well pleased to feel some minimal compliance. She gazed at the bleeding crucifix on the wall or the serenely cold china madonna on the dresser, but she never refused him, for she knew that his salvation depended on her service and prayers, and that her own sanctity, like the Blessed Virgin's, was measured by the performance of God's will. God's will was of far greater concern than even John Patrick.

Thus she left her husband's bed every morning at five to attend the early mass with the nuns; her closest friend, "old maid" Mary O'Meara; a scattered two dozen other devout women; and two or three effeminate men she did not admire. At first John Patrick had protested her daily departure, not admitting his need to feel her warmth next to him, but insisting protectively that she required more sleep.

"I can sleep for all eternity," she said softly.

She would have honored any other request, but God came first, and there was no way on heaven or earth to dissuade her. At times he held her tightly and feigned heavy sleep, but she fought her way free. Occasionally he pretended sickness, and then she would attend to his needs quickly and go off to mass in the new Oldsmobile he had taught her to drive. Finally, he gave up and accepted her going to mass as he did his own job.

She was transformed when she entered the old brick church. With its vaulted arches and huge plaster pillars, the smell of incense and the creaking of oiled wooden floors, it gave her a few moments of peace, without interruptions or babies to attend or coffee to make. Her face became like that of a child. Her lips, normally thin and drawn tight to hide an overbite that had always embarrassed her, relaxed with the fullness of a passion John Patrick would never know. The blue eyes glowed and stared rapturously at the giant crucifix suspended behind the altar. She readied her missal like a teacher preparing for class, read the special prayers on holy cards gathered since childhood in Chicago. Then came the organ and the ancient Gregorian melodies of the Kyrie and the Gloria and the triumphant preface chant that had startled Mozart, the solemn Pater Noster that brought her close to tears. There was no greater joy. She made her way to communion, calling out in her heart *Domine, non sum dignus* and thrilling to the soft strum of the organ's Adoro Te . . .

The office transformed him as the church did her. His booming good-morning and always new Irish palaver about "so much beauty in a single room" or "how lucky can a man get" reduced the female office staff to giggles. Even his firmness, when reports were late or quarterly rating charts incorrect, made him attractive. He had an incredible mind for figures, could multiply or divide complicated problems in his head, and stored endless statistics of insurance rates and projected costs almost effortlessly.

His private secretary, Doris, was secretly in love with him and found his dramatic dictations of letters an eloquent delight. Although forced out of school in seventh grade to help support his family, John Patrick had an impressive vocabulary and perfect grammar. He was exceptionally clean, had manicures with his twice-monthly haircut, and dressed handsomely. Always a fresh white shirt and appropriate tie, shoes shined, rusty hair flattened as much as the stubborn curls would allow. He held his head proudly, tilted almost arrogantly, and usually opened his mouth when he smiled. He liked his own looks, especially the proud, prominent nose that gave immense character to his face and justified a touch of swagger when he walked . . .

A month later he bought a house despite the alarmist talk of troubled economic conditions and an end to prosperity. He surprised Margaret one evening after work by inviting her and the children out for a ride.

"Dinner's in the oven—"

"It'll keep," he said. "I feel like taking a ride on such an evening."

She feared he had been drinking with his new friend, Mike McNulty, a short, stocky ex-middleweight he had met at a football game.

They drove to a Dutch neighborhood in the south end of Kirkwood, hardly two blocks from where J. R. Harris lived, at the fringe of Protestant affluence.

"Beautiful houses here," he mused aloud.

"That's not important," she said. "We have everything we need." She didn't admit that she wanted a refrigerator to replace the dripping old icebox that was rotting the linoleum.

He stopped the car in front of a corner house that had brick wainscoting and an enclosed front porch. There was a front and side yard and a separate garage. A neat hedge surrounded the entire property and a peach and a cherry tree bloomed gracefully in separate yards. Small evergreens flanked the front porch and contrasted elegantly with the fresh white paint. It was two stories with an attic and basement and half again as big as the house they were renting.

"That's a fine house," he said. "Let's take a look."

"My God in heaven, John. You might get shot just wandering around." Now she was certain he had been drinking.

He picked up Jack and walked to the front entrance. Margaret did not move from the car, and little Jim was crying. She prayed aloud when John Patrick walked up on the porch.

He shouted to her. "It's empty, Margaret, let's take a look." He disappeared inside with Jack.

Still she did not understand, and she feared for his welfare. She slid out of the car with the baby and walked nervously up the front steps, reassuring herself that the children afforded protection. Her heart almost stopped when she saw the open door and realized he had stepped inside.

"For God's sake, John," she hissed. "What on earth has happened to you?"

Then he came to the front door with the beaming smile that had won her love at Lake Winnebago.

"How do you like it? It's empty. I think I'll buy it."

"Don't talk foolish, John, we never could afford it." She walked inside cautiously, as if she were robbing a bank.

"Dear God, it's beautiful," she whispered.

There were refinished hardwood floors and a living room fireplace with an ivory painted mantel. A formal dining room with double windows and wide window seats, a bright kitchen, and three bedrooms upstairs. The basement was large, though unfinished, with a fruit cellar and a coal bin.

Margaret was speechless, giggling like a little girl now, delighted by the daring escapade that reminded her of their courtship, still not realizing that the house was hers.

When he used the toilet upstairs she was frantic. He put his arms around her and smiled that proud smile again, and then she burst into tears of joy.

"O John, John, but so expensive!"

"It's too late now," he said. "We'll move in next week. And I've ordered a refrigerator."

There was no brooding that night as he ate seconds of pot roast and peas, gravy and apple pie. After a third cup of coffee and another cigarette, he helped her bathe the children and they talked till almost midnight about the business he would have, all his own, and the place in the country besides.

For once she only listened, delighted that they had room for all the children God might send and worrying if her lust for a refrigerator had been sinful.

"I only wish my mother had lived to see it." It was one of the rare times she made such a request.

Then they went to bed and he made love to her. With special gentleness and as much pleasure as she had ever allowed herself. When he was finally asleep, she slipped from bed to ask God's forgiveness for her enjoyment and thanked Him for the new house. Then she cuddled next to her husband and set the alarm for early mass.

She prayed more fervently when the Depression came crashing down in October 1929. Although Kirkwood, with its furniture factories, paper mills, and chemical plants, its apple orchards, dairy farms, and celery marshlands, was not nearly as scarred as the larger Michigan cities that depended on the automobile, the impact was, nevertheless, dramatic. The Audit Bureau cut back employees and with them John Patrick's salary. Still he did not admit his concern as he brooded in the new leather recliner he had bought along with Margaret's refrigerator. "A chair worthy of Doyle himself," he had joked.

Now he was not joking. It was a tense struggle to survive from day to day. Gene Tunney's retirement from boxing and a vacant heavyweight throne seemed inconsequential although Notre Dame's continuing dominance of college football under Knute Rockne gave John Patrick consistent energy to hold up his head in Kirkwood. No Depression could change that, nor could it ever force his fierce pride to admit aloud that he was frightened. He even permitted himself to gloat over the bungling "medicine ball" administration of pudgy Herbert Hoover with his Quaker background. Al Smith would have handled it all.

Somehow, with the money they had saved and Margaret's fierce management, they were able to endure and keep the new house. But there could be no thought of starting a new business or buying an old one. Or of having more children. Margaret did not agree with his decision about children as he uttered it one brooding evening as he sat in the brown leather recliner. To have a dozen children was, for her, a small enough sacrifice for ignoring the convent. Yet, to her credit, she would never have disputed her husband's judgment if he had not introduced a condom into their bedroom the week after Jim was weaned. Although she had never seen one, she instinctively knew it was evil, and she blessed herself nervously.

"My God in heaven, John Patrick!"

"It's a way of not having children for a while."

He was embarrassed, but it had never occurred to him that it was really wrong.

There had been no discussions in Saint Raphael's pulpit about birth control. Informed Catholics may have known the law, but Margaret was too naïve to have wondered, and John Patrick believed he only had to be a faithful husband and a good father. He had never heard the pope's opinion, nor did he care about it. Thus when Margaret turned from him, as much perhaps from fear as from any spiritual rejection, he became furious. The condom shriveled and fell on the sheets and Margaret grasped her rosary.

"For God's sake, Margaret, I'm a man!"

"We can deny ourselves and be grateful for what we have."

"Damn it. I am grateful, but we're entitled!"

"If Father Doyle says it's—"

He shouted, ripping the condom to shreds, "Doyle doesn't run my bedroom! You're my wife!"

She was trembling, then crying, and the two boys were crying besides. "What's it all worth if we go to hell?"

He charged from the bedroom and slammed the door. The crucifix fell to the floor and Margaret gasped in horror. As she arose to replace the crucifix and sprinkle holy water from the small ivory font by the door, John Patrick poured himself some bourbon, smuggled from Canada by McNulty's brother, and sat for several hours in his recliner. The sadness engulfed him until even the beautiful new house had lost its luster. Tears formed in his eyes but would not fall. Then he heard Jim crying and brought him in and held him tenderly, rocking him in the chair until he gurgled softly in his father's arms. He put his son back in the crib and fell asleep on the couch.

That night, something changed in their marriage.

Several other children are born to John and Margaret including one son who will enter the priesthood and be torn between the calling of the spirit and the yearning of the flesh.

Read the complete Bantam Book, available September 1st, 1979, wherever paperbacks are sold.